The Sound
&
the Furry:

The Complete
Hoka Stories

Books by Poul Anderson

Genesis
The Guardians of Time
The High Crusade
Starfarers
Tau Zero
Three Hearts and Three Lions
The Time Patrol
War of the Gods

Books by Gordon R. Dickson

Dorsai!
The Dragon and the Fair Maid of Kent
The Dragon and the George
The Final Encyclopedia
Necromancer
Soldier Ask Not
The Tactics of Mistake
Timestorm

The Sound & the Furry:

The Complete Hoka Stories

Hoka! Hoka! Hoka!
Hokas Pokas!

POUL ANDERSON &
GORDON R. DICKSON

SCIENCE
FICTION

Published by arrangement with
Baen Publishing Enterprises
P.O. Box 1188
Wake Forest, NC 27587

Publishing history:
Hoka! Hoka! Hoka! First Baen printing November 1998
Hokas Pokas! First Baen printing February 2000
First SFBC printing March 2001

Visit us online at *www.sfbc.com*

Printed in the United States of America

The Sound
&
the Furry:

The Complete
Hoka Stories

Table of Contents

Hoka! Hoka! Hoka!

Table of Contents

PROLOGUE

From the *Encyclopaedia Galactica*, 11th edition:

TOKA: Brackney's Star III. The sun (NSC 7-190853426) is of type G2, located in Region Deneb, approximately 503 light-years from Sol. . . . The third planet appears Earthlike, to a sufficiently superficial observer. . . . There are three small moons, their League names being Uha, Buha, and Huha. As is customary in the case of inhabited planets, these derive from a major autochthonous language (see NOMENCLATURE: Astronomical). It was discovered too late that they mean, respectively, "Fat," "Drunk" and "Sluggish." . . .

At least "Toka" means "Earth." However, indigenous tongues have become little more than historical curiosities, displaced by whatever Terrestrial speech suits the role of the moment. . . .

Two intelligent species evolved, known today as the Hokas and the Slissii. The former are quasi-mammalian, the latter reptiloid. . . . Conflict was ineluctable. . . . It terminated after human explorers had come upon the system and the Interbeing League took charge. . . . In effect, the Slissii were bought out. Abandoning their home world *en masse*, they became free wanderers throughout civilization, to its detriment. (See SLISSII. See also COMPUTER CRIME; CONFIDENCE GAMES; EMBEZZLEMENT; GAMBLING: Crooked; MISREPRESENTATION; POLITICS.)

The ursinoid Hokas generally stayed in place. No nation of theirs refused to accept League tutelage, which of course has had the objective of raising their level of civilization to a point where autonomy and full membership can be granted. Rather, they all agreed with an eagerness which should have warned the Commissioners. . . .

The fact is that the Hokas are the most imaginative race of beings in known space, and doubtless in unknown space too. Any role that strikes their fancy they will play, individually or as a group, to the limits of the preposterous and beyond. This does not imply deficiency of intellect, for they are remarkably quick to learn. It does not even imply that they lose touch with reality; indeed, they have been heard to complain that reality often loses touch with them. It does demonstrate a completely protean personality. Added to that are a physical strength and energy astonishing in such comparatively small bodies. Thus, in the course of a few short years, the "demon teddy bears," to use a popular phrase for them, have covered their planet with an implausible kaleidoscope of harlequin societies describable only by some such metaphor as the foregoing. . . .

THE SHERIFF OF CANYON GULCH

It had been a very near thing. Alexander Jones spent several minutes enjoying the simple pleasure of still being alive.

Then he looked around.

It could almost have been Earth—almost, indeed, his own North America. He stood on a great prairie whose dun grasses rolled away beneath a high windy sky. A flock of birds, alarmed by his descent, clamored upward; they were not so very different from the birds he knew. A line of trees marked the river, a dying puff of steam the final berth of his scoutboat. In the hazy eastern distance he saw dim blue hills. Beyond those, he knew, were the mountains, and then the enormous dark forests, and finally the sea near which the *Draco* lay. A hell of a long ways to travel.

Nevertheless, he was uninjured, and on a planet almost the twin of his own. The air, gravity, biochemistry, the late-afternoon sun, could only be told from those of home with sensitive instruments. The rotational period was approximately 24 hours, the sidereal year nearly 12 months, the axial tilt a neat but not gaudy $11^1/_2$ degrees. The fact that two small moons were in the sky and a third lurking somewhere else, that the continental outlines were an alien scrawl, that a snake coiled on a nearby rock had wings, that he was about 500 light-years from the Solar System—all this was mere detail. The veriest bagatelle. Alex laughed at it. The noise jarred so loud in this emptiness that he decided a decorous silence was more appropriate to his status as an officer and, by Act of Parliament as ratified locally by the United States Senate, a gentleman. Therefore he straightened his high-collared blue naval tunic, ran a nervous hand down the creases of his white naval trousers, buffed his shining naval boots on the spilled-out naval parachute, and reached for his emergency kit.

He neglected to comb his rumpled brown hair, and his lanky form did not exactly snap to attention. But he was, after all, quite alone. Not that he intended to remain in that possibly estimable condition. He shrugged the heavy packsack off his shoulders. It had been the only thing he grabbed besides the parachute when his boat failed, and the only thing he really needed. His hands fumbled it open and he reached in for the small but powerful radio which would bring help.

He drew out a book.

It looked unfamiliar, somehow . . . had they issued a new set of instructions since he was in boot camp? He opened it, looking for the section on Radios, Emergency, Use of. He read the first page he turned to:

"—apparently incredibly fortunate historical development was, of course, quite logical. The relative decline in politico-economic influence of the Northern Hemisphere during the later twentieth century, the shift of civilized dominance to a Southeast Asia-Indian Ocean region with more resources, did not, as alarmists at the time predicted, spell the end of Western civilization. Rather did it spell an upsurge of Anglo-Saxon democratic and libertarian influence, for the simple reason that this area, which now held the purse strings of Earth, was in turn primarily led by Australia and New Zealand, which nations retained their primordial loyalty to the British Crown. The consequent renascence and renewed growth of the British Commonwealth of Nations, the shaping of its councils into a truly world—even interplanetary—government, climaxed as it was by the American Accession, has naturally tended to fix Western culture, even in small details of everyday life, in the mold of that particular time, a tendency which was accentuated by the unexpectedly early invention of the faster-than-light secondary drive and repeated contact with truly different mentalities, and has produced in the Solar System a social stability which our forefathers would have considered positively Utopian and which the Service, working through the Interbeing League, has as its goal to bring to all sentient races—"

"Guk!" said Alex.

He snapped the book shut. Its title leered up at him:

EMPLOYEES' ORIENTATION
MANUAL
by Adalbert Parr,
Chief Cultural Commissioner
Cultural Development Service
Foreign Ministry
of the
United Commonwealths
League City, N.Z., Sol III

"Oh, no!" said Alex.

Frantically, he pawed through the pack. There must be a radio . . . a raythrower . . . a compass . . . one little can of beans?

He extracted some 5000 tightly bundled copies of CDS Form J-16-LKR, to be filled out in quadruplicate by applicant and submitted with attached Forms G776802 and W-2-ZGU.

Alex's snub-nosed face sagged open. His blue eyes revolved incredulously. There followed a long, dreadful moment in which he could only think how utterly useless the English language was when it came to describing issue-room clerks.

"Oh, hell," said Alexander Jones.

He got up and began to walk.

He woke slowly with the sunrise and lay there for a while wishing he hadn't. A long hike on an empty stomach followed by an uneasy attempt to sleep on the ground, plus the prospect of several thousand kilometers of the same, is not conducive to joy. And those animals, whatever they were, that had been yipping and howling all night sounded so damnably *hungry*.

"He looks human."

"Yeah. But he ain't dressed like no human."

Alex opened his eyes with a wild surmise. The drawling voices spoke . . . English!

He closed his eyes again, immediately. "No," he groaned.

"He's awake, Tex." The voices were high-pitched, slightly unreal. Alex curled up into the embryonic position and reflected on the peculiar horror of a squeaky drawl.

"Yeah. Git up, stranger. These hyar parts ain't healthy right now, nohow."

"No," gibbered Alex. "Tell me it isn't so. Tell me I've gone crazy, but deliver me from its being real!"

"I dunno." The voice was uncertain. "He don't talk like no human."

Alex decided there was no point in wishing them out of existence. They looked harmless, anyway—to everything except his sanity. He crawled to his feet, his bones seeming to grate against each other, and faced the natives.

The first expedition, he remembered, had reported two intelligent races, Hokas and Slissii, on this planet. And these must be Hokas. For small blessings, give praises! There were two of them, almost identical to the untrained Terrestrial eye: about a meter tall, tubby and golden-furred, with round blunt-muzzled heads and small black eyes. Except for the stubby-fingered hands, they resembled nothing so much as giant teddy bears.

The first expedition had, however, said nothing about their speaking English with a drawl. Or about their wearing the dress of Earth's 19th-century West.

All the American historical stereofilms he had ever seen gabbled in Alex's mind as he assessed their costumes. They wore—let's see, start at the top and work down and try to keep your reason in the process—ten-gallon hats with brims wider than their own shoulders, tremendous red bandannas, checked shirts of riotous hues, Levis, enormously flaring chaps, and high-heeled boots with outsize spurs. Two sagging cartridge belts on each plump waist supported heavy Colt six-shooters which almost dragged on the ground.

One of the natives was standing before the Earthman, the other was mounted nearby, holding the reins of the first one's—well—his animal. The beasts were about the size of a pony, and had four hoofed feet . . . also whiplike tails, long necks with beaked heads, and scaly green hides. But of course, thought Alex wildly, of course they bore Western saddles with lassos at the horns. Of course. Who ever heard of a cowboy without a lasso?

"Wa'l, I see yo're awake," said the standing Hoka. "Howdy, stranger, howdy." He extended his hand. "I'm Tex and my pardner here is Monty."

"Pleased to meet you," mumbled Alex, shaking hands in a dream-like fashion. "I'm Alexander Jones."

"I dunno," said Monty dubiously. "He ain't named like no human."

"Are yo' human, Alexanderjones?" asked Tex.

The spaceman got a firm grip on himself and said, spacing his words with care: "I am Ensign Alexander Jones of the Terrestrial Interstellar Survey Service, attached to HMS *Draco*." Now it was the Hokas who looked lost. He added wearily: "In other words, I'm from Earth. I'm human. Satisfied?"

"I s'pose," said Monty, still doubtful. "But we'd better take yo' back to town with us an' let Slick talk to yo'. He'll know more about it. Cain't take no chances in these hyar times."

"Why not?" said Tex, with a surprising bitterness. "What we got to lose, anyhow? But come on, Alexanderjones, we'll go on to town. We shore don't want to be found by no Injun war parties."

"Injuns?" asked Alex.

"Shore. They're comin', you know. We'd better sashay along. My pony'll carry double."

Alex was not especially happy at riding a nervous reptile in a saddle built for a Hoka. Fortunately, the race was sufficiently broad in the beam for their seats to have spare room for a slim Earthman. The "pony" trotted ahead at a surprisingly fast and steady pace. Reptiles on Toka—so-called by the first expedition from the word for "earth" in the language of the most advanced Hoka society—seemed to be more highly evolved than in the Solar System. A fully developed four-chambered heart and a better nervous system made them almost equivalent to mammals.

Nevertheless, the creature stank.

Alex looked around. The prairie was just as big and bare, his ship just as far away.

" 'Tain't none o' my business, I reckon," said Tex, "but how'd yo' happen to be hyar?"

"It's a long story," said Alex absent-mindedly. His thoughts at the moment were chiefly about food. "The *Draco* was out on Survey, mapping new planetary systems, and our course happened to take us close to this star, your sun, which we knew had been visited once before. We thought we'd look in and check on conditions, as well as resting ourselves on an Earth-type world. I was one of the several who went out in scoutboats to skim over this continent. Something went wrong, my engines failed and I barely escaped with my life. I parachuted out, and as bad luck would have it, my boat crashed in a river. So—well—due to various other circumstances, I just had to start hiking back, toward my ship."

"Won't yore pardners come after yo'?"

"Sure, they'll search—but how likely are they to find a shattered wreck on the bottom of a river, with half a continent to investigate? I could, perhaps, have grubbed a big SOS in the soil and hoped it would be seen from the air, but what with the necessity of hunting food and all . . . well, I figured my best chance was to keep moving. But now I'm hungry enough to eat a . . . a buffalo."

"Ain't likely to have buffalo meat in town," said the Hoka imperturbably. "But we got good T-bone steaks."

"Oh," said Alex.

"Yo' wouldn't'a lasted long, hoofin' it," said Monty. "Ain't got no gun."

"No, thanks to—Never mind!" said Alex. "I thought I'd try to make a bow and some arrows."

"Bow an' arrers—Say!" Monty squinted suspiciously at him. "What yo' been doin' around the Injuns?"

"I ain't—I haven't been near any Injuns, dammit!"

"Bows an' arrers is Injun weapons, stranger."

"I wish they was," mourned Tex. "We didn't have no trouble back when only Hokas had six-guns. But now the Injuns got 'em too, it's all up with us." A tear trickled down his button nose.

If the cowboys are teddy bears, thought Alex, *then who—or what—are the Indians?*

"It's lucky for yo' me an' Tex happened to pass by," said Monty. "We was out to see if we couldn't round up a few more steers afore the Injuns get here. No such luck, though. The greenskins done rustled 'em all."

Greenskins! Alex remembered a detail in the report of the first expedition: two intelligent races, the mammalian Hokas and the reptilian Slissii. And the Slissii, being stronger and more warlike, preyed on the Hokas—

"Are the Injuns Slissii?" he asked.

"Wa'l, they're ornery, at least," said Monty.

"I mean . . . well . . . are they big tall beings, bigger than I am, but walking sort of stooped over . . . tails and fangs and green skins, and their talk is full of hissing noises?"

"Why, shore. What else?" Monty shook his head, puzzled. "If yo're a human, how come yo' don't even know what a Injun is?"

They had been plop-plopping toward a large and noisy dust cloud. As they neared, Alex saw the cause, a giant herd of—uh—

"Longhorn steers," explained Monty.

Well . . . yes . . . one long horn apiece, on the snout. But at least the red-haired, short-legged, barrel-bodied "cattle" were mammals. Alex made out brands on the flanks of some. The entire herd was being urged along by fast-riding Hoka cowboys.

"That's the X Bar X outfit," said Tex. "The Lone Rider decided to try an' drive 'em ahead o' the Injuns. But I'm afeered the greenskins'll catch up with him purty soon."

"He cain't do much else," answered Monty. "All the ranchers, just about, are drivin' their stock off the range. There just ain't any place short o' the Devil's Nose whar we can make a stand. I shore don't intend tryin' to stay in town an' hold off the Injuns, an' I don't think nobody else does either, in spite o' Slick an' the Lone Rider wantin' us to."

"Hey," objected Alex, "I thought you said the, er, Lone Rider was fleeing. Now you say he wants to fight. Which is it?"

"Oh, the Lone Rider what owns the X Bar X is runnin', but the Lone Rider o' the Lazy T wants to stay. So do the Lone Rider o' Buffalo Stomp, the Really Lone Rider, an' the Loneliest Rider, but I'll bet they changes their minds when the Injuns gets as close to them as the varmints is to us right now."

Alex clutched his head to keep it from flying off his shoulders. "How many Lone Riders are there, anyway?" he shouted.

"How should I know?" shrugged Monty. "I knows at least ten myself. I gotta say," he added exasperatedly, "that English shore ain't got as many names as the old Hoka did. It gets gosh-awful tiresome to have a hundred other Montys around, or yell for Tex an' be asked which one."

They passed the bawling herd at a jog trot and topped a low rise. Beyond it lay a village, perhaps a dozen small frame houses and a single rutted street lined with square-built false-fronted structures. The place was jammed with Hokas—on foot, mounted, in covered wagons and buggies—refugees from the approaching Injuns, Alex decided. As he was carried down the hill, he saw a clumsily lettered sign:

WELCOME TO CANYON GULCH
Pop. Weekdays 212
Saturdays 1000

"We'll take yo' to Slick," said Monty above the hubbub. "He'll know what to do with yo'."

They forced their ponies slowly through the swirling, pressing, jabbering throng. The Hokas seemed to be a highly excitable race, given to arm-waving and shouting at the top of their lungs. There was no organization whatsoever to the evacuation, which proceeded slowly with its traffic tie-ups, arguments, gossip exchange, and exuberant pistol shooting into the air. Quite a few ponies and wagons stood deserted before the saloons, which formed an almost solid double row along the street.

Alex tried to remember what there had been in the report of the first expedition. It was a brief report, the ship had only been on Toka for a couple of months. But—yes—the Hokas were described as friendly, merry, amazingly quick to learn . . . and hopelessly inefficient. Only their walled sea-coast towns, in a state of bronze-age technology, had been able to stand off the Slissii; otherwise the reptiles were slowly but steadily conquering the scattered ursinoid tribes. A Hoka fought bravely when he was attacked, but shoved all thought of the enemy out of his cheerful mind whenever the danger was not immediately visible. It never occurred to the Hokas to band together in a massed offensive against the Slissii; such a race of individualists could never have formed an army anyway.

A nice, but rather ineffectual little people. Alex felt somewhat smug about his own height, his dashing spaceman's uniform, and the fighting, slugging, persevering human spirit which had carried man out to the stars. He felt like an elder brother.

He'd have to do something about this situation, give these comic-opera creatures a hand. Which might also involve a promotion for Alexander Braithwaite Jones, since Earth wanted a plentiful supply of planets with friendly dominant species, and the first report on the Injuns—Slissii, blast it!—made it unlikely that they could ever get along with mankind.

A. Jones, hero. Maybe then Tanni and I can—

He grew aware that a fat, elderly Hoka was gaping at him, together with the rest of Canyon Gulch. This particular one wore a large metal star pinned to his vest.

"Howdy, sheriff," said Tex, and snickered.

"Howdy, Tex, old pal," said the sheriff obsequiously. "An' my good old sidekick Monty too. Howdy, howdy, gents! Who's this hyar stranger—not a *human*?"

"Yep, that's what he says. Whar's Slick?"

"Which Slick?"

"*The* Slick, yo'—yo' sheriff!"

The fat Hoka winced. "I think he's in the back room o' the Paradise Saloon," he said. And humbly: "Uh, Tex . . . Monty . . . yo'll remember yore old pal come ee-lection day, won't yo'?"

"Reckon we might," said Tex genially. "Yo' been sheriff long enough."

"Oh, thank yo', boys, thank yo'! If only the others will have yore kind hearts—" The eddying crowd swept the sheriff away.

"What off Earth?" exclaimed Alex. "What the *hell* was he trying to get you to do?"

"Vote ag'in him come the next ee-lection, o' course," said Monty.

"Against him? But the sheriff . . . he runs the town . . . maybe?"

Tex and Monty looked bewildered. "Now I really wonder if yo're human after all," said Tex. "Why' the humans themselves taught us the sheriff is the dumbest man in town. Only we don't think it's fair a man should have to be called that all his life, so we chooses him once a y'ar."

"Buck there has been *ee*-lected sheriff three times runnin'," said Monty. "He's *really* dumb!"

"But who is this Slick?" cried Alex a trifle wildly.

"The town gambler, o' course."

"What have I got to do with a town gambler?"

Tex and Monty exchanged glances. "Look, now," said Monty with strained patience, "we done allowed for a lot with yo'. But when yo' don't even know what the officer is what runs a town, that's goin' just a little too far."

"Oh," said Alex. "A kind of city manager, then."

"Yo're plumb loco," said Monty firmly. "*Everbody* knows a town is run by a town gambler!"

Slick wore the uniform of his office: tight pants, a black coat, a checked vest, a white shirt with wing collar and string tie, a diamond stickpin, a derringer in one pocket and a pack of cards in the other. He looked tired and harried; he must have been under a tremendous strain in the last few days, but he welcomed Alex with eager volubility and led him into an office furnished in vaguely 19th-century style. Tex and Monty came along, barring the door against the trailing, chattering crowds.

"We'll rustle up some sandwiches for yo'," beamed Slick. He offered Alex a vile purple cigar of some local weed, lit one himself, and sat down behind the rolltop desk. "Now," he said, "when can we get help from yore human friends?"

"Not soon, I'm afraid," said Alex. "The *Draco* crew doesn't know about this. They'll be spending all their time flying around in search of me. Unless they chance to find me here, which isn't likely, they won't even learn about the Injun war."

"How long they figger to be here?"

"Oh, they'll wait at least a month before giving me up for dead and leaving the planet."

"We can get yo' to the seacoast in that time, by hard ridin', but it'd mean takin' a short cut through some territory which the Injuns is between us and it." Slick paused courteously while Alex untangled that one. "Yo'd hardly have a chance to sneak through. So, it looks like the only way we can get yo' to yore friends is to beat the Injuns. Only we can't beat the Injuns without help from yore friends."

Gloom.

To change the subject, Alex tried to learn some Hoka history. He succeeded beyond expectations, Slick proving surprisingly intelligent and well-informed.

The first expedition had landed thirty-odd years ago. At the time, its report had drawn little Earthly interest; there were so many new planets in the vastness of the galaxy. Only now, with the *Draco* as a forerunner, was the League making any attempt to organize this frontier section of space.

The first Earthmen had been met with eager admiration by the Hoka tribe near whose village they landed. The autochthones were linguistic adepts, and between their natural abilities and modern psychography had learned English in a matter of days. To them, the humans were almost gods, though like most primitives they were willing to frolic with their deities.

Came the fatal evening. The expedition had set up an outdoor stereoscreen to entertain itself with films. Hitherto the Hokas had been interested but rather puzzled spectators. Now, tonight, at Wesley's insistence, an old film was reshown. It was a Western.

Most spacemen develop hobbies on their long voyages. Wesley's was the old American West. But he looked at it through romantic lenses; he had a huge stack of novels and magazines but very little factual material.

The Hokas saw the film and went wild.

The captain finally decided that their delirious, ecstatic reaction was due to this being something they could understand. Drawing-room comedies and interplanetary adventures meant little to them in terms of their own experience, but here was a country like their own, heroes who fought savage enemies, great herds of animals, gaudy costumes—

And it occurred to the captain and to Wesley that this race could find very practical use for certain elements of the old Western culture. The Hokas had been farmers, scratching a meager living out of prairie soil never meant to be plowed; they went about on foot, their tools were bronze and stone—they could do much better for themselves, given some help.

The ship's metallurgists had had no trouble reconstructing the old guns, Colt and derringer and carbine. The Hokas had to be taught how to smelt iron, make steel and gunpowder, handle lathes and mills; but here again, native quickness and psychographic instruction combined to make them learn easily. Likewise they leaped at the concept of domesticating the wild beasts they had hitherto herded.

Before the ship left, Hokas were breaking "ponies" to the saddle and rounding up "longhorns." They were making treaties with the more civilized agricultural and maritime cities of the coast, arranging to ship meat in exchange for wood, grain, and manufactured goods. And they were gleefully slaughtering every Slissii warband that came against them.

As a final step, just before he left, Wesley gave his collection of books and magazines to the Hokas.

None of this had been in the ponderous official report Alex read: only the notation that the ursinoids had been shown steel metallurgy, the use of chemical weapons, and the benefits of certain economic forms. It had been hoped that with this aid they could subdue the dangerous Slissii, so that if man finally started coming here regularly, he wouldn't have a war on his hands.

Alex could fill in the rest. Hoka enthusiasm had run wild. The new way of life was, after all, very practical and well adapted to the plains—so why not go all the way, be just like the human godlings in every respect? Talk English with the stereofilm accent, adopt human names, human dress, human mannerisms, dissolve the old tribal organizations and replace them with ranches and towns—it followed very naturally. And it was so much more fun.

The books and magazines couldn't circulate far; most of the new gospel went by word of mouth. Thus certain oversimplifications crept in.

Three decades passed. The Hokas matured rapidly, a second generation which had been born to Western ways was already prominent in the population. The past was all but forgotten. The Hokas spread westward across the plains, driving the Slissii before them.

Until, of course, the Slissii learned how to make firearms too. Then, with their greater military talent, they raised an army of confederated tribes and proceeded to shove the Hokas back. This time they would probably continue till they had sacked the very cities of the coast. The bravery of individual Hokas was no match for superior numbers better organized.

And one of the Injun armies was now roaring down on Canyon

Gulch. It could not be many kilometers away, and there was nothing to stop it. The Hokas gathered their families and belongings from the isolated ranch houses and fled. But with typical inefficiency, most of the refugees fled no further than this town; then they stopped and discussed whether to make a stand or hurry onward, and meanwhile they had just one more little drink. . . .

"You mean you haven't even *tried* to fight?" asked Alex.

"What could we do?" answered Slick. "Half the folks 'ud be ag'in the idea an' wouldn't have nothin' to do with it. Half o' those what did come would each have their own little scheme, an' when we didn't follow it they'd get mad an' walk off. That don't leave none too many."

"Couldn't you, as the leader, think of some compromise—some plan which would satisfy everybody?"

"O' course not," said Slick stiffly. "My own plan is the only right one."

"Oh, Lord!" Alex bit savagely at the sandwich in his hand. The food had restored his strength and the fluid fire the Hokas called whiskey had given him a warm, courageous glow.

"The basic trouble is, your people just don't know how to arrange a battle," he said. "Humans do."

"Yo're a powerful fightin' outfit," agreed Slick. There was an adoration in his beady eyes which Alex had complacently noticed on most of the faces in town. He decided he rather liked it. But a demi-god has his obligations.

"What you need is a leader whom everyone will follow without question," he went on. "Namely me."

"Yo' mean—" Slick drew a sharp breath. *"Yo'?"*

Alex nodded briskly. "Am I right, that the Injuns are all on foot? Yes? Good. Then I know, from Earth history, what to do. There must be several thousand Hoka males around, and they all have some kind of firearms. The Injuns won't be prepared for a fast, tight cavalry charge. It'll split their army wide open."

"Wa'l, I'll be hornswoggled," murmured Slick. Even Tex and Monty looked properly awed.

Suddenly Slick began turning handsprings about the office. "Yahoo!" he cried. "I'm a rootin', tootin' son of a gun, I was born with a pistol in each hand an' I teethed on rattlesnakes!" He did a series of cartwheels. "My daddy was a catamount and my mother was a alligator. I can ran faster backward than anybody else can run forrad, I can jump over the outermost moon with one hand tied behind me, I can fill an inside straight every time I draw, an' if any sidewinder here says it ain't so I'll fill him so full o' lead they'll mine him!"

"What the hell?" gasped Alex, dodging.

"The old human war-cry," explained Tex, who had apparently resigned himself to his hero's peculiar ignorances.

"Let's go!" whooped Slick, and threw open the office door. A tumultuous crowd surged outside. The gambler filled his lungs and roared squeakily:

"Saddle yore hosses, gents, an' load yore six-guns! We got us a human, an' he's gonna lead us all out to wipe the Injuns off the range!"

The Hokas cheered till the false fronts quivered around them, danced, somersaulted, and fired their guns into the air. Alex shook Slick and wailed: "—no, no, you bloody fool, not now! We have to study the situation, send out scouts, make a plan—"

Too late. His impetuous admirers swept him out into the street. He couldn't be heard above the falsetto din. He tried to keep his footing and was only vaguely aware of anything else. Someone gave him a six-shooter, and he strapped it on as if in a dream. Someone else gave him a lasso, and he made out the voice: "Rope yoreself a bronc, Earthman, an' let's go!"

"Rope—" Alex grew groggily aware that there was a corral just behind the saloon. The half-wild reptile ponies galloped about inside it, excited by the noise. Hokas were deftly whirling their lariats forth to catch their personal mounts.

"Go ahead!" urged the voice. "Ain't got no time to lose."

Alex studied the cowboy nearest him. Lassoing didn't look so hard. You held the rope here and here, then you swung the noose around your head like *this*—

He pulled and came crashing to the ground. Through whirling dust, he saw that he had lassoed himself.

Tex pulled him to his feet and dusted him off. "I . . . I don't ride herd at home," he mumbled. Tex made no reply.

"I got a bronc for yo'," cried another Hoka, reeling in his lariat. "A real spirited mustang!"

Alex looked at the pony. It looked back. It had an evilly glittering little eye. At the risk of making a snap judgment, he decided he didn't like it very much. There might be personality conflicts between him and it.

"Come on, let's git goin'!" cried Slick impatiently. He was astraddle a beast which still bucked and reared, but he hardly seemed to notice.

Alex shuddered, closed his eyes, wondered what he had done to deserve this, and wobbled over to the pony. Several Hokas had joined to saddle it for him. He climbed aboard. The Hokas released the animal. There was a personality conflict.

Alex had a sudden feeling of rising and spinning on a meteor that twisted beneath him. He grabbed for the saddle horn. The front feet came down with a ten-gee thump and he lost his stirrups. Something on the order of a nuclear shell seemed to explode in his vicinity.

Though it came up and hit him with unnecessary hardness, he had never known anything so friendly as the ground just then.

"Oof!" said Alex and lay still.

A shocked, unbelieving silence fell on the Hokas. The human hadn't been able to use a rope—now he had set a new record for the shortest time in a saddle—*what sort of human was this, anyway?*

Alex sat up and looked into a ring of shocked fuzzy faces. He gave them a weak smile. "I'm not a horseman either," he said.

"What the hell are yo', then?" stormed Monty. "Yo' cain't rope, yo' cain't ride, yo' cain't talk right, yo' cain't shoot—"

"Now hold on!" Alex climbed to somewhat unsteady feet. "I admit I'm not used to a lot of things here, because we do it differently on Earth. But I can outshoot any man . . . er, any Hoka of you any day in the week and twice on Sundays!"

Some of the natives looked happy again, but Monty only sneered. "Yeah?"

"Yeah. I'll prove it." Alex looked about for a suitable target. For a change, he had no worries. He was one of the best raythrower marksmen in the Fleet. "Throw up a coin. I'll plug it through the middle."

The Hokas began looking awed. Alex gathered that they weren't very good shots by any standards but their own. Slick beamed, took a silver dollar from his pocket, and spun it into the air. Alex drew and fired.

Unfortunately, raythrowers don't have recoil. Revolvers do.

Alex went over on his back. The bullet broke a window in the Last Chance Bar & Grill.

The Hokas began to laugh. It was a bitter kind of merriment.

"Buck!" cried Slick. "Buck . . . yo' thar, sheriff . . . c'mere!"

"Yes, sir, Mister Slick, sir?"

"I don't think we need yo' for sheriff no longer, Buck. I think we just found ourselves another one. Gimme yore badge!"

When Alex regained his feet, the star gleamed on his tunic. And, of course, his proposed counter-attack had been forgotten.

* * *

He mooched glumly into Pizen's Saloon. During the past few hours, the town had slowly drained itself of refugees as the Injuns came horribly closer; but there were still a few delaying for one more drink. Alex was looking for such company.

Being official buffoon wasn't too bad in itself. The Hokas weren't cruel to those whom the gods had afflicted. But—well—he had just ruined human prestige on this continent. The Service wouldn't appreciate that.

Not that he would be seeing much of the Service in the near future. He couldn't possibly reach the *Draco* now before she left—without passing through territory held by the same Injuns whose army was advancing on Canyon Gulch. It might be years till another expedition landed. He might even be marooned here for life. Though come to think of it, that wouldn't be a lot worse than the disgrace which would attend his return.

Gloom.

"Here, sheriff, let me buy yo' a drink," said a voice at his elbow.

"Thanks," said Alex. The Hokas did have the pleasant rule that the sheriff was always treated when he entered a saloon. He had been taking heavy advantage of the custom, though it didn't seem to lighten his depression much.

The Hoka beside him was a very aged specimen, toothless and creaky. "I'm from Childish way," he introduced himself. "They call me the Childish Kid. Howdy, sheriff."

Alex shook hands, dully.

They elbowed their way to the bar. Alex had to stoop under Hoka ceilings, but otherwise the rococo fittings were earnestly faithful to their fictional prototypes—including a small stage where three scantily clad Hoka females were going through a song-and-dance number while a bespectacled male pounded a rickety piano.

The Childish Kid leered. "I know those gals," he sighed. "Some fillies, hey? Stacked, don't yo' think?"

"Uh . . . yes," agreed Alex. Hoka females had four mammaries apiece. "Quite."

"Zunami an' Goda an' Torigi, that's their names. If I warn't so danged old—"

"How come they have, er, non-English names?" inquired Alex.

"We had to keep the old Hoka names for our wimmin," said the Childish Kid. He scratched his balding head. "It's bad enough with the men, havin' a hundred Hopalongs in the same county . . . but how the hell can yo' tell yore wimmin apart when they're all named Jane?"

"We have some named 'Hey, you' as well," said Alex grimly. "And a lot more called 'Yes, dear.' "

His head was beginning to spin. This Hoka brew was potent stuff.

Nearby stood two cowboys, arguing with alcoholic loudness. They were typical Hokas, which meant that to Alex their tubby forms were scarcely to be distinguished from each other. "I know them two, they're from my old outfit," said the Childish Kid. "That one's Slim, an' t'other's Shorty."

"Oh," said Alex.

Brooding over his glass, he listened to the quarrel for lack of anything better to do. It had degenerated to the name-calling stage. "Careful what yo' say, Slim," said Shorty, trying to narrow his round little eyes. "I'm a powerful dangerous hombre."

"You ain't no powerful dangerous hombre," sneered Slim.

"I am so too a powerful dangerous hombre!" squeaked Shorty.

"Yo're a fathead what ought to be kicked by a jackass," said Slim, "an' I'm just the one what can do it."

"When yo' call me that," said Shorty, "smile!"

"I said yo're a fathead what ought to be kicked by a jackass," repeated Slim, and smiled.

Suddenly the saloon was full of the roar of pistols. Sheer reflex threw Alex to the floor. A ricocheting slug whanged nastily by his ear. The thunder barked again and again. He hugged the floor and prayed.

Silence came. Reeking smoke swirled through the air. Hokas crept from behind tables and the bar and resumed drinking, casually. Alex looked for the corpses. He saw only Slim and Shorty, putting away their emptied guns.

"Wa'l, that's that," said Shorty. "I'll buy this round."

"Thanks, pardner," said Slim. "I'll get the next one."

Alex bugged his eyes at the Childish, Kid. "Nobody was hurt!" he chattered hysterically.

"O' course not," said the ancient Hoka. "Slim an' Shorty is old pals." He spread his hands. "Kind o' a funny human custom, that. It don't make much sense that every man should sling lead at every other man once a month. But I reckon maybe it makes 'em braver, huh?"

"Uh-huh," said Alex.

Others drifted over to talk with him. Opinion seemed about equally divided over whether he wasn't a human at all or whether humankind simply wasn't what the legends had cracked it up to be. But in spite of their disappointment, they bore him no ill will and stood him drinks. Alex accepted thirstily. He couldn't think of anything else to do.

It might have been an hour later, or two hours or ten, that Slick came into the saloon. His voice rose over the hubbub: "A scout just brung me the latest word, gents. The Injuns ain't no more'n five miles away an comin' fast. We'll all have to git a move on."

The cowboys swallowed their drinks, smashed their glasses, and boiled from the building in a wave of excitement. "Gotta calm the boys down," muttered the Childish Kid, "or we could git a riot." With great presence of mind, he shot out the lights.

"Yo' fool!" bellowed Slick. "It's broad daylight outside!"

Alex lingered aimlessly by the saloon, until the gambler tugged at his sleeve. "We're short o' cowhands an' we got a big herd to move," ordered Slick. "Get yoreself a *gentle pony* an' see if yo' can help."

"Okay," hiccoughed Alex. It would be good to know he was doing something useful, however little. Maybe he would be defeated at the next election.

He traced a wavering course to the corral. Someone led forth a shambling wreck of a mount, too old to be anything but docile. Alex groped after the stirrup. It evaded him. "C'mere," he said sharply. "C'mere, shtirrip. Ten-*shun!* For'ard marsh!"

"Here yo' are." A Hoka who flickered around the edges . . . ghost Hoka? Hoka Superior? the Hoka after Hoka? . . . assisted him into the saddle. "By Pecos Bill, yo're drunk as a skunk!"

"No," said Alex. "I am shober. It's all Toka whish ish drunk. So only drunks on Toka ish shober. Tha's right. Yunnershtan'? Only shober men on Toka ish uh drunks—"

His pony floated through a pink mist in some or other direction. "I'm a lo-o-o-one cowboy!" sang Alex. "I'm thuh loneliesh lone cowboy in these here parts."

He grew amorphously aware of the herd. The cattle were nervous, they rolled their eyes and lowed and pawed the ground. A small band of Hokas galloped around them, swearing, waving their hats, trying to get the animals going in the right path.

"I'm an ol' cowhand, from thuh Rio Grande!" bawled Alex.

"Not so loud!" snapped a Tex-Hoka. "These critters are spooky enough as it is."

"You wanna get 'em goin', don'cha?" answered Alex. "We gotta get going. The greenskins are coming. Simple to get going. Like this. See?"

He drew his six-shooter, fired into the air, and let out the loudest screech he had in him. "Yahoo!"

"Yo' crazy fool!"

"Yahoo!" Alex plunged toward the herd, shooting little and shouting. "Ride 'em, cowboy! Get along, dogies! Yippee!"

The herd, of course, stampeded.

Like a red tide, it suddenly broke past the thin Hoka line. The riders scattered, there was death in those thousands of hoofs, their universe was filled with roaring and rushing and thunder. The earth shook!

"Yahoo!" caroled Alexander Jones. He rode behind the longhorns, still shooting. "Git along, git along! Hiyo, Silver!"

"Oh, my God," groaned Slick. "Oh, my God! The tumbleweed-headed idiot's got 'em stampeded *straight toward the Injuns—*"

"After 'em!" shouted a Hopalong-Hoka. "Mebbe we can still turn the herd! We cain't let the Injuns git all that beef!"

"An' we'll have a little necktie party too," said a Lone Rider-Hoka. "I'll bet that thar Alexanderjones is a Injun spy planted to do this very job."

The cowboys spurred their mounts. A Hoka brain had no room for two thoughts at once. If they were trying to head off a stampede, the fact that they were riding full tilt toward an overwhelming enemy simply did not occur to them.

"Whoopee-ti-yi-yo-o-o-o!" warbled Alex, somewhere in the storm of dust.

Caught by the peculiar time-sense of intoxication, he seemed almost at once to burst over a long low hill. And beyond were the Slissii.

The reptile warriors went afoot, not being built for riding—but they could outrun a Hoka pony. The tyrannosaurian forms were naked, save for war paint and feathers such as primitives throughout the galaxy wear, but they were armed with guns as well as lances, bows, and axes. Their host formed a great compact mass, tightly disciplined to the rhythm of the thudding signal drums. There were thousands of them . . . and a hundred cowboys, at most, galloped blindly toward their ranks.

Alex saw none of this. Being behind the stampede, he didn't see it hit the Injun army.

Nobody really did. The catastrophe was just too big.

When the Hokas arrived on the scene, the Injuns—such of them as had not simply been mashed flat—were scattered over the entire visible prairie. Slick wondered if they would ever stop running.

"At 'em, boys!" he yelled. "Go mop 'em up!"

The Hoka band sped forward. A few small Injun groups sounded their war-hisses and tried to rally for a stand, but it was too late, they were too demoralized, the Hokas cut them down. Others were chased as they fled, lassoed and hog-tied by wildly cheering teddy bears.

Presently Tex rode up to Slick. Dragging behind his pony at a lariat's end was a huge Injun, still struggling and cursing. "I think I got their chief," he reported.

The town gambler nodded happily. "Yep, you have. He's wearin' a high chief's paint. Swell! With him for a hostage, we can make t'other Injuns talk turkey—not that they're gonna bother this hyar country for a long time to come."

As a matter of fact, Canyon Gulch has entered the military textbooks with Cannae, Waterloo, and Xfisthgung as an example of total and crushing victory.

Slowly, the Hokas began to gather about Alex. The utter awe shone in their eyes.

"*He* done it," whispered Monty. "All the time he was playin' dumb, he knew a way to stop the Injuns—"

"Yo' mean, make 'em bite the dust," corrected Slick solemnly.

"Bite the dust," agreed Monty. "He done it singlehanded! Gents, I reckon we should'a knowed better'n to go mistrustin' o' a . . . *human*!"

Alex swayed in the saddle. A violent sickness gathered itself within him. And he reflected that he had caused a stampede, lost an entire herd of cattle, sacrificed all Hoka faith in the Terrestrial race for all time to come. If the natives hanged him, he thought grayly, it was no more than he deserved.

He opened his eyes and looked into Slick's adoring face.

"Yo' saved us," said the little Hoka. He reached out and took the sheriff's badge off Alex's tunic. Then, gravely, he handed over his derringer and playing cards. "Yo' saved us all, human. So, as long as yo're, here, yo're the town gambler o' Canyon Gulch."

Alex blinked. He looked around. He saw the assembled Hokas, and the captive Slissii, and the trampled field of ruin . . . why, why— they had won!

Now he could get to the *Draco*. With human assistance, the Hoka race could soon force a permanent peace settlement on their ancient foes. And Ensign Alexander Braithwaite Jones was a hero.

"Saved you?" he muttered. His tongue still wasn't under very close control. "Oh. Saved you. Yes, I did, didn't I? Saved you. Nice of me." He waved a hand. "No, no. Don't mention it. *Noblesse oblige,* and all that sort of thing."

An acute pain in his unaccustomed gluteal muscles spoiled the effect. He groaned. "I'm walking back to town. I won't be able to sit down for a week as it is!"

And the rescuer of Canyon Gulch dismounted, missed the stirrup, and fell flat on his face.

"Yo' know," murmured someone thoughtfully. "maybe that's the way humans get off their hosses. Maybe we should all—"

INTERLUDE I

**Foreign Ministry
of the
United Commonwealths**

Cultural Development Service
Earth Headquarters
Interdepartmental No. 19847364
2/3/75

FROM: Adalbert Parr, Chief Cultural Commissioner

TO: Hardman Terwilliger, Head Administrator, Personnel Office, New Cultures Section, Extraterrestrial Adjustment and Assignment Branch

SUBJECT: Tokan Autochthones, Development of, Cultural

REFERENCES: (a) TISS Report 17281, (b) TISS Report 28485, (c) Prelim. Psych. Rep. 12971-B, (d) CDS Regs. (rev.), Vol. XVIII, Sec. 49, Par. 2-c

1. You are hereby advised that the Tokan ursinoids, as originally reported in Ref. (a) and subsequently in Ref. (b), have agreed to send a delegation to EHQ to consider guidance. Details in Ref. (b), especially as regards mineral deposits on planet and strategic location of star in area where civilization is rapidly expanding, indicate that acceptance of such status by the aforementioned is highly

desirable from the standpoint of achieving the objectives of the League and this Service.

2. Of course, the party of six whom HMS *Draco* of Ref. (b) have brought to Sol can legally speak only for their own small city-states, but empirical evidence given in Ref. (c) suggests that no great difficulty will be experienced in co-ordinating the rest of the planet once such a foothold has been gained.

3. The Tokan delegation is now in quarantine Callisto Reception Center, but is expected to reach Earthport Prime on 5th inst. at 0947 hours GMT.

4. You are therefore directed to prepare suitable quarters and entertainment for the aforementioned with a view to inducing them to accept ward status for their people, stressing the preferability of our protection and guidance to whatever precarious and backward autonomy their nations may possess at the moment.

5. In accordance with Ref. (d), you are further directed to nominate a suitable plenipotentiary in event of affirmative decision by Tokans.

6. However, Refs. (a), (b), and (c) do show this to be quite an unusual case. It is by no means certain that any of our own career personnel would be an ideal choice for the position, but rather someone already possessing a degree of familiarity with the Tokan situation is to be recommended for at least temporary appointment.

AP/grd

Foreign Ministry
of the
United Commonwealths

Cultural Development Service

Earth Headquarters

Interdepartmental No. 19847372

2/3/75

FROM: Hardman Terwilliger, P.O., N.C.S., E.T.A.A.B.

TO: Adalbert Parr, C.C.C.

SUBJECT: Tokan Autochthones, Entertainment of and Plenipotentiary for, Arrangement of

REFERENCES: (a) Interd. No. 19847364, (b) TISS Personnel File J-965731-s3

1. Note is hereby taken of Ref. (a).
2. In compliance therewith, have arranged suitable quarters for Tokan delegation in the Official Hostel, and appointed Miss Doralene Rawlings of my personal staff Official Hostess to the aforementioned.
3. In view of allegedly unusual Tokan character and recommendation that experienced persons be found to deal with them, have also arranged with TISS HQ to borrow Ensign Alexander Braithwaite Jones to serve as Official Host. As shown in Ref. (b), Ensign Jones has probably had more experience with Tokans than any other available human. Indeed, he is doubtless an expert on their psychology, though showed commendable modesty in disclaiming any such abilities whatsoever when his furlough was cancelled with orders to report to undersigned.
4. Your recommendation noted re appointment of plenipotentiary; but must remind your office that, while it possesses powers of review, all actual appointments fall under jurisdiction of this office, which must follow its own judgment exclusively.

HT/pa

DON JONES

"Don't go—" said Tanni Hostrup, kissing Alexander Jones frantically.

"I've got to—" said Alex, kissing Tanni frantically.

"You mustn't—"

"I must—"

"I love you so much—"

"I love you too—"

We will spare you the rest of this dialogue. One reconciliation between lovers is very much like another.

The trouble was that while Tanni was a highly desirable specimen, both physically—being the possessor of long sunlight-colored hair, eyes like North Martian summer skies, a pertly beautiful face and a figure describable objectively by a complex assemblage of high-order curves and subjectively by an explosion in a fireworks factory—and mentally, being spirited, intelligent, cultured, and good-humored . . . she suffered from one minor vice which recent circumstances had blown into a major one. (If this sentence is complicated, it is because a girl like Tanni touches off extremely complicated reactions in a healthy man like Alex.)

She was unreasonably jealous.

Though stunning, she had only emerged of late from a gawky and lonesome adolescence. The scars of insecurity were not quite healed over. They showed as a too-quick readiness to assume that her fiancé lived up to the roving reputation of all spacemen.

Now actually, in spite of writing poems now and then, Alex was a rather steadfast young chap. But his record, as far as Tanni was concerned, was against him.

On a sunny afternoon two years before, he had been spending furlough time in Krog's Fish Restaurant in Copenhagen. Tanni walked by just as a capitalized Meal was commencing. Alex abandoned a cold glass of Hof and a plate of Limfjord oysters to take off after her—an infallible sign of true love. The same love lent his tongue an unaccustomed glibness. Though the immediate result, a whispered "Ja, *min elskede*" while the Tivoli roller-coaster poised for an especially fell swoop, was excellent: its long-range effects were troublesome. If this American spaceman could win her so swiftly, brooded Tanni, why would not the same techniques work elsewhere? The laws of nature are constant, even on the remotest planets.

She did him an injustice. He had, in fact, been looking for a job which would pay enough for him to get married and also permit him to live with his wife, instead of merely visiting her on meager Earthside leaves. So far he had not succeeded.

We have now given Alex and Tanni enough time to say their goodbyes. After all, they expected to meet again the next day.

He kissed her a last lingering once and stepped through the door, over the flange, onto the elevated walkway. It soared in one magnificent arch from this apartment building to the League hostel where Alex was quartered; the view of towers, traffic, sky, and New Zealand's distant mountains was famous throughout the civilized galaxy; but Alex turned to wave at the blonde girl in the door.

"Who's the blossom?" inquired a familiar husky voice at his shoulder.

He glanced around. A foreboding chill twined about his vertebrae. This was an unusual phenomenon, for the Canadian lass, Doralene Rawlings, was generally believed to raise the temperature three degrees C. in any room where men were present. She was tall, strong, supple, red-haired, green-eyed, unmistakably mammalian, and addicted to skin-tight tunics and half-kneelength skirts. Alex, however, had had his troubles on her account.

"My fiancée," he said coldly. "We're engaged."

"It figures," said Doralene. She took his arm in her normal companionable manner. "Well, let's get back and make ready for the occasion, eh?"

"Please!" Alex pulled away from her. "You don't understand," he added when she gave him a hurt look. "That party the other night . . . you remember, we got to talking on the terrace, and then you wanted me to learn that new dance—"

"Which one?" she asked. "I was showing you several. You've been away from Earth a long time, spaceman, and you had a lot to catch up on."

Alex blushed. "I mean the . . . the one you said was derived from the Pilsudski's Star III fertility rite."

"Oh, yes." Doralene sighed reminiscently. "That one."

"That one," said Alex, "happened to be what you were teaching me when Tanni found us. She'd just gotten back to Earth herself after a good many months—vacationing on New Podunk—and, well—" He shuffled his feet. "I only got matters straightened out today."

"Oh, I see." Doralene smiled compassionately. "I'm sorry." She cocked her head at him. "You know, Alex, you're cute."

And, with that impulsiveness which so many men found so delightful, she kissed him.

"Yipe!" said Alex.

"Oh, dear," said Doralene. "I forgot."

"Well, please see to it that you remember." Alex began walking very fast toward the hostel. Her long smooth legs matched his strides easily.

"After all," he fumbled, "I thought you and, er, Hardman Ter-williger were, uh—"

"Him?" Doralene laughed. "Hardman better go up five grades in the Service before he starts talking to *me* about love." She stretched herself voluptuously. "I don't understand why you're in such a rush to get married, Alex. Play the field a while longer—like me. Hardman's only useful for wangling me soft assignments like this one." Then, for just a moment, quite a different light flickered in her eyes, and she added with unnecessary quickness: "Oh, don't think I'm mercenary about it. I do like him. He's kind of cute in a stuffed-shirt way. Almost like your Hokas."

"They're not *my* Hokas," clipped Alex. "And as for their being cute, I could tell you a thing or two!"

"Nonsense," said Doralene, shaking back her mane of ruddy hair. "They're just pure cuteness, with their adorable button noses and little round tummies, sitting there all in a row and simply eating up that opera. I'm quite unprofessional about them."

Alex jumped.

"Opera?" he demanded sharply. "You don't mean . . . horse opera?"

"Why, no. The San Francisco Opera was in town, and I took them down to see it a couple of nights ago. *Don Giovanni*." She stared at him. "What's the matter with horse operas?"

Alex gulped. "They react to stories about cowboys and Indians," he said.

So far things had gone smoothly enough. The delegation was not from the Wild West but from the more prosperous and socially advanced confederation of maritime city-states. Apart from a tendency to wear striped pants, top hats, and morning coats everywhere—even to bed—the Hokas had been very well-behaved.

Alex realized, however, that he had been quite derelict in his duty. The assignment was to keep the delegates happy . . . but calm. Introduce them in the most favorable way to the amenities of civilization. Persuade them to accept low status and the long upward grind toward full acceptance, autonomy, and League membership.

But when she heard he was on Earth, Tanni had taken an apartment right in the city to be near him. And, well, Doralene had been very kind about squiring his charges around for him. But of course, if trouble came up while he was neglecting his task, it could mean court-martial, dishonorable discharge, and even an ensign's lousy pay was better than no pay at all—

He entered the enormous hostel building with Doralene and took the gravshaft up to the floor where he, she, and the Hokas had their adjoining suites. As he stepped into the ornate corridor, a light flashed and a robotic voice said: "Ensign Jones, sir, there is an urgent call for you." With the remorseless literal-mindedness of all machinery, a portable visio unit had already rolled up to save the few seconds it would take him to get inside his own quarters.

"Oh?" Wondering, Alex stepped forward.

"I better go on ahead," said Doralene. "Have to get our Hokas all tidied up for this dinner tonight."

"Right." Alex nodded and bent over the visio. Tanni's face sprang onto the screen. There were big pathetic tears in her eyes. There was also a cannibalistic screech in her voice.

"Alex!"

"Eep!" said Alex.

"I saw you with that woman!"

"Yipe! But . . . but darling—" stammered Alex. "It was only Doralene . . . you never let me explain before, but she works with me—lives right here—"

"WHAT?"

"Oh, Lord! Look, she's assigned to, this job with me—"

"Why?"

"Why . . . why . . . well, I need an assistant . . . well, actually, just between the two of us, she has pull with Hardman Terwilliger and—"

"And she used it to get assigned to a job with you. I know!" Tanni's charming Danish accent became less suggestive of dances on the greensward than of a Viking chief telling his men to break out the battle axes. "Well, she's not going to get away with it. I'm coming right over there and—"

"You can't!" yelped Alex. "It's against regulations! I'll be court-martialled if they find a woman in my rooms—"

"Except that Doralene woman, of course," snarled Tanni.

"But she *works* here!"

"What does she work at, besides you?"

"Look here," gabbled Alex, "there are these Victorian-type regulations on the books. Left over from the Puritan Party administration fifty years ago. Ordinarily they're just ignored . . . so much ignored that no one's ever bothered to change them. But Terwilliger—my supervisor while I'm on this blasted assignment—well, he heard about that episode at the party too. The one with, well, us, you know. He won't admit it, but he's obviously in love with Doralene . . . wildly jealous. He told me if I ever broke the morality regulations he'd report me to my CO for dereliction of duty and—and—oh, gosh, he's coming over here now! Tonight! Dinner party for the Hokas—supposed to be small, intimate thing between alien delegates and CDS official—can you see how you'd foul the whole thing up by making a scene and—"

"I don't care!"

"No! Wait! Wait, Tanni, honey, please!" wailed Alex. "Listen, you've got it all wrong. Doralene told me herself she isn't interested in getting married. She's just playing the field—"

"*Oh!*" shrieked Tanni.

And cut the connection.

After a frantic attempt to call back, Alex turned and sprinted for the door of the Tokan suite.

"Doralene!" he howled, bursting in. "You've got to help me—you—us . . . huh?"

The place seemed to be deserted by all except one small Hoka.

Somehow, this pudgy being had gotten dressed in crimson trunk hose, black velvet doublet, puff-sleeved shirt, cloak, and boots, not to forget the tall plumed hat which he now removed from his panda-like head in order to sweep the carpet with a low bow.

"Ah, Illustrissimo!" he squeaked. The English which he had learned so recently and so well had suddenly become thickly accented, with a tendency to wander off into bars of melody. "You are returned."

"Of course I are returned . . . am returned . . . I'm back!" puffed Alex. "Where's Miss Rawlings? What's happened to the others? Why are you all costumed up like that, Ardu?"

"Ah, 'Lustrissimo!" warbled the Hoka reproachfully. "Do you not recognize your faithful Leporello?"

"Lepo—huh?"

"Your servant, Don Giovanni. Your assistant in the unnumbered amorous escapades which have made you the terror of husbands and fathers from Lisbon to Athens." The Hoka struck a pose with one hand extended and the other on his pot belly, and burst into song:

"Gaily he within is sporting.
I must keep off all intrusion,
For his lordship needs seclusion—"

"Stop!" yelled Alex. And as the Hoka obediently quit singing, he rattled: "You mean me? Don Giovanni? I'm Don Giovanni?"

"In the Spanish sometimes referred to as Don Juan," amplified the self-appointed Leporello.

Alex clutched after reality, which seemed to be eluding him. "But that's just an opera!"

"Cospetto! Has your lordship been so trounced by an indignant husband that your lordship's memory has failed him?"

"No such thing!" screamed Alex. "Where's Miss Rawlings?"

"Hist!" said Leporello slyly, laying a stubby finger to his black nose. "Ah, the beautiful Zerlina."

"All right," gritted Alex. "The beautiful Zerlina. Where is she?"

Leporello stood on tiptoe and whispered hoarsely: "She is within."

"Within? Within what, for Betelgeuse's sake?"

"Within your chambers, of course, Illustrissimo."

"My chambers?" Alex charged off, skidded to a halt, decided that her chambers—oops, rooms!—were meant, and turned left in the hallway instead of right.

Mozartian tweedlings came through the door as he leaned on the chime button. "Doralene!" he cried "Open up! What's happening here?"

The door was flung wide. Five Hokas stood there in Renaissance costume, violins tucked under their chins or flutes to their lips or—"Seducer! Ravisher! Cuckolder!" they squeaked.

One of them put down his oboe, drew a wicked-looking rapier, and lunged. "Help!" yelled Alex, giving ground.

Leporello came trotting forth, slammed the door in the faces of his fellow delegates, and called soothingly: "Excellencies, Excellencies! It is no use. My master, that rascal, has just made his escape."

They seemed willing enough to accept this. The music resumed and one of them broke into an aria swearing vengeance upon a certain unknown assailant and murderer.

"Whew!" shuddered Alex. "What's got into them?"

"The Signor means Don Ottavio and the other husbands, fathers, brothers, and lovers of the women he has ruined?" asked Leporello.

"Yes . . . I mean no! Now, look here! What's become of Doralene?"

"Did I not inform your lordship, the beautiful damsel was in his chambers?" replied Leporello. He dug his elbow familiarly into Alex's ribs, and winked. "Surely your lordship would not wish her to be any place else, would your lordship?"

"Oh, NO!" Alex smote his brow.

"That's what I thought," beamed Leporello.

Alex spun about, reached the door of his own rooms, jerked it open, and charged through. "Doralene!" he yelled from the entry. "Where are you?"

"Alex?" trilled a voice from further in. "I'm here."

He dashed ahead, braked, and yipped. Her voice had come from his bathroom.

"What are you doing in there?" he shouted. "What's going on here? Have those Hokas gone crazy?"

A happy feminine laugh bubbled through the panels. "Aren't they cute?" purred Doralene. "They were just wild about that opera. Of course, I'd already told them they were Earth's guests and could send out for anything they wanted, so they must have called the library and a costumer and a music shop and—"

"But . . . you mean they *believe* all this?"

"Well, more or less, Alex. Haven't you read the preliminary psychological reports? It seems that Hokas have a hitherto unknown type of mind—given to accepting any colorful fantasy as if it were real . . . nobody knows, yet, whether they actually and literally believe it at the time, or just play a role to the hilt, but it comes to the same thing. They're also very quick to learn anything at all, so—"

Alex held tight to his whirling head.

"Oh, by the way," went on Doralene carelessly. "Hardman just called. He's got an emergency session later tonight, so we're going to have dinner early. He ought to be here any minute now."

"Now?" squeaked Alex. He got a fresh grip on himself. "But what are you doing in my bathroom?"

"Taking a shower, of course," replied Doralene's voice. "I couldn't dress in my own suite with the Hokas falling all over me. They were waiting for Don Giovanni . . . isn't it just darling? . . . they're convinced he'll show up sooner or later in any young woman's chambers. I'll be out in a minute—that is," her voice finished cheerfully, "unless you want to come in and scrub my back."

"Yipe!" said Alex.

"Do you mean yipe—yes, or yipe—no?" inquired Doralene's voice.

"I mean yipe n—"

Bong, bing, bong went the doorchimes.

"Wait!" cried Alex in agony. "Don't move— I mean, don't come out!"

"Why not?"

"Never mind why not!" Alex dashed off.

As he re-entered his living room, he heard Tanni's wrathful tones from the entry. "Where is he?"

"Mean you my master?" wavered Leporello's high-pitched recitative.

"I mean him, that deceitful . . . that deserter—" She choked.

"Ah!" said Leporello wisely. "You must be Donna Elvira."

"What?"

"Come, come, Zelenza, I am privy to all my master's secrets."

"You're what?" said Tanni. Her English was fluent, but had its limitations as yet.

"My master," said Leporello, misunderstanding. "Don Giovanni. Sometimes in the Spanish referred to as Don Juan."

"Don Juan!" "claimed Tanni in a fire-breathing manner. "Yes, that's just what he is! A miserable, deceitful Don Juan."

"Are you Spanish, too?" asked Leporello, interested.

Tanni burst into tears.

"Ah!" said Leporello. "Time for me to sing the comforting aria." His voice soared:

"Gentle lady, this list I would show you
Of the fair ones my master has courted:
Here you'll find them all duly assorted
In my writing, will't please you to look.
In fair Italy, six hundred and forty,
Germany, two hundred and thirty-one,
A hundred in France—"

Shaken, Alex tiptoed backward. If he could only find a way out—

With a sudden feeling of shock, he checked himself and shook his head to clear it. What was this fantastic spell the Hokas seemed to cast? It must be their own hypnotic solemnity. For a minute he had actually been thinking of himself as Don Giovanni.

This was intolerable! Was he a man or a figment of some Hoka's inflamed imagination? Wheeling about, he marched back into the living room. Tanni had just entered, brushing Leporello aside.

"Alex!" She hesitated, with fire in her eyes.

Bong, bing, bong went the door again, followed a second later by the booming voice of Hardman Terwilliger, unseen in the entry. "Well, well, well! And where is everybody?"

"Yipe!" gasped Alex. "Tanni, hide! It's him!"

"Never mind him," she said, grimly. "This Hoka has been telling me some things about you and what I want to know is—"

With visions of court-martial dancing through his head to the sound of muffled drums, Alex pushed her into Leporello's arms. "Hide her!" he whispered. "Get rid of her . . . lock her in the study at the rear. . . . I'll explain later, darling—"

"I—" Tanni got no further. Leporello's hand closed about her mouth and Leporello's astonishing Hoka strength lifted her off her feet. He whisked her away barely in time.

Terwilliger entered the living room, carrying a package. He was a heavy-set ginger-haired man in his late thirties, who had never quite decided whether a bluff comradely heartiness or a stiff official dignity was more suitable. The former would in fact have been the most natural to him, but some fifteen years of climbing the bureaucratic stairway had left their mark.

His red face split in a hail-fellow let's-let-bygones-be-bygones smile. "Hello, there, Jones!" he trumpeted. "Got a cooler for this? Magnum of champagne I brought along, for you and Doralene and myself. Understand the, ah, Tokans prefer their native beverage, but no reason for us to stint ourselves, eh? Daresay the catering machines will fix a decent enough dinner, but, the appropriation doesn't allow for champagne, so, tum-te-tum . . . take care of your stomach, I always say, and your stomach will take care of you."

Alex bolted an artificial grin to his own face. "Thank you, sir," he wheezed. "Ah (pant, pant) . . . excuse my not being in uniform . . . you did come unexpectedly early."

"Quite all right, quite all right." Terwilliger rubbed his hands and looked about him. "Pleasant digs here, eh? Cut above spaceship on Survey, what? Is Dory ready yet?"

"Dory? Er . . . Miss Rawlings? She's getting dressed, I, I believe—" said Alex, casting a worried glance down the hall toward his bathroom door.

"Ah? Dressing? Ho, ho!" said Terwilliger, turning, if possible, a shade redder in the face than usual. "Perhaps I ought to take her a glass of the gloom-chaser, eh? Haw!" He dug Alex in the ribs, sending the younger man tottering off balance. "I say, what a woman, eh? What a shape! What—"

"I'd better put this bottle in the cooler," said Alex, and dashed for the kitchen.

He swerved just in time to avoid colliding with Doralene, as she stepped out of his bedroom clad in a shimmering dinner gown which hugged her form like a mountain climber not quite able to reach the ultimate peaks.

"Oops! Watch it, boy," she said. "Where's the fire—oh, hullo, Hardy."

Alex looked around, swallowing. Terwilliger's rubicund features appeared to have lost some of their good humor. His eyes swiveled from Alex to Doralene to the bedroom door and back.

"How do you do," he said frozenly.

"Ha, ha!" said Alex. "Guess what happened! The Hokas took over Dor— Miss Rawlings' rooms, so she had to dress in mine. Isn't that funny?"

"Ha-ha!" laughed Doralene.

"Ha!" said Terwilliger.

"What did you say, Hardy?" cooed Doralene.

"Just 'ha,' " snapped Terwilliger. "Man has a right to say 'ha' if he wants to, eh?"

"What's wrong with you, anyway?" asked the girl.

"Nothing wrong with me!"

"Oh yes, there's something wrong with you—"

"Will the gentlefolk have a small drink before dinner?" fluted Leporello, emerging from the kitchen. The savory odors which followed him showed that the catering service robots were hard at work on the meal. Leporello carried a tray bearing three tall glasses and a bottle of extraterrestrial manufacture.

As he passed Alex, he said in a *sotto voce* audible for several meters: "I have locked the importunate damsel away to await your pleasure, Illustrissimo."

"What's this?" Terwilliger started.

"Oh, that!" floundered Alex. *"The Importunate Damsel.* Novel by, uh, Wolfgang Amadeus. Very interesting. Lend it to you when I'm through with it— Have a drink!"

He took one off the tray himself. Automatically, the other two humans followed suit. Terwilliger raised his stonily, took a sip, choked, and lowered it with tears in his prominent pale eyes.

"A native Tokan beverage?" he asked in a strangled voice.

"Uh . . . yes," said Alex wretchedly, after tasting and wincing. "It's pretty strong—not quite to Terrestrial taste. . . . I'll get some Dubonnet or—"

"No, no," said Terwilliger. In a rough aside: "Don't you know, you bloody fool, you never refuse a non-League alien's gift? No telling how some of 'em will react. We'll drink this if it burns our guts out."

"It could be worse, really," murmured Doralene around a thoughtful sip. But then, she was a very husky young woman.

"Ah, Ser Masetto," burbled the Hoka servant to Terwilliger, "take courage. You may only be a peasant, but what is rank compared to honest worth? What, even, is the disgrace in losing your beloved to my master? There is no woman living who could resist him."

"*Eh?*" exploded Terwilliger.

"Er . . . excuse me . . . put the champagne in the cooler," mumbled Alex. "Ardu—Leporello, I mean—a word with you."

When they were in the kitchen, he demanded the key to the study. Leporello broke out another bottle and followed him down the short passageway, remarking that Donna Elvira would need consolation.

Alex unlocked the door. Tanni stood there with sparks in her lovely eyes and small jets of steam appearing to come from her chiseled nostrils. "Well!" she began.

"Now, wait—" croaked Alex. "Here; honey, take this—" Blindly, he snatched the bottle from Leporello and thrust it into her hands. "I'm sorry," he gibbered, "but you shouldn't have come in the first place . . . could ruin me . . . you've got to keep quiet, lie doggo in here till Terwilliger goes home. Then we can straighten out this mess."

"But—" protested Tanni.

"Do you want to get me court-martialled?" groaned Alex.

He closed the door in her face and sped back to the living room.

The conversation between Terwilliger and Doralene had grown somewhat acrimonious in his brief absence. As he entered, a shrill "Now you look here, Hardman Terwilliger—" broke off, and the two stared glumly at their glasses. The boss raised his with a defiant air and tossed the contents off at a gulp. The effect was spoiled by his choking as said contents sank its claws into his gullet. Doralene sneered, swallowed her own drink likewise, and didn't turn a single red hair.

"Uh . . . is dinner ready yet, Leporello?" groped Alex.

"At once, Signor," bowed the Hoka. "And their other Excellencies?"

"What other Excellencies?"

"The husbands, brothers, fathers, and lovers of the women you have seduced, ravished, and—"

"Yes, yes, of course," interrupted Alex as Terwilliger turned his head to stare at him.

"Then best that your Excellency wear this mask." Leporello whipped a black domino from his doublet and extended it. Alex put it on in a numbed, unthinking fashion. Leporello trotted out the main door to give the word.

A swelling chorus of *Finch'han dal vino* rose and five Hokas poured in, engulfed the humans for a moment, and washed on into the dining room, still singing.

"What's been going on here, anyway?" demanded Terwilliger. "What's all this with costumery and . . . and opera, and masks, and—"

"Oh, don't be such a bore, Hardy," said Doralene. She giggled. "I think it's fun."

Terwilliger bristled. "Oh, so I'm a bore now, am I?"

"No . . . yes . . . don't *be* like this!"

"I'll be any way I jolly well please," said Terwilliger sullenly. He poured himself another glassful, grabbed the bottle by the neck, and marched on into the dining room. Alex escorted Doralene, as if through a lobster-and-ice-cream dream.

It would have seemed a pleasing sight under happier circumstances: the snowy tablecloth, the glittering silver, the candles, the bottles, the gaily clad Hokas seated there waving their instruments, swilling merrily, and extemporizing a drinking song full of grace notes. The RoboServs rolled about offering appetizers, not too badly handicapped by Leporello's assistance, and sunset light streamed through the tall plastic windows. It ought to have been a picture of gracious living.

Terwilliger sat down at the head of the table and took a moody gulp of liquor. Doralene sat at his right and took a moody gulp for herself. Alex, at his left, sweating under the mask, realized that the Hoka hell-brew was taking effect on them. Already it had numbed taste buds and judgment enough so that they didn't understand what they were drinking and what a wallop was being prepared.

"Wouldn't you like to switch to this vermouth?" he suggested.

"No," said Terwilliger.

"Well, the clear soup looks good—"

"Don't want any clear soup."

"Perbacco!" squeaked the sword-bearing Hoka who had apparently assumed the part of Don Ottavio. "This Masetto is a man of parts. He would rather drink than eat. Drink to Ser Masetto!"

"Ah," said another Hoka pityingly, "who would not seek to drown his sorrows, whose intended bride is soon to be seduced by the unspeakable villain Don Giovanni . . . if, indeed, she has not already succumbed to his lure?"

"What?" barked Terwilliger, jerking in his chair. "What's going on here?"

"I don't know," said Doralene, perhaps a bit to quickly.

Terwilliger's eyes narrowed as he stared at her. "Who is this Giovanni chap, anyhow?" he demanded.

"Ah," said Don Ottavio, "who, indeed?" He looked straight at Alex's dominoed face. "Perhaps you, anonymous sir, know where we may find the villain to punish him for his crimes?"

"No," said Alex weakly. "He went that-a-way . . . I mean, no, I don't."

"It's no use, anyway," said the mournful Hoka. "There is no mortal man who can overcome Don Giovanni. You are but inviting your own death, Don Ottavio."

"Nevertheless," said Don Ottavio firmly, "I have sworn vengeance." He hopped up on his chair, put one foot on the table, spread his arms dramatically, and burst into song:

> *"Che giuramento, oh Dei!*
> *Che giuramento, oh Dei!*
> *Che barbarao momento!*
> *Tra cento affetti e cento—"*

"Uh . . . er . . . see here," shouted Alex above the racket. "Terwilliger . . . ah . . . this is supposed to be an official dinner, and I haven't yet presented the delegates—"

"Yes," said Terwilliger darkly, tossing off another draught. "It was *supposed* to be an official dinner."

"Have some salad?" pleaded Alex as a tray rolled by with the next course.

"What use is salad?" mumbled Doralene, draining her glass and singing to Leporello to refill it. "I should sit here and listen to a certain gazabo crunching salad in his big fat mouth?"

"May I ask to what gazabo you refer, Miss Rawlings?" said Terwilliger with elaborate overtones.

"Never mind," said Doralene. "It might not be polite to say."

Terwilliger quivered. His eyes swung to Alex and grew smoky.

"You!" he rasped.

"Me?" said Alex.

"You!" repeated Terwilliger, breathing heavily.

"Leave him alone!" said Doralene.

Terwilliger returned his bleared gaze to her. "Ah so!" he said. "Now it comes out! Dressing in here—*ha!*"

"Oh!" cried Doralene. "Are you insin— are you insin-shin—" She drew herself up in her seat. Her décolletage, already strained, threatened to burst its moorings altogether. "How dare you!"

"Why, Miss Rawlings, what *are* you thinking of?" leered Terwilliger unpleasantly.

"Now, now, wait—" sputtered Alex. "I don't undersand—I didn't have anything to do with—"

"My master speaks truth, Ser Masetto," murmured Leporello, leaning over Terwilliger's shoulder to pour him another glassful. "He was out seducing another wench at the time."

"*What?*" roared Terwilliger.

"Excuse us, Masetto," piped a couple of Hokas. They got up and brushed past him and toddled out of the room.

"WHAT'S GOING ON HERE?" bellowed Terwilliger. "What you been doing behind my back, Jones? Are you an incompetent, a lecher, a lechment incompeter . . . an incompeter lech . . . or . . . or both? What is all this?"

"I'd better check on them," stammered Alex. He scrambled to his feet and dove after the two Hokas who had left.

Shuddering, he inspected the inner doors. Noises came from his bedroom. He entered.

A large statue in green marble loomed by the dresser. He recognized it as belonging to the Progress of Man series which lined the tenth-floor main corridor. This one represented John W. Campbell. Somehow . . . oh God . . . *when* had the Hokas stolen it?

The two whom he sought stood with brushes and a bucket of whitewash, happily splashing it on the statue.

"What are you doing?" choked Alex.

"Ah, Signor," beamed one. "Obviously matters are approaching a climax. It seems only proper that we prepare the statue of the Commandant for an appropriately ghastly entrance."

"No!" Alex snatched the bucket away from them. "Absolutely not. We don't do that."

"Why not, Signor?" asked a small wide-eyed being.

"Because . . . because . . . it's not the first of the month," said Alex desperately. "Statues of Commandants only get whitewashed on the first of the month, not like statues of Admirals, who get whitewashed on the fifteenth or the twentieth. That's because Admirals have more salt on them—" He realized suddenly that he was babbling, and with a strong effort pulled himself together. "Now do go back to the dinner party," he begged.

Somewhat disappointed, but willing as always to oblige, the painters obeyed. Alex stood for a moment wondering where he could put the bucket—no use leaving temptation around—ah, yes. He took it into the bathroom and balanced it precariously on the medicine chest, out of the short Hoka reach.

Loud, disputatious human voices came from the dining room. Alex was in no hurry to intervene. He slipped down the little hallway and stuck his head in the study door. It would not have surprised him much to have gotten it bitten off.

A warm and wobbly shape collapsed softly on his neck. "Oh, Alesh," breathed Tanni. "Sh' been sho long—"

Alex stared at her. She stared back, through tangled golden locks. She giggled. "Oh, Alesh," she said. "Alesh, dear, tha' li'l bottle shtuff . . . so *strong* . . . hol' onna me, honey—"

His eyes lit on the half-emptied bottle. He saw it had not, as he had assumed, been blown on Earth. The label said:

OLD PANTHER SWEAT
Made in Montana by Panthers

"Oh, no!" he moaned.

"Oh, yes," said Tanni. "Kiss me."

"JONES!" thundered Terwilliger. "Where are YOU? C'mere!"

"Sig du elsker mig," pleaded Tanni.

"JONES!"

"Now . . . now just sit here . . . I'll be right back—just take it easy—" Somehow, Alex untangled himself from his suddenly octopus-like beloved and stumbled back to the living room.

Terwilliger, his face hardly distinguishable from the boiled lobster which Leporello was urging on him, sat weaving in his chair. He fixed a swollen and bloodshot eye on Alex. "Jones!" he woofed. "Where you been?"

"Oh . . . the Commandant . . . whitewash, you know," stuttered Alex with a feeble smile, sliding back into his seat.

"Whash— whish— Be. That. As. It. May. Jones," said Terwilliger, "I hold you responsible. High times I looked— I mean, *high time* I looked inna conditions here. Noss gregligence! Underculture aliens . . . prospec'ive wards o' League, d'you hear, allowed t' run riot an' . . . run riot. Mos' reprehensible." He sat for a moment repeating "reprehensible," obviously to be sure he had it right. The Hokas joined in with voice and instruments, and an impromptu cantata was getting under way when Terwilliger shifted gears and went on:

"Al'ays had . . . sof' spot f' you, Jones. But now . . . neglec' o' duty . . . slip me this rotgut, hope make me drunk so I wouldn' notice . . . highly immoral, lecher an' so forth—Nothin' personal, un'erstan'!" he added quickly. "Nothin' personal. If you've ruined woman I love—nothin' personal . . . feel sorry f' you, Doralene, him an' his hundreds of, uh, uh—"

"Paramours, Signor," supplied Leporello.

"Thank you. Paramours. You'll be outvoted, I'm afraid, Doralene. But i'sh your business." Terwilliger climbed slowly to his feet. "If I report you f' dereliction o' duty, Jones . . . recommen' court-martial— nothin' personal. Don' misun'erstan'. 'S jus' f' good o' the Service." He turned majestically on his heel. It was a well-chosen exit line, marred only by the fact that he kept on turning and asked plaintively: "Which way's uh bathroom?"

"Not love," snuffled Doralene into her glass. "Go up five grades 'fore talk to me o' love. Suffed shtirt . . . stuffed shirt! Cute, though. Could'a loved him—" She began to cry. Terwilliger gyrated slowly out.

"Doralene!" howled Alex, oblivious to the interested gaze of the surrounding Hokas. "Doralene, what happened?"

He stood up as she came tearfully around the table. "Quarrel," she said. "Shirred stuff! *Believed* wha' those Hokas was sayin'— Oh, Alex!" And throwing her arms about his neck and her face against his tunic, she broke into noisy sobs.

"Doralene . . . now, Doralene, please—" he begged.

A Valkyrie shriek interrupted him. He yanked his eyes around and saw Tanni advancing on them.

"Bravo!" cheered the Hokas.

"*That woman!*" bawled Tanni. "All uh time I was waitin' and waitin' for you, all alone, you an!— Oh!"

"Whozis?" queried Doralene, fuzzy-voiced.

"My dear Ottavio," murmured one of the Hokas, "considering how the ladies cluster about him could it be that our mysterious masked friend is none other than . . . him?"

"*Cospetto!*" A furry hand dropped to a sword. "Think you so?"

"*Ye-e-e-e-es,*" said another Hoka in A flat.

"*I happen* t' be Ens'n Jones' fian-she," said Tanni to Doralene.

"Oh, izzat so?" said Doralene, still holding on to Alex.

"It is past time we had our revenge, Signores," said a Hoka, "I, for one, don't like being cuckolded."

"But you're not married, Don Vittorio," pointed out another one reasonably. "How do you know if you haven't tried—"

"Yes," said Tanni. "That izzo."

"Now, girls," chattered Alex. "Girls, girls—"

"Wanna make somethin' of it, beanpole?" growled Doralene.

"Beanpole!" screamed Tanni. "Why, you fat frump—"

"After all," said a Hoka, "it's my honor that's at stake."

"How did it get there?" asked Don Vittorio.

"I have my suspicions," said the first one, darkly.

A crash from the inner suite was followed by a weird, strangled, gargling cry. The humans half turned to see what it was. But they had too much else to think about.

"What did you call me?" spat Doralene.

"The thing is," said Don Ottavio, "how can I discover his true identity as long as he has that mask on?"

"I call' you uh frat fump," said Tanni, returning to the pressing business at hand.

"You could ask him to take it off," suggested Don Vittorio.

"Why, you li'l squirt—" snarled Doralene.

"Girls, girls, girls!" Alex wrung his hands.

"Pardon me." Someone tugged at his sleeve. He looked down into Don Ottavio's round golden-furred face.

"Yes?" he asked.

"Would you do me the favor of removing your mask, sir?" requested the Hoka.

"How 'ud you enjoy uh poke inna nose?" said Tanni.

"Girls, girls—" Absently, Alex removed the domino "Tanni, Dory, now wait, wait just a—"

"Perbacco! 'Tis he! At the villain! Hew him down!"

With a roar of epithets, the Hokas came swarming around the table at Alex. Don Ottavio's rapier whizzed in front of his nose. He yelped and jumped back. The other Hokas formed a line, cleared their throats, and broke into the Soldiers' Chorus from *Faust.*

Don Ottavio halted his ominous advance. "That doesn't sound right, Signores," he complained.

"I know," said Don Vittorio. "But we haven't really had time to prepare—"

"Ho-yo-to-ho?" suggested the smallest Hoka.

Don Ottavio turned and bowed at Alex. "Perhaps your Excellency knows a suitably bloodthirsty chorus to which to meet your doom?" he inquired politely.

Frantic, Alex looked about for a weapon. He didn't know if the

Hokas would really kill him or not—they were the kindliest race he had ever met, ordinarily, but they were so hopped up on this grand opera jag right now that— He backed into a corner.

"No!" cried Tanni, running toward him. "Stop that, you little monster! Don't you dare!"

Leporello caught her by the arms. "Don't worry, Zelenza," he said. "Your honor is about to be avenged. He never paid me enough anyway."

Tanni kicked and writhed to no avail. "But I don't want my honor avenged!" she sobbed.

"Dammit," shouted Alex, "her honor doesn't *need* avenging! I'm not— I didn't—"

He broke off. So did the Hokas. One and all stood frozen at the noises coming toward the room . . . the sound of slow, heavy footfalls.

Through the door, arms extended, grisly white, tottered a Shape.

It was Hardman Terwilliger, liberally coated with whitewash.

"Blop-blup-bluh!" he said, waving his dripping hands at them.

The Hokas' eyes lit up.

"The Man in Stone!" squeaked Don Ottavio. "The Commandant!"

Happily shrilling dismay, he and his friends fell back from the apparition. Leporello dived conscientiously under the table. "Help!" cried Don Vittorio.

"I'm palsied with fright," said another. "See how I tremble."

"I'm shuddering, myself," said the one beside him in a confidential tone. "It's more gruesome."

The smallest Hoka went rigid as a board and, holding his stance, toppled over backward to land with a thud. Stiff on the carpet, he opened one beady black eye.

"I fainted," he explained, and closed it again.

Alex's lurching brain made a final convulsive leap.

One way to straighten out this mess—at least to save a few fragments—

He sprang past the petrified girls, to the table. One hand seized a bottle of the murderous Hoka liquor and emptied it on the floor. Another threw a candle on top of it. A cool but satisfactorily hellish blue alcohol flame jumped up.

He reeled back to the gaping Terwilliger. "Quick!" he whispered. "When I fall, drag me out of here."

"Eh? What?" sputtered the bureaucrat. "Wha's uh meanin' o' this, Jones? What—" His eyes fell on Tanni, standing beside Doralene. "My God," he whispered in awe. "The man's insatiable."

"Drag me off to eternal damnation, you idiot!" hissed Alex.

Terwilliger remained dazed. Alex swore under his breath. Then he emitted one last, anguished scream and fell against the whitewashed man, throwing the shoulder block he had learned on the football fields of the Academy. Don Giovanni and the Statue went crashing out the dining room door.

All kindly gods be praised! As he got an arm around Terwilliger's throat to keep him quiet, Alex heard Tanni—his own dear sweet intelligent wonderful Tanni, sobered by his need of her—pick up the cue. She stepped to the door, closed it, and cried in an awful voice:

"Such is the end of those who do evil! To such an end, the wicked have ever come and ever will!"

The Hokas must have retrieved their instruments, for as Alex struggled with Terwilliger, he heard the operatic finale rise to a doomful burst and die away again.

It was followed by thunderous clapping and squeaky cries of: *"Da capo!"*

"No, dear friends," said Tanni. "It is all over now. Don Giovanni has perished as he so richly deserved. Now hadn't you better go to your rooms and get a good night's sleep?"

"Sì, Zelenza," agreed Leporello.

"After all, tomorrow you will be having all kinds of important conferences with high interplanetary officials."

"Mysterious conferences?"

"Very mysterious."

"Then goodnight, Miss Hostrup," said Ardu gallantly.

Small feet pattered out through the main door.

Alex released Terwilliger. "Shall we join the ladies?" he panted.

"You'll pay for this, Jones!" stormed Terwilliger as they went back into the living room. "Discredit whole mission . . . make a farce . . . slip me this rotgut—" His wandering eye came to light on a disheveled Tanni and Doralene, who were wearily accepting coffee from a RoboServ. "Yes, an' lechery . . . drag in blondes soon's m' back's turned—"

"Shut up!" roared Alex.

The whitewash rose on Terwilliger's neck. "What?"

"I said shut up." Alex strode over to Tanni and put an arm about her waist. She sighed and snuggled up to him. "Miss Hostrup happens to be my fiancée. I haven't done a damned thing I shouldn't have, and you'd have known it if you weren't so filthy-minded suspicious, and I can prove it. If you'd known what you were supposed to know about Hoka psychology, you'd never have believed those yarns. And I didn't ask for this job in the first place. It was your big bright idea to yank me in off my furlough and hand it to me."

"But—"

"Shut up, I said! I'm not through with you yet, Terwilliger. You never gave me any restrictions to observe in entertaining the Hokas, so this mess tonight is your fault, and it was Miss Hostrup and I who pulled your isotopes out of the pile. I didn't try to get you drunk, either, you melodramatic excuse-monger. Did I hold you by the nose and pour that wet lightning down your throat? I did not. I even asked you to drink something else. I didn't upset a pail of whitewash on my own clumsy head and track up this suite, either!"

Alex stepped forward, fists doubled. "Terwilliger," he finished, "if you want to try and make trouble for me, go ahead. Just go ahead! I've got the real story of what happened here tonight, with witnesses, and I can spread it from here to the Lesser Magellanic Cloud!"

"That's telling him, sweetheart," said Tanni.

"Uh," said Doralene with rather less enthusiasm.

Terwilliger turned pale beneath his whitewash. "So!" he said. "It's blackmail!"

As a matter of fact, it was, and Alex felt ashamed of himself. But he couldn't see any alternative. He had, after all, been neglecting this assignment in order to be with Tanni—that much could be proven, if Terwilliger did press charges—so the only thing to do was silence the man with the threat of making him a galactic laughing-stock.

"Shall we say . . . a bargain?" puffed Alex in what he hoped was a suitably villainous manner.

Terwilliger began to swell alarmingly. "No," he said thickly, "we shall not."

His voice rose to a quarterdeck bellow. *"Publish and be damned! The Service is muh career, but if y' think I got so li'l honor that I'd give in t' blackmail—"*

"Sweetheart!" trilled Doralene, hurling herself into his arms.

"Huh?" said Terwilliger after he had picked himself up.

Doralene wiped whitewash off her face. "Oh, darling," she said, "here I always thought you were jus' a shuffed stirt—"

"Perhaps I am a snuffed skirt," said Terwilliger doggedly, "but thuh fack remains—"

"Oh, but you aren't! I see it now. You're a *man!* Oh, darlin', you don' wanna make a big mess o' things an' get y'self in trouble an' poor Alex an' Tanni . . . they're in love, darling, jus' like us!"

"Like us?" whispered Terwilliger, not daring to believe.

Doralene squelched into his arms. Silently, Alex and Tanni left the room.

They were in the study, half an hour or so later, when Terwilliger knocked on the door and entered.

"Ah," he beamed, scattering good humor and flakes of dried white-wash. "Ah, there, Jones. No hard feelings, I trust? There's something that just occurred to me. How would you like to be a plenipotentiary—?"

INTERLUDE II

**Foreign Ministry
of the
United Commonwealths**

Cultural Development Service
Earth Headquarters
5/5/75

Ens. Alexander B. Jones (TISS, ret.) New Cultures Section, E.A.A.B.
CDS Building Prime, Annex 18
League City, N.Z.

My dear Mr. Jones:

Enclosed is your official appointment as Plenipotentiary of the Interbeing League to Culture X-73-Z-218-r, otherwise known (in English translation of the indigenous name) as the Five and a Half Cities, said culture being located on the planet officially designated Toka or Brackney's Star III. You will note that your jurisdiction will automatically be expanded to include any other societies on this world which may apply for ward status; and the preliminary studies and propaganda results indicate that all autochthonous nations will be eager to do so as soon as exposed to League civilization. Thus your territory should, within a few years at most, include the entire planet. My heartiest congratulations and best wishes for a long and successful career in the Service.

As an "old hand" "who knows the ropes," and by way of duty from seniors such as myself to "new chums" such as yourself, perhaps I may be permitted to extend a *verbum sapienti,* as it were. A great tradition binds us of the CDS together—not only here at Earth Headquarters, but wherever the flag of civilization waves, and even on airless worlds where the flag of civilization does not wave at all. Little honored and unsung (except, of course, on Thrrrwhilia, whose inhabitants have somewhat of a mania for musical limericks), we carry on our daily rounds, long-suffering but unrelenting in our efforts to raise the primitive. And of all fully civilized races, it is humankind, the predominant species whose culture sets the tone of the entire League, that most feels the impact of *noblesse oblige.*

You have now joined us in assuming the Earthman's Burden.

We must remind ourselves, always and forever, to be patient with the innocent sub-civilized being. We shall often find his attitude uncosmic, his mind naively fumbling in its attempt to grasp the nuances of that which we teach him. He gazes at us with clear unknowing eyes that plead with us to show him the right way, the civilized way—the way, in short, of the Interbeing League. We must not fail that trust.

Perhaps he will seem slow to adopt our ways. Especially at first, he will tend to be shy, retiring, afraid to push himself forward, to suggest things to us. And when this happens, we must draw him out of himself. (N.B.: The use of this metaphor is not recommended in the presence of shelled or carapaced beings.) We must take him by the hand (or paw, or tentacle, as the case may be); we must put his small, hesitating shoulder or equivalent thereof to the wheel of progress, encouraging him in his faltering attempts to adopt our most basic ways while simultaneously guarding him against those aspects of civilization which are beyond his present ability to understand and/or cope with.

It is a hard task. We who labor in this vineyard will not gather the fruits of those same trees we plant; it takes more than one lifetime to elevate a whole world to readiness for full status, autonomy, and representation in the League. Our chief reward is the rich sense of personal achievement; the knowledge that ultimately, however much some of them at present may resent certain necessary restrictions, we shall each have the undying gratitude of an entire intelligent species; and, in the words of that great poet whose prescient spirit animates our entire endeavor, "the judgment of your peers!"—i.e., your fellows in the Service.

For the present, then, I leave you with the motto of the Service, which is now yours: *Whatsoever a man soweth, that shall he also reap.* (Gal., vi, 7)

Very truly yours,
Adalbert Parr
Chief Cultural Commissioner

N.B.: Immediately upon arrival at your post of duty, you will complete Forms W-43921-j, G-64390, and X-89-A-7645, and return them to this office.

AP/grd

IN HOKA SIGNO VINCES

"Snort!" snorted Alexander Jones.

"What, dear?" inquired Tanni.

"It's those Pornians," he grumbled from behind the newsfax sheet he was holding, still damp off the subspace receiver. "They've finished building that battleship, and now they're putting her into space."

"How awful!" said Tanni musically.

Alex lowered the newssheet and gazed fondly at her blonde beauty. He could never quite get over the exaltation of being married to her. And when in addition, he—still a very young man, only a few months ago mere ensign in Survey—was made plenipotentiary, with the rank and pay of an ambassador, it was not even a very believable situation.

So far his duties had been light: to reside here in the coastal city-state Mixumaxu, introducing the natives gradually to modern technology, leading them toward the eventual formation of their own world government, and so on. Of course, as the Terrestrial cultural mission expanded their activities and brought more of the planet under his supervision, the work would increase; already there were a fiendish lot of reports to file. And even ambassadorial quarters on a new planet were not quite the ideal home for a recent bride, and the Hokas were—well—a little odd, to say the least. But it could have been a lot worse, too. Mixumaxu was fairly civilized, and had a delightful climate. The Hokas, far from chafing at their subordinate status, were falling all over themselves to be friendly and helpful and . . . yes, their only fault was that excessive enthusiasm, too much imagination, too much tendency to go hog-wild over any new concept, too little ability to distinguish fiction from fact—

"I think that's terrible," said Tanni indignantly. "You'd think the other planetary governments would get together and stop them."

"What?" asked Alex, jerked back from his musings.

"Those Pornians and their space dreadnaught."

"Oh, that!" said Alex. "Well, you see, the trouble is, after the last war all the civilized races agreed to complete disarmament except for small interplanetary police forces. There's no military to speak of anywhere in the known parts of the galaxy, and the taxpayers wouldn't stand for any. Damn fool thing, too—" Alex started to fume again. "We need some kind of *interstellar* police to stop fanatic racialists like those Pornians from building weapons. Why, something like this ship could spoil a hundred years of peace and goodwill, start an armaments race and wreck the League—" He got to his feet. "Where's the subspace video? I want to see what Earth Headquarters has to say in today's bulletins."

The newsfax was sent from a local bureau a mere fifty light-years away; only by straining his ambassadorial salary could Alex afford a receiver for programs sent all the way from Earth.

"I put it on the porch, dear," said Tanni. "That program the Hokas like so much—you know, *Tom Bracken of the Space Patrol*—it was on and they came to see it like they do every day."

Alex frowned at her. "I hope you didn't leave the circuits open, honey," he said. "You know the Hokas aren't supposed to have contact with anything too modern at this stage of their development."

"I locked it on that one channel," she reassured him. "They can only get the children's programs."

Alex sighed with relief and went out and wheeled in the video. The Hokas were just too blinking inventive, among their other faults. He wished Earth Headquarters hadn't been so quick about allowing them limited trade rights. A few unscrupulous traders could start furnishing them with stuff they shouldn't get for the next twenty years.

He tuned the video to EHQ and sat through an hour of official bulletins. But there was nothing of importance. Pornia was so far from Earth that a lethargic government couldn't appreciate the danger. But it was within a few light-years of Toka, and Alex was acutely aware of that fact. This was not the first time he had grumbled about the situation, to his wife or even to some of the Hokas. You'd think the human race's own history would have convinced it that militarism must be nipped in the bud, but—

He sighed, switched off the set, and yawned. Presently he and Tanni turned out the lights and went to bed.

* * *

Alex was just falling off to sleep when there was small tap on the window. For a moment, he tried drowsily to ignore it, but it came again.

"Hist," whispered a Hoka voice through the opening.

Alex cursed, swiveled his eyes toward Tanni, and saw that she was already asleep. He signalled silence to the bear-like face which pressed its damp black nose against the pane. "Just a minute," he murmured. "I'll be right out."

Growling to himself, he dressed clumsily in the dark and went out on the porch. One moon was up, almost full. In its bright glow he could see two Hokas waiting for him.

Surprise brought him up short, and his breath hissed between his teeth. Gone were the floppy boots, peak hats, and bell-covered motley of the local folk dress. The two that faced him had adorned their portly bodies with gray tunics, tight whipcord riding breeches, Sam Browne belts, jackboots, and goggled metal helmets. And holstered by the side of each was a—

"What are you doing with those," squeaked Alex. His heart tried to climb out of his mouth. "Where'd you get Holman raythrowers?"

They paid no attention. Solemnly, the larger Hoka saluted.

"Coordinator Jones," he said in the English which was rapidly becoming the world language of Toka, "the expedition is ready."

"What expedition?" cried Alex. "Look here, Buntu—"

"Sir," said the Hoka stiffly, "I am now Captain Jax Bennison of the Space Patrol, at your service." He clicked his heels and saluted again.

"Great jumping rockets!" exclaimed the other Hoka. "Don't tell me the Coordinator didn't recognize you?"

"It's the moonlight, probably," said the first Hoka. "All clear and on green now, Coordinator?"

"I—I—" stammered Alex.

"Aye, aye!" repeated Jax Bennison crisply. "No time to lose, then. We lift gravs at 2330 hours. Follow us, sir."

The Hokas set rapidly off and Alex, his brain spinning, hurried after them. He didn't understand one part of this—but if it ever got back to Earth that he had allowed Holman raythrowers to get into the hands of aborigines— His brow beaded with cold sweat at the thought.

The Hokas led the way down narrow, cobbled streets between high-walled houses. The city was quiet, asleep it seemed. But the guards at the old defensive wall saluted and opened the gates for them. "Good hunting, Patrolmen," said one.

Outside, there was a broad empty field used for the infrequent spaceship landings. In the moonlight, Alex, saw that more than a hundred Hokas, uniformed like the two of them, were lined up at attention.

But it was on the large shape behind them that his staggering mind focused.

"My courier boat!" he wailed. "What have you done to her?"

The once sleek shape of the *Tanni Girl* was now hacked and scarred. Holes had been cut the length of her sides and the muzzles of primitive gunpowder cannon projected beyond the air-seals. Her name had been painted out and the cognomen *Fearless* replaced it; below were the words *Space Patrol Ship Number One* and a large white star.

Alex made three long strides and caught up with Captain Jax Bennison, who was saluting an elderly Hoka recognizable as a town official. But this one was now dressed in a blue tunic, gold braid, cutlass, and cocked hat.

"What's the idea?" barked Alex hysterically. "My ship—"

Jax pointed to the ornate shield with the legend *Space Patrol* that he wore on his breast.

"Sorry, sir," he answered, "but you know the rights of the Patrol. Patrolmen may requisition whatever is needed just by showing their badges."

"Who said so?" raged Alex.

"Tom Bracken of the Space Patrol, sir," said Jax. "He says it every day on the video."

Cocked-Hat saluted in his turn. "We knew that you, sir, as Supreme Coordinator, would approve," he said. "Fleet Admiral Ron Bronz at your command, sir."

"The danger is imminent, sir," added the second Hoka.

"The Malevonians are obviously preparing the great push, and yet the Patrol Fleet seems to be elsewhere. We could do nothing but organize our own branch of the Patrol to stop the enemy." He clicked heels. "Executive Officer Lon Meters at your command, sir."

Alex turned wildly to Admiral Ron Bronz. "What are you *doing?*" he spluttered.

"Admiral's inspection before the Patrol embarks," said the old Hoka. His cocked hat slipped down over his muzzle and he raised it with an irritated gesture. "Damn that tailor. Wouldn't surprise me if he was a Malevonian agent." His voice barked out over the waiting ranks of teddy bears. "Ten-SHUN! Inspection will proceed."

Solemnly, he and Captain Jax went down the line touching the nose of each spaceman to see that it was cold and moist. Alex groaned.

"All in good health, sir," said the admiral as returned. "All clear and on green." His cocked hat slipped down again. Alex found it strangely disconcerting to be addressing now a face and now a hat.

"But—but—but—" he stammered.

Lon Meters leaned over and said to Jax Bennison in a clearly audible whisper: "Something wrong with the Coordinator, Captain? You suppose the Malevonians have gotten control of his mind?"

"Of course not," said Jax. "They wouldn't dare. It's just his crusty way. He has a rough exterior but a heart of gold."

Admiral Bronz turned to Alex. "Well, sir, the men are ready," he reported. "Would you make a brief but touching speech before they take off?"

A hundred furry countenances turned expectantly to Alex where he stood in the moonlight. He raised a shaky voice: "This nonsense has got to stop!"

"That's right, sir," beamed Captain Jax. "We've got to stop the enemy."

"Go home to your wives and families!" screamed Alex, trying to rouse a sense of domestic duty. "Go home to your fireside brides!"

"Aye," shrilled the admiral. "When peace has come to the galaxy, we shall return to our homes."

"You've got your own work to do—" pleaded Alex.

"*Aye! Aye!*" The falsetto cheers seemed to shake the city walls. "We've got to stop the foe!"

"Form ranks!" barked Captain Jax. "Forward march!"

A hundred Hokas faced the boat and tramped toward its airlock. A hundred voices lifted in song.

> "*Off we go, into the vacuum yonder,*
> *Climbing high, into the black,*
> *Shaking out ee-vil with fire and thunder,*
> *Blasting down to the attack!*
> *All the wo-o-orlds watch us in wonder*
> *Till our mi-i-ission is done.*
> *We'll ride on high throughout the sky,*
> *For nothing can stop Patrol Ship Number One!*"

"You encouraged them marvelously well, sir," said the admiral.

"Stop!" screamed Alex. He raced after the marching Hokas, trying to stem the tide.

"The Coordinator!" yelled Lon Meters in a burst of happiness. "The Coordinator himself has decided to come with us!"

Before Alex could catch his breath, he was caught up in the onward sweep. The press of a hundred solid little bodies forced him into the boat, up a companionway and onto the bridge. He heard the airlock clang shut behind him. There was no chance to open it again; all passages were jammed tight with shining-eyed Hokas.

Captain Jax strapped himself into the pilot chair while Alex was still gibbering. "Ready to blast," called a voice from the intercom. The engines growled.

"Ready to blast," echoed Captain Jax.

"Stop!" shrieked Alex, recognizing in panic what was about to happen. "Stop, I say!"

Nobody heard him. Captain Jax pulled the drive switch. Since he had not cut in the acceleration compensators, and Alex was not harnessed in place, the human was thrown back against a bulkhead and smashed into unconsciousness.

"Are you all right, sir?"

Fuzzily, with ringing head, Alex struggled back to awareness. Through bleared eyes, he saw that he was alone on the bridge with Jax and Lon. They were bending anxiously over him.

"Here," said Jax, extending a flask. "Have a pull of Old Spaceman."

No matter what name it went under, Hoka liquor was potent stuff. Alex felt a measure of strength flow back into him with a gulp. He pulled his lanky frame up against the artificial gravity till he stood more or less erect. Then he glared.

"Sorry, sir," apologized the exec, Lon. "We didn't realize you were too busy planning our strategy to have prepared for takeoff."

Alex clenched his teeth. "Where are we?" he mumbled.

"Sir," replied the captain, "we don't know. After we went through the space warp, we lost orientation."

"Huh?" said Alex. "Went through the what?"

"The space warp, sir," explained Lon Meters.

"Oh," said Alex. For a moment the solemnity of the small Hoka was so convincing that he found himself wondering if the four years of astrogation courses he had taken had not perhaps been negligent in not mentioning this phenomenon.

"Well, then," said Captain Jax blandly, "you realize that we must be in a totally unfamiliar part of space. Maybe even in another universe. Observe." He pointed to the viewscreen and the black, starry sky it showed. Alex goggled. Some of the constellations had certainly changed, though not much.

The human's brain began to function once more; he could almost feel it sweating. Video programs never mentioned the elaborate mathematics of astrogation, so the Hokas must have assumed that you simply aimed your spaceship where you wanted it to go. Finding themselves unable to locate their position, they had leaped to the conclusion that a space warp—whatever that might be—had thrown them off course.

In fact, once they began taking the Tom Bracken program literally, everything else followed with a relentless kind of logic. The Pornian menace—they must have equated that with these Malevonians who, not content with mere rearmament, were apparently out to conquer the universe. They must have decided that the ostensible human plenipotentiary was really the Supreme Coordinator of the Space Patrol in disguise. Then they went ahead and organized their own unit and—and—

Oh, no!

"Where are we headed?" he asked.

"Sir?" said Lon Meters.

"Top secret," snapped Captain Jax quickly. "Exec Meters, close your eyes and put your hands over your ears." The other complied.

"We had this Pornia in mind, sir," resumed the captain. "It seems to be the local center of enemy operations. But now that we're lost—"

"Well—" Alex was slowly recovering his equilibrium. "Never mind. We're first going to have to figure out just where we are."

"That's what I thought we were going to have to do," said Captain Jax. "Exec Meters, you can open your eyes and ears. Do you think you can locate us, sir?"

A vision of the paper work involved in that little chore floated through Alex's head. As if it didn't ache enough already! "I think so," he groaned.

"Excellent, Coordinator," said Captain Jax. "You take over the chart room, and meanwhile the rest of us will maneuver the ship around and look for enemies."

"Oh, Lord," said Alex dismally. But there didn't seem to be much he could do about it; and even at trans-light velocities, interstellar space is so big that their chances of barging into a star or planet were negligible. As for the boat, these roboticized models all but handled themselves, which was the reason a few semi-trained Hokas had been able to get her under way.

"Of course," said Captain Jax, "the Malevonians may be any place. Perhaps even now we are in the heart of their stronghold. If—"

He was interrupted by a grizzled Hoka in an acid-stained smock who came indignantly into the bridge. "Sir," he squeaked, "you've got to do something about that chief engineer."

"Do what?" asked the captain.

"How should I know?" cried the newcomer, shaking his fists and dancing with rage. "Feed him to the bems. Make him walk the plank. Anything, just so he'll quit bothering me!"

"I don't believe you've met this man, sir," whispered Lon Meters to Alex. "Dr. Zarbovsky, our scientist. Quite mad, of course—but a genius."

"But if he's mad," said Alex, "then why—"

"Every Patrol ship has a mad scientist, sir, as you well know," said Lon firmly. "Tom Bracken's, for instance."

"How can I build a new-type disintegrator if the engineer won't let me have the busbars from the drive unit?" screamed Dr. Zarbovsky. "Answer me that!"

Alex stepped into the breach. "There should be extra busbars in the storeroom," he said diplomatically.

"In the storeroom," murmured Dr. Zarbovsky. "I never thought of that!" He hurried out again.

Jax and Lon looked awestruck at Alex. "What a brain!" breathed the exec.

"He wouldn't be Coordinator if he didn't have one," said Jax proudly.

"I wonder," whispered Lon, "I wonder if he's a mutant?"

"I'm getting out of here!" snarled Alex. He slammed the door behind him. The two Hoka officers looked affectionately in his direction.

"A crusty exterior," said Lon, "but a heart of gold. Eh, Jax?"

"On green, Lon," agreed the captain.

For the fortieth time, Alex's coffee cup leaped into the air and splashed on the floor as the boat's gravity beams ripped her through another sudden change of direction. Red-eyed from forty-eight hours with little sleep, he slammed his stylus down on the latest sheet of calculations and started to get up.

A burry voice grumbled over the intercom: "Engine rroom to brridge. Chief Engineerr MacTavish speaking. Wha' the hell d'ye think ye're doing? Can ye no keep the ship on a level coorse forr five minutes straight?"

"Sorry, Angus," replied Captain Jax soothingly. "We're dodging invisible space torpedoes."

Alex slumped back over the chart room desk, burying his face in his hands.

"Oh, no," he moaned. "Oh, no, no, no, no, no."

He lit a cigaret with trembling fingers, thinking that at least this lunatic ride would soon be over. Be brave, he told himself. Chin up and all that sort of thing. Just a few more hours.

Once he had pinpointed the boat in space, it had not been hard to calculate a path to Pornia's sun. Now they were inside the Pornian System, moving at sub-light speed toward the only inhabited planet. The Hokas had naturally been enthusiastically in favor of going there to do battle.

Well, they'd land, and then he'd turn them over to the Pornians who, possessing a military force, could arrest them and return them to Toka. It was a dirty trick for him to play on his little friends, but he had no choice. You just couldn't allow this boatful of . . . of permanent children to go batting around the galaxy.

An obbligato of Hoka voices filtered to him over the intercom from the bridge.

"Rough section of space, this, captain."

"Space is like that, Lon. If the space tides don't get you, the radiation madness does. You dodge a meteor to find yourself trapped in a Sargasso of deadly space weed. And if you manage to battle your way out of that by some miracle, you emerge to find yourself blasting on all jets straight into the middle of the Malevonian fleet."

Alex closed his eyes and hung on to the coffee-stained calculation sheets—the data needed to land on Pornia. He thought bitterly that there might be a cupful of cosmic dust between them and the next star, but that was all that could be expected. . . .

"Then there's pirates—"

"Like that one bearing down on us now?"

"Don't be jet-happy, Lon. No pirate would dare attack a Patrol ship."

"Well, if he isn't a pirate, what's he doing with the skull and crossbones painted on his ship?"

"I don't see any skull and crossbones."

"Well, I can't see the skull either, but look at those red bloody crossbones on that white field."

"Great jumping comets, Lon, you're right! Attention, all gun crews! Attention, all gun crews! Stand by for battle!"

Struck by a sudden horrible suspicion, Alex flicked on the chart room's little viewscreen. Swimming in the nearby void was a long spaceship with a red cross large on its side.

"Stop!" roared Alex. "That's a hospital ship!"

He exploded out of the room and whizzed toward the bridge. Halfway there, he tripped over a small white-smocked figure.

"Damn interference!" squeaked Dr. Zarbovsky. "Can't let a mad scientist alone for a minute." Then, recognizing Alex's sprawled form: "Oh, sorry, sir. I was just coming to see you. Where can I get a one-farad condenser?"

"Go to the devil," raged Alex, picking himself up.

"But we don't have a devil on this ship," said Dr. Zarbovsky plaintively.

Alex was already running down the corridor. He burst into the bridge and skidded to a halt before the communications board.

"Do you wish to take over, sir?" asked Jax.

"I sure do," gasped Alex.

His fingers danced over the board as he sent a call to the other ship.

The image of a Pornian—two meters tall, snake-limbed, with a flat green face sticking out of a high gold-braided collar—formed on the screen. "What's up?" it demanded in the English of the spaceways. "Who are you?"

"Never mind that," said Alex impolitely. "Let me speak to your captain."

"Who are you?" repeated the Pornian in a stiff tone. "We are the Pornian Navy's hospital ship *Sudbriggan.* Identify yourself, or else as aliens without passports you are liable to detention."

"Detention?" said Alex blankly. He hadn't realized the arrogance of the new militarist government had gone that far. "You're kidding!"

The Pornian's countenance turned chartreuse with anger. "Do you insult me?" he hissed. "You are under arrest. Stand by to be boarded."

Alex had a spine-chilling vision of himself explaining to Earth Headquarters just how he and a hundred of his wards came to be interned by the government of a notoriously touchy planet.

"Never mind," he said. "I was just about to leave."

Jumping up from the screen, he stepped over to the control panel. He was reaching for the main secondary-drive switch when a thunderous explosion rocked the *Fearless.* Alex felt himself hurled to the floor, his nose sideswiping a table on the way down.

He rose, wiping blood from his face, and glared at Captain Jax. "What happened now?" he yelled.

"Why, we opened fire," said the Hoka, pointing to the viewscreen. It showed a portion of the *Fearless'* exterior as well as the open sky. Smoke was whiffing into space from the cannon mouths. "We didn't get the pirate Malevonian, though," he added regretfully. "His force shield must already have been up."

If anybody, anywhere in the cosmos, has invented the legendary force screen, the Astrogation Improvement Authority of the Interbeing

League will be very anxious to meet him, her, it, or xu. Alex took another horrified look at the Pornian ship. It was taking off sunward at full acceleration. The clumsy solid cannonballs had done no more than scratch its armored hull, but the captain had evidently had the fright of his life.

The image of an Earth Headquarters Cultural Development Board was replaced in Alex's unhappy mind by the picture of an Interbeing League courtroom and one A. Jones on trial for armed assault. Since space piracy, being utterly impractical, had never occurred, perhaps the old laws about hanging pirates were still on the books. At the very least, no plenipotentiary who went around shooting up hospital ships could reasonably expect to keep his position. A certain dignity is demanded in such an office.

Out of the welter of thoughts there was only one that emerged with any clarity. And that was to catch the Pornian before he could officially report what had happened, explain, apologize, and ask him not to file charges.

"Full thrust ahead!" he bellowed, vaulting into the pilot chair and throwing down the grav-drive switch.

The Hokas whooped with joy.

"Trust us, Coordinator!" shouted Captain Jax. "They won't escape!"

—And the *Fearless* took off in pursuit.

The Lord High Admiral of the Pornian Navy thundered at the shaken, tentacled figure in the screen before him.

"What?"

"Help! Help!" cried the figure. "Hospital ship *Sudbriggan* reporting. There's a Space Patrol ship after me!"

"A what?" cried the Lord High Admiral.

"Space Patrol Ship Number One," choked the figure. It added breathlessly: "They've got a secret weapon."

"What do you mean, Space Patrol ship?" roared the Admiral. "There's no such thing as a Space Patrol."

"There is too!" shrieked the captain of the *Sudbriggan*. The Pornian Navy had not been in existence long enough to become well grounded in military courtesy. "And it's gaining."

Ferociously, the Lord High Admiral punched a button. The communications center of the huge dreadnaught answered him.

"Give me a long-range tracer," rapped the Admiral. "Find out what's behind this idiot."

Communications Center obliged.

* * *

"Fearless calling *Sudbriggan,"* gasped Alexander Jones into an unresponsive screen. "Come in, *Sudbriggan. Please* come in, *Sudbriggan!"*

The set flickered to life with the terrified figure of a Pornian who must be the exec of the hospital ship. He was waving his eye-stalks, too agitated to find English words.

"Get me your captain," said Alex. "I want your captain."

"N-n-no," stammered the officer. "We shall defend our captain to the l-last enlisted man."

"Then your Admiral," said Alex hoarsely. His contorted face looked more ferocious than he knew. "I must see your Admiral right away. This business has got to be stopped!"

"Eek," said the officer.

"I'm doing my best," pleaded Alex, "but if you don't get me through to your Admiral I can't answer for the consequences."

The Pornian paled at this bloodthirsty threat and switched off his receiver.

"Hey!" shouted Alex. "Come back there!"

"Never mind, Coordinator," said Captain Jax. "We're overhauling him."

The *Sudbriggan* was a glinting speck, lost among the stars, but a glance at the radar tracker told Alex that the courier boat was, indeed, gaining on the slower hospital ship. He mopped his brow in some relief. His chance of catching the other vessel in time to mollify its skipper and prevent a report looked pretty good after all. He began turning over in his mind the form his apology would take.

He had assumed that the *Sudbriggan* had taken off in a random sunward direction, and had no idea that the backbone of the Pornian Navy was close at hand. Consequently, the dreadnaught took him completely by surprise.

One minute, the viewscreen gleamed only with stars. Then all at once, looming up and growing with hideous speed, was the titanic figure of the space battleship, gun turrets glimmering ominously in the light of the distant sun.

"What is this farce?" demanded the Lord High Admiral angrily, looking at the boat in his tracer screen. He could make out the legend Space Patrol Ship Number One on its bow. What was it, and why was so minute a thing hurling itself so viciously on the great, and invincible super-dreadnaught?

He twined his boneless hands thoughtfully. Something occurred to him. What was it the captain of the *Sudbriggan* had said?

Secret weapon!

"Fire guns!" bawled the suddenly panic-stricken Admiral, clutching the intercom mike. "Fire torpedo! Fire One, fire Two, fire Three! Fire everything! Shoot that ship down before it hits us!"

Gun crews who have looked on their drills as a sort of pleasant exercise, are not at their peak when suddenly ordered without even the preamble of a battle alert to fire their weapons. Such an unexpected command breeds a certain amount of confusion. Nevertheless, they did their best.

Atomic explosions began to blossom about the hurtling *Fearless,* but in the vacuum of space a shell has to make a direct hit to do any significant harm. Therefore the guns gave way to the space torpedoes that leaped out at the enemy, each as big as the courier boat itself.

Now this was unfortunate. The torpedoes were equipped with the latest tracking devices to find their own targets. But it had been assumed that such targets would be destroyers, at the very least, since nothing smaller could possibly menace the new battleship. So simple preventive circuits had also been installed to keep them from homing on each other.

Thus when they reached the *Fearless* and matched velocities and accelerations, they didn't know what to do next. They trailed undecidedly after the Hoka ship, their computers clicking madly. One computer must have gone insane, for that torpedo blew itself up. The rest moved hesitantly toward their own ship.

The Admiral shivered in his quarters, gripping the arms of his chair and praying for a hit and regretting the day he had ever let the Racialist Party leaders talk him into figureheading the Navy. His wife had warned him against it and his wife always knew best. It was all very well strutting around in gold braid; but he might have suspected there would be a catch to it. And sure enough there was.

He might have known there was a real Space Patrol. He might have known a bloodthirsty race like the humans wouldn't really let a peaceful world like his own get away with a little rearming.

"Please," prayed the Admiral, rolling his eye-stalks toward the ceiling of his cabin. "Please. A direct hit. Just one."

"But I only want to apologize!" yelled Alex into the blank communicator screen, holding frantically onto the board while the *Fearless* rocked to the nearby explosions. *"Sudbriggan.* Dreadnaught. Anybody. It's all a mistake. I just want to apologize, dammit!"

"What's the old man up to?" Lon Meters asked Captain Jax as they both clung to their pilot chairs.

"I can't tell you," replied the captain with a knowing wink. "But

I'll give you this much of a hint. Underneath that bluff exterior, the Coordinator's mighty shrewd. *Mighty* shrewd."

"Oh," said the exec. They nodded understandingly together.

All good things must come to an end; and the famous Space Patrol-Pornian battle was no exception. Aboard the enormous ship they opened a safety port to admit the fleeing *Sudbriggan*. It flashed inside, but before they could close the port again, the *Fearless,* moving too fast for Alex to stop her in time, had also entered.

If it had not been for the fantastic safety devices inside the dreadnaught, the episode would have ended then and there. But as it was, the absorber fields channeled the terrific kinetic energy of the two vessels into the dreadnaught's accumulators, and they lay inert in the belly of the monster. The port clanged to behind them.

The torpedoes decelerated as their circuits informed them that they were almost upon their mother craft. They milled about in space, their computers gibbering. One torpedo, perhaps equipped with a better-than-average "brain," went up and sniffed at the safety port, wagging its tail rather wistfully.

The *Sudbriggan* had been the first to enter. Its crew boiled from the airlock and scrambled toward the safety of the dreadnaught's interior. A few minutes later, Alex opened the lock of the *Fearless* and stuck his nose out. He jerked it hastily back as a raybeam shot past it and splattered on the hull of the Patrol boat. This was too much. After being shanghaied, kept up for two nights to make calculations, threatened with internment, and shot at, Alex finally lost his temper. He went storming back to the bridge.

"Give me a raythrower!" he roared.

"Hadn't you better get into a suit first, sir?" asked Lon Meters.

Alex did a double take. All along the main corridor, he could see the Hokas scrambling into things that looked like a cross between a spacesuit and a set of medieval armor. The exec was holding out one tailored more nearly to human proportions.

"What?" said Alex.

"Combat armor, sir," said Captain Jax proudly. "We used the ship's tools and made it out of the spare meteor plating in the hold."

Alex goggled. The labor in fashioning the suits must have been heartbreaking. Even given the ship's machine tools, the collapsed steel of meteor plating was almost unworkable. For a second he wavered between, admiration and a desire to blow his top at this latest outrage on his property. Then he remembered the near-singe his nose had taken, and began donning the armor without a word.

"Battle ax," said Captain Jax.

"Battle ax," repeated the exec, handing a wicked-looking double-bitted weapon to Alex.

"Raythrower," said the captain.

"Raythrower," repeated the exec, offering a gun.

Alex grabbed the Holman with his first real enthusiasm since this trip started. A smile was forming on his lips when he realized that the object was entirely too heavy to be what it appeared to be.

He inspected it. "What's this?" he demanded.

"The raythrower, sir?" Captain Jax looked a little crestfallen. "We had some trouble with them, Coordinator. We sent off our boxtops according to orders over the video, but when we got these, they wouldn't shoot."

"Sabotage," supplied Lon Meters.

"Exactly," said the captain. "So we fixed them up to fire regular bullets like the Western shooting irons. You see—"

He pressed the firing button on his imitation Holman, and a slug whanged off the low ceiling of the bridge. Alex ducked before remembering that his new clothes were bullet proof. He straightened, groaned as he looked at the clumsy weapon, and then, with a sigh, holstered it and clumped his way toward the airlock. At least his present equipment would protect him until he could get to some Pornian officer and explain the case—

But his last feeble intentions of legality were destroyed when he led his Hokas into the first corridor branching from the entry port. A barrage of rays from behind a hastily erected wall of office furniture made his armor glow and sparkle. He tingled with the shock of secondary radiation.

Plainly, the aliens weren't going to give him a chance to parley.

"That's enough!" he bellowed in a rage, his voice coming weirdly from the air holes in the top of his helmet. "Let's clean up the whole blinking ship!"

And he charged forward like a miniature tank, using the sheer mass of his armor to break through the barricade and send the defenders scooting before him in terror.

"The old man's finally got his dander up," said the exec to the captain.

"Yep," answered Jax. "That he has. But let me tell you something, boy. Underneath that dander there's a heart of pure, eighteen-carat, solid gold!"

*   *   *

The true story of the cleaning up of the Pornian dreadnaught will never be adequately told, for words are insufficient to describe it.

For a century or more, no civilized entity had been seriously threatened by organized violence. On top of this fact was another: that the advanced military minds who designed this battleship would have tut-tutted in horror if they had been asked how the crew was to defend it against a boarding party. With icy politeness they would have pointed out that boarding vanished with wooden ships, and that no enemy vessel could approach within three thousand kilometers of this giant without being destroyed. Thus few of the crew had hand guns, and fewer still knew how to use them. So everywhere through the huge ship could be seen shrieking herds of tall Pornians fleeing before one or two small armored figures waving battle axes. It was like a host of Frankenstein dolls let loose in an enormous home for old ladies. Such of the crew of the dreadnaught as was not assailed—and after all, a hundred Hokas could reach only a fraction of the total acreage inside—stayed by its posts, shivering and hoping there would be no orders to counterattack.

To be sure, there was one center of resistance. When the news reached the Admiral that the crew of the Space Patrol boat had effected an entrance, he gathered his personal staff around him on the bridge and resolved to die fighting. His followers unlimbered a mobile disintegrator, trained it on the doorway, and waited.

Meteor plating is good protection against hand guns. But it is about as useful as wet cardboard against the full power of a mobile disintegrator. Alex, leading a dozen Hokas around a bend in the main corridor, came full upon the bridge. The Pornians let off a panicky, ill-timed bolt which tore a hole through three floors above. Alex beat a hasty retreat, struggling to restrain the Hokas, who were all for rushing the gun.

"Look," he said grimly, when he finally had them settled down, "are Jax and Lon here?"

"Here, Coordinator."

"On green—I mean, aye, aye, sir."

"Well, look," said Alex. "That mobile unit isn't like a hand gun—that is, it doesn't have a self-contained power source. It gets its energy from a cable run directly to the ship's generators." As a former TISS man, Alex had of course been given training in the Solar Guard. "Now, what I want you to do is hunt around for the central power control room—it ought to be on this level—and pull every switch you find there. One of them should shut off the juice to that mobile."

The two little armored figures nodded their anonymous heads and toddled off down the corridor. Alex and the rest sat down to wait.

"Mighty smart, the old man," said Lon Meters as they trudged along. "Imagine him knowing the way Malevonian ships are put together."

"There isn't much that goes on in the universe that the Coordinator of the Space Patrol doesn't know," replied Jax Bennison complacently. "Why, I imagine nobody will ever know how many spy rays the old man has in places, and how many undercover agents at work."

"Lonely life, though," said Lon sadly. "Can't trust anyone, the old man can't. The responsibility for the safety of all civilization rests on his shoulders." He paused, then went on: "Which of us do you think he's picked to take his place when his time comes?"

They had, by now, explored up and down several halls and looked into a number of luxurious apartments for the top officers of the dreadnaught. Now they came to a small door with a sign stencilled on it in the spatial English:

DANGER
DO NOT ENTER

"Ah-ha," said Lon.

"This'll be it," said Jax. He swung his battle ax at the lock, and the door—being unlocked—bounced open. They stepped inside.

"Yep," said Captain Jax, looking about him with satisfaction at the ranked masses of levers, wheels, buttons, and switches. "This is it, all right. Executive Meters, you take that side and I'll take this."

They started yanking levers.

Coughing, choking, sneezing, and gurgling, the Lord High Admiral of the Pornian Navy sloshed his way forward to surrender.

"My sword, sir," he said with what dignity he could summon up.

Alex accepted it.

"The ship, sir, is yours," coughed the Admiral. Then his official manner broke down "But if turning on the fire extinguisher sprinklers, the fumigation system, the leak-detector smoke system, the emergency radionic-heating system, the emergency refrigeration system, and directing the sewers into the deck-flushing system isn't a dirty way to fight, I'd like to know what is."

Alex ignored his resentment.

"The terms for your surrender are these," he began sternly.

"Yes, sir," said the Admiral in a meek voice.

"Your government will dismantle this dreadnaught and build no more ships of the line."

"Yes, sir," said the Admiral. "I, for one, will be happy to get back to civilian life—"

"You will disband the navy."

"Glad to, sir."

"You will inform Earth Headquarters of your decisions in these matters, but will not specify the reasons or mention this battle. That is classified information."

"Yes, sir."

"And you will inform the Racialist Party on Pornia that the Space Patrol, which owes allegiance to no race or system, but is dedicated to the upholding of law and order throughout the galaxy, takes a dim view of their government and demands another planet-wide election wherein other Pornian parties shall be given a fair chance to run for office."

The Admiral gulped.

"Well—I—yes, sir, I guess I can do that. Under the circumstances."

"Okay, fine," said Alex. Signalling the armored figures around him to follow, he turned on his heel and went back toward the entry port.

When the *Fearless* was finally settled down on her return trip, Alex called the Hokas together and, speaking over the intercom, addressed them all.

"Gentlemen of the Space Patrol," he said crisply, "our mission is accomplished. Well done! But now I must inform you that there will be no more expeditions of the Patrol for an indefinite time."

"None?" asked Captain Jax in a wistful tone.

"None," said Alex, tossing the keys of the control panel in one hand and clamping firmly onto them as they landed back in his palm. "The Space Patrol is being disbanded as of now until such time as another threat to the galaxy brings us forth to scour the evildoer from the stars and the space between the stars."

There was a moment's sad quietude. Then the exec, Lon Meters, spoke up.

"But what's going to become of you, sir?" he asked sympathetically.

"That," said Alex, unable to disguise a slight quaver in his voice, "is what I am just about to find out."

He waved bravely to the assembled Hoka officers and dismissed them from the bridge and shut the door on them. The new long-range subspace communicator which the dreadnaught's technicians had installed for him glowed as his trembling fingers put in a call. While the Hoka at the switchboard in far-off Mixumaxu routed his beam, he licked dry lips and ran a shaky finger under his collar.

The figure of Tanni appeared on the screen. Her arms folded implacably as she recognized him.

"Well," she said, "and just where have you been?"

Weakly, Alexander Jones started to explain.

INTERLUDE III

Plenipotentiary of the
Interbeing League
Planet Toka

HEADQUARTERS OFFICE   CITY OF MIXAMAXU

Interoffice No. X-73-Z-218-r-478-R

11/10/75

FROM: Alexander B. Jones, Plenipotentiary

TO: Adalbert Parr, C.C.C.

SUBJECT: Allegations concerning Tokan conduct with respect to reported interstellar piracy

REFERENCES: (a) EHQ-X-73-Z-218-r-261-RQ, (b) Proc. Gal. Psych. Assn., viii, 5, 221-296

ENCLOSURE: (a) CDS Acct. P-3547-291

1. Reply is hereby made to Ref. (a), your inquiry concerning small armed vessel somewhat unreliably reported to have committed piracy in this galactic section, said vessel having allegedly identified itself in English as belonging to a so-called "Space Patrol" and been asserted to bear a crew rumored to possess a slight resemblance to the Hokas under my care.
2. Since I hesitate to accuse Terrestrial diplomatic and intelligence officers of having uncritically swallowed the wild hoax of some

intoxicated or possibly deranged Pornian outcast, I beg leave to confess myself at a loss to explain these statements.

3. As reference to the files will show, the Hokas are assigned to Class D, and are therefore by definition totally incapable of building a secondary-drive vessel, or operating one without trained assistance. As for the far-fetched hypothesis advanced—not, I am sure, by yourself—in Ref. (a), Par. 16, that a Hoka gang appropriated my courier boat, I can only point out that the mysterious damage which it suffered shortly prior to the time of the episode in question makes this most improbable, to put it mildly. (Expense account for repairs attached, Encl. (a).) To the additional rumor that there was, among these Hokoid individuals, a humanoid bearing a small similarity to myself, I offer either an indignant denial or the suggestion of erroneous testimony. After all, it is well known that one humanoid looks very much like another humanoid to the average non-humanoid. (Documentation in Ref (b).)

4. However, the entire question as concerns the planet Toka can be disposed of merely on a common-sense level. What reasonable person could seriously entertain the notion that a mere handful of Class D primitives aboard a mere courier boat could conceivably overwhelm a dreadnaught armed (like all dreadnaughts) to the teeth? I note that Ref. (a), Par. 7, mentions that a certain Pornian Admiral has been hospitalized for nervous overstrain consequent to this by-no-means-proven episode. Does that sound like the result of an encounter of a ranking member of a Class A civilization with my cheerful, friendly, innocent little Class D wards? I leave the question to your judgment.

5. As noted in Par. 2 above, I do not pretend to understand the cause of these rumors, but I would suggest that either the Pornians were somewhat overwrought or else the affair is a case of mistaken identity, possibly involving some as yet unknown race.

ABJ/eek

**Foreign Ministry
of the
United Commonwealths**

Cultural Development Service
Earth Headquarters
Interoffice No. EHQ-X-73-Z-218-r-262
12/11/75

FROM: Adalbert Parr, C.C.C.
TO: A. Jones, Plenipotentiary, Mixumaxu, U.X., Brackneys Star III
SUBJECT: Reported activity in Pornian region
REFERENCES: (a) X-73-Z-218-r-478-R

1. Note has been taken of Ref. (a), and said reply to inquiries made is hereby judged satisfactory.
2. I should particularly like to commend you for the brilliant suggestion in Ref. (a), Par. 5. I have taken the matter up with higher echelons, who have in turn brought it to the attention of the League Council itself. A search for these aliens, who know English and possess a Space Patrol but have nevertheless remained undiscovered by us, is now under way.
3. Obviously, this is a matter of vital importance to the League. In view of the fact the aliens' action was, at least in its results, not so much piratical as pro-libertarian and anti-militaristic, I saw fit to expand your suggestion a trifle, and my own memorandum has received favorable consideration. Therefore the League is acting on the tentative assumption that the aliens belong to an elder race of Great Galactics—that the Space Patrol is maintained by their Observers—and that our civilization would have much to learn from them if contact can somehow be established.
4. My own office has, accordingly, been commended for its zeal. Thus the entire Cultural Development Service benefits from your originality, which reflects great credit on you.
5. A copy of this letter will be placed in your 201 file.

AP/grd

THE ADVENTURE OF
THE MISPLACED HOUND

Whitcomb Geoffrey was the very model of a modern major operative. Medium tall, stockily muscular, with cold gray eyes in a massively chiseled, expressionless face, he was quietly dressed in purple breeches and a crimson tunic whose slight bulge showed that he carried a Holman raythrower. His voice was crisp and hard as he said: "Under the laws of the Interbeing League, you are required to give every assistance to a field agent of the Interstellar Bureau of Investigation. Me."

Alexander Jones settled his lean length more comfortably behind the desk. His office seemed to crackle with Geoffrey's dynamic personality; he felt sure that the agent was inwardly scorning its easygoing sloppiness. "All right," he said. "But what brings you to Toka? This is still a backward planet, you know. Hasn't got very much to do with spatial traffic." Remembering the Space Patrol episode, he shuddered slightly and crossed his fingers.

"That's what you think!" snapped Geoffrey. "Let me explain."

"Certainly, if you wish," said Alex blandly.

"Thanks, I will," said the other man. He caught himself, bit his lip, and glared. It was plain that he thought Alex much too young for the exalted position of plenipotentiary. And in fact Alex's age was still, after nearly ten years in this job, well below the average for a ranking CDS official.

After a moment, Geoffrey went on: "The largest problem the IBI faces is interstellar dope smuggling, and the most dangerous gang in that business is—or was—operated by a group of renegade ppussjans from Ximba. Ever seen one, or a picture? They're small, slim fellows, cyno-centauroid type: four legs and two arms, spent years trying to track down this particular bunch of dream peddlers. We finally located their headquarters and got most of them. It was on a planet of Yamatsu's Star, about six light-years from here. But the leader, known as Number Ten—"

"Why not Number One?" asked Alex.

"Ppussjans count rank from the bottom up. Ten escaped, and has since been resuming his activities on a smaller scale, building up the ring again. We've *got* to catch him, or we'll soon be right back where we started.

"Casting around in this neighborhood with tracer beams, we caught a spaceship with a ppussjan and a load of nixl weed. The ppussjan confessed what he knew, which wasn't much, but still important. Ten himself is hiding out alone here on Toka—he picked it because it's backward and thinly populated. He's growing the weed and giving it to his confederates, who land here secretly at night. When the hunt for him has died down, he'll leave Toka, and space is so big that we might never catch him again."

"Well," said Alex, "didn't your prisoner tell you just where Ten is hiding?"

"No. He never saw his boss. He merely landed at a certain desolate spot on a large island and picked up the weed, which had been left there for him. Ten could be anywhere on the island. He doesn't have a boat of his own, so we can't track him down with metal detectors; and he's much too canny to come near a spaceship, if we should go to the rendezvous and wait for him."

"I see," said Alex. "And nixl is deadly stuff, isn't it? Hm-m-m. You have the coordinates of this rendezvous?"

He pushed a buzzer. A Hoka servant entered, in white robes, a turban, and a crimson cummerbund, to bow low and ask: "What does the sahib wish?"

"Bring me the big map of Toka, Rajat Singh," said Alex.

"He's been reading Kipling," said Alex apologetically. It did not seem to clear away his guest's puzzlement.

The coordinates intersected on a large island off the main continent. "Hm," said Alex, "England. Devonshire, to be precise."

"Huh?" Geoffrey pulled his jaw up with a click. An IBI agent is never surprised. "You and I will go there at once," he said firmly.

"Remember your duty, Jones!"

"Oh, all right. I'll go. But you understand," added the younger man diffidently, "there may be a little trouble with the Hokas themselves."

Geoffrey was amused. "We're used to that in the IBI," he said. "We're well-trained not to step on native toes."

Alex coughed, embarrassed. "Well, it's not exactly that—" he stumbled. "You see . . . well, it may be the other way around."

A frown darkened Geoffrey's brow. "They may hamper us, you mean?" he clipped. "Your function is to keep the natives non-hostile, Jones."

"No," said Alex unhappily. "What I'm afraid of is that the Hokas may try to help us. Believe me, Geoffrey, you've no idea of what can happen when Hokas take it into their heads to be helpful."

Geoffrey cleared his throat. He was obviously wondering whether or not to report Alex as incompetent. "All right," he said. "We'll divide up the work between us. I'll let you do all the native handling, and you let me do the detecting."

"Good enough," said Alex, but he still looked doubtful.

The green land swept away beneath them as they flew toward England in the plenipotentiary's runabout. Geoffrey was scowling. "It's urgent," he said. "When the spaceship we captured fails to show up with its cargo, the gang will know something's gone wrong and send a boat to pick up Ten. At least one of them must know exactly where on the island he's hiding. They'll have an excellent chance of sneaking him past any blockade we can set up." He took out a cigaret and puffed nervously. "Tell me, why is the place called England?"

"Well—" Alex drew a long breath. "Out of maybe a quarter million known intelligent species, the Hokas are unique. Only in the last few years have we really begun to probe their psychology. They're highly intelligent, unbelievably quick to learn, ebullient by nature . . . and fantastically literal-minded. They have difficulty distinguishing fact from fiction, and since fiction is so much more colorful, they don't usually bother. Oh, my servant back at the office doesn't consciously believe he's a mysterious East Indian; but his subconscious has gone overboard for the role, and he can easily rationalize anything that conflicts with his wacky assumptions." Alex frowned, in search of words. "The closest analogy I can make is that the Hokas are somewhat like small human children, plus having the physical and intellectual capabilities of human adults. It's a formidable combination."

"All right," said Geoffrey. "What's this got to do with England?"

"Well, we're still not sure just what is the best starting point for the development of civilization among the Hokas. How big a forward step should the present generation be asked to take? More important, what socio-economic forms are best adapted to their temperaments and so on? Among other experiments, about ten years ago the cultural mission decided to try a Victorian English setup, and chose this island for the scene of it. Our robofacs quickly produced steam engines, machine tools, and so on for them . . . of course, we omitted the more brutal features of the actual Victorian world. The Hokas quickly carried on from the start we'd given them. They consumed mountains of Victorian literature—"

"I see," nodded Geoffrey.

"You begin to see," said Alex a little grimly. "It's more complicated than that. When a Hoka starts out to imitate something, there are no half measures about it. For instance, the first place we're going to get the hunt organized is called London, and the office we'll contact is called Scotland Yard, and—well, I hope you can understand a nineteenth-century English accent, because that's all you'll hear."

Geoffrey gave a low whistle. "They're that serious about it, eh?"

"If not more so," said Alex. "Actually, the society in question has, as far as I know, succeeded very well—so well that, being busy elsewhere, I haven't had a chance to keep up with events in England. I've no idea what that Hoka logic will have done to the original concepts by now. Frankly, I'm scared!"

Geoffrey looked at him curiously and wondered whether the plenipotentiary might not perhaps be a little off-balance on the subject of his wards.

From the air, London was a large collection of peak-roofed buildings, split by winding cobbled streets, on the estuary of a broad river that could only be the Thames. Alex noticed that it was being remodeled to a Victorian pattern: Buckingham Palace, Parliament, and the Tower were already erected, and St. Paul's was halfway finished. An appropriate fog was darkening the streets, so that gas lamps had to be lit. He found Scotland Yard on his map and landed in the court, between big stone buildings. As he and Geoffrey climbed out, a Hoka bobby complete with blue uniform and bulging helmet saluted them with great deference.

" 'Umans!" he exclaimed. "H'I sye, sir, this must be a right big case, eh what? Are you working for 'Er Majesty, h'if h'I might myke so bold as ter awsk?"

"Well," said Alex, "not exactly." The thought of a Hoka Queen Victoria was somewhat appalling. "We want to see the chief inspector."

"Yes, sir!" said the teddy bear. "H'Inspector Lestrade is right down the 'all, sir, first door to yer left."

"Lestrade," murmured Geoffrey. "Where've I heard that name before?"

They mounted the steps and went down a gloomy corridor lit by flaring gas jets. The office door indicated had a sign on it in large letters:

FIRST BUNGLER

"Oh no!" said Alex under his breath.

He opened the door. A small Hoka in a wing-collared suit and ridiculously large horn-rimmed spectacles got up from behind the desk.

"The plenipotentiary!" he exclaimed in delight. "And another human! What is it, gentlemen? Has—" He paused, looked in sudden fright around the office, and lowered his voice to a whisper. "Has Professor Moriarty broken loose again?"

Alex introduced Geoffrey. They sat down and explained the situation. Geoffrey wound up with: "So I want you to organize your—CID, I imagine you call it—and help me track down this alien."

Lestrade shook his head sadly. "Sorry, gentlemen," he said. "We can't do that."

"Can't do it?" echoed Alex, shocked. "Why not?"

"It wouldn't do any good," said Lestrade, gloomily. "We wouldn't find anything. No, sir, in a case as serious as this, there's only one man who can lay such an arch-criminal by the heels. I refer, of course, to Mr. Sherlock Holmes."

"Oh, NO!" said Alex.

"I beg your pardon?" asked Lestrade.

"Nothing," said Alex, feverishly wiping his brow. "Look here—Lestrade—Mr. Geoffrey here is a representative of the most effective police force in the Galaxy. He—"

"Come now, sir," said Lestrade, with a pitying smile. "You surely don't pretend that he is the equal of Sherlock Holmes. Come, come, now!"

Geoffrey cleared his throat angrily, but Alex kicked his foot. It was highly illegal to interfere with an established cultural pattern, except by subtler means than argument. Geoffrey caught on and nodded as if it hurt him. "Of course," he said in a strangled voice. "I would be the last to compare myself with Mr. Holmes."

"Fine," said Lestrade, rubbing his stubby hands together. "Fine. I'll take you around to his apartment, gentlemen, and we can lay the problem before him. I trust he will find it interesting."

"So do I," said Alex, hollowly.

* * *

A hansom cab was clopping down the foggy streets and Lestrade hailed it. They got in, though Geoffrey cast a dubious look at the beaked, dinosaurian reptile which the Hokas called a horse, and went rapidly through the tangled lanes. Hokas were abroad on foot, the males mostly in frock coats and top hats, carrying tightly rolled umbrellas, the females in long dresses; but now and then a bobby, a red-coated soldier, or a kilted member of a Highland regiment could be seen. Geoffrey's lips moved silently.

Alex was beginning to catch on. Naturally, the literature given these—Englishmen—must have included the works of A. Conan Doyle, and he could see where the romantic Hoka nature would have gone wild over Sherlock Holmes. So they had to interpret everything literally; but who had they picked to be Holmes?

"It isn't easy being in the CID, gentlemen," said Lestrade. "We haven't much of a name hereabouts, y'know. Of course, Mr. Holmes always gives us the credit, but somehow word gets around." A tear trickled down his furry cheek.

They stopped before an apartment building in Baker Street and entered the hallway. A plump elderly female met them. "Good afternoon, Mrs. Hudson," said Lestrade. "Is Mr. Holmes in?"

"Indeed he is, sir," said Mrs. Hudson. "Go right up." Her awed eyes followed the humans as they mounted the stairs.

Through the door of 211-B came a horrible wail. Alex froze, ice running along his spine, and Geoffrey cursed and pulled out his raythrower. The scream sawed up an incredible scale, swooped down again, and died in a choked quivering. Geoffrey burst into the room, halted, and glared around.

The place was a mess. By the light of a fire burning in the hearth, Alex could see papers heaped to the ceiling, a dagger stuck in the mantel, a rack of test tubes and bottles, and a "V.R." punched in the wall with bullets. It was hard to say whether the chemical reek or the tobacco smoke was worse. A Hoka in dressing gown and slippers put down his violin and looked at them in surprise. Then he beamed and came forward to extend his hand.

"Mr. Jones!" he said. "This is a real pleasure. Do come in."

"Uh—that noise—" Geoffrey looked nervously around the room.

"Oh, that," said the Hoka, modestly. "I was just trying out a little piece of my own. Concerto in Very Flat for violin and cymbals. Somewhat experimental, don't y'know."

Alex studied the great detective. Holmes looked about like any

other Hoka—perhaps he was a trifle leaner, though still portly by
human standards. "Ah, Lestrade," he said. "And Watson—do you mind
if I call you Watson, Mr. Jones? It seems more natural."

"Oh, not at all," said Alex, weakly. He thought the real Watson—
no, dammit, the Hoka Watson!—must be somewhere else; and the
natives' one-track minds—

"But we are ignoring our guest here, whom I perceive to be in Mr.
Lestrade's branch of the profession," said Holmes, laying down his
violin and taking out a big-bowled pipe.

IBI men do not start; but Geoffrey came as close to it as one of his
bureau's operatives had ever done. He had no particular intention of
maintaining an incognito, but no officer of the law likes to feel that his
profession is written large upon him. "How do you know that?" he
demanded.

Holmes' black nose bobbed. "Very simple, my dear sir," he said.
"Humans are a great rarity here in London. When one arrives, thus,
with the estimable Lestrade for company, the conclusion that the problem is one for the police and that you yourself, my dear sir, are in some
way connected with the detection of criminals, becomes a very proba-
ble one. I am thinking of writing another little monograph— But sit
down, gentlemen, sit down, and let me hear what this is all about."

Recovering what dignity they could, Alex and Geoffrey took the
indicated chairs. Holmes himself dropped into an armchair so overstuffed that he almost disappeared from sight. The two humans found
themselves confronting a short pair of legs beyond which a button
nose twinkled and a pipe fumed.

"First," said Alex, pulling himself together, "let me introduce Mr.—"

"Tut-tut, Watson," said Holmes. "No need. I know the estimable
Mr. Gregson by reputation, if not by sight."

"Geoffrey, dammit!" shouted the IBI man.

Holmes smiled gently. "Well, sir, if you wish to use an alias, there
is no harm done. But between us, we may as well relax, eh?"

"H-h-how," stammered Alex, "do you know that he's named Gregson?"

"My dear Watson," said Holmes, "since he is a police officer, and
Lestrade is already well known to me, who else could he be? I have
heard excellent things of you, Mr. Gregson. If you continued to apply
my methods, you will go far."

"Thank you," snarled Geoffrey.

Holmes made a bridge of his fingers. "Well, Mr. Gregson," he
said, "let me hear your problem. And you, Watson, will no doubt want
to take notes. You will find pencil and paper on the mantel."

Gritting his teeth, Alex got them while Geoffrey launched into the story, interrupted only briefly by Holmes' "Are you getting all this down, Watson?" or occasions when the great detective paused to repeat slowly something he himself had interjected so that Alex could copy it word for word.

When Geoffrey had finished, Holmes sat silent for a while, puffing on his pipe. "I must admit," he said finally, "that the case has its interesting aspects. I confess to being puzzled by the curious matter of the Hound."

"But I didn't mention any hound," said Geoffrey numbly.

"That is the curious matter," replied Holmes. "The area in which you believe this criminal to be hiding is Baskerville territory, and you didn't mention a Hound once." He sighed and turned to the Scotland Yard Hoka. "Well, Lestrade," he went on, "I imagine we'd all better go down to Devonshire and you can arrange there for the search Gregson desires. I believe we can catch the 8:05 out of Paddington tomorrow morning."

"Oh, no," said Geoffrey, recovering some of his briskness. "We can fly down tonight."

Lestrade was shocked. "But I say," he exclaimed. "That just isn't done."

"Nonsense, Lestrade," said Holmes.

"Yes, Mr. Holmes," said Lestrade, meekly.

The village of St. Vitus-Where-He-Danced was a dozen thatch-roofed houses and shops, a church, a tavern, set down in the middle of rolling gray-green moors. Not far away, Alex could see a clump of trees which he was told surrounded Baskerville Hall. The inn had a big signboard announcing "The George and Dragon," with a picture of a Hoka in armor spearing some obscure monster. Entering the low-ceilinged taproom, Alex's party were met by an overawed landlord and shown to clean, quiet rooms whose only drawback was the fact that the beds were built for one-meter Hokas.

By then it was night. Holmes was outside somewhere, bustling around and talking to the villagers, and Lestrade went directly to bed; but Alex and Geoffrey came back downstairs to the taproom. It was full of a noisy crowd of Hoka farmers and tradesmen, some talking in their squeaky voices, some playing darts, some clustering around the two humans. A square, elderly native introduced as Farmer Toowey joined them at their table.

"Ah, lad," he said, "it be turrible what yeou zee on the moor o' nights." And he buried his nose in the pint mug which should have held beer but, true to an older tradition, brimmed with the fiery liquor this high-capacity race had drunk from time immemorial. Alex, warned by past experience, sipped more cautiously at his pint; but Geoffrey was sitting with a half-empty mug and a somewhat wild look in his eyes.

"You mean the Hound?" asked Alex.

"I du," said Farmer Toowey. "Black, 'tis, an' bigger nor any bullock. And they girt teeth! One chomp and yeou'm gone."

"Is that what happened to Sir Henry Baskerville?" queried Alex. "Nobody seems to know where he's been for a long time."

"Swall'd um whole," said Toowey, darkly, finishing his pint and calling for another one. "Ah, poor Sir Henry! He was a good man, he was. When we were giving out new names, like the human book taught us, he screamed and fought, for he knew there was a curse on the Baskervilles, but—"

"The dialect's slipping, Toowey," said another Hoka.

"I be zorry," said Toowey. "I be oold, and times I forget masel'."

Privately, Alex wondered what the real Devonshire had been like. The Hokas must have made this one up out of whole cloth.

Sherlock Holmes entered in high spirits and sat down with them. His beady black eyes glittered. "The game is afoot, Watson!" he said. "The Hound has been doing business as usual. Strange forms seen on the moors of late— I daresay it's our criminal, and we shall soon lay him by the heels."

"Ridic'lous," mumbled Geoffrey. "Ain't—isn't any Hound. We're affer dope smuggler, not some son of—YOWP!" A badly thrown dart whizzed by his ear.

"Do you have to do that?" he quavered.

"Ah, they William," chuckled Toowey. "Ee's a fair killer, un is."

Another dart zoomed over Geoffrey's head and stuck in the wall. The IBI man choked and slid under the table—whether for refuge or sleep, Alex didn't know.

"Tomorrow," said Holmes, "I shall measure this tavern. I always measure," he added in explanation. "Even when there seems to be no point in it."

The landlord's voice boomed over the racket. "Closing time, gentlemen. It is time!"

The door flew open and banged to again. A Hoka stood there, breathing hard. He was unusually fat, and completely muffled in a long black coat; his face seemed curiously expressionless, though his voice was shrill with panic.

"Sir Henry!" cried the landlord. "Yeou'm back, squire!"

"The Hound," wailed Baskerville. "The Hound is after me!"

"Yeou've na cause tu fee-ar naow, Sir Henry," said Farmer Toowey. " 'Tis Sheerlock Holmes unself coom own to track yan brute."

Baskerville shrank against the wall. "Holmes?" he whispered.

"And a man from the IBI," said Alex. "But we're really after a criminal lurking on the moors—"

Geoffrey lifted a tousled head over the table. "Isn't no Hound," he said. "I'm affer uh dirty ppussjan, I am. Isn't no Hound nowheres."

Baskerville leaped. "It's at the door!" he shrieked, wildly. Plunging across the room, he went through the window in a crash of glass.

"Quick, Watson!" Holmes sprang up, pulling out his archaic revolver. "We'll see if there is a Hound or not!" He shoved through the panicky crowd and flung the door open.

The thing that crouched there, dimly seen by the firelight spilling out into darkness, was long and low and black, the body a vague shadow, a fearsome head dripping cold fire and snarling stiffly. It growled and took a step forward.

"Here naow!" The landlord plunged ahead, too outraged to be frightened. "Yeou can't coom in here. 'Tis closing time!" He thrust the Hound back with his foot and slammed the door.

"After him, Watson!" yelled Holmes. "Quick, Gregson!"

"Eek," said Geoffrey.

He must be too drunk to move, Alex thought. Alex himself had consumed just enough to dash after Holmes. They stood in the entrance, peering into darkness.

"Gone," said the human.

"We'll track him down!" Holmes paused to light his bull's-eye lantern, button his long coat, and jam his deerstalker cap more firmly down over his ears. "Follow me."

No one else stirred as Holmes and Alex went out into the night. It was pitchy outside. The Hokas had better night vision than humans and Holmes' furry hand closed on Alex's to lead him. "Confound these cobblestones!" said the detective. "No tracks whatsoever. Well, come along." They trotted from the village.

"Where are we going?" asked Alex.

"Out by the path to Baskerville Hall," replied Holmes sharply. "You would hardly expect to find the Hound anyplace else, would you, Watson?"

Properly rebuked, Alex lapsed into silence, which he didn't have the courage to break until, after what seemed an endless time, they came to a halt. "Where are we now?" he inquired of the night.

"About midway between the village and the Hall," replied the voice of Holmes, from near the level of Alex's waist. "Compose yourself, Watson, and wait while I examine the area for clues." Alex felt his hand released and heard the sound of Holmes moving away and rustling about on the ground. "Aha!"

"Find something?" asked the human, looking nervously around him.

"Indeed I have, Watson," answered Holmes. "A seafaring man with red hair and a peg leg has recently passed by here on his way to drown a sackful of kittens."

Alex blinked. "What?"

"A seafaring man—" Holmes began again, patiently.

"But—" stammered Alex. "But how can you tell that?"

"Childishly simple, my dear Watson," said Holmes. The light pointed to the ground. "Do you see this small chip of wood?"

"Y-yes, I guess so."

"By its grain and seasoning, and the type of wear it has had, it is obviously a piece which has broken off a peg leg. A touch of tar upon it shows that it belongs to a seafaring man. But what would a seafaring man be doing on the moors at night?"

"That's what I'd like to know," said Alex.

"We may take it," Holmes went on, "that only some unusual reason could force him out with the Hound running loose. But when we realize that he is a redheaded man with a terrific temper and a sackful of kittens with which he is totally unable to put up for another minute, it becomes obvious that he has sallied forth in a fit of exasperation to drown them."

Alex's brain, already spinning somewhat dizzily under the effect of the Hoka liquor, clutched frantically at this explanation, in an attempt to sort it out. But it seemed to slip through his fingers.

"What's all that got to do with the Hound, or the criminal we're after?" he asked weakly.

"Nothing, Watson," reproved Holmes sternly. "Why should it have?"

Baffled, Alex gave up.

Holmes poked around for a few more minutes, then spoke again. "If the Hound is truly dangerous, it should be sidling around to overwhelm us in the darkness. It should be along very shortly. Hah!" he rubbed his hands together. "Excellent!"

"I suppose it is," said Alex, feebly.

"You stay here, Watson," said Holmes, "and I will move on down the path a ways. If you see the creature, whistle." His lantern went out and the sound of his footsteps moved away.

Time seemed to stretch on interminably. Alex stood alone in the darkness, with the chill of the moor creeping into his bones as the liquor died within him, and wondered why he had ever let himself in for this in the first place. What would Tanni say? What earthly use would he be even if the Hound should appear? With his merely human night vision, he could let the beast stroll past within arm's reach and never know it. Of course, he could probably hear it. . . .

Come to think of it, what kind of noise would a monster make when walking? Would it be a *pad-pad,* or a sort of *shuffle-shuffle-shuffle* like the sound on the path to his left?

The sound—*Yipe!*

The night was suddenly shattered. An enormous section of the blackness reared up and smashed into him with the solidity and impact of a brick wall. He went spinning down into the star-streaked oblivion of unconsciousness.

When he opened his eyes again, it was to sunlight streaming through the leaded windows of his room. His head was pounding, and he remembered some fantastic nightmare in which—hah!

Relief washing over him, he sank back into bed. Of course. He must have gotten roaring drunk last night and dreamt the whole weird business. His head was splitting. He put his hands up to it.

They touched a thick bandage.

Alex sat up as if pulled on a string. The two chairs which had been arranged to extend the bed for him went clattering to the floor. "Holmes!" he shouted. "Geoffrey!"

His door opened and the individuals in question entered, followed by Farmer Toowey. Holmes was fully dressed, fuming away on his pipe; Geoffrey looked red-eyed and haggard. "What happened?" asked Alex, wildly.

"You didn't whistle," said Holmes reproachfully.

"Aye, that yeou di'n't," put in the farmer. "When they boor yeou in, tha face were white nor a sheet, laike. Fair horrible it were, the look on tha face, lad."

"Then it wasn't a dream!" said Alex, shuddering.

"I—er—I saw you go out after the monster," said Geoffrey, looking guilty. "I tried to follow you, but I couldn't get moving for some reason." He felt gingerly of his own head.

"I saw a black shape attack you, Watson," added Holmes.

"I think it was the Hound, even though that luminous face wasn't there. I shot at it but missed, and it fled over the moors. I couldn't pursue it with you lying there, so I carried you back. It's late afternoon now—you slept well, Watson!"

"It must have been the ppussjan," said Geoffrey with something of his old manner. "We're going to scour the moors for him today."

"No, Gregson," said Holmes. "I am convinced it was the Hound."

"Bah!" said Geoffrey. "That thing last night was only—was only—well, it was not a ppussjan. Some local animal, no doubt."

"Aye," nodded Farmer Toowey. "The Hound un were, that."

"Not the Hound!" yelled Geoffrey. "The ppussjan, do you hear? The Hound is pure superstition. There isn't any such animal."

Holmes wagged his finger. "Temper, temper, Gregson," he said.

"And stop calling me Gregson!" Geoffrey clutched his temples. "Oh, my head—!"

"My dear young friend," said Holmes patiently, "it will repay you to study my methods if you wish to advance in your profession. While you and Lestrade were out organizing a futile search party, I was studying the terrain and gathering clues. A clue is the detective's best friend, Gregson. I have five hundred measurements, six plaster casts of footprints, several threads torn from Sir Henry's coat by a splinter last night, and numerous other items. At a conservative estimate, I have gathered five pounds of clues."

"Listen." Geoffrey spoke with dreadful preciseness. "We're here to track down a dope smuggler, Holmes. A desperate criminal. We are not interested in country superstitions."

"I am, Gregson," smiled Holmes.

With an inarticulate snarl, Geoffrey turned and whirled out of the room. He was shaking. Holmes looked after him and tut-tutted. Then, turning: "Well, Watson, how do you feel now?"

Alex got carefully out of bed. "Not too bad," he admitted. "I've got a thumping headache, but an athetrine tablet will take care of it."

"Oh, that reminds me—" While Alex dressed, Holmes took a small flat case out of his pocket. When Alex looked that way again, Holmes was injecting himself with a hypodermic syringe.

"Hey!" cried the human. "What's that?"

"Morphine, Watson," said Holmes. "A seven percent solution. It stimulates the mind, I've found."

"Morphine!" Alex cried. Here was an IBI man currently present for the purpose of running down a dope smuggler and one of his Hokas had just produced— "OH, NO!"

Holmes leaned over and whispered in some embarrassment: "Well, actually, Watson, you're right. It's really just distilled water. I've written off for morphine several times, but they never send me any. So—well, one has one's position to keep up, you know."

"Oh," Alex feebly mopped his brow. "Of course."

While he stowed away a man-sized dinner, Holmes climbed up on the roof and lowered himself down the chimney in search of possible clues. He emerged black but cheerful. "Nothing, Watson," he reported. "But we must be thorough." Then, briskly: "Now come. We've work to do."

"Where?" asked Alex. "With the search party?"

"Oh, no. They will only alarm some harmless wild animals, I fear. We are going exploring elsewhere. Farmer Toowey here has kindly agreed to assist us."

"S'archin', laike," nodded the old Hoka.

As they emerged into the sunlight, Alex saw the search party, a hundred or so local yokels who had gathered under Lestrade's direction with clubs, pitchforks and flails to beat the bush for the Hound—or for the ppussjan, if it came to that. One enthusiastic farmer drove a huge "horse"-drawn reaping machine. Geoffrey was scurrying up and down the line, screaming as he tried to bring some order into it. Alex felt sorry for him.

They struck out down the path across the moor. "First we're off to Baskerville Hall," said Holmes. "There's something deucedly odd about Sir Henry Baskerville. He disappears for weeks, and then reappears last night, terrified by his ancestral curse, only to dash out onto the very moor which it is prowling. Where has he been in the interim, Watson? Where is he now?"

"Hm—yes," agreed Alex. "This Hound business and the ppussjan—do you think that there could be some connection between the two?"

"Never reason before you have all the facts, Watson," said Holmes. "It is the cardinal sin of all young police officers such as our impetuous friend Gregson."

Alex couldn't help agreeing. Geoffrey was so intent on his main assignment that he just didn't take time to consider the environment; to him, this planet was only a backdrop for his search. Of course, he was probably a cool head ordinarily, but Sherlock Holmes could unseat anyone's sanity.

Alex remembered that he was unarmed. Geoffrey had a raythrower, but this party only had Holmes' revolver and Toowey's gnarled staff. He gulped and tried to dismiss thoughts of the thing that had slugged him last night. "A nice day," he remarked to Holmes.

"It is, is it not? However," said Holmes, brightening up, "some of the most bloodcurdling crimes have been committed on fine days. There was, for example, the Case of the Dismembered Bishop—I don't believe I have ever told you about it, Watson. Do you have your notebook to hand?"

"Why, no," said Alex, somewhat startled.

"A pity," said Holmes. "I could have told you not only about the Dismembered Bishop, but about the Leaping Caterpillar, the Strange Case of the Case of Scotch, and the Great Ghastly Case—all very interesting problems. How is your memory?" he asked suddenly.

"Why—good, I guess," said Alex.

"Then I will tell you about the Case of the Leaping Caterpillar, which is the shortest of the lot," commenced Holmes. "It was considerably before your time, Watson. I was just beginning to attract attention with my work; and one day there was a knock on the door and in came the strangest—"

"Here be Baskerville Hall, laike," said Farmer Toowey.

An imposing Tudoresque pile loomed behind its screen of trees. They went up to the door and knocked. It opened and a corpulent Hoka in butler's black regarded them with frosty eyes. "Tradesmen's entrance in the rear," he said.

"Hey!" cried Alex.

The butler took cognizance of his humanness and became respectful. "I beg your pardon, sir," he said. "I am somewhat near-sighted and— I am sorry, sir, but Sir Henry is not at home."

"Where is he, then?" asked Holmes, sharply.

"In his grave, sir," said the butler, sepulchrally.

"Huh?" said Alex.

"His grave?" barked Holmes. "Quick, man! Where is he buried?"

"In the belly of the Hound, sir. If you will pardon the expression."

"Aye, aye," nodded Farmer Toowey. "Yan Hound, ee be a hungry un, ee be."

A few questions elicited the information that Sir Henry, a bachelor, had disappeared one day several weeks ago while walking on the moors, and had not been heard from since. The butler was surprised to learn that he had been seen only last night, and brightened visibly. "I hope he comes back soon, sir," he said. "I wish to give notice. Much as I admire Sir Henry, I cannot continue to serve an employer who may at any moment be devoured by monsters."

"Well," said Holmes, pulling out a tape measure, "to work, Watson."

"Oh, no, you don't!" This time Alex asserted himself. He couldn't see waiting around all night while Holmes measured this monstrosity of a mansion. "We've got a ppussjan to catch, remember?"

"Just a little measurement," begged Holmes.

"No!"

"Not even one?"

"All right." Jones relented at the wistful tone. "Just one."

Holmes beamed and, with a few deft motions, measured the butler.

"I must say, Watson, that you can be quite tyrannical at times," he said. Then, returning to Hoka normal: "Still, without my Boswell, where would I be?" He set off at a brisk trot, his furry legs twinkling in the late sunlight. Alex and Toowey stretched themselves to catch up.

They were well out on the moor again when the detective stopped and, his nose twitching with eagerness, leaned over a small bush from which one broken limb trailed on the ground. "What's that?" asked Alex.

"A broken bush, Watson," said Holmes snappishly. "Surely even you can see that."

"I know. But what about it?"

"Come, Watson," said Holmes, sternly. "Does not this broken bush convey some message to you? You know my methods. Apply them."

Alex felt a sudden wave of sympathy for the original Dr. Watson. Up until now he had never realized the devilish cruelty inherent in that simple command to apply the Holmesian methods. Apply them—how? He stared fiercely at the bush, which continued to ignore him, without being able to deduce more than that it was (a) a bush and (b) broken.

"Uh—a high wind?" he asked hesitantly.

"Ridiculous, Watson," retorted Holmes. "The broken limb is green; doubtless it was snapped last night by something large passing by in haste. Yes, Watson, this confirms my suspicions. The Hound has passed this way on its way to its lair, and the branch points us the direction."

"They be tu Grimpen Mire, a be," said Farmer Toowey dubiously. "Yan mire be impassable, un be."

"Obviously it is not, if the Hound is there," said Holmes. "Where it can go, we can follow. Come, Watson!" And he trotted off, his small body bristling with excitement.

They went through the brush for some minutes until they came to a wide boggy stretch with a large signboard in front of it.

GRIMPEN MIRE
FOUR MILES SQUARE
DANGER!!!!!!

"Watch closely, Watson," said Holmes. "The creature has obviously leaped from tussock to tussock. We will follow his path, watching for trampled grass or broken twigs. Now, then!" And bounding past the boundary sign, Holmes landed on a little patch of turf, from which he immediately soared to another one.

Alex hesitated, gulped, and followed him. It was not easy to progress in jumps of a meter or more, and Holmes, bouncing from spot to spot, soon pulled away. Farmer Toowey cursed and grunted behind Alex. "Eigh, ma oold boons can't tyke the leaping na moor, they can't," he muttered when they paused to rest. "If we'd knowed the Mire were tu be zo much swink, we'd never a builted un, book or no book."

"You made it yourselves?" asked Alex. "It's artificial?"

"Aye, lad, that un be. 'Twas in the book, Grimpen Mire, an' un swall'd many a man doon, un did. Many brave hee-arts lie asleep in un deep." He added apologetically: "Ow-ers be no zo grimly, though un tried hard. Ow-ers, yeou oonly get tha feet muddy, a-crossing o' 't. Zo we stay well away fran it, yeou understand."

Alex sighed.

The sun was almost under the hills now, and long shadows swept down the moor. Alex looked back, but could not make out any sign of Hall, village, or search party. A lonesome spot—not exactly the best place to meet a demoniac Hound, or even a ppussjan. Glancing ahead, he could not discern Holmes either, and he put on more speed.

An island—more accurately, a large hill—rose above the quaking mud. Alex and Toowey reached it with a final leap. They broke through a wall of trees and brush screening its stony crest. Here grew a wide thick patch of purple flowers. Alex halted, looked at them, and muttered an oath. He'd seen those blossoms depicted often enough in news articles.

"Nixl weed," he said. "So this is the ppussjan hideout!"

Dusk came swiftly as the sun disappeared. Alex remembered again that he was unarmed and strained wildly through the gathering dimness. "Holmes!" he called. "Holmes! I say, where are you, old fellow?" He snapped his fingers and swore. *Damn! Now I'm doing it!*

A roar came from beyond the hilltop. Jones leaped back. A tree stabbed him with a sharp branch. Whirling around, he struck out at the assailant. "Ouch!" he yelled. "Heavens to Betsy!" he added, though not in precisely those words.

The roar lifted again, a bass bellow that rumbled down to a savage snarling. Alex clutched at Farmer Toowey's smock. "What's that?" he gasped. "What's happening to Holmes?"

"Might be Hound's got un," offered Toowey, stolidly. "We hears un eatin', laike."

Alex dismissed the bloodthirsty notion with a frantic gesture. "Don't be ridiculous," he said.

"Ridiculous I may be," said Toowey stubbornly, "but they girt Hound be hungry, for zartin sure."

Alex's fear-tautened ears caught a new sound—footsteps from over the hill. "It's—coming this way," he hissed.

Toowey muttered something that sounded like "dessert."

Setting his teeth, Alex plunged forward. He topped the hill and sprang, striking a small solid body and crashing to earth. "I say, Watson," came Holmes' dry, testy voice, "this really won't do at all. I have told you a hundred times that such impetuosity ruins more good police officers than any other fault in the catalogue."

"Holmes!" Alex picked himself up, breathing hard. "My God, Holmes, it's you! But that other noise—the bellowing—?"

"That," said Holmes, "was Sir Henry Baskerville when I took the gag out of his mouth. Now come along, gentlemen, and see what I have found."

Alex and Toowey followed him through the nixl patch and down the rocky slope beyond it. Holmes drew aside a bush and revealed a yawning blackness. "I thought the Hound would shelter in a burrow," he said, "and assumed he would camouflage its entrance. So I merely checked the bushes. Do come in, Watson, and relax."

Alex crawled after Holmes. The tunnel widened into an artificial cave, about two meters high and three square, lined with a spray-plastic—not too bad a place. By the vague light of Holmes' bull's-eye, Alex saw a small cot, a cookstove, a radio transceiver, and a few luxuries. The latter, apparently, included a middle-aged Hoka in the tattered remnants of a once-fine tweed suit. He had been fat, from the way his skin hung about him, but was woefully thin and dirty now. It hadn't hurt his voice, though—he was still swearing in a loud bass unusual for the species, as he stripped the last of his bonds from him.

"Damned impertinence," he said. "Man isn't even safe on his own grounds any more. And the rascal had the infernal nerve to take over the family legend—*my* ancestral curse, dammit!"

"Calm down, Sir Henry," said Holmes. "You're safe now."

"I'm going to write to my M.P.," mumbled the real Baskerville. "I'll tell him a thing or two, I will. There'll be questions asked in the House of Commons, egad!"

Alex sat down on the cot and peered through the gloom. "What happened to you, Sir Henry?" he asked.

"Damned monster accosted me right on my own moor," said the

Hoka, indignantly. "Drew a gun on me, he did. Forced me into his noisome hole. Had the unmitigated gall to take a mask of my face. Since then he's kept me on bread and water. Not even fresh bread, by Godfrey! It—it isn't British! I've been tied up in this hole for weeks. The only exercise I got was harvesting his blinking weed for him. When he went away, he'd tie me up and gag me—" Sir Henry drew, an outraged breath. "So help me, he gagged me *with my own school tie!*"

"Kept as slave and possibly hostage," commented Holmes. "Hm. Yes, we're dealing with a desperate fellow. But Watson, see here what I have to show you." He reached into a box and pulled out a limp, black object with an air of triumph. "What do you think of this, Watson?"

Alex stretched it out: a plastimask of a fanged monstrous head, grinning like a toothpaste ad. When he held it in shadow, he saw the luminous spots on it. The Hound's head!

"Holmes!" he cried. "The Hound is the—the—"

"Ppussjan," supplied Holmes.

"How do you do?" said a new voice, politely.

Whirling around, Holmes, Alex, Toowey, and Sir Henry managed, in the narrow space, to tie themselves in knots. When they had gotten untangled, they looked down the barrel of a raythrower. Behind it was figure muffled shapelessly in a great, trailing black coat, but with the head of Sir Henry above it.

"Number Ten!" gulped Alex.

"Exactly," said the ppussjan. His voice had a Hoka squeakiness, but the tone was cold. "Fortunately, I got back from scouting around before you could lay an ambush for me. It was pathetic, watching that search party. The last I saw of them, they were headed for Northumberland."

"They'll find you," said Alex, with a dry voice. "You don't dare hurt us."

"Don't I?" asked the ppussjan, brightly.

"I zuppoze yeou du, at that," said Toowey.

Alex realized sickly that if the ppussjan's hideout had been good up to now, it would probably be good until his gang arrived to rescue him. In any case, he, Alexander Braithwaite Jones, wouldn't be around to see.

But that was impossible. Such things didn't happen to him. He was League plenipotentiary to Toka, not a character in some improbable melodrama, waiting to be shot. He—

A sudden wild thought tossed out of his spinning brain: "Look here, Ten, if you ray us you'll sear all your equipment here too." He had to try again; no audible sounds had come out the first time.

"Why, thanks," said the ppussjan. "I'll set the gun to narrow-beam." Its muzzle never wavered as he adjusted the focusing stud. "Now," he asked, "have you any prayers to say?"

"I—" Toowey licked his lips. "Wull yeou alloo me to zay one poem all t' way through? It have given me gree-at coomfort, it have."

"Go ahead, then."

"By the shores of Gitchee Gumee—"

Alex knelt too—and one long human leg reached out and his foot crashed down on Holmes' lantern. His own body followed, hugging the floor as total darkness whelmed the cave. The raybeam sizzled over him—but, being narrow, missed and splatted the farther wall.

"Yoiks!" shouted Sir Henry, throwing himself at the invisible ppussjan. He tripped over Alex and went rolling to the floor. Alex got out from underneath, clutched at something, and slugged hard. The other slugged back.

"Take that!" roared Alex. "And that!"

"Oh, no!" said Sherlock Holmes in the darkness. "Not again, Watson!"

They whirled, colliding with each other, and groped toward the sounds of fighting. Alex clutched at an arm. "Friend or ppussjan?" he bellowed.

A raybeam scorched by him for answer. He fell to the floor, grabbing for the ppussjan's skinny legs. Holmes climbed over him to attack the enemy. The ppussjan fired once more, wildly, then Holmes got his gun hand and clung. Farmer Toowey yelled a Hoka battle cry, whirled his staff over his head, and clubbed Sir Henry.

Holmes wrenched the ppussjan's raythrower loose. It clattered to the floor. The ppussjan twisted in Alex's grasp, pulling his leg free. Alex got hold of his coat. The ppussjan slipped out of it and went skidding across the floor, fumbling for the gun. Alex fought the heavy coat for some seconds before realizing that it was empty.

Holmes was there at the same time as Number Ten, snatching the raythrower from the ppussjan's grasp. Ten clawed out, caught a smooth solid object falling from Holmes' pocket, and snarled in triumph. Backing away, he collided with Alex. "Oops, sorry," said Alex, and went on groping around the floor.

The ppussjan found the light switch and snapped it. The radiance caught a tangle of three Hokas and one human. He pointed his weapon. "All right!" he screeched. "I've got you now!"

"Give that back!" said Holmes indignantly, drawing his revolver.

The ppussjan looked down at his own hand. It was clutching Sherlock Holmes' pipe.

Whitcomb Geoffrey staggered into the George and Dragon and grabbed the wall for support. He was gaunt and unshaven. His clothes were in rags. His hair was full of burrs. His shoes were full of mud. Every now and then he twitched, and his lips moved. A night and half a day trying to superintend a Hoka search party was too much for any man, even an IBI man.

Alexander Jones, Sherlock Holmes, Farmer Toowey, and Sir Henry Baskerville looked sympathetically up from the high tea which the landlord was serving them. The ppussjan looked up too, but with less amiability. His vulpine face sported a large black eye, and his four-legged body was lashed to a chair with Sir Henry's old school tie. His wrists were bound with Sir Henry's regimental colors.

"I say, Gregson, you've had rather a thin time of it, haven't you?" asked Holmes. "Do come have a spot of tea."

"Whee-ar's the s'arch party, lad?" asked Farmer Toowey.

"When I left them," said Geoffrey, dully, "they were resisting arrest at Potteringham Castle. The earl objected to their dragging his duckpond."

"Wull, wull, lad, the-all ull be back soon, laike," said Toowey, gently.

Geoffrey's bloodshot eyes fell on Number Ten. He was too tired to say more than: "So you got him after all."

"Oh, yes," said Alex. "Want to take him back to Headquarters?"

With the first real spirit he had shown since he had come in, Geoffrey sighed. "Take him back?" he breathed. "I can actually leave this planet?"

He collapsed into a chair. Sherlock Holmes refilled his pipe and leaned his short furry form back into his own seat.

"This has been an interesting little case," he said. "In some ways it reminds me of the Adventure of the Two Fried Eggs, and I think, my dear Watson, that it may be of some small value to your little chronicles. Have you your notebook ready? . . . Good. For your benefit, Gregson, I shall explain my deductions, for you are in many ways a promising man who could profit by instruction."

Geoffrey's lips started moving again.

"I have already explained the discrepancies of Sir Henry's appearance in the tavern," went on Holmes implacably. "I also thought that the recent renewed activity of the Hound, which time-wise fitted in so well with the ppussjan's arrival, might well be traceable to our criminal. Indeed, he probably picked this hideout because it did have such a legend. If the natives were frightened of the Hound, you see, they would be less likely to venture abroad and interfere with Number Ten's activities; and anything they did notice would be attributed to the Hound and dismissed by those outsiders who did not take the superstition seriously. Sir Henry's disappearance was, of course, part of this program of terrorization; but also, the ppussjan needed a Hoka face. He would have to appear in the local villages from time to time, you see, to purchase food and to find out whether or not he was being hunted by your bureau, Gregson. Watson has been good enough to explain to me the process by which your civilization can cast a mask in spray-plastic. The ppussjan's overcoat is an ingenious, adaptable garment; by a quick adjustment, it can be made to seem either like the body of a monster, or, if he walks on his hind legs, the covering of a somewhat stout Hoka. Thus, the ppussjan could be himself, or Sir Henry Baskerville, or the Hound of the Baskervilles, just as it suited him."

"Clever fella," murmured Sir Henry. "But dashed impudent, don't y'know. That sort of thing just isn't done. It isn't playing the game."

"The ppussjan must have picked up a rumor about our descent," continued Holmes. "An aircraft makes quite a local sensation. He had to investigate and see if flyers were after him and, if so, how hot they might be on his trail. He broke into the tavern in the Sir Henry disguise, learned enough for his purposes, and went out the window. Then he appeared again in the Hound form. This was an attempt to divert our attention from himself and send us scampering off after a nonexistent Hound—as, indeed, Lestrade's search party was primarily doing when last heard from. When we pursued him that night, he tried to do away with the good Watson, but fortunately I drove him off in time. Thereafter he skulked about, spying on the search party, until finally he returned to his lair. But I was already there, waiting to trap him."

That, thought Alex, was glossing the facts a trifle. However—

Holmes elevated his black nose in the air and blew a huge cloud of nonchalant smoke. "And so," he said smugly, "ends the Adventure of the Misplaced Hound."

Alex looked at him. Damn it—the worst of the business was that Holmes was right. He'd been right all along. In his own Hoka fashion, he had done a truly magnificent job of detection. Honesty swept Alex off his and he spoke without thinking.

"Holmes—by the Lord Harry, Holmes," he said, "this—this is sheer genius."

No sooner were the words out of his lips than he realized what he had done. But it was too late now—too late to avoid the answer that Holmes must inevitably give. Alex clutched his hands together and braced his tired body, resolved to see the thing through like a man. Sherlock Holmes smiled, took his pipe from between his teeth, and opened his mouth. Through a great, thundering mist, Alexander Jones heard THE WORDS.

"Not at all. *Elementary, my dear Watson!*"

INTERLUDE IV

**Plenipotentiary of the
Interbeing League
Planet Toka**

2/3/85

Mr. Hardman Terwilliger
2011 Maori Towers
League City, N.Z., Sol III

Dear Hardman,

Good to hear from you—and many thanks for the booties. They're just the right size, says Tanni, though since this is now our third offspring, I maintain with some authority that human babies come in pretty standardized lots. How are your own kids, and Dory? Give them our regards. Congratulations on your promotional transfer to the CDS inspection office. Any chance of your being the next inspector who'll come to review my progress? No, I guess not—your job will be mostly Earthside, evaluating the reports of poor devils like me. It was decent of you to write unofficially, concerning that complaint about my alleged religious intolerance. I do hate sweating out governmentalese for our mutual Great White Father, Parr. It's one reason why I sometimes think of resigning, in spite of a long stay here on Toka. The Hokas themselves, of course, are another reason or fifty.

No one who hasn't spent time with these furry little demons of mine seems to realize their capabilities. Between you and me and the circular file, I believe the Testing Section goofed dramatically when they pegged this race for a mere Stage D, back in the beginning. They failed to take into account the paralyzing effect of a geological era (?) of armed competition with the Slissii. Now that that damper has been taken off—but come to think of it, I doubt if you know what happened to the Slissii. You'll need the information in your new post, but rather than send you through a decade's worth of reports, here's the gist of it.

They're an odd race. In general temperament and character, they are everything the Hokas are not, cold, calculating, xenophobic, as if nature had struck a needed balance between good and evil on this planet. (Though that, of course, is a purely anthropomorphic value judgment. I daresay the Slissii are kind to their own families.) Early in the game it became clear that we could never make an agreement with them that they'd respect; man has to deal with Hokas on this planet, or no one. But since I could supply my own wards, the Five and a Half Cities, with gunpowder weapons—an inducement, among others, which helped get all the rest of the Hoka nations to accept ward status—the Slissii tribes were totally defeated in a few years.

Meanwhile, their aristocrats had been studying the galactic situation for all they were worth. By the time their last confederation surrendered to the Hoka . . . well, let's face it, to the United States Cavalry and the Royal Canadian Mounted Police . . . they knew what to do. So they were to be Injuns? All right. They became Noble Savages. They wrote pamphlets about the Vanishing Tokan. A very bad novel by one of them, *The Last of the Reptiles,* became a planet-wide best seller. They invented rain dances and charged admission. They wrung tears from the Hoka leaders and, against my strongest advice, some of the best oil lands on this world for reservations.

Soon they were all hog-rich, and presently their leaders weaseled a Class A rating out of the Testing Section. I have some evidence that they cheated outrageously on the tests, but for Pete's sake, don't check up on that! We're well rid of them. You see, as Class A's they can go anywhere they wish, so now practically the entire species is playboying it through the known galaxy, with sidelines in crooked stock, cardsharping and so on.

Don't conclude from this that they are more intelligent than the Hokas. I suspect it's actually the other way around, though the leaping Hoka imagination obscures the fact. Damn it. I've been given an impossible job! A Hoka is *not* a miniature human being, and all my attempts to make him one have blown up in my face.

Which brings me to this complaint of religious discrimination made against me by the Bedrock Fundamentalist Church. You're damn well right I refused their missionaries permission to operate on Toka. This is not intolerance. Any faith that wants to proselytize here is welcome, and many have done so; but there are certain reasonable restrictions which must be observed.

Can you imagine what would happen if I admitted a band of preachers who not only read from the Old Testament—and won't give our local rabbis a chance to explain the details—but hand out illustrated biographies of Oliver Cromwell?

Heigh-ho. Earthman's Burden and all that sort of thing. It's late now, and I have a big day ahead of me, so I'll close. We're being threatened with a spate of piracy, and tomorrow I have to investigate a Venetian claim that Captain Nemo had been sinking their gondolas.

All the best,
Alex

YO HO HOKA!

Alexander Jones was in trouble again. His lean form strode through narrow, cobbled streets between half-timbered houses, automatically dodging horse-drawn carriages. The "horses" were dinosaurian monstrosities, but otherwise Plymouth was a faithful small-scale copy of what the Hokas thought its original had been, circa 1800 A.D. in Earth's England. (This *England* was not to be confused with the Tokan Great Britain, which had been brought up to a Victorian level of civilization.)

The natives who thronged the streets made a respectful way for him, closing in again behind. He heard the awed whispers: "Bli'me, it's the Plenipotentiary 'imself! . . . Look thar, Alf, ye'll allus remember ye saw the great Jones wid yer own blinkin' eyes. . . . Wonder wot e's after? . . . Prob'ly Affairs of State. . . . Yus, ye can see that on the poor lad, it's mykin' 'im old afore 'is time . . ." These citizens were variously dressed: cocked hats, tailcoats, knee breeches; burly dock wallopers in carefully tattered work clothes; red-coated musketeers; long skirts on the females; and no few males in striped jerseys and bell-bottomed trousers, for Plymouth was a major base of His Majesty's Navy.

Now and then Alex's lips moved. "Old Boney," he muttered. "I keep telling them and telling them there isn't any Napoleon on this planet, but they won't believe me! Damn Old Boney! Blast these history books!"

He turned in at the Crown and Anchor, went through a noisy bar where Hokas sat puffing churchwardens and lying about their exploits with many deep-sea oaths, and proceeded up a narrow stair. The room which he had engaged was clean, though the furniture was inconvenient for a human with twice the Hoka height and half the breadth of beam. Tanni looked up at him from a crudely printed newspaper with horror in her eyes. She had left the children with their nurse, to accompany him here.

"Alex!" she cried. "Listen to this, dear. They're getting violent— killing each other!" She read from the *Gazette*, "Today the notorious highwayman Dick Turpin was hanged on Tyburn Hill—"

"Oh, that," said Alex, relieved. "Turpin gets hanged every Thursday. It's wonderful sport for all."

"But—"

"Didn't you know? You can't hurt a Hoka by hanging him. Their neck musculature is too strong in proportion to their weight. If hanging hurt Dick Turpin, the police would never do it. They're proud of him."

"Proud!"

"Well, he's part of this eighteenth-century pattern they're trying so hard to follow, isn't he?" Alex sat down and ran a hand through his hair. He was sometimes surprised that it hadn't turned gray yet.

"Poor dear," said Tanni sympathetically. "How did it go?" They had flown here only today from Mixumaxu, and she was still a little puzzled as to the nature of their mission.

"I couldn't get any sense out of the Admiralty Office at all," said Alex. "They kept babbling about old Boney. I can't convince them that these pirates represent a real menace."

"How did it ever happen, darling? I thought the imposed cultural patterns were always modified so as to exclude violence."

"Oh, yes, yes . . . but some dimwit out in space learned how the Hokas go for Earth fiction and smuggled some historical novels into this sector. Pirates, forsooth!" Alex grinned bitterly. "You can imagine what the idea of swaggering around with a cutlass and a Jolly Roger could do to a Hoka. The first I heard, there were a couple of dozen ships turned pirate, off to the Spanish Main . . . wherever on Toka they've decided *that* is! So far no trouble, but they're probably fixing to attack some place like the Bermuda we've established."

"Criminals?" Tanni frowned, finding it hard to believe of her little friends.

"Oh, no. Just . . . irresponsible. Not really realizing it'll mean bloodshed. They'll be awfully sorry later. But that'll be too late for us, sweetheart." Alex looked gloomily at the floor. "Once Headquarters learns I've permitted a war-pattern to evolve on this planet, I'll be out on my ear and blacklisted from here to the Lesser Magellanic Cloud. My only chance is to stop the business before it blows up."

"Oh, dear," said Tanni inadequately. "Can't they understand? I'd like to give those bureaucrats back home a piece of—"

"Never mind. You have to have iron-bound regulations to run a civilization the size of ours. It's results that count. Nobody cares much how I get them, but get them I must." Alex got up and began rummaging in their trunk.

"What are you looking for?" asked Tanni.

"That green beard . . . the one I wore to the Count of Monte Cristo's masquerade ball last week . . . thought it'd come in handy." Alex tossed articles of apparel every which way, and Tanni sighed. "You see, I've already been to the Admiralty in my proper *persona,* and they wouldn't order out the fleet to catch those pirates—said the routine patrols were adequate. Going over their heads, through Parliament and the King, would take too long. . . . Ah, here!" He emerged with a hideous green beard, fully half a meter in length.

"I'll go direct to Lord Nelson, who's in town," he went on. "It's best to do it incognito, to avoid offending the Admiralty; this beard is disguise enough, not being included in the Hokas' Jones-Gestalt. Once alone with him, I'll reveal myself and explain the situation. He's pretty level-headed, I'm told, and will act on his own responsibility." He put the beard to his chin and the warmth of his body stuck it as fast as a natural growth—more so, for the synthetic fibers could not be cut or burned.

Tanni shuddered at the loathsome sight. "How do you get it off?" she asked.

"Spirits of ammonia. All right, I'm on my way again." Alex stooped to kiss her and wondered why she shrank away. "Wait around till I get back. It may take a while."

The foliage flapped around his chest as he went downstairs. "Scuttle my hatches!" said someone. "What is it?"

"Seaweed," theorized another. "He's been too long underwater."

Alex reached the dock and stared over the tangle of rigging and tall masts which lay beyond. The Hokas had built quite a sizable navy in expectation of imminent Napoleonic invasion, and HMS *Intolerable* lay almost side by side with *Incorrigible* and *Pinafore.* Their mermaid figureheads gleamed gilt in the light of the lowering sun—that is, Alex assumed the fishtailed Hoka females to be mermaids, though the four mammaries were so prominent as to suggest ramming was still standard naval practice. He couldn't see where the *Victory* was. Casting about for assistance, he spotted a patrol of sailors swinging along with a burly little Hoka in the lead. "Ahoy!" he yelled.

The patrol stepped smartly up to him, neat in their English Navy uniforms. "Tell me," said Alex, "how do I get out to the flagship? I must see Admiral Lord Nelson at once."

"Stow my top-hamper!" squeaked the leader. "You can't see the Admiral, mate. 'Tain't proper for a common seaman to speak to the Admiral unless spoken to first."

"No doubt," said Alex. "But I'm not a common seaman."

"Aye, that you are, mate," replied the other cheerfully. "Pressed right and proper as a common seaman, or me name's not Billy Bosun."

"No, no, you don't understand—" Alex was beginning, when the meaning filtered through to him. *"Pressed?"*

"Taken by the press gang of Billy Bosun for His Majesty's frigate *Incompatible,"* said the Hoka. "And a fair bit of luck for you, mate. The worst hell-ship afloat, not counting the *Bounty,* and we sail on patrol in two hours. Toss the prisoner into the gig, men."

"No! Wait!" yelled Alex, frantically trying to pull his beard loose. "Let me explain! You don't know who I am. You can't—"

As he himself had remarked, the Hoka musculature is amazingly strong. He landed on his head in the bottom of the gig and went out like a light.

"Pressed man to speak with you, Cap'n Yardly," said Billy Bosun, ushering Alex into the captain's cabin.

The human blinked in the light from the cabin portholes and tried to brace himself against the rolling of the ship. He had been locked in the forward hold all night, during which time HMS *Incompatible* had left Great Britain far behind. He had gotten over a headache and a tendency to seasickness, but was wild with the thought that every minute was, taking him farther from Tanni and his desperately urgent mission. He stared at the blue-coated, cocked-hatted Hoka who sat behind a desk facing him, and opened his mouth to speak; but the other beat him to it.

"Does, does he?" growled Captain Yardly. The fur bristled on his neck. "Thinks he signed on for a pleasure cruise, no doubt! We'll teach him different, b'gad, won't we, Bosun?"

"Aye, sir," said Billy, stiffly.

"Wait, Captain Yardly!" cried Alex. "Let me just have a word with you in private—"

"Private, eh? Private, damme!" exploded the Hoka. "There's no such thing as privacy aboard a King's ship. Ain't that right, Bosun?"

"Aye, aye, sir."

"But if you'll just listen to me for a moment—" wailed Alex.

"Listen, b'gad! I don't listen to men, do I, Bosun?"

"Aye, aye, sir."

"Nothing in the articles of war that makes it my duty to listen! My duty's to flog, b'gad; keelhaul, damme; drive the mutinous dogs till they drop. Stap my vitals, eh, Bosun?" Captain Yardly snorted with indignation.

"Aye, aye, sir."

Alex took a firm grip on his temper. He reminded himself that there was no use arguing with a Hoka once he had decided to play a certain role. The only way to handle him was to act along. Alex forced his face into a meek expression.

"Sorry, Captain," he said. "The truth is, I've come to confess that I'm not what I appear to be."

"Well, that's different!" huffed the officer. "Nothing against my listening to a man's confession as long as I flog him afterwards anyway."

Alex gulped, and quickly continued: "The truth is, Captain, this green beard of mine is false. You probably think I'm one of these outworlders you see occasionally, but without it, you'd recognize me at once. I'll bet you can't guess who I really am."

"Done!" roared the captain.

"Huh?" said Alex.

"I wager I can guess who you are. Your name's Greenbeard."

"No—no—"

"Said so yourself."

"No, I said—"

"SILENCE!" thundered the captain. "You've lost your wager. No carping, damme. It's not done. Not sporting at all. I'm appointing you first mate, Mr. Greenbeard, in accordance with regulations—"

"Regulations?" stammered Alex. "What regulations?"

"Pressed man always appointed first mate," snorted Captain Yardly, "in spite of his well-known sympathy for the crew. Got sympathy for the crew, haven't you?"

"Well . . . I suppose so . . ." stammered Alex, weakly— "I mean . . . what kind of first mate would I be— No, wait, I'm all mixed up. I mean—"

"No back talk, if you please!" interrupted the Hoka. "Step lively and drive her smartly, Mr. Greenbeard. We're headed 'round the Horn and I want no malingerers aboard."

"The Horn?" goggled Alex.

"You heard me, Mr. Greenbeard."

"But—" protested Alex, wildly, as Billy Bosun started pulling him by main force out of the cabin. "How . . . how long a voyage is this supposed to be?"

The captain's face dropped suddenly into an unhappy embarrassed expression.

"That depends," he said morosely, "on which way we go."

And he turned and vanished through a connecting door into the inner cabin. His voice came back, somewhat muffled: "Clap on all sail, Mr. Greenbeard, and call me if the weather freshens."

The words were followed by what sounded like a sob of desperation.

Giving up further argument as a bad job, Alex went back on deck. A stiff breeze drove the *Incompatible* merrily over a sea which sparkled blue, to the sound of creaking boards and whining rigging. The crew moved industriously about their tasks, and Alex hoped he wouldn't be needed to direct them. He could pilot a spaceship between the stars, but the jungle of lines overhead baffled him.

Probably he wasn't essential, though. He was simply part of the pattern which the Hokas followed so loyally. In the same way, all that talk about gruesome punishment must be just talk—the Navy felt it was expected of them. Which was, however, small consolation, since the same blind devotion would keep the ship out here for as long as the orders said. Without this eternally cursed beard, Alex could easily take command and get back to shore; but he couldn't get rid of the beard until he was ashore. He had a sense of futility.

As he walked along the deck, his eyes lit on a completely incongruous figure leaning on one of the deck guns. This was a Hoka in shirt and trousers of coarse cloth, leather leggings, a chain-mail coat, a shaggy cape, a conical helmet with huge upcurving horns and an interminable sword. A pair of very large and obviously fake yellow mustaches drooped from underneath his nose. He looked mournful.

Alex drew up to the anachronism, realizing he must be from the Viking-culture area in the north and wondering how he had gotten here. "Hello," he said. "My name's Jo—" He stopped; it was useless to assert his identity until he got that triply damned spinach off his face—"Greenbeard."

"Pleased to meet yü," said the viking in a high-pitched singsong. "Ay ban Olaf Button-nose from Sveden. Have yü ever been to Constantinople?"

"Well—no," said Alex, taken somewhat aback.

"Ay vas afraid yü hadn't," said Olaf, with two large tears running down into his mustache. "Nobody has. Ay come sout' and signed on here, hoping ve vould touch at Constantinople, and ve never do."

"Why did you want to—" began Alex, fascinated.

"To yoin the Varangian Guard, of course," said Olaf. "Riches, loot, beautiful vimmen, lusty battles, ha, Odin." He shed two more tears.

"But—" Alex felt a twinge of compassion. "I'm afraid, Olaf, that there isn't any Constantinople on this planet."

"How do yü know, if yü never been there?"

"Why, because—" Alex found the conversation showing the usual Hoka tendency to get out of hand. He gritted his teeth.

"Now, look, Olaf, if I *had* been there, I'd be able to tell you where it was, wouldn't I?"

"Ay hope yü vould," said Olaf, pessimistically.

"But since I *haven't* been there, I can't tell you where it is, can I?"

"Exactly," said Olaf. "Yü don't know. That's yust what Ay vas telling yü."

"No, no, *no!*" yelled Alex. "You don't get the point—"

At this moment, the door to the captain's cabin banged open and Yardly himself came popping out on deck.

"Avast and lay forrad!" he bellowed. "All hands to the yards! Aloft and stand by to come about! We're standing in to round the Horn."

There was a stampeding rush, a roar, and Alex found himself alone. Everybody else had gone into the rigging, including the helmsman and captain. Alex turned hesitantly to one of the masts, changed his mind and ran to the bows. But there was no land in sight.

He scratched his head and returned amidships. Presently everyone came down again, the crew growling among themselves. Captain Yardly slunk by Alex, avoiding his eyes and muttering something about "slight error—happen to anyone—" and disappeared back into his cabin.

Olaf returned, accompanied by Billy Bosun. "Wrong again," said the viking gloomily.

"Rot me for a corposant's ghost, if the crew'll take much more o' this," added Billy.

"Take more of what?" inquired Alex.

"The captain trying to round the Horn, sir," said Billy. "Terrible hard it is, sir."

"Are they afraid of the weather?" asked Alex.

"Weather, sir?" replied Billy. "Why, the weather's supposed to be uncommon good around the Horn."

Alex goggled at him. "Then what's so hard about rounding it?"

"Why, nothing's hard about *rounding* it," said Billy. "It's *finding* it that's so hard, sir. Few ships can boast they've rounded the Horn without losing at least part of their crew from old age first."

"But doesn't everybody know where it is?"

"Why, bless you, sir, of course everybody knows; it doesn't move around. But we do. And where are we?"

"Where are we?" echoed Alex, thunderstruck.

"Aye, sir, that's the question. In the old days, if we were here we'd be about one day's sail out of Plymouth on the southwest current."

"But that's where we are."

"Oh, no, sir," said Billy. "We're in the Antarctic Ocean. That's why the captain thought he was close to the Horn. That is, unless he's moved us since."

Alex gave a wordless cry, turned, and fled to the captain's cabin. Inside it, Yardly sat at a desk mounded high with sheets of calculations. There was a tortured look on his furry face. On the bulkhead behind him was an enormous map of Toka crisscrossed with jagged pencil lines.

"Ah, Mr. Greenbeard," he said in a quavering voice as he looked up. "Congratulate me. I've just moved us three thousand miles. A little matter of figuring declination in degrees east instead of degrees west." He glanced anxiously at Alex. "That sounds right, doesn't it?"

"Ulp!" said Alex.

In the following four days, the human gradually came to understand. In earlier times, native ships had found their way around the planet's oceans by a familiarity with the currents and prevailing winds, but with the technology of 1800 had come the science of navigation and since then no Hoka would be caught dead using the old-fashioned methods. With the new, some were successful and some were not. Lord Nelson, it was said, was an excellent navigator. So was Commodore Hornblower. Others had their difficulties. Captain Yardly's was that while he never failed to take a proper sight with his sextant, he invariably mistrusted the reading he got and was inclined to shift his figures around until they looked more like what he thought they should be. Also, he had a passion for even numbers, and was always rounding off his quantities to more agreeable amounts.

Under this handicap, the physical ship sailed serenely to her destination, guided by a non-navigating crew who automatically did the proper things in the old fashion at the proper time. But the hypothetical ship of Captain Yardly's mathematical labors traversed a wild and wonderful path on the map, at one time so far at sea that there was not enough fresh water for them to make land alive, at another time perched high and dry on the western plains of Toka's largest continent. It was not strange that the captain had a haunted look.

All of which was very unsettling to the crew who, however willing to give him the benefit of the doubt, were finding it somewhat of a strain even on their elastic imaginations to be told they were in the tropics one moment and skirting the south polar ice cap the next. Their nerves were on edge. Moreover, Alex discovered, the consensus among them was that the captain was becoming too obsessed with his navigation to pay proper attention to the running of the ship. No one had been hanged for several weeks, and there hadn't been a keelhauling for over a month. Many a Hoka standing on the sun-blistered deck cast longing glances at the cool water overside and wished he would be keelhauled (which was merely fun on a planet without barnacles). There was much fo'c'sle talk about what act could be committed dastardly enough to rate the punishment.

"If you want a swim, why don't you just fall overboard?" asked Alex of Billy Bosun on the fourth day.

The Hoka's beady eyes lit up, and then saddened again. "No, sir," he said wistfully. "It's contrary to the articles of war, sir. Everybody knows British sailors can't swim a stroke."

"Oh, well," said Alex, helpfully. "If you've got scruples—" He picked up the boatswain and tossed him over the rail. Billy splashed into the sea with a howl of delight.

"Shiver my timbers!" he roared gleefully, threshing around alongside and blowing spouts of water into the air. "I'm murdered! Help! Man overboard!"

The crew came boiling up on deck. Small furry bodies began to go sailing into the sea, yelling something about rescue. The second mate started to lower a boat, decided to pitch the nearest sailor into the ocean instead, and followed him.

"Heave to!" yelled Alex, panic-stricken. "Man—er—men overboard! Bring her about!"

The helmsman spun the wheel and the ship pivoted into the wind's eye with a rattle of canvas. Whooping, he overbalanced, and fell. His joyously lamenting voice joined the chorus already resounding below.

The door to the captain's cabin flew open. Yardly rushed out. "Avast!" he cried. "Belay! What's about, here?" He headed for the rail and stared downward.

"We're drowning!" the crew informed him, playing tag.

"Belay that!" shouted the captain. "Avast drowning immediately. Call yourselves British seamen, do you? Mutinous dogs, I call you. Treacherous, mutinous dogs! Quarrelsome, treacherous, mutinous dogs! Careless, quarrel—"

He looked so hot and unhappy in his blue coat and cocked hat that Alex impulsively picked him up and threw him over the side.

He hit the water and came up spouting and shaking his fist. "Mister Greenbeard!" he thundered. "You'll hang for this. This is mutiny!"

* * *

"But we don't have to hang him, do we?" protested Alex.

"Blast my bones, Cap'n Greenbeard," said Billy, "but Yardly was a-going to hang you."

"Ay don't see how yü can avoid it," said Olaf, emptying sea water out of his scabbard. "Ve ban pirates now."

"Pirates!" yelped Alex.

"What else is left for us, Cap'n?" asked Billy. "We've mutinied, ain't we? The British Navy'll never rest till ve're hunted down."

"Oh well," said Alex, wearily. If hanging the ex-captain was considered part of the pattern, he might as well play along. He turned to the two seamen holding Yardly. "String him up."

They put a noose around Yardly's neck and politely stepped back. He took a pace forward and surveyed the crew, then scowled blackly and folded his arms.

"Treacherous, ungrateful swine!" he said. "Don't suppose that you will escape punishment for this foul crime. As there is a divine as well as a Hoka justice—"

Alex found a bollard and seated himself on it with a sigh. Yardly gave every indication of being good for an hour of dying speech. The human relaxed and let the words flow in one ear and out the other. A sailor scribbled busily, taking it all down for later publication in a broadside.

"—this causeless mutiny—plotted in secret—ringleaders did not escape my eye—some loyal hearts and true poisoned by men of evil— forgive you personally, but cannot—sully the British flag—cannot meet my eye—in the words of that great man—"

"Oh, no!" said Alex involuntarily, but Billy was already giving the captain the pitch on his boatswain's whistle.

"Oh, my name it is Sam Hall, it is Sam Hall
Yes, my name it is Sam Hall, it is Sam Hall. . . ."

Like most Hokas, the captain had a rather pleasant tenor, Alex reflected, but why did they all have to sing "Sam Hall" before being hanged?

"Now up the rope, I go, up I go. . . ."

Alex winced. The song came to an end. Yardly wandered off on a sentimental side issue, informed the crew that he had had a good home and loving parents, who little suspected he would come to this, spoke a few touching words concerning his little golden-furred daughter ashore, wound up by damning them all for a pack of black-hearted scoundrels, and in a firm voice ordered the men on the end of the rope to do their duty.

The Hokas struck up a short-haul chanty, and to the tune of "Haul Away, Joe" Yardly mounted to the yard-arm. The crew paled and fainted enthusiastically as for five minutes he put on a spirited performance of realistic twitches, groans, and death rattles—effective enough to make Alex turn somewhat the same shade as his beard. He was never sure whether or not something at this stage had gone wrong and the Hoka on the rope was actually being strangled. Finally, however, Yardly hung limp. Billy Bosun cut him down and brought him to the captain's cabin, where Alex signed him up under the name of Black Tom Yardly and sent him forward of the mast.

Thus left in charge of a ship which he had only the foggiest notion of how to run, and a crew gleefully looking forward to a piratical existence, Alex put his head in his hands and tried to sort out matters.

He was regretting the mutiny already. Whatever had possessed him to throw the captain of a British frigate overboard? He might have known such a proceeding would lead to trouble. There was no doubt Yardly had been praying for an excuse to get out of his navigational duties. But what could Alex have done once his misguided impulse had sent Yardly into the ocean? If he had meekly surrendered, Yardly would probably have hanged him . . . and Alex did not have a Hoka's neck muscles. He gulped at the thought. He could imagine the puzzlement of the crew once they had cut him down and he didn't get up and walk away. But what good is a puzzled Hoka to a dead plenipotentiary? None whatsoever.

Moreover, not only was he in this pickle, but five days had gone by. Tanni would be frantically flying around the world looking for him, but the chance of her passing over this speck in the ocean was infinitesimal. It would take at least another five days to get back to Plymouth, and hell might pop in Bermuda meanwhile. Or he might be seized in the harbor if someone blabbed and strung up as a mutineer before he could get this green horror off his chin.

On the other hand—

Slowly, Alex got up and went over to the map on the bulkhead. The Hokas had been quick to adopt Terrestrial place names, but there had, of course, been nothing they could do about the geographical dissimilarity of Toka and Earth. The West Indies here were only some 500 nautical miles from Great Britain; HMS *Incompatible* was almost upon them now, and the pirate headquarters at Tortuga could hardly be more than a day's sail away. It shouldn't be too hard to find and the buccaneer fleet would welcome a new recruit. Maybe he could find some ammonia there. Otherwise he could try to forestall the raid, or sabotage it, or something.

He stood for several minutes considering this. It was dangerous, to be sure. Cannon, pistols, and cutlasses, mixed with Hoka physical energy and mental impulsiveness, were nothing a man wanted close to him. But every other possibility looked even more hopeless.

He went to the door and called Olaf. "Tell me," he said, "do you think you can steer this ship in the old-fashioned way?"

"To be sure Ay can," said the Viking, "Ay'm old-fashion myself."

"True," agreed Alex. "Well, then, I'm going to appoint you first mate."

"Ay don't know about that, now," interrupted Olaf, doubtfully. "Ay don't know if it ban right."

"Of course," said Alex, hastily, "you won't be a regular first mate. You'll be a Varangian first mate."

"Of course Ay will!" exclaimed Olaf, brightening. "Ay hadn't t'ought of that. Ay'll steer for Constantinople."

"Well—er—remember we don't know where Constantinople is," said Alex. "I think we'd better put in at Tortuga first for information."

Olaf's face fell. "Oh," he said sadly.

"Later on we can look for Constantinople."

"Ay suppose so."

Seldom had Alex felt so much like a heel.

They came slipping into the bay of Tortuga about sunset of the following day, flying the skull-and-crossbones which was kept in the flag chest of every ship just in case. The island, fronded with tropical trees, rose steeply over an anchorage cluttered with a score of armed vessels; beyond, the beach was littered with thatch huts, roaring bonfires, and swaggering pirates. As their anchor rattled down, someone whooped from the crow's nest of the nearest vessel: "Ahoy, mates. Ye're just in time. We sail for Bermuda tomorry."

Alex shivered, the green beard and the thickening dusk concealing his unbuccaneerish reaction. To the eagerly swarming crew, he said: "You'll stay aboard till further orders."

"What?" cried Black Tom Yardly, outraged. "We're not to broach a cask with our brethren of the coast? We're not to fight bloody duels, if you'll pardon the language, and wallow in pieces of eight and—"

"Later," said Alex. "Secret mission, you know. You can break out our own grog, bosun." That satisfied them, and they lowered the captain's gig for him and Olaf to go ashore in. As he was rowed away from the *Incompatible,* Alex heard someone start a song about a life on the ocean wave, in competition with someone else who, for lack of further knowledge, was endlessly repeating, "Yo-ho-ho—and a bottle of rum—" *They're happy*, thought Alex.

"What yü ban going to do now?" inquired Olaf.

"I wish I knew," said Alex, forlornly. The little Viking, with his skepticism about the whole pirate pattern, was the only one he could trust at all, and even to Olaf he dared not confide his real hopes. Such as they were.

Landing, they walked through a roaring, drunken crowd of Hokas trying to look as villainous as possible with the help of pistols, knives, cutlasses, daggers, sashes, earrings, and nose-rings. The Jolly Roger flew over a long hut within which the Captains of the Coast must be meeting; outside squatted a sentry who was trying to drink rum but not succeeding very well because he would not let go of the dagger in his teeth.

"Avast and belay there!" shrilled this freebooter, lurching erect and drawing his cutlass as Alex's bejungled face came out of the gloom. "Halt and be run through!"

Alex hesitated. His sea-stained tunic and trousers didn't look very piratical, he was forced to admit, and the cutlass and floppy boots he had added simply kept tripping him up. "I'm a captain too," he said. "I want to confer with my . . . er . . . confreres."

The sentry staggered toward him, waving a menacing blade. Alex, who had not the faintest idea of how to use a sword, backed up. "So!" sneered the Hoka. "So ye'll not stand up like a man, eh? I was tol' t' run anybody through what came near, and damme, I will!"

"Oh, shut up," said Olaf wearily. His own sword snaked out, knocking the pirate's loose. That worthy tried to close in with his dagger, but Olaf pushed him over and sat on him. "Ay'll hold him here, skipper," said the Viking. Hopefully, to his squirming victim: "Do know the vay to Constantinople?"

Alex opened the door and walked in, not without trepidation. The hut was lit by guttering candles stuck in empty bottles, to show a rowdy group of individuals seated around a long table. One of them, with a patch over his eye, glared up. "Who goes?" he challenged.

"Captain Greenbeard of the *Incompatible,*" said Alex firmly. "I just got in."

"Oh, well, siddown, mate," said the pirate. "I'm Cap'n One-eye, and these here is Henry Morgan and Flint and Long John Silver and

Hook and Anne Bonney and our admiral La Fontaine, and—" someone clapped a hand over his mouth.

"Who's this?" squeaked La Fontaine from under his cocked hat. Twenty pairs of Hoka eyes swiveled from him to Alex and back again.

"Why, scupper and gut me!" growled another, who had a hook taped to the end of his hand. "Don't ye know Cap'n Greenbeard?"

"Of course not!" said La Fontaine. "How could I know a Cap'n Greenbeard when there ain't any such man? Not in any of the books, there ain't. I'll wager he's John Paul Jones in disguise."

"I resent that!" boomed a short Hoka, bouncing to his feet. "Cap'n Greenbeard's my cousin!" And he stroked the black, glossy, but obviously artificial beard on his chin.

"Blast me, nobody can say that about a friend of Anne Bonney," added the female pirate. She was brilliantly bedecked in jewels, horse pistols, and a long gown which she had valiantly tried to give a low-cut bodice. A quadrimammarian Hoka needed two bodices, one above the other, and she had them.

"Oh, very well," grumbled La Fontaine. "Have a drink, cap'n, and help us plan this raid."

Alex accepted a tumbler of the fiery native distillation. The Hokas' fantastic capacity for beverage alcohol he was well aware of, but he hoped to go slow and, in view of the long head start the others had, stay halfway sober. Maybe he could master the situation somehow. "Thanks," he said. "Have one yourself."

"Don't mind if I do, mate," said La Fontaine amiably, tossing off another half liter. "Hie!"

"Is there any spirits of ammonia here?" asked Alex.

One-eye shifted his patch around to the other orb and looked surprised. "Not that I know of, mate," he said. "Should be some in Bermuda, though. Ye want it for polishing up treasure before burying it?"

"Let's come to order!" piped Long John Silver, pounding his crutch on the table. His left leg was strapped up against his thigh. "By the Great Horn Spoon, we have to make some plans if we're going to sail tomorrow."

"I, er, don't think we should start that soon," said Alex.

"So!" cried La Fontaine triumphantly. "A coward, is it? Rip my mainto'gallantstuns'l if I think ye're fit to be a Captain o' the Coast. Hic!"

Alex thought fast. "Shiver my timbers!" he roared back. "A coward, am I? I'll have your liver for breakfast for that, La Fontaine! What d'ye take me for, a puling clerk? Stow me for a—a—sea chest if I think a whitefaced stick like yourself is fit to be admiral over the likes of us. Why," he added, cunningly, "You haven't even got a beard."

"Whuzzat got to do with it?" asked La Fontaine muzzily, falling into the trap.

"What kind of admiral is it that hasn't got a hair to his chin?" demanded Alex, and saw the point strike home to the Hokas about him.

"Admirals don't have to have beards," protested La Fontaine.

"Why, hang, draw, and quarter me!" interrupted Captain Flint. "Of course admirals have to have beards. I thought everybody knew that." A murmur of assent went up around the table.

"You're right," said Anne Bonney. "Everybody knows that. There's only two here fit to command the fleet: Cap'n Blackbeard and Cap'n Greenbeard."

"Captain Blackbeard will do very well," said Alex graciously.

The little Hoka got to his feet. "Bilge me," he quavered, "if I ever been so touched in m'life before. Bung me through the middle with a boarding pike if it ain't right noble of you, Cap'n Greenbeard. But amongst us all, I can't take an unfair advantage. Much as I'd be proud to admiral the fleet, your beard is a good three inches longer'n mine. I therefore resigns in your favor."

"But—" stammered Alex, who had expected anything but this.

"That's fantastic!" objected La Fontaine, tearfully. "You can't pick a man by his beard—I mean—it isn't—you just can't!"

"La Fontaine!" roared Hook, pounding the table. "This here council o' pirate captains is following the time-honored procedure o' the Brethren o' the Coast. If you wanted to be elected admiral, you should ha' put on a beard afore you came to meeting. I hereby declares the election over."

At this last and cruelest cut, La Fontaine fell speechless. "Drawer!" shouted Henry Morgan. "Flagons all around to drink to the success of our venture."

Alex accepted his warily. He was getting the germ of an idea. There was no chance of postponing the raid as he had hoped; he knew his Hokas too well. But perhaps he could blunt the attack by removing its leadership, both himself and La Fontaine. . . . He reached over and clapped the ex-chief on the shoulder. "No hard feelings, mate," he said. "Come, drink a bumper with me, and you can be admiral next time."

La Fontaine nodded, happy again, and threw another down his gullet. "I like a man who drinks like that!" shouted Alex "Drawer, fill his flagon again! Come on, mate, drink up. There's more where that came from."

"Split my mizzenmast!" put in Hook. "But that's a neat way o' turning it, Admiral! 'More where that came from.' Neat as a furled sail. True, too."

"Oh, well," said Alex, bashfully.

"Here, drawer, fill up for Admiral Greenbeard," cried Hook. "That's right. Drink deep, me hearty. More where this came from. Haw!"

"Ulp!" gulped Alex. Somehow he got it down past shriveling tonsils. "Hoo-oo-oo!"

"Sore throat?" asked Anne Bonney solicitously.

"More where that came from," bellowed Hook. "Fill up!"

Alex handed his goblet to La Fontaine. "Take it, mate," he said generously. "Drink my health."

"Whoops!" said the ex-admiral, tossed it off, and passed out.

"Yo, heave ho," said Billy Bosun. "Up you come, mate."

They hoisted the limp figure of La Fontaine over the rail of the *Incompatible*. Alex, leaning heavily on Olaf, directed operations.

"Lock 'm in m' cabin," he wheezed. "Hois' anchor and set sail for Bermuda." He stared toward a sinking moon. Toka seemed suddenly to have acquired an extra satellite. "Secret mission, y' know. Fi-ifteen men on a dead-ead man's chest—"

"Sling a hammock on deck for the captain," ordered Billy. "He don't seem to be feeling so well."

"Yo-ho-ho and a bottle of rum," warbled Alex.

"Aye, aye, sir," said Billy, and handed him one.

"Woof!" groaned Alex and collapsed. The night sky began majestically revolving around him. Shadowy sails reached out to catch the offshore breeze. The *Incompatible* moved slowly from the harbor. Alex did not see this. . . .

Bright sunlight awakened him. He lay in his hammock until the worst was over, and then tried to sort things out. The ship was heeling to a steady wind and the sounds of sail-flap, rigging-thrum, plank-creak and crew-talk buzzed around him. Rising, he saw that they were alone in the great circle of the horizon. In the waist, the starboard watch were sitting about telling each other blood-curdling tales of their piratical exploits. Black Tom Yardly, as usual, was outdoing all the rest.

Alex accepted breakfast from the cook, lit the captain's pipe in lieu of a cigaret, and considered his situation. It could be worse. He'd gotten away with La Fontaine, and they should be in Bermuda shortly after sunset. There would be time to warn it and organize its defenses; and the pirates, lacking both their accustomed and their new admiral, would perhaps botch the attack completely. He beamed and called to his first mate. "Mr. Button-nose!"

Olaf approached. "Ay give yü good morning," he said gravely.

"Oh? Well, the same to you, Olaf," replied Alex. There was a certain air of old world courtesy about the small Viking which seemed to be infectious. "What kind of speed are we making?"

"About ten dragon's teeth," said Olaf.

"Dragon's teeth?" repeated Alex, bewildered.

"Knots, yü would say. Ay don't like to call them knots, myself. It don't sound Varangian."

"Fine, fine," smiled Alex. "We should be there in no time."

"Vell, yes," said Olaf, "only Ay suppose ve must heave to, now."

"Heave to?" cried Alex. "What for?"

"So yü can have a conference vit' the other captains," said Olaf, pointing astern. Alex spun on his heel and stared along the creamy wake of the *Incompatible*. There were sails lifting over the horizon. The pirate fleet!

"My God!" he exclaimed, turning white. "Pile on all sail!" Olaf looked at him surprised. "Pile on all sail!"

Olaf shook his round head. "Veil, Ay suppose yü know best," he said tiredly, and went off to give the necessary orders.

The *Incompatible* leaped forward, but the other ships still crept up on her. Alex swallowed. Olaf returned from heaving the log.

"Twelve dragon's teeth," he informed Alex reproachfully.

It was not a pleasant day for Admiral Greenbeard. In spite of almost losing his masts, he could not distance the freebooters, and the gap continued to narrow. Toward sunset, the other ships had almost surrounded him. The islands of Bermuda were becoming visible, and as darkness began to fall the whole fleet rounded the headland north of Bermuda City Bay. Lights twinkled on the shore, and the Hokas crowding the shrouds set up a lusty cheer. Resignedly, Alex ordered his crew to heave to. The other craft did likewise, and they all lay still.

Alex waited, chewing his fingernails. When an hour had passed and nothing happened except sailors hailing each other, he hunted up Olaf. "What do you think they're waiting for?" he asked nervously.

The bear-like face leaned forward out of shadow. "Ay don't t'ink," said Olaf. "Ay know. They're vaiting for yü to signal the captains aboard your flagship. The qvestion is, what are yü waiting for?"

"Me? Summon *them?*" said Alex. "But they were chasing us!"

"Ay vould not call it shasing," said Olaf. "Since yü ban admiral, they vould not vant to pass yü up."

"No, no, Olaf." Alex lowered his voice to a whisper. "Listen, I was trying to escape from them."

"Yü vere? Then yü should have said so," declared Olaf strongly. "Ay ban having a terrible time—yust terrible—to keep from running avay from them vit' all sails set."

"But why did you think they were following us?" raved Alex.

"Vy, what should they be doing?" demanded Olaf. "Yü ban admiral. Naturally, ven we leave for Bermuda, they're going to follow yü."

Speechless, Alex collapsed on a bollard. After a while he stirred feebly.

"Signal all captains to report aboard for conference," he said in a weak voice.

"Gut and smoke me!" thundered Captain Hook, as the chiefs crowded around a table arranged on the poop. "Slice me up for hors d'oeuvres, but you're a broom-at-the-mast sailor, Admiral Greenbeard. We had to clap on all canvas to keep you in sight."

"Oh, well," said Alex, modestly.

"Blast my powder magazine if I ever seen anything like it. There you was, flying through the water like a bloody gull; and at the same time I could have laid me oath you was holding the ship back as hard as you could."

"Little sailing trick. . . ." murmured Alex.

"Blind me!" marveled Hook. "Well, to business. Who's to lead the attack on the fort, Admiral?"

"Fort?" echoed Alex blankly.

"You knows how it is," said Hook. "They got cannon mounted on that fort which juts out into the bay. We'll have to sail past and give 'em a broadside to put 'em out of action. Then we can land and sack the town before Lord Nelson, blast his frogs and facings, shows up."

"Oh," said Alex. He was thinking with the swiftness of a badly frightened man. Once actual fighting started, Hokas would be getting killed—which, quite apart from any natural sympathy, meant the end of his tenure as plenipotentiary. If he himself wasn't knocked off in the battle. "Well. . . ." he began slowly. "I have another plan."

"Hull and sink me!" said Long John Silver. "A plan?"

"Yes, a plan. We can't get by that fort without getting hurt. But one small boat can slip in easily enough, unobserved."

"Stab me!" murmured Captain Kidd in awe. "Why, that's sheer genius."

"My mate and I will go ashore," went on Alex. "I have a scheme to capture the mayor and make him order the fort evacuated." Actually, his thoughts extended no further than warning the town and getting this noxious vegetation off his face. "Wait till I signal you from the jetty with lanterns how you're to arrive. One if by land and two if by sea."

"Won't go, Admiral," said Anne Bonney. She waved into the darkness, from which came the impatient grumbling of the crews. "The men won't brook delay. We can't hold 'em here more than a couple of hours. Then we'll have to attack or face a mutiny."

Alex sighed. His last hope of avoiding a fight altogether, by making the fleet wait indefinitely, seemed to have gone glimmering. "All right," he agreed hollowly. "Sail in and land the men. Don't fire on the fort, though, unless it shoots first, because I may be able to empty it, the way I suggested."

"Scupper and split me, but you're a brave man," said Hook. "Chop me up for shark bait if I think we could ha' done anything without you."

"Thanks," gritted Alex. This last was the unkindest cut of all.

The other Hokas nodded and mumbled agreement. Hero worship shone in their round black eyes.

"I moves we drinks to the Admiral's health," boomed Flint. "Steward! Fetch the flagons for—"

"I'd better leave right away," said Alex hurriedly.

"Nonsense!" said Henry Morgan. "Who ever heard of a pirate doing anything sober?"

"Psssh!" said Alex, rapping on the window of the mayor's residence. Muffled noises came from the garden behind, where Olaf had tied up the guards who would never have permitted a green-bearded stranger to approach.

The window opened and the mayor, an exceedingly fat Hoka, pompous in ruffles and ribbons, looked out, square into the nauseous tangle of hair beyond.

"Eek!" he said.

"Hic!" replied Alex, holding on to the sill while the official mansion waltzed around him.

"Help!" cried the mayor. "Sea monsters attacking! Drum up the guard! Man the battlements. Stow the belaying pins!"

He was quite obviously preparing to launch his not inconsiderable weight from the window at Alex, when a familiar golden head appeared over his shoulder.

"Alex!" gasped Tanni. "Where have you been?"

"Pressed pirate," said Alex, reeling. "Admiral Greenbeard. Help me in. Hic!"

"Drunk again," said Tanni resignedly, grabbing his collar as he scrambled over the sill. She loved her husband; she had been scouring the planet in search of him, had come here as a forlorn hope; but it is hard to shed joyful tears over a green beard quaking with hiccups.

"Mayor Bermuda," mumbled Alex. "British gen'leman. En'ertain th' lady. Ge' me anti-alco—anti-alco—alkyho—yo-ho-ho an' a bo'le o' rum—"

Tanni left him struggling with the word and went off after a sober-pill. Alex got it down and shuddered back to normal.

"Whoof!" he exclaimed. "That's better. . . . Tanni, we're in one hell of a spot. Pirates—"

"The pirates," she said firmly, "can wait until you get that thing off your face." She extended a bottle of ammonia and a wad of cotton.

Thankfully, Alex removed the horror and gave them the story. He finished with: "They're too worked up to listen to me now, even in my character of plenipotentiary. They'll be landing any minute. But if we don't offer resistance, there'll at least be no bloodshed. Let them have the loot if they must."

"Come, come," said the mayor. "It's out of the question. Out of the question entirely."

"But they outnumber your garrison!" spluttered Alex.

"Beastly fellows," agreed the mayor happily, lighting a cigar.

"You can't possibly fight them off. The only thing to do is surrender."

"Surrender? But we're British!" explained the mayor patiently.

"Damn it, I order you to surrender!"

"Impossible," said the mayor doggedly. "Absolutely impossible. Contrary to Colonial Office Regulations."

"But you're bound to lose."

"Gallantly," pointed out the mayor.

"This is stupid!"

"Naturally," said the mayor, mildly. "We're muddling through. Muddle rather well, if I do say so myself."

Alex groaned. Tanni clenched her fists. The mayor turned to the door. "I'd better have the soldiers informed," he said.

"No . . . wait!" Alex leaped to his feet. Something had come back to him. *Chop me up for shark bait if I think we could ha' done anything without you.* And the others had agreed . . . and once a Hoka got an idea in his head, you couldn't blast it loose. . . . His hope was wild and frail, but there was nothing to lose. "I've got a plan."

"A plan?" The mayor looked dubious.

Alex saw his error. "No, no," he said hastily. "I mean a ruse."

"Oh, a *ruse!*" The mayor's eyes sparkled with pleasure. "Excellent. Superb. Just the sort of thing for this situation. What is it, my dear plenipotentiary?"

"Let them land unopposed," said Alex. "They'll head for your palace here, of course, first."

"Unopposed?" asked the mayor. "But I just explained—"

Alex pulled out his cutlass and flourished it. "When they get here, I'll oppose them."

"One man against twenty shiploads of pirates?"

Alex drew himself up haughtily. "Do you imply that I, your plenipotentiary, can't stop twenty ships?"

"Oh, no," said the mayor. "Not at all. By all means, my dear sir. Now, if you'll excuse me, I must have the town crier inform the people. They'd never forgive me if they missed such a spectacle." He bustled away.

"Darling!" Tanni grabbed his arm. "You're crazy. We don't have so much as a raythrower—they'll kill you!"

"I hope not," said Alex, bleakly. He stuck his head out the window. "Come in, Olaf. I'll need your help."

The corsair fleet moved in under the silent guns of the fort and dropped anchor at the quay. Whooping, shouting, and brandishing their weapons, the crews stormed ashore and rushed up the main street toward the mayor's palace. They were mildly taken aback to see the way lined with townsfolk excitedly watching and making bets on the outcome, but hastened on roaring bloodthirsty threats.

The palace lay inside a walled garden whose gate stood open. Nearby, the redcoats of the garrison were lined up at attention. Olaf watched them gloweringly: it was his assignment to keep any of them from shooting. Overhead, great lanterns threw a restless yellow light on the scene.

"Fillet and smoke me, but there's our admiral!" shouted Captain Hook as the tall green-bearded figure with drawn cutlass stepped through the gateway. "Three cheers for Admiral Greenbeard!"

"Hip, hip, hooray!" Echoes beat against the distant rumble of surf. The little round pirates swarmed closer, drawing to a disorderly halt as they neared their chief.

"Aha, me hearties!" cried Alex. "This is a great day, for the Brethren of the Coast. I've got none less than Alexander Jones, the plenipotentiary of Toka, here, and I'm about to spit him like a squab!" He paused. "What, no cheers?"

The pirates shuffled their feet.

"What?" bellowed Alex. "Speak up, you swabs. What's wrong?"

"Stab me!" mumbled Hook. "But it don't seem right to spit the plenipotentiary. After all he done for this planet."

Alex felt touched, but redoubled the ferocity of his glare.

"If it's glory you're after, Admiral," contributed Captain Kidd, "blast me if I'd waste time on the plenipotentiary. There's no glory to be gained by spitting him. Why, he's so feeble, they say he has to have a special chair to carry him around."

This description of the one small luxury Alex had purchased after three years of saving—a robot chair for his office—so infuriated him that he lost his temper completely.

"Is that so?" he yelled. "Well, it just happens that he's challenged me to a duel to the death, and I'm not going to back out. And you scuts will stay there and watch me kill him and like it!"

"No, I won't have it," cried a soldier, raising his musket. Olaf took it away from him, tied it into a knot, and gave it back.

Alex ducked inside the portal, where Tanni and the mayor waited in the garden, still muttering furiously to himself.

"What's wrong now, dear?" asked Tanni, whitefaced.

"Blankety-blanks," snarled Alex. "For two cents I'd kill myself, and then see how they'd like it!" He stamped over to a large brass urn that had been placed in readiness.

"*En garde!*" he roared, fetching it a lusty swipe with his cutlass. "Take that!"

The gathered pirates jumped nervously. Billy Bosun tried to go through the gateway to see what was happening, but Olaf picked him up and threw him over the heads of Henry Morgan and One-eye. "Private matter," said the Viking imperturbably.

Viciously, Alex battered the clamoring urn with his blade, meanwhile yelling imprecations. "Don't try to get away! Stand and fight like a man! Aha! Take that, me hearty!"

Hammering away, he fumbled in his pocket with his free hand and brought out some ammonia-soaked cotton. The beard came loose and he gave it to Tanni, who was dabbing him with ketchup here and there, as he shouted in a slightly lower pitch.

"Is that so? Take that yourself! And that, Greenbeard! Didn't know, did you"—he thrust his clean-shaven face around the edge of the gate—"that I was on the fencing team as a boy?"

Impulsively, the pirates cheered.

"As well," said Alex, circling back out of view and belaboring the urn, "as having my letter in track and swimming. I could have made the basketball team too, if I'd wanted. Take that!"

Hurriedly, he stuck the beard back on and signaled for more ketchup.

"Bum and blister me," be swore, backing a little ways out of the gate and scowling horribly at the buccaneers, "but you've a tricky way about you, Jones. But it won't save you. The minute I trap you in a corner I'll rip you up for bait. Take that!" He stepped out of sight again. "Ouch!" he cried in the lower voice.

The pirates looked sad. "It don't seem right," muttered Long John Silver. "It just never come to me, like, that people might get hurt."

Captain Hook winced at the din.

"Aye," he said, shakily. "What've we gotten ourselves into, mates?"

"Don't be too cocky, Greenbeard!" cried Alex, appearing with a bare chin and lunging while Tanni struck the urn. "Actually, I've got muscles of steel. Take that! And that! And that!"

Vanishing again, he fetched the urn three ringing blows, dropped his cutlass, and clapped the beard back onto his face, giving vent to a spine-freezing scream.

"You got me!" he yammered. Clasping ketchup-soaked hands over his heart, he reeled across the gateway, stopping before the terrified visage of the pirates.

"Oh," he groaned. "I'm done for, mates. Spitted in fair and equal combat. Who'd ha' thought the plenipotentiary was such a fighter? Goodby, mates. Clear sailing. Anchors aweigh. Don't look for my body. Just let me crawl off and die in peace."

"Goodby," wept Anne Bonney, waving a handkerchief at him. The whole buccaneer band was dissolving into tears.

Alex staggered out of sight, removed his beard, and breathed heavily for a while. Then he picked up his cutlass and strode slowly out the gate and looked over his erstwhile followers.

"Well, well," he said scornfully. "What have we here? Pirates?"

There was a pause.

"Mercy, sir!" wept Captain Hook, failing to his knees before the conqueror of the terrible, the invincible, the indispensable Greenbeard, "We was just having our bit of fun, sir."

"We didn't mean nothing," pleaded Flint.

" 'Specially to get nobody hurt," added Billy Bosun.

"Silence!" commanded Alex. "Do you give up?" There was no need to wait for an answer. "Very well. Mister Mayor, you will have these miscreants hanged at dawn. Then put them on their ships and let them go. And"—he scowled at the pirates—"see that you all behave yourselves hereafter!"

"Y-y-y-es sir," said Black Tom Yardly.

Alex felt someone shyly plucking at his sleeve. He looked around, and saw it was the mayor.

"Oh . . . I don't know." The mayor looked up at him. Wistfulness edged his tone. "They weren't so bad, now were they, sir? I think we owe 'em a vote of thanks, damme. These colonial outposts get infernally dull."

"Why, thank'ee, mayor," said Anne Bonney. "We'll come sack you any time."

Alex interrupted hastily. Piracy seemed to have become an incurable disease, but if you can't change a Hoka's ways, you can at least make him listen to reason . . . on his own terms.

"Now hear this," he decreed loudly. "I'm going to temper justice with mercy. The Brethren of the Coast may sack Bermuda once a year, but there must be no bloodshed—"

"Why should there be?" asked the mayor, surprised.

"—and the loot must be returned undamaged."

"Slice and kipper me!" exclaimed Captain Hook indignantly. "Of course it'll be returned, sir. What d'ye think we are—thieves?"

Festivities lasted through all the next day, for the pirates, of course, had to sail away into the sunset. Standing on a terrace of the palace garden, his arm about Tanni and the mayor nearby, Alex watched their masts slip over the horizon.

"I've got just one problem left," he said. "Olaf. The poor fellow is still hanging around, trying to find someone who knows the way to Constantinople. I wish I could help."

"Why, that's easy, sir," said the mayor. "Constantinople's only about fifty miles due south of here."

"What?" exclaimed Alex. "No, you're crazy. That's the Kingdom of Natchalu."

"It was," nodded the mayor. "Right up till last month it was. But the queen is a lusty wench, if you'll pardon the expression, madam, and was finding life rather dull until a trader sold her some books which mentioned a, hm," the mayor coughed delicately, "lady named Theodora. They're still getting reorganized, but it's going fast and—"

Alex set off at a run. He rounded the corner of the house and the setting sun blazed in his, eyes. It gilded the helmet and byrnie of Olaf Button-nose, where he leaned on his sword, gazing out to sea.

"Olaf!" cried Alex.

The Hoka Viking turned slowly to regard the human. In the sunset, above the droop of his long blond mustaches, his face seemed to hold a certain Varangian indomitability.

INTERLUDE V

**Plenipotentiary of the
Interbeing League
Planet Toka**

HEADQUARTERS OFFICE   CITY OF MIXUMAXU

7/6/86

Mr. Adalbert Parr
Chief Cultural Commissioner
EHQ of CDS
League City, N.Z., Sol III

Dear Mr. Parr :

Thank you for your personal letter of the 10th ult., inquiring about second-hand reports that I contemplate resigning my office. I will answer your questions just as informally and off the record, as I have not yet reached any definite decision.

I realize that what you are pleased to term my "unmatchable knowledge of the race based on years of experience" would be hard to duplicate; and I realize what damage might be done to Hoka society by someone lacking such qualifications. Were the matter as simple as this, I would certainly remain at my post; for I care for the little fellows as if they were my own children.

But I have been increasingly nagged by a very basic doubt—a doubt of the value, even the rightness, of the Service's very *raison d'être*. Is it possible that our problem of "civilizing backward planets" is only a subtler form of the old, discredited imperialism of Earth's brutal past? Have I merely been turning my wards into second-rate humans, instead of first-rate Hokas? I don't know. In spite of all our pretentious psychocultural tests, I doubt if anyone really knows.

But leaving this aside, there is also a personal horn to my dilemma. Ordinary human flesh and nerves can only stand so much. I am tired of becoming Mr. Chips or Tarzan on a minute's notice. There are wild moments in which I see myself lighting a huge bonfire of all the books on this planet, and dancing before it. Yet, paradoxically, I find growing within myself a kind of Hokaishness—an awful sort of addiction to these childlike heroisms.

Am I in danger of losing my humanness? I did not realize what years of Tokan liquor had done to me until, on a recent vacation trip to Gelkar, I absentmindedly drank off an entire pitcher of martinis, taking it merely for a tall tumbler of the local mineral water. Consciously, I remain myself—most of the time—I think—but is my subconscious becoming an alcoholic? On the same trip, I was sight-seeing in Callipygia City, when a visiting Klkr'n arachnoid took me for a Gelkarite policeman; and I have grown so used to falling into different roles that I confidently directed him to some place I myself had never heard of before; and when I left for home two days later, the poor chap was still missing.

At one time, as you know, I had high hopes of bringing the Hokas, practically single-handed, to a sane, sober, and civilized condition where their talents could fully serve the Interbeing League. But I see now, quite apart from all my doubts mentioned above, that the task is too big. And I do have my own family, as well as my sanity, to consider.

Therefore I welcome the arrival of Inspector Brassard, whom I have been notified to expect soon. If he can give the situation here a clean bill of health, I shall very probably step aside for a new man with a new viewpoint to try his luck on the Hokas.

                                        Yours truly, Alexander Jones.

THE TIDDLYWINK WARRIORS

The whole trouble began with Jorkins Brassard, Cultural Development Inspector from Earth Headquarters. Or perhaps you should blame the bureaucratic tradition in general. But a rigid set of rules is necessary if the League is to civilize some thousands of new planets in a gradual and humane fashion. Therefore the blame goes back to the inventors of gravity control and the faster-than-light secondary drive. However, if they had not done what they did, history would have been different and Alexander Jones would never have been born. This is getting us nowhere, so we shall leave the onus on the well-meaning but dogmatic head of Jorkins Brassard.

His tour of the frontier worlds had brought him, complete with military escort, to Toka, where he landed in Mixumaxu. The subspace radio had announced his coming, and preparations consonant with his exalted rank had been made.

Emerging from his ship, Brassard blinked in the hot sunshine. He was a balding red-faced man, sweaty in dress uniform, with a promising pot belly that he yanked in whenever he remembered it. A score of crisp young marines followed. They paused on the gangway and stared in most unmilitary stupefaction. They had not been expecting a double column of knights in full armor, mounted on dinosaurian monstrosities, sitting rigid with lances aloft except when someone broke formation to oil himself.

A group of Hokas trotted up and surrounded the Earthmen as these came slowly down to the field. This bunch wore scarlet coats, purple capes, blue trousers with gold frogging, jack-boots with spurs, cocked hats and ceremonial swords. They were preceded by a Scottish bag-pipe corps.

Their leader bowed so his black nose almost touched the ground. "Welcome to Toka, sirs," he squeaked in fluent English.

"Uh . . . thank you . . . but who are these?" Brassard waved at me knights.

"Those are your honor guard, sir," beamed the chief. His breast glittered blindingly with medals. "There was some argument over who should have the privilege. It nearly came to a fight between the United States Cavalry and the Varangian Guard. But then King Arthur allied himself with the Black Watch and overawed the others."

"I see," murmured Brassard faintly. "But who are you?"

"Sir!" The Hoka drew himself up with a touch of hauteur. "We're the Secret Service, of course. Now, if you please, sir, we'll take you to His Excellency."

It was a slow ride through the old city's narrow streets, under peaked tile roofs and between cheering crowds, to the metal and plastic tower of the League Office. The vehicle was a perfectly good electric groundcar, but protocol seemed to demand it should be drawn by the reptilian "horses." Brassard and his men sighed with relief when they had got past a native sentry in full Samurai costume and into the cool interior of the new building.

Alex met them in the reception room. After the formalities, he apologized. "I'm afraid my wife isn't here, Inspector. We'll have to bach it. But I have an excellent Hoka chef—hired him away from Louis XIV."

"Oh," said Brassard. Recovering himself: "Doesn't matter. Just here to check up. Routine. I'll want to see your records, visit a few spots, make a report to EHQ." He sighed and sipped the aperitif which a Hoka in full footman's livery had just handed him. "Earthman's burden. Not easy. Sure you understand."

"Of course," said Alex, and wondered if it would be mutual.

Tanni Jones was a loyal wife, as well as a blonde and beautiful one, but she had declared that one more official function would unfunction her. Alex sympathized and suggested they send the children to the Hoka London to watch Parliament; he had hopes of government careers for them, and this was an unparalleled education in how not to conduct such business. "And maybe you'd like to take a flitter and run outsystem."

"Yes." Tanni smoothed her dress over her hips and winced. "I've been meaning to go to Gelkar anyway, the reconditioning center."

"What off Earth for?" demanded Alex.

"Do you realize I've put on three kilos?" she answered "None of my clothes will fit me any longer. I can get a ten-day treatment there."

Alex could see no difference in her, but had been married long enough not to admit that. She did have a slight tendency to plumpness and fought it bitterly.

"All right," he agreed, and went on to instruct her in the handling of a spaceship: run on normal gravs until well out of the system, than switch to secondary for the two-day voyage to Gelkar, and always trust your autopilot no matter what your senses tell you. She had flown before, but Alex had firm prejudices.

He saw her off and went back to prepare for Brassard's arrival.

The bureaucrat went through his files first, a dull business. They had been at it for a day, and it was four days after Tanni's departure, when the news of catastrophe came.

Alex was sitting and smoking in a heap of papers, listening to acrid criticism of his methods. "Not done at all. You know very well census figures should be under P for Population. Cross-reference. Regulations." At that, he was getting off lightly.

The Secret Service chief came into the office on the run, tangled with his sword, and skidded across the floor. Somehow he got his head jammed into the waste-basket. Alex dragooned Brassard into pulling on the legs while he held the container. The Hoka emerged with a pop and looked wildly about him.

"Sabotage!" he hissed.

The beady eyes glittered suspiciously at Brassard. "Has he been cleared?"

The inspector huffed. "Of course I've been cleared."

The chief scratched his head. "But have the people who cleared you been cleared?" he asked.

"Never mind," sighed Alex. "I'll vouch for him."

The chief looked under the desk, opened a few cabinet drawers, and checked under the tenth-story window. Then he came back and drew Alex's ear down to his muzzle. Cupping his hands, he whispered hoarsely: "Visio call for you, sir."

"Oh." Alex was hardened, after a dozen years on Toka. "Excuse me, Mr. Brassard." He went out, took a gravshaft to the fifth level, and tuned in the buzzing subspatial transceiver.

Tanni's face swam into the screen. It was streaked with dirt, her long golden hair was tangled, and tears furrowed the dust. In the background, against the flitter control panel, Alex saw a squat non-human figure with what appeared to be a weapon.

"Oh, Alex!" wailed Tanni.

His initial horror lessened when he realized she was unhurt. And at least the boat's communicator was working. "What happened?"

"I . . . I've crashed," she said.

Alex gaped. "Where?"

"On Telko—"

"How in space did that happen?" he yelped.

"I tried to . . . cut in past the sun to build up speed!" she sniffled. "I came too close, and it was either fall in toward Telko or overload the cooling system—"

Alex snorted indignantly. "How many tines have I told you to lay off that close-orbit stunt? Women astrogators!"

Tanni wiped her eyes. "I tried to land for another start," she went on shakily. "Northern peninsula . . . b-but you know I c-c-can't land without a GCA beam."

Alex glowered. "How badly is it damaged?"

"Th-the flitter? I don't know. It just w-w-won't fly."

"Well," grumbled Alex. "Broadcast a signal so I can find you. I'll get you in the courier boat."

"Yes . . ." whispered Tanni. "And come quick, darling."

His fears stirred anew. "Is something really wrong?"

"The—the natives."

"Are they threatening you?" shouted Alex. His heart popped into his mouth. The natives of Telko had not molested the few visitors to their planet so far, but they were known to be warlike.

"No-o-o-o!" wailed Tanni. "Worse!"

"Worse!"

"They think I'm a—a—goddess, or a mascot, or something."

"Well," he asked slowly, "what's wrong with that?"

"But they keep feeding me and feeding me. They won't let me eat the boat supplies. They almost stuff their own food down my mouth. It was all I could do to be allowed to come here and call you."

"Oh . . . that's all right," said Alex with a shudder of relief. "Telkan food has vitamin deficiencies, but a few days of it won't hurt you."

"But there's something in it! High calories or something. I'm putting on kilos and kilos. Alex, you've got to come right away!"

"You ought to be glad it's not poisoned," said the man unfeelingly. Most of him was turned to the worried planning of a rescue expedition. A few raythrowers would get rid of the Telks if they'd not listen to reason, but it could be a ticklish operation.

Tanni burst into tears and softened his heart. "It's all right, dear," he said soothingly. "Remember, Inspector Brassard is here with a military escort. We'll pull you out in a couple of days at most."

The Telk in the background laid an impatient hand on her shoulder. She gulped and blew a trembling kiss. Then she was led out of sight.

It was ridiculous, really. Telko was in the same planetary system as Toka, being the next world sunward. But Alex, on speaking terms with the natives of planets a thousand light-years removed, had never been there and knew almost nothing about it. Nobody did.

The reason, though, was simple. Telko was a hot, cloudy world with a voracious life, terrestroid to only six points of classification. That meant you wouldn't be killed outright by eating its food, but you would suffer from the complete lack of Vitamins A, B, C, and E.

Furthermore, the natives were an unpromising lot. On their single continent, they had only one language, its dialects mutually comprehensible; but they were split into thousands of tribes with wildly different cultures. One point all the Telks had in common: they loved battle. It was instinctive, a hangover from ages when they had fought wild beasts barehanded. Unless he could take something sharp-edged at least once a month and go out and kill somebody, a Telk pined away.

So, after a few scientific studies, they were left alone. They were certainly not a race among whom you'd want to park your wife.

Alex came into the office at full speed. Brassard looked up from a sheaf of reports and asked querulously: "What's this about the Heisenberg Uncertainty Principle?"

"Tanni—" panted Alex.

"Don't interrupt me! I want to know. Important to get serious xenological survey of original autochthonous cultures. How else can we know best course for natives? Here I—don't interrupt, I say!—I have report from xenologist. Tried to study untouched Hoka village. Took statistics, asked questions, standard approved methods. Comes back babbling about impossibility of getting results due to Heisenberg Uncertainty Principle. What's the explanation?"

Alex braced himself. He was beginning to understand Brassard's mind. It was worthy of a Hoka, except for lacking the Hoka *joie de vivre*. "The fellow should have known better," he said between his teeth. "I warned him."

"But what happened?"

"What would you expect? Here you had a Hoka tribe whose first exposure to human culture was a xenologist. You know how they go overboard for anything new. They started asking *him* questions about tribal customs and sex practices. They followed him around and took notes. They decided his watch was an ancestral totem and— Oh, never mind. Now they're making nuisances of themselves all over the planet. Will you listen to me for a change?"

Rapidly, Alex outlined the situation.

Brassard drummed impatiently on the desk top. "Well," he asked, when the younger man had run down, "what d'you want, hey?"

"Your help, of course! We've got to go rescue my wife!"

"Sorry. Inspector not permitted to use force on any natives unless directly threatened. Colonial Office Regulations, Vol. XXXVIII, Sec. 12, Par. 3-b."

"Then I'll go!" screamed Alex. "I'll rescue her myself!"

Brassard pressed the buzzer. "Rescue?" he barked. "What d'you mean, rescue? No charging in there with modern weapons and decimating the natives, Jones."

"B-b-but they won't give her up otherwise!"

"Then we'll send a commission. Yes, commission. That's what we'll send. Have one out there in a month. Two months at the latest. Long as I'm inspector in charge of this region there'll be no exposing of Class W planets to any weapons above Class 6."

A couple of Brassard's men appeared in the doorway in response to the buzzer. "Not sure I trust you, Jones," said the bureaucrat. "Have to sequester your sidearms. Better remove secondary-drive units from your boats, too, so you can't go outsystem for mercenary soldiers."

"But those vitamin deficiencies," pleaded Alex. "In two months she'll have scurvy and—and weigh three hundred kilos—"

"Sorry," said Brassard. "Earthman's burden. I'm not unreasonable, though. Go to Telko yourself if you like and see what you can do. I'll push hard for commission to negotiate if you fail."

Alex wavered, rebellion hot within him. But there were two strong marines in the doorway. Also— In his mind's eye he saw a picture of his lovely wife, captive, sadly stuffing herself and putting on weight. But right beside it, his mind's eye was placing another vision of Tanni growing thin and wan on his meager ensign's pension, which was all he would have if he got broken from his present job rather than resigning with honors.

Maybe he should rely on the government after all. But if the commission failed, Tanni was doomed . . . assuming she hadn't already gone out of her head from watching herself balloon and done something desperate. No!

Class 6 weapons—Wait, simple gunpowder was Class 5, wasn't it? He could round up some Hokas to help. The cowboys of the Western plains? No, it would take weeks to gather enough of them . . . *Hey!*

Very formally, Alexander Jones applied in triplicate for permission to attempt a rescue with Tokan auxiliaries. Equally formally, Jorkins Brassard stamped his OK. Then the plenipotentiary went out to the spacefield, where a sympathetic but rule-bound marine turned his emasculated courier boat over to him and watched it dwindle eastward in the sky.

Alex had not specified what auxiliaries he would use.

Toka had one desert. Once outworld traders had discovered what a market there was here for second-rate historical novels, it was inevitable that this desert would be populated by Arabs and the French Foreign Legion.

Alex landed outside Sidi Bel Abbès, a cluster of flat-roofed mud huts in an oasis. A kilometer or so beyond it lay the main Legion outpost, the Tricolor drooping over its walls. Everywhere else was rock and sand, glimmering under a brilliant sun.

A few portly figures in kaftan and burnoose watched him as he hurried through the streets. Once he collided with one of the brontosaurian beasts locally supposed to be a camel. He was rather dazed, both by the crisis and the hypno he had taken en route—all available information on Telko. A knowledge of its dialects swirled through his head, mixed with technical dissertations on the biochemistry and its rapid action (that must be why Tanni was getting fat so fast) and a recording of a bloodthirsty folk song.

Arriving at the civil governor's mansion, he was led at once to that worthy. It was cool and dim in the office, but the Hoka stuck firmly by his sun helmet. He had also glued spiked mustaches and a goatee to his face.

"Ah, M'sieur L'Ambassadeur!" he cried, rising with a sweeping gesture that knocked a vase off his desk. *"Quel honneur! Bienvenu!"*

"Hoog whah hogoo—" panted Alex. "Damn! I mean, how do you do. Look, M. LaFontanelle, I've got troubles."

"Tiens!" The governor waved his arm nonchalantly and upset a floor lamp. "Something has occurred, then?" Like nearly all Hokas, he spoke good English, but as a Frenchman considered it his duty to throw in an accent.

"My wife—" began Alex, and stopped. The fewer beings told about Tanni's humiliating plight, the better; it would be enough to raise the Legion.

"Ah," said the governor, drawing a sharp breath. "Your lady?"

"She—er—well, I guess I better not talk about it," stumbled Alex.

"But of course!" cried LaFontanelle, raising his hands in horror. "My poor friend! It is *La Légion Etrangère* you wish, *hein?"*

Startled at such prescience, Alex could only nod. "Come with me," said the governor, laying a furry hand on his. There were tears in the black button eyes. Dazedly, Alex permitted himself to be led out toward the fortress.

He had been here before, to make sure that the Legion and the Arab Hokas were not killing each other. They weren't; there was no grudge between them, in fact, a brisk trade, though they felt obliged to exchange occasional shots. But the Arabs preferred to skulk behind sand dunes and be highlighted against the setting sun on camelback, while the French—true to the tradition of Legionnaire marksmanship—never fired at less than 500 meters; and their black powder rifles, though producing the loud report and heavy smoke prized by Hokas, had an extreme range of about half that.

Guards in blue tunic, white breeches, red sash and kepi presented arms as the governor and the plenipotentiary hurried in through the gates. Beyond lay a dusty courtyard littered with adobe buildings. Toward the largest of these Alex was conducted, and found himself standing before the desk of the elderly commandant. "Here you are, *mon vieux,*" said LaFontanelle.

"*Qu'est-que-c'est-que-ca?*" rattled the commandant.

"*La Femme—*" said the governor.

"*Non!*" The officer's jaw dropped.

"Mais oui."

"Avec un autre—un plus jeune—"

"*On ne le dit pas, cependant. . . .*" said the governor, nodding knowingly. The other Hoka nodded also and took out a printed form.

"Brassard!" muttered Alex between clenched jaws.

"*Ah, Brassard son nom-de-guerre.*" The commandant wrote it down. "If you will sign here—" Alex scribbled his name without stopping to think. The commandant beamed, leaned across the desk and shook the human's hand. "Congratulations, *mon brave,*" he burbled. "You are now a Legionnaire. Report to Sergeant LeBrute."

"What?" yelped Alex, coming out of his daze. "What did you say?"

The commandant rubbed his hands and smiled in a fatherly fashion. "You are joining the Foreign Legion to forget."

"What do you mean?" shouted Alex. "I can't join the French Foreign Legion! I'm the League Plenipotentiary!"

"He tests us," nodded the governor of the commandant. "Ah, my friend, one knows how to preserve a secret. One understands you wish to forget. Ah, the frailty of woman." He sighed. "A word, a glance, and their heart is turned. No, Private Brassard, your secret is safe with me."

"And with *la Légion*," said the Hoka behind the desk. "Fear not, Private Brassard. What you were before entering is a secret that you may bury with you. The Legion asks no questions. The Legion will release you to no one," he turned his head. "Sergeant LeBrute!"

The door opened and a burly little Hoka came in.

"Wait!" cried Alex desperately, the sudden awful realization sweeping over him that he had slipped into another of those situations that beset his path on Toka like pools of quicksand. "You can't do this to me! I tell you, I belong to Earth!"

"Once, perhaps," replied the commandant. "Now you belong to La Belle France. It matters not what you were before joining. . . . Another *bleu,* Sergeant LeBrute. Take it out."

"*Cochon!*" bawled the sergeant, trying hard to get a sadistic rasp into his squeaky voice. "*Nom d'un chameau!* Come along now!" And with the usual Hoka strength, so greatly disproportionate to their size, he clamped hold of Alex's collar and dragged him easily out as the human kicked and struggled and screamed for justice.

The governor twirled his mustache and wiped a tear from his eye.

"Ah," he said. "How well he pretends. *Un brave.* But underneath, his heart is breaking for the wife who has deceived him."

"*Naturellement,*" replied the commandant.

They got out a bottle marked *Chablis,* poured, and raised glasses solemnly.

"Remain there, *bleu misérable!*" said Sergeant LeBrute, tossing Alex onto a hard cot and stamping out.

The man sat up and looked around. He was in some kind of barracks, with several Legionnaires sitting about. None of them looked very surprised; they must get some odd types here, even for this planet.

"Bit of a brute, that Sergeant LeBrute," observed an Oxford accent. Alex turned to see an aristocratic-mannered Hoka on the adjoining cot, who continued: "Allow me to introduce myself. Cecil Fotheringay-Phipp Alewyn Smith. You'll find the Legion isn't such a bad spot, old man. Of course, they march you till you drop, the food is terrible, the Arabs torture you to death if they catch you, the officers and non-coms are sadistic beasts, and you associate with the scum of the earth—but on the whole, it's not a bad life."

"Oh?" said Alex, feebly. He knew from his survey that it was mostly just talk: Hokas who had read P. C. Wren thought it was expected of them, but were much too kindly to put it into practice. Still, soldiering here could be rugged, and there was Tanni—

"No, indeed," went on the English Hoka. "Our platoon, for example, is fairly representative. Right next to you on the other side is Rastignon, whom we playfully call the Murderer."

Alex jumped and became aware of the other Hoka, sitting and sharpening his bayonet on a whetstone. "I am, too!" he squeaked, and by the usual native courtesy his whopper was taken at face value.

"Next to him," went on Smith, "is LeRat, a scum of the Paris sewers type. Next to him is Alf Sniggs, a scum of the London sewers type. That mysterious fella playing with ink and paper at the table is Le Forgeur. Beyond him, that enormously strong and brutal-looking chap is Giuseppe Fortissimo." To the untrained eye, he was indistinguishable from the other round-bellied ursinoids. "Over in the corner—"

The Hoka he was pointing at looked up and suddenly broke into song. "My name is John Wellington Wells, I'm a dealer in magic and spells—"

"Mad, poor fellow," sighed Smith. "We call him Les Ciseaux, or in English, The Scissors. That sullen chap beside him is Kurt Wilhelm Schwartzmann von und zu Griffentaffel, a typical Prussian beast. At least, he would be typical if he weren't the only one on Toka."

The Legionnaire in question leaped onto his feet, clicked his heels and shouted: *"Achtung!"* He wore the standard uniform, but had added a monocle.

Alex shook his head, dazedly. "How does a Prussian beast get into the French Foreign Legion?" he asked in a numb voice.

"Ach!" sighed von und zu Griffentaffel. "It vas *schrecklich.* I had read about Bismark, *verstehen Sie?* I vanted to machen all der odder *deutsche* Hokas into ein *Landswehr.* Nobody listened." He took off his monocle to let a tear fall from his eye. "Vot good iss it to be ein Prussian beast mit spiked helmet und all, ven effery time I shouten *'Achtung!'* efferybody else chust clicken der beer steins und singen *'In München steht ein Hofbräuhaus'?* I am ein failure." He collapsed into tears.

Alex sighed and got back to his own troubles. "Look here, Smith," he said, "my wife—"

"Tut, tut, old chap," interrupted the Hoka. "No need to tell your story. In the Legion, one doesn't ask. A code of sorts, don't y'know."

"But you don't understand! My wife—"

"Of course, of course," said Smith. "A word is sufficient. Wives. Women. The ladies. Gentlemen, the Queen!" He stood up suddenly, raised his hand as if to propose a toast, caught himself, and sat down. "What am I doing?" he asked shakily. "Excuse me, old boy. You arouse old memories."

Alex slumped. He was getting nowhere.

* * *

That evening he was issued a uniform and told by Sergeant LeBrute, with many oaths, to put it on. Since it was meant for a Hoka and Alex was rather tall and lanky, even for a human, the effect can be imagined. He spent an unhappy night, and the next morning—after breakfast, which was coffee and French bread—his platoon was called out at a gruesome hour for a work detail.

He gulped when he saw what it was. His sleek courier boat was now the property of the Legion, and had been hauled into the fortress grounds. Nobody knew how to fly it, or cared. But the commandant was interested in its temperature-regulating coils.

It seemed that Sidi Bel Abbès did a lively trade in beer with the Arabs. These Hokas had heard vaguely that Bedouins don't drink, and abstained from the 180-proof rotgut the French fondly consumed as wine. But no Hoka could imagine life without alcohol, so they settled for homebrew beer. The daily consumption of this by the average Bedouin was awesome. The commandant decided to use the boat's coils in fermenting the mixture. Great vats of it were installed, and hundreds of bottles put in the hold for later use.

"*Bleus misérables!* Idler! *Cochon! Chameau! Vache! Hommard!*" Sergeant LeBrute scurried up and down, shouting curses at the platoon. Now and then he kicked them. This did not hurt a well-padded Hoka, but Alex was built differently. In any event, a man does not enjoy turning his own spaceboat into a brewery. He spent a seething day and returned exhausted to his barracks at the end of it.

As darkness fell, he lay on his cot and brooded. This was ridiculous. And poor Tanni! But how the devil was he going to get out of it?

His eyes wandered about the lantern-lit room, where the Legionnaires sat telling enormous lies about the heat and thirst they had suffered in the desert, and the girls in the Casbah. He could get no help from them; they were enjoying their roles too much . . . No—wait! An idea struck him.

He hurried over to the table where Le Forgeur was copying a fifty-franc note with considerable skill. "Er—pardon me," he said.

" 'Allo," said the Hoka, amiably.

"Er—look—you couldn't possibly whip me up a discharge from the Legion, could you?"

"A discharge?" echoed Le Forgeur, looking up in astonishment. "*Mais, mon ami,* there are no discharges in the Legion. One deserts."

"One does?"

"*Exactement.* And if one is caught, one is sent to the penal battalion."

"Ulp!" said Alex.

Le Forgeur got up, alight with the quick heady enthusiasm of his race. "Is it that you intend perhaps to desert?" he cried. *"Alors,* I will accompany you."

"Huh?" said Alex. "You?"

A friendly hand fell on his arm. "If you're going to desert, old man," said Smith, "you'll need the help of an old hand who knows the desert. I'll come too. No, no thanks, I insist."

"Ach, to see Alt Heidelberg again!" said von und zu Griffentaffel. "I vill come mit."

"Buono! Bravo!" shouted Giuseppe Fortissimo. "Napoli! Vesuvio! Ice cream! La Scala!" And he broke into opera at the top of his lungs: *"Sì, fuggiam da queste mura . . . !"*

"Oh, no!" moaned Alex, as they all crowded around him.

"This way," whispered Alex.

He led the file of Hokas toward the shadowy form of his courier boat.

"Quiet now," he cautioned, opening the airlock.

"Bleus misérables!" shrilled a voice, splitting the night, and the rotund figure of Sergeant LeBrute popped up to confront him. "Aha! *Deserting!"*

Alex swallowed his heart and thought fast.

"No, no, mon . . . er . . . sergeant," he said. "Secret mission—I mean patrol. Yes, that's it. We're a patrol—out to get lost!"

"A lost patrol!" cried LeBrute. Even in the dark, Alex could see his eyes shine with sudden excitement. "Ah, *mes enfants,* you will need Sergeant LeBrute to guide you."

"B-but—" stammered Alex.

"Silence! C'est un fait accompli. I, Sergeant LeBrute, am now in command. *En avant, marche!"*

"Into the boat," supplemented Alex, hurriedly.

"Into the *bâteau,"* agreed the noncom.

One by one, they crowded in.

Well . . . he had got his auxiliaries, though not precisely in the way he had planned. Alex set the autopilot for Telko and ran spaceward at full acceleration. The Hokas were too preoccupied with staring out at the stars and speculating on their mission to give much trouble. Alex had a chance to review his hypnotically acquired knowledge.

The trouble was, the northern peninsula on which Tanni had crashed was completely unknown. Cut off from the rest of the continent by a rugged mountain range, it had developed its own cultures, whatever they might be; all you could be sure of was (a) the language; (b) the technology, primitive iron-working, and agriculture; and (c) a state of continuous warfare. Well, he'd have to play by ear. The platoon had its rifles, such as they were. And his anachronistic charges had recently led Alex to develop skill with sword, bow and lance, if it came to that.

He called to mind the Telk physiognomy. An average male was a bit taller than a Hoka and even broader, one mass of muscle under a green skin, nude except for assorted cutlery. He had four powerful arms, and his stocky bowlegs ended in prehensile-toed feet which could serve as hands. The head was round, hairless, bat-eared, with small yellow eyes protected by bony ridges, mouth and nose contained in a porcine snout. Formidable characters, but—

At top acceleration, with gravitic fields to protect against pressure, the boat reached Telko in a few hours. Alex dove beneath the cloud layer to find himself under a gloomy sky and over a sullen, tideless ocean. When he located the single continent, he followed its jungled shores to the peninsula, and there he picked up Tanni's broadcast signal and homed on it.

The peninsula was a stony waste, thinly covered with scrub brush and tilled fields. The mountains ran out into steep hills. At their foot, Alex saw a flash of metal and swooped low. The flitter stood there, its drive-cones smashed. It was inside the thick earth walls of a village whose rounded huts resembled igloos more than anything else. There was no sign of life, but he thought it best not to land within the settlement at once. He might get shot full of arrows.

Casting about, he saw a large ruined structure some two kilometers south, on a hilltop—a similar village, but wrecked and deserted in some war or other. It would do for a base. He set the boat down behind its walls and cut the engines.

The lost patrol poured out with glad cries. They were in a courtyard overgrown with native plants, mostly tubers. A warm dry wind blew upon them, and the eternal clouds lay moodily overhead. It looked like a good situation. Alex was somewhat startled, therefore, when he emerged to see Sergeant LeBrute prowling about with a worried expression. The platoon was posted on the wall facing the other village, rifles ready.

"What's wrong?" asked the human.

The sergeant spat. "Name of a name of a name of a name of a— uh—"

"Name?" suggested Alex.

"Merci. Name!" finished the sergeant. "But we will never from here emerge alive, *bleu."*

Alex did a double take. This was no attitude to find in those he expected to overcome the Telks.

"Nonsense!" he replied. "Why, we'll walk right out of here—"

"Bleu misérable!" stormed LeBrute. "Do you contradict me? This is Zinderneuf—the fort which perishes to the last man!"

"But—but—"

"Silence, cochon!" LeBrute turned away. "Rastignon, Sniggs, you are detailed to the kitchen. Prepare these plants for eating."

"Wait—" screeched Alex, remembering Tanni's experience and seeing the Hokas and himself, grossly overweight, rolling around on the earth like helpless basketballs. "The . . . the Arabs have poisoned the fort's food supply. Use the stores in the galley of the boat."

He sighed with relief when the sergeant conceded the point, and went back himself to try calling Tanni. Somewhat to his surprise, the communicator responded and her distracted face looked out at him. He noticed that it had grown fuller.

"Alex!" she gasped. "Where are you?"

"I'm here," said Alex. "I mean, I'm on Telko. I just landed in this old ruin up the hill. I've got some Legionnaires with me— But how are you?"

"I—" she choked back a sob. "I'm still eating."

"How much do you weigh now?"

"Don't ask me that!" she shrieked.

"Well . . . you're in the flitter again, I see."

"Yes. But—Alex, you came just at the right moment. The Telks won't let me go without fighting like devils. But they have a new war on now. The hill tribes are invading and the village warriors are out to fight them. I've been left here in the flitter, nobody but the females to guard me. If you hurry—"

"I'll see," said Alex, dubiously. "Sit tight, sweetheart."

He rushed outside, his brain humming.

"Mes amis!" he shouted. "Join me! We must hasten! The Arabs have got Cigarette, the daughter of the Legion, locked up over there. We've just time to rescue her!"

Hoka faces fell. But to Alex's dismay, not one of them moved.

"What are you waiting for?" he demanded. "Come on!"

"Hélas!" sobbed Sergeant LeBrute.

"Hélas?" asked Alex.

"Oui, hélas," said Rastignon the murderer in a choked voice. *"La*

pauvre petite. Quel dommage that one so young and beautiful should perish while *les soldats de la Légion* stand helplessly by."

"Helpless!" squeaked Alex.

"Oui," said Sergeant LeBrute. "Helpless. Our duty is to defend this post to the last man. We may not abandon it. Cigarette is a child of the Legion. She will understand. She will die thinking of La Belle France and singing the Marseillaise."

"The hell she will!" snarled Alex, grabbing his rifle. "All right, I'll go alone."

"Halt!" ordered Sergeant LeBrute, aiming at him. *"Ne pas bouger!"*

"What do you mean, *ne pas bouger?*" cried Alex. "I certainly won't *ne pas bouger.* I—"

"Silence, bleu!" bellowed LeBrute. "It is your duty to die like the rest of us on the wall of Zinderneuf. If you attempt a rescue of Cigarette, I will order the platoon to open fire on you."

"At less than 500 meters?" asked Alex.

LeBrute put down his rifle and scratched his head. Taking a perhaps unfair advantage of his confusion, the human made a dash for the wall.

But he barely got one leg over it when a roar from the hills petrified him. Out of a nearby defile poured a good two thousand battling creatures. The village Telks were in grim retreat, and the hillmen after them. In moments, the fight had spilled across the plain and there was no hope of escaping Zinderneuf.

Alex goggled. He had never seen a combat like this. Not a sword or a spear in sight. The natives were fighting with—Yipe!—eggbeaters, scissors, tennis balls, pipes, spoons and mousetraps!

After a while, the man began to understand.

The eggbeaters, a defensive weapon like the medieval pike, had sharp blades on the end of a three-meter shaft, turned by a crank. The scissors were for clipping off an enemy's head or hand. Only a four-armed Telk could have wielded such monstrosities. The mousetraps were oversized affairs, big enough to catch a bear, thrown in the path of an advancing army. The spoons were enormous ladles, dipped into pots of corrosive acid which was splattered at the foe. The rubber-like balls held needles which must be poisoned, and were sent bouncing into opposing ranks by Telks with carefully developed calluses on their hands. The pipes were of Gargantuan dimensions, smoked by certain warriors who blew great greasy clouds; a flaw of the wind gave

Alex a whiff and sent him from the wall, coughing, weeping and swearing. Their "tobacco" must be some noxious weed to which the pipemen had cultivated an immunity.

And he was supposed to rescue Tanni from this!

"They collide!" shouted Le Forgeur. "They come together with force of the extreme and slaughter indescribable!"

"Whoops!" said Alf Sniggs. "H'I sye, they ain't 'arf fightin', are they?"

"Buck up, old chap," advised Smith. "Remember the playing fields of Eton."

"Well," yelled Alex, desperately, "Come on, then!"

Smith raised his eyebrows. "But these *aren't* the playing fields of Eton," he pointed out.

Helplessly, Alex watched the battle surge past his stronghold. There was another corps among the villagers, who now formed a rear-guard while the rest streamed inside their walls. These Telks spat something into their horny hands and spunged them at the foe—objects which even the raging hillmen avoided. One skittered over the ramparts of Zinderneuf, and Alex got a close look at it: a small metal disk with sharp edges that glistened with some poison.

He buried his face in his hands. "Oh, no," he groaned. "Oh, no, not tiddlywinks!"

By littering the ground with these missiles, the villagers covered their retreat and got safely home. The great wooden gates slammed shut as the enemy poured up. Spoonmen made it discouraging to walk about under the walls, and the invaders withdrew sullenly, dragging their casualties along.

Carried away by enthusiasm, Smith hopped up and gave three cheers for the defenders; then, remembering his British sportsmanship, he politely added three cheers for the attackers.

They heard him. Snouted faces turned around, yellow eyes glistened balefully, a harsh war cry lifted—and as one, the barbarians charged at this new object.

"*Aux armes!*" yelled LeBrute, gleefully. "*Formez vos bataillons! Marchons! Un pour tous et tous pour un!*"

Rifles cracked as the Telks swarmed close. Alex saw a number of direct hits. Only—they didn't do any damage! A punctured Telk was bowled over, but picked himself up and resumed his advance. That damned rapid biochemistry—blood clotted almost instantly—black powder rifles just weren't any good here!

For a moment, shears gleamed before him as a warrior mounted the wall. Then Giuseppe Fortissimo pushed him off. Doggedly, the

Telk climbed up again, to be pushed off again. This might have gone on indefinitely, but the charge spent itself and the hillmen drew back, grumbling. They might not be seriously hurt by bullets, but the shock was painful.

For a moment, Telk and Hoka glared at each other. There was a hurried conference among the barbarian leaders, and one native was sent forward. He walked on his hands with feet in the air and a scrap of cloth in his mouth.

LeBrute looked puzzled. "Name of an adequate little red wine," he muttered. "What is it he does, that one?"

"Parley, old bean," guessed Smith astutely. "Must be their idea of a flag of truce, don't y'know . . . shows he's completely disarmed."

"Ah, so!" Sergeant LeBrute sprang up on the wall. His round, furry face looked down on the envoy, who stood upright.

"*Eh bien?*" snapped Sergeant LeBrute.

"*Hoog, whag, waag!*" said the Telk.

"*Qu'est-ce que vous dîtes?*"

"Waag ah hoog wha hoog."

"*Jamais! Nous sommes soldats de la Légion!*"

"Wugh wugh wahaag!"

"*Cochon! Nous n'avons pas peur. Nous ne savons pas ce que c'est que la peur!*"

"Whog!"

"*Vache!*"

"One has to give the devil his due," whispered Smith to Alex. "A sadistic oaf, our sergeant, but he has courage. I'll wager it's not often that someone has stood up to that Telk and told him off in just those words."

Alex climbed up beside the Hoka noncom. This was getting nowhere. He broke in, speaking Telkan, and LeBrute spat a final "*Chameau!*" and stood aside.

The conversation was brief and to the point. His Most Heathen Majesty, Illustrious King-Emperor of Whaa, Magnificent Duke of Hoog-Guggl, Incomparable Lord of the Marsh Marches, Warrior of the Order of Wug, Protector of the Gods, Hereditary Head-snipper of the Tribes of Gung and Wuh, Earl of the High Whaag, Commander of Skuggwah, the Very-Invincible-And-Much-To-Be-Feared-Whose-Tread-Shakes-The-Earth-And-Whose-Burps-Are-Thunder-In-The-Hills, Hooglah Hooglah Hooglah Gungwhoo Whog Hooglah XVII, offered alliance to the furbearing strangers against the impious village of Gundersnath which had not only refused him his rightful tribute, but had demanded tribute from *him*. In exchange for what petty but perhaps amusing assistance they might give, the furbearing stranger would get a small share of the loot. If they refused this generous offer of His Most Heathen Majesty, half of them would be hanged without mercy, and the rest beheaded without reprieve. A reply was requested at their earliest convenience.

Alex, describing himself as Ambassador Plenipotentiary and Extraordinary of the Most Terrible and Carnivorous Empire Of Earth, accepted, on condition that he should have the hairless, two-armed female held prisoner by the admittedly vile and unspeakable Gundersnathians. This was agreed, and the envoy walked off on his hands.

"*Bien!*" snapped Sergeant LeBrute. "What was said?"

Alex explained. "It's our only chance to get at that village," he added.

"*Non!*" cried the Hoka. "Have I not told you, we are here to defend this fortress *à l'outrance?*"

"Oh, but this is different," said Alex, hastily. "We'll be making a sally."

"*Bleu misérable!*" screamed LeBrute. "Have you the impudence to give advice to your sergeant?"

"Yes," said Alex.

"Excellent!" said LeBrute. "What courage! I shall recommend you for a decoration. Let us sally, therefore, at once." And he leaped off the wall and started toward the hillmen, crying, "*Marchons! Vive la France!*"

The rest followed. Alex dashed back into the boat to call Tanni and give her the word. It would be slaughter if he tried to land directly; nor was a vessel this size maneuverable enough to be used as a weapon in itself, say to knock enemy soldiers off the walls. But if his allies could storm the village—

A rank smell assailed his nose. He heard a seething behind the after bulkhead. Flinging it open, he was horrified to see the vats of green beer foaming and boiling. The entire engine room was one vast mass of suds.

"Oh, no," whimpered Alex.

That Telkan biochemistry again. Airborne yeasts—?

He tested the engines nervously, finding them unharmed behind their insulation. Despite her fears for him, Tanni was somewhat hurt at the briefness of her husband's message. But she did not have to speak from a cabin filled with the odor of 500 liters of sour beer.

Hooglah Hooglah Hooglah Gungwhoo Whog Hooglah XVII was not optimistic. He had tried another charge and seen it reel back from the walls of Gundersnath. The village was amply provisioned, but the hillmen had no supplies and could not live off this barren country. Anyhow, the fiery Telk temperament did not include the patience for a siege.

As night fell, the army camped around the settlement, their fires twinkling through the dense gloom, and sang defiant songs to drown out the jeers therefrom. Alex listened to one because it had a rather pleasant little melody.

> *"Ha, carrion birds*
> *shall batten on them—*
> *belly gashes,*
> *guts and blood! Eggbeaters howl;*
> *heads shall roll;*
> *the foe shall tread*
> *on tiddlywinks!"*

The king paced murkily before his own fire. Its red light shimmered off the scissors of his guards. A dozen assorted knives rattled at his waist. The Legionnaires sat nearby, smoking vicious cigarets—that much was authentically French—and yarning about their desperate adventures in the trackless Sahara. Alex paced side by side with the king, even more worried than he. The effect was like a tall palm walking next to a stumpy cactus.

"Had we but some long-range weapon," grumbled the Telk. " 'Tis their spoonmen and tiddlywinkers up on the walls which will not let us near enough to bash in the gates. Were I not the mightiest butcher the world had known, I'd give up and go kill somebody else. I may do it anyway."

Alex gulped. "Our rifles—" he suggested.

"Bah!" said the king. " 'Tis a good idea, having weapons which shoot from afar, but yours only make holes a cub would laugh at. It takes a broad cutting edge, see you, to lay those wights out."

Alex considered introducing the longbow. But no—it would take days to make enough, nor would a Telk submit to the intensive training required—nor did he and Tanni have that much time.

John Wellington Wells, alias Les Ciseaux, pushed back his kepi and said plaintively: "Ah, for some wine!"

"An excellent idea, *mon brave,*" answered Sergeant LeBrute. "Rastignon, Sniggs, Fortissimo, fetch us the old and rare."

"Pardon, Sergeant," said Le Forgeur, unhappily. "But there is no wine."

"No wine!"

The Legionnaires looked thunderstruck. Too late, Alex remembered that he had left Toka without a supply of the potent liquor which was so much a part of everyday Hoka life.

"We are wineless!" sobbed LeRat. "It is the end of the universe."

"No—wait—" Alex spoke hurriedly, before they should get completely demoralized. "We do have some beer on the boat, you know."

"*Bière?*" snorted LeBrute. His moist black nose wrinkled.

"It's better than nothing."

"*Ach, Bier!*" sighed von und zu Griffentaffel ecstatically. "*Alt Heidelberg! Ach, du lieber Augustine—*"

The other Hokas, shouting above his song, agreed with Alex and sent a party to get some flasks. When it arrived, King Hooglah snatched a bottle, sniffed it, sipped, and threw it away in disgust. "Not poisonous," he growled.

The bottle hit the ground and exploded, scattering shrapnel. Alex dove for the dirt. When he looked up, the Hokas were calmly gulping their own ration.

"It is of a nothing," said LeBrute reassuringly. "It is but that here the fermentation is so rapidly proceeding. Be of good courage, Private Brassard."

"*Brassard!*" Alex jumped with blood in his eye. He had endured being railroaded into the Legion, making his boat a brewery, crossing space, fighting aliens . . . but to call him Brassard was beyond endurance. Snatching a bottle, he lifted it to break LeBrute's head.

Just in time, he stopped himself. Shaken, the flask jetted a stream of evil-smelling foam over his tunic. But—

"Your Majesty!" he croaked. "Your Majesty!"

In the gray dawn of Telko, Hooglah's army attacked again.

It came in a solid wave, howling, brandishing its weapons. Pouring down the slope and across the plain, demoniac, their feet shaking the earth like the ponderous unstoppable advance of the incoming tide, the hill warriors rushed at the defenders.

But in front of them was a line of special troops, to the number of a hundred. Each member held a tightly corked beer bottle in each of his upper hands, and had a bag full of them into which his lower hands could dip. And each wooden cork had a knife blade driven into it by the tang.

At the head of the assault charged King Hooglah with his guards. There, too, was the French Foreign Legion—Alex could not hold them back, and something forbade him to linger in the rear when his Hokas were going to war.

Up on the walls, now, he could see the Gundersnath garrison. The wind was at his back, so there were no pipemen; but spoons waved ominously over bubbling pots, and tiddlywinks were already bouncing to meet him.

Alex sweated and tried not to swallow his tongue. He had seen what those edges, whetted and venomous, could do. But beyond the enemy, he saw the metallic gleam of the flitter holding Tanni.

They were almost at the stronghold when Hooglah roared a battle cry and lifted his eggbeater in signal. Alex stole a glance behind him.

He saw the beermen shake their flasks, brace them against the upper shoulders, and take aim, all in one motion. He did not see the corks come out—those traveled nearly as fast as a rifle bullet—but he saw the silver jet of liquid and foam that arrowed from the mouths of the bottles and sprayed across the foe.

The knife blades whistled among the defenders. They did not make fatal wounds, but were enough to put a Telk *hors de combat* for a few hours. Spoonmen and tiddlywinkers dropped. Their line grew ragged.

"Once more into the breach, dear friends!" squeaked Smith.

"*Allons, enfants!*" cried LeBrute, popping away with his rifle. He ignored a gob of acid spattering within centimeters of him. Hokas did not lack courage. "*Aux armes! Marchons! Voilà!*"

"*Donnerwetter!*" cheered von und zu Griffentaffel. "*Vorwärts! Drang nach Osten!*" He broke into *Die Beiden Grenadiere,* in competition with Guiseppe Fortissimo who was singing *Di quella pira,* complete with high C's.

Again the cosmos exploded. And again. And again. The beermen stood like machines, grabbing out bottles, shaking, aiming, firing, sweeping the walls clean. And meanwhile a hundred of their comrades were battering down the gates.

As the invaders swarmed through, Alex found himself whirled off with his Hokas. He glimpsed snatches of the fight, Telk against Telk with what they considered conventional weapons. In spite of all the activity, there were surprisingly few casualties. A fair number were hopping about scratching frantically with all four arms where the ladled acid had got to them, but they seemed too tough for serious damage. Near the flitter, a hill Telk with oversize shears was energetically trying to cut a village Telk in half. He was not succeeding, the victim's six flailing limbs knocking the blades aside as fast as they approached.

The excitement of the battle carried Alex away as he clubbed his rifle and led the Hokas toward the flitter.

"Sally on!" he cried.

"*Chargeons!*" agreed LeBrute, slamming a Telk into the air.

"And a left!" whooped Alex. "And a right! Let 'em have it! Yea, team! Brrrackety-ax, co-ax, co—oh, hello, dear. We've come to rescue you." He hung on the airlock of the flitter and gasped for breath.

"Alex!" cried Tanni, emerging. She had definitely put on weight, but not to any serious extent as yet. So far she had just achieved a look of pleasantly bouncy plumpness. Her tunic and skirt, however, were already strained to the bursting point and had begun to give at the seams in discreet places.

"Back, now!" said Alex. "Return to the boat!" He added quickly: "The lost patrol has accomplished its mission. Now we must get the secret papers back to headquarters."

The Hokas formed a square about Tanni and slugged their way to the gate. There they halted.

The flight was ending, more and more Gundersnath Telks standing on their hands and waving their feet in the air. But it was urgent to escape, lest King Hooglah turn on his allies.

Nevertheless, the ground for half a kilometer outside was strewn with tiddlywinks.

The Legionnaires milled nervously. "What are you waiting for?" bawled Alex. He was still half berserk.

"Out there, *mon vieux—*" LeBrute pointed.

"We have shoes on, what?" ventured Smith. "They may protect us. Then again, they may not. What say, eh, what, what, what?"

Alex swept Tanni into his arms and led a dash. His voice lifted in a howl:

"Damn the tiddlywinks! Full speed ahead!"

A bright and cheerful sun shone on the parade ground of the Foreign Legion at Sidi Bel Abbès, and on the troops drawn up in dress uniform. The Lost Patrol stood in front, Sergeant LeBrute almost bursting his buttons with pride. The entire platoon was being awarded the Croix de Guerre, and he had the Legion of Honor.

Jorkins Brassard hovered unhappily about. He had enforced the regulations about weapons, but there were also regulations about needlessly exposing wards of the League to danger. Alex bore no special grudge; still, with the inspector under his thumb, he could be sure of a glowing report to Earth Headquarters.

Near Tanni and her husband, the Hoka governor twirled his mustaches diffidently.

"How can Madame forgive me?" he asked. "For my . . . indelicate assumption, *c'est à dire.*"

"You're forgiven," said Tanni graciously.

Alex ducked as a button popped off LeBrute's tunic.

"I am so sorry," went on the governor. *"Naturellement,* one has torn up the enlistment papers—" He stammered in embarrassment.

"That's all right," said Alex, not to be outdone.

"I would never have leaped to such an erroneous conclusion," said LaFontanelle, "but—"

"But what?" asked Tanni.

"Madame must understand," said the little Hoka. "It is only that I am so French."

"Monsieur l'Ambassadeur de la Terre Alexander Braithwaite Jones!" said the commandant of the Legion formally.

Alex stepped forward with equal stiffness. The commandant adjusted his épaulettes, stood on tiptoe, and pinned the red rosette on the man's chest.

"Mon brave!" said the commandant.

He kissed Alex on both cheeks.

Humans and Hokas present were treated to the sight of the Cultural Development Plenipotentiary, representative and official arm of the United Commonwealths, which is the mightiest state within an Interbeing League of a hundred thousand suns, blushing like a schoolboy.

INTERLUDE VI

Plenipotentiary of the
Interbeing League
Planet Toka

HEADQUARTERS OFFICE   CITY OF MIXUMAXU

9/9/86

Mr. Hardman Terwilliger
2011 Maori Towers
League City, N.Z., Sol III

Dear Hardman,

This is a somewhat hasty note, but you'll soon see the reasons for that. Briefly, I'm shipping out for Earth in a few weeks, and the preparations are keeping me busier than a one-armed octopus.

The fact is, I've changed my mind about resigning my position here. Exposure to your man Brassard, while generally instructive, has convinced me that possibly the Hokas would be better off under my wing than someone else's.

Also, those doubts I've expressed to you are being resolved. Thinking over all my years here, I see them as basically a sturdy, brave, independent little folk; their protean imaginativeness merely plays like a brilliant flickering light over a fundamental solid strength.

"Cultural imperialism" or not, I don't think the Service program—in my hands, anyhow—can hurt them. At worst, it will only involve them in a certain amount of waste motion. Their very adaptability is a protection against losing their racial heritage. It is, also, the special talent by which they may one day succeed us as the political leaders of the galaxy. Don't laugh at the thought! Feel free to shudder, but don't laugh.

What also bothered me was the feeling that I was accomplishing nothing. I didn't want to be a party to the Hokas remaining in Class D for the standard minimum fifty years. They have met every other requirement for upgrading—at least to Class C. It's quite possible that I may see them attain full status in my own lifetime, which would make all my troubles worthwhile.

Accordingly, I used the threat of resigning, even after I'd changed my mind, as a club on Parr. So he's waived the fifty-year rule, and I'm taking a Hoka delegation to Earth to apply for advancement.

We have a Galactic Series Baseball game coming up shortly, but after that I'll be on my way. And when you meet my Hokas again, I'm sure you'll be amazed at how civilized they've become. I do think I've pounded some sanity into them—even if it has been my own sanity, pulled up by the roots!

Must close now. Be seeing you. Our love to Dory.

Best,
Alex

JOY IN MUDVILLE

"Pla-a-a-ay *ball!*"

The long cry echoed through the park as Alexander Jones, plenipotentiary of the Interbeing League to the planet Toka, came through the bleacher entrance. Out on the field the pitcher wound up in a furry whirl of arms and legs and let go. Somehow the batter managed to shift his toothpick, grip the bat, and make ready while the ball was streaking at him. There was a clean crisp *smack* and the ball disappeared. The batter selected a fresh toothpick, stuck it in his mouth, jammed his hands in his pockets, and started a leisurely stroll around the diamond.

Alexander Jones was not watching this. He had heard the crack of the bat and seen the ball vanish; but following that there had been only a vague impression of something that roared by him and smashed into the bench above in a shower of splinters. As a former Interstellar Survey man, Alex was *ex officio* a reservist in the Solar Guard, and the promptness and decisiveness with which he hit the dirt now would have brought tears of fond pride to the eyes of his superior officers had they been there to see it.

However, they were not, and after holding his position for several seconds, Alex lifted a cautious head. Nobody else was up to bat; it looked safe to rise. He dusted himself off while glancing over the field.

It was spotted with small round forms, tubby, golden-furred, ursine-faced, the Hoka natives of the planet Toka. They were all in uniform, the outfit of long red underwear, shortsleeved shirts, loose abbreviated trousers, and peaked caps which had been traditional for baseball since it was invented back on Earth. Even if most of the races throughout the known Galaxy which now played the game were not even remotely human, they all wore some variation of the costume. Alexander Jones often wondered if his kind might not, in the long run, go down in history less as the originators of space travel and the present leaders of the Interbeing League than as the creators of baseball.

Mighty Casey, the planet's star batter, had completed his home run—or home saunter—and returned to the benches. Lefty was warming up before he tried himself against The Babe. Professor, the intellectual outfielder, was at his post, keeping one eye on the diamond while the other studied a biography of the legendary George Herman Ruth. Beyond the bleachers, the high tile roofs of Mixumaxu lifted into a sunny sky. The Teddies were practicing, the day was warm, the lark on the wing, the snail on the thorn.

Putzy, the manager of the team, trotted worriedly up to Alex. He had been called something like Wishtu before the craze reached his planet; but the Hokas, perhaps the most adaptable race in the universe, the most enthusiastic innovators, had taken over names, language—everything!—from their human idols. Though of course they tended to be too literal-minded . . .

"Ya all right?" he demanded. He had carefully cultivated hoarseness into his squeaky voice. "Ya didn't get a concussion or nuttin'?"

"I don't think so," answered Alex a little shakily. "What happened?"

"Ah, it wuz just mighty Casey," said Putzy. "We allus try a new pitcher out on him. Shows him he's gotta woik when he's up wit' duh Teddies."

"Er—yes," said Alex, mapping his brow. "He isn't going to hit any more this way, is he?"

"He knocks dat kind every time," said Putzy with pardonable smugness.

"Every time?" retorted Alex maliciously. "Did you ever hear the original poem of 'Casey At the Bat'?"

Putzy leaped forward, clapped a furry hand to Alex's mouth, and warned in a shaking whisper: "Don't never say dat! Geez, boss, ya don't know what duh sound of dat pome does to Casey. He ain't never got over dat day in Mudville!"

Alex winced. He might have known it. The Hoka mind was about as *sui generis* as a mind can get: quick, intelligent, eager, but so imaginative that it could hardly distinguish between fact and fiction and rarely bothered. Remembering other facets of Hoka-assimilated Earth culture—the Wild West, the Space Patrol, Sherlock Holmes, the Spanish Main, *la Légion Étrangère*—Alex might have known that the one who had adopted the role of mighty Casey would get so hypnotized by it as to start believing the ballad had happened to him personally.

"Never mind," he said. "I came over to get you. The Sarennians just arrived at the spaceport and their manager's due at my office in half an hour. I want you there to meet him."

"Okay," said Putzy, sticking an enormous cigar into his mouth. Alex shuddered as he lit up; tobacco grown on Toka gets strong enough to walk. They strolled out together, the pudgy little Hoka barely reaching the waist of the lean young human. Alex's runabout was waiting; it swung them above the walled city toward the flashy new skyscraper of the League Mission.

Seen from above, the town was a curious blend of the ancient and the ultramodern. As a technologically backward race, the Hokas were supposed to be introduced gradually to Galactic civilization; until they had developed so far, they were to be gently guarded from harming themselves or being harmed by any of the more advanced peoples. Alex, as League plenipotentiary, had the job of guide and guardian. It paid well and was quite a distinction; but he sometimes wondered if it wasn't making him old before his time. If the Hokas were just a little less individualistic and unpredictable—

The runabout set itself down on a landing flange of the skyscraper and Alex led the way inside. Ella, his native secretary, nodded at him from an electrowriter. There was a cigaret in her lipsticked mouth, but the effect of her tight blouse was somewhat spoiled for him by the fact that Hokas have twice the lactational equipment of humans. She was competent, but her last job had been with Mixumaxu's leading Private Eye.

Entering the inner office with Putzy, Alex flopped into a chair and put his feet on the desk. "Sit down," he invited. "Now look, before the Sarennian manager comes, I want to have a serious talk with you. It's about financing the team."

"We're doing okay," said Putzy, chewing on his cigar.

"Yes," said Alex grimly. "I know all about that. Your arrangement with these self-appointed outlaws in the so-called Sherwood Forest."

"It's fair enough," said Putzy. "Dey all get free passes."

"Nevertheless," said Alex after gulping for air, "things have got to be put on a more regular basis. Earth Headquarters likes the idea of you . . . people playing ball, it's a good way to get you accustomed to meeting other races, but *I'm* responsible for your accounts. Now I have a plan which is a little irregular, but I do have discretionary powers." He reached for some papers. "As you know, there are valuable uranium deposits on this planet which are being held in trust for your people; they're being robotmined, and the proceeds have been going into the general planetary development fund. But there are enough other sources of income for that, so I've decided to divert the uranium mines to the Teddies' use. That will give you an income out of which to pay for necessities." He paused and frowned. "—and that does *not* include toothpicks for Casey!"

"But he's gotta have toot'picks!" cried the manager, shocked. "How kin he waggle a toot'pick wit'out—"

"He can buy his own," said Alex sternly. "Salaries are paid to the team, you know. The same goes for that bookworm outfielder of yours, Professor—let him pay for his own books if he must read while he plays."

"Okay, okay. But we gotta have a likker fund. Duh boys gotta have deir snort."

Alex gave in on that. The fieriness of the Hoka distillation and the capacity of its creators were a Galactic legend. "All right. Sign here, Putzy. Under the law, native property has to be in native hands, so this gives you title to those mines, with the right to receive income from them and dispose of it as you see fit. Sometime next week I'll show you how to keep books."

The manager scrawled his name as Ella stuck her head in the door. She never would use the office annunciator. "A monster to see you, chief," she said in a loud whisper.

"Ask him to wait a minute, will you?" said Alex. He turned to Putzy. "Now look, please be as polite as you can when the Sarennian comes in. I don't want any trouble."

"What's duh lowdown on dem, anyway?" inquired Putzy. "All I know is we play 'em here next mont' for duh Sector pennant."

"They—well, I don't know." Alex coughed. "Just between us, I don't like them much. It isn't their appearance, of course; I've been friends with weirder beings than they are. It's something in their culture, something ruthless. . . . They're highly civilized, full members of the League and so on, but it's all that the rest of the planets can do to restrain their expansionism. By hook or by crook, they want to take over the leadership." He brightened. "Oh, well, we're only going to play ball with them."

"*Only?*" cried Putzy, aghast. "What's so only about it? Man, dis is for duh Sector pennant. Dis ain't no bush-league braggle. Dis is a crooshul serious!"

Alex shrugged. "All right, so it is." But he could sympathize with his charges. The Hokas had come far and fast in a mere ten years. It would mean a lot to them to win Sector championship.

The Galactic Series necessarily operated under some rather special rules. In a civilization embracing thousands of stars and still expanding, one year just wasn't enough to settle a tournament. The Series had been going on for more than two centuries now. On the planets local teams contended in the sub-series for regional championships; regions fought it out for continental victories, and continents settled the planetary supremacy. Then there were whole systems, and series between systems, all going on simultaneously. . . . Alex's brain reeled at the thought.

Extrapolating present expansion of the League frontiers, sociologists estimated that the play-off for the Galactic Pennant would occur in about 500 years. It looked very much as if the Toka Teddies might be in the running then. In one short decade, their energy and enthusiasm had made them ready to play Sarenn for the Sector pennant. The sector embraced a good thousand stars, but Toka had by-passed most of these by defeating previously established multistellar champions.

"If we lose," said Putzy gloomily, "back to duh bush leagues for anudder ten-twen'y years, and mebbe we'll never get a chanst at duh big game." He cheered up. "Ah, who's worrying? Casey ain't been struck out yet, and Lefty got a coive pitch dat's outta dis univoise."

Alex pressed a button and spoke into the annunciator. "Send the gentlebeing in, Ella." He rose politely; after all, Ush Karuza, manager of the Sarenn Snakes, was a sort of ambassador.

The monster squished in. He stood well over two meters high, on long, clawed legs; half a dozen ropy tentacles ending in strong boneless fingers circled his darkly gleaming body under the ridged, blubbery-faced head. Bulging eyes regarded Alex with a cold, speculative stare, but he bowed courteously enough. "Your sservant, ssir," he murmured in tolerably good English.

"Welcome . . . ah . . . Mr. Karuza," said Alex. "May I introduce Putzy Ballswatter, the manager of the Teddies? Won't you sit down?"

Putzy rose and the two beings nodded distantly at each other. Ush Karuza sniffed and unfolded a trapeze-like arrangement he was carrying. When he had draped himself over this, he lay waiting.

"Well," said Alex, swinging into the little speech he had prepared, "I'm sure you two will get along famously—"

Putzy, who had been staring at Ush Karuza, muttered something to himself.

"Did you say something, Putzy?" asked Alex.

"Nuts!" said Putzy.

"Hiss!" hissed the Sarennian.

"Well, as I was saying," continued Alex hurriedly, "you'll get along famously as you ready yourselves for the big contest—"

Putzy seemed on the verge of speaking again.

"—in your *separate* training camps," went on Alex loudly, "at *good* distances from each other—" Under the rules, a team playing off its own world had to have a month's training on the other planet to accustom itself to the new conditions. There was also a handicapping system so complicated that no human brain could master it.

Alex knew what the trouble was this time. It was something he had kept carefully to himself since first learning that the Teddies were to play the Snakes. The fact was that the Sarennians bore a slight but unfortunate resemblance to the Slissii, the reptile race which had been the Hokas' chief rival for control of Toka from time immemorial till men arrived to help out; and the fur on the little manager's neck had risen visibly at the mere sight of his opposite number.

What was worse, Ush Karuza seemed to be experiencing a like reaction toward Putzy. Even as Alex watched, the tentacled monster produced a small bottle which he opened and wafted gently before his nose like a disdainful dandy of the Louis Quinze period on Earth. For a second, Alex merely blinked, and then a whiff from the bottle reached his own nostrils. He gagged.

Putzy's sensitive nose was wrinkling too. Ush Karuza came as close to smirking as a being with fangs in its mouth could.

"Ah . . . merely a little butyl mercaptan, ssirss," he hissed. "Our atmosphere containss a ssimilar compound. It iss nessessary to our metabolissm. Quite harmless, to man and Hoka."

"Um . . . ugh . . . ah?" said Alex brightly. Out of the corner of his eye he saw Putzy grind out his dead cigar in the ashtray and dig another one twice the size out of his baggy uniform shirt. He fired it up. Butyl mercaptan sallied forth to meet and mingle with blue noisome clouds of smoke.

"Ah sssso!" mumbled Karuza furiously and began to waft his bottle more energetically.

Puff! Puff! Puff! went Putzy.

"Gentlebeings, gentlebeings, please!" wheezed Alex, taking the heavy paperweight away from the Hoka.

Venomously hissing, Ush Karuza was uncorking a second bottle while Putzy crammed more cigars into his mouth.

Things were off to a fine start.

Alexander Jones came staggering home to his official residence that night in a mood to be comforted by his beautiful blonde wife, Tanni. But the house was empty, she having taken the children for a few days to the Hoka Bermuda for its annual sack by pirates (a notable social event on Toka), and dinner was served by the Admirable Crichton with his usual nerve-wracking ostentation. It was only afterward, sitting alone in the study with a Scotch and soda, that Alex's ganglia stopped vibrating.

The study was a comfortable book-lined room with a cheerful fire, and when he had slipped into a dressing gown and placed himself before the desk, Alex realized that privacy was just what he needed. He pressed the door-lock button, opened a secret drawer, and got out a sheaf of papers.

Let not the finger of scorn be pointed at Alexander Jones. The most amiable, conscientious, thoroughly normal young men still have their hidden vices; perhaps these outlets are what keep them on their orbits, and surely Alex had more troubles than most who shoulder the Earthman's burden. What the universe needs is more candor, more tolerance and understanding of human weakness. The truth is that Alexander Jones was a poet.

Like most great creative artists, he was frustrated by the paradoxes of public taste. As a Solar Guardsman, he had achieved immortality by his poetic gifts. It was he who had originated the limerick about the spaceman and girl in free fall, as well as the Ballad of the Transparent Spacesuits, and these shall live forever. Yet they were merely the sparks of his careless youth and he now winced to recall them. His spirit was with the Avantist Revival; his idols had never been known outside of a select clique: Rimbaud, Baudelaire, cummings, Eliot, Cogswell. From time to time the interstellar mails carried manuscripts signed J. Alexander to the offices of *microcosm: the minuscule magazine.* So far, they had also carried the manuscripts back. But a shoulderer of the Earthman's burden is not easily discouraged.

Alex took a long drink, placed stylus to paper, and began writing:

> *the circumambient snake surrounds the pal-*
> *pitating tarry fever-dream of uncertain dis-*
> *tortions and Siva screams and mutters*
> *unheard vacillations: now? then?*
> *Perhaps later, it is hot today.—*

The visio set interrupted him with a buzz. He swore and pressed the *Accept* button. The features of a rather woozy-looking Hoka appeared on the screen.

"Hi-yah, bosh," said the apparition.

"Putzy!" cried Alex. "You're drunk!"

"I am not," Putzy replied indignantly, momentarily reeling out of screen range, "Shober as a judge," he said, reappearing. "Coupla liters ish all I had. Wouldn't make a pup drunk. It's dis yer stuff Ush Karuza smokes when he's shelebratin'. Dese Sarennians don' drink. Dey just smokes uh stuff. Makes me kinda light-headed—smellin' it—" Putzy went over backwards.

Climbing back into view, he said with heavy gravity: "I called y'up t' tell ya shumfin. You said be nice to Karuza, di'n'ya?"

"Yes?" said Alex, a dreadful premonition seizing him.

"Thash what I thought ya said. Well, listen. Like yuh said, we wen' out for li'l drink. Had li'l talk, like yuh said we should. We got t' talkin' shop, shee, an' I tol' him 'bout dose uranium mine rights. Right away he wan'ed ta bet me some salt mines on Sarenn against 'em. So I did."

"You did?" yelped Alex.

"Sure I did. Signed duh papers an' all. Di'n' ya say be nice to him? But listen—" Putzy beckoned mysteriously and Alex leaned forward, shaking. Putzy went on in a whisper. "Here's duh t'ing. Not on'y has I made him happy, but we got us some salt mines."

"How come?" moaned Alex.

"Because!" said Putzy strongly, driving his point home with a stubby finger jabbed into the screen before him. "Because he don' know it yet, but duh Teddies is gonna win."

"Is that so?" barked Alex.

"Sure, ah' yuh know why?"

Alex shook his head numbly. "No, why?"

"Because," said Putzy triumphantly, "duh Snakes is gonna lose."

He beamed. "Jush t'ought ya'd like to know, bosh. So long."

"Hey!" screamed Alex. "Come back here!"

He was too late. The screen was blank.

"Oh, *no!*" he gasped. "Not this!"

For a wild instant, his only thought was of *quotation at the water-front*. It had been shaping up so nicely! Wouldn't he ever get a chance to write something really significant?

Then he settled back to realities and wished he hadn't.

Tottering to his office the next morning after a sleepless night, he took an athetrine tablet and called the Mission library to send up Volume GAK-GAR of *Basic Interstellar Law*. When he received it, he turned to the section on gambling between beings from different planets. He had to find out if the bet Putzy had made with Karuza could be legally collected or not. The legislation in question turned out to be full of such witty statements as, "The above shall apply to all cases covered by Smith vs. Xptui except in such cases as are covered by Sections

XCI through CXXIII inclusive"—each of these with its own quota of exceptions and references. After two hours, he was still no closer to an answer.

He sighed, sent Ella out for more coffee, and was just settling down to a fresh assault on the problem when there was a sort of swirl in the air before him and a semi-humanoid specimen with an enormous bald head topping a spindly little body materialized in his visitors' chair.

"Greetings, youth!" boomed the newcomer. "My visualization of the cosmic all implies that you are surprised. Do not be so. Be advised that I am Nicor of Rishana, who is to umpire the forthcoming contest between Toka and Sarenn."

Alex recovered from his astonishment. The Rishanans, the most intellectual race in the known Galaxy, were almost legends. They could be lured from their home only by a problem impossible for lesser races to solve. Such was any game governed by the 27 huge volumes of the Interstellar Baseball Association rules; as a result, Rishanans invariably officiated in the Series as umpires.

Otherwise they ignored the rest of the Galaxy and were ignored by it. Undoubtedly they had a lot on the ball—for instance, whatever tiny machine or inborn psionic ability permitted them to project themselves through space at will; but since nobody really misses the brains he doesn't have, the rest of the League had never fallen prey to any sort of inferiority complex. Indeed, most beings felt rather sorry for the poor dwarfs. Since the Rishanans felt rather sorry for the poor morons, everybody was happy.

Inspiration came to Alex. "May I ask you a question, sir?" he begged.

"Of course you may ask a question," snapped Nicor. "Any ego may ask a question. What you really wish to know is whether I will answer the question." He paused and looked uncertain. "Or have you already asked me the question? Time is a variable, you know."

"No, I didn't know," said Alex politely.

"Yes, indeed," thundered the voice of that incredible ancient being. "As determined by Sonrak's hypothesis. But come, come, youth—the question."

"Oh, er, yes." Alex pointed to the law book. "I'm having a little trouble with a small point here. Just a—heh! heh!—a theoretical question, you know, sir. If a Hoka bet a Sarennian some Tokan land, and lost, could the—er—say the Sarennian collect?"

"Certainly," snapped Nicor. "That is, he would collect by respective substitute."

"I beg your pardon?"

"You need not apologize for inferior mentality. In effect, the Hokas, being wards of the League, would be protected; but as plenipotentiary and responsible individual, you would have to pay the winner an equivalent amount."

"What?" cried Alex as the assessed valuation of the uranium mines—a fourteen-digit figure—reeled before him.

He heard the explanation through a blur. The extreme libertarians who had drawn up the League Constitution had protected ordinary citizens right and left but deliberately placed high officials on a limb. In this case, a judgment in equity would send him to the Sarennian salt mines for—oh, in view of the new longevity techniques, about fifty years, turning his wages over to Ush Karuza. The working conditions were not too bad unless one happened to have a distaste for the odor of the mercaptans.

"Well, well, enough of this pleasant but unprofitable chit-chat, youth," finished Nicor. "Let us be off to the ball game."

"What game?" asked Alex weakly. "The pennant game isn't for another month."

"Tut-tut," improved Nicor. "Don't interrupt. I am, of course, both forgiving and gracious. Perhaps you think an intellectual like myself has no sense of humor. So many beings fall into the misapprehension. Certainly I have a sense of humor. Of course it is more subtle than yours; and naturally I am not amused by the crude horseplay of lesser intelligences. In fact," went on Nicor, his brow darkening, "that is the main trouble with beings of small development. They do not take the cosmic all seriously enough. No dignity, youth, no dignity."

"But wait a minute—" broke in Alex.

"Don't interrupt! As an intelligence of the quaternary class, you cannot possibly make an interruption of sufficient importance to interfere with a statement emanating from an intelligence of my class. As I was saying . . . Dignity. Dignity! That is what is so painfully lacking in the younger races." A thundercloud gathered on his face. "When I think of the presumption of those few rash individuals who have dared to question my—MY!—decisions upon the baseball field—But I am sure your charges will be guilty of no such indiscretion."

Alex rocked in his chair. If there was any sport the Hokas loved with a pure and undying love, it was umpire-baiting.

"As for your quaint belief that this is not the day of the game," continued Nicor, "I could hardly expect you to know. You irresponsible children never know. When I was your age, I used to have to get up every morning and figure time as a variable to fourteen decimal places before I could start my day's calculations. We didn't have Sonraks in those days to help us. The trouble with you present youths is that you have it too easy. Surely you do not think I would put myself in the ridiculous position of having to realign myself for thirty days in the future? Naturally, I devoted only one point eight percent of my reasoning power to this business of establishing my spatio-temporal coordinates, but it is inconceivable that I should fail. No, no, rest assured that this is the day of the game."

Alex pointed a mute finger at the chronopiece on the wall. Nicor whirled and stared at it.

"What?" he roared with a volume that shook the office. "Am I to be given the lie by a mechanical? Am I to be outfaced by a planet? Am I to be maladjusted by a cosmic integral of the square root of minus one over log log tangent X, theta R squared over N dx from zero to infinity? Blast Sonrak! Damn the mis-placed decimal point! Time is not a variable!"

And with an explosion that rocked the room, he vanished.

Now, it seemed, everything depended on the Teddies winning the game. Alex visited the Hoka ball park and tried to make Putzy institute more rigorous training. The Hokan idea of practice was to let Casey swat a few wild ones while the basemen and fielders sat down, puffing cigars, tilting jugs to their lips, and chatting lightly of this and that. To Alex's protests that the Snakes were bound to get some hits when they came up to bat, Putzy retorted that Lefty would fan them or, failing that, fielders with the speed of the Professor would easily tag them out. Alex gave up.

He made an excuse to drop in on the Sarennian training camp. The visitors were good, no denying that: their main advantage was their terrific tentacle spread, handy for nabbing flying balls; and when the pitcher was winding up, you couldn't see what kind of pitch was coming among all those arms, or even what arm it was coming from. But they lacked the Hoka swiftness and hitting power. Alex—who had spent long hours under a hypnoteacher cramming himself with baseball lore—decided that one set of advantages just about offset the other, so that there would be no handicapping.

Ush Karuza looked positively gloating under his superficial good manners, and Alex began to get suspicious. Considering the ambitions of Sarenn, there was probably more at stake than the pennant and a bet. Returning to his office, the man consulted the Service roster and found that a Sarennian was now at the top of the list of those waiting for ambassadorial vacancies and, if Toka's plenipotentiary were removed, would probably get the job. Sarenn being fairly close to the Tokan sun while Earth was far away, it wouldn't take long for the new chicf to gain complete control of the planet for his people without attracting too much attention at Headquarters.

And a plenipotentiary sent to the salt mines would naturally not retain his position.

Alex looked hollowly into space. He didn't even have Tanni to comfort him; she had messaged an intention to stay on a while in Bermuda and he agreed, not wishing to torment her with worry which might turn out to be needless. His carefully guided planet was headed for tyrannous foreign rule; he was headed for the same; *microcosm* had just returned *Greeks En Brochette*. . . .

There is an old saying that, "The optimist declares this is the best of all possible worlds; the pessimist is afraid he's right." Alex agreed.

The big day dawned bright and clear and hot. Since early morning, a colorful throng of Hokas had been flocking into the ball park. They had come not only from Mixumaxu and its neighboring city-states, but reflected the varied impact of human culture on their entire planet. A booted and spurred cowboy sat next to a top-hatted Victorian gentleman; a knight in armor clanked past a tubby Space Patrolman; a sashed character with a skull and crossbones on his cocked hat grumbled saltily, "Scupper my mizzenmast!" as he tripped on his cutlass. One part of the stands was reserved for Sarennian spectators, a silent and impassive mass of tentacles.

As Alex walked across the field to his official seat in the Hoka dugout, he scowled. The substitutes were all present and accounted for, but where was the regular team?

"Hot dogs, pop cawn, soda pop!" bawled a vendor in the stands above. "Getcha pop here, folks. Can't kill duh umpire wit'out a pop bottle!"

Alex's worried eyes traveled across the dusty ground to the center of the infield. Nicor of Rishana was already there, leaning on the bookcase containing the 27 volumes of rules. There was a grim look on his face which might have been caused by thoughts of Sonrak, and a slightly withdrawn expression in his eyes as he mentally scanned the field from all necessary points of view. This psionic ability had enabled the number of umpires to be reduced to one, even as the easy exhaustion of some races had forced changes in the rules governing substitutions.

"Where's our team?" muttered Alex. "They're late already."

The buzz from the bleachers became a chant. "We want the Teddies. We want the Teddies. We want the Teddies."

Then there was a ragged cheer as the famous nine came into sight—not from the locker room, but from the main gate. Even at that distance, Alex saw how they staggered. Leading the way Ush Karuza, looking smug and supporting Putzy, who was singing something about somebody called Adeline. Alex broke into a cold sweat.

Putzy lurched up to him while the rest of the team was calling cheery greetings to their friends in the stands and forcing autographed balls on them. "Hi-ya," burbled the Hoka manager, collapsing into Alex's arms. "I gotta tell ya shumfin. We got dese Sarennians all wrong. Good ol' Ush, he's all right. Ya know what he done? He took us all out dis mornin' an' stood us to duh bigges' dinner in town. All duh steak an' French fries we could eat. Whoops!" He lost his grip and sat down suddenly. "T'ink I'll take li'l nap." His beady eyes closed.

Alex glared at the Snake manager. "Is this your idea of fair play?" he asked. "Drugging our team. Umpire!"

Nicor flickered in mid-air and appeared beside them. "What is it, youth?"

"This—" Alex pointed shakily at Ush Karuza. "This *gentlebeing* took our men out and drugged them with that stuff he smokes."

"My dear ssir!" protested the monster. "It iss merely a mild sstimulant that we Ssarennianss ssmoke for pleasure. I am not accountable if it affectss our little friendss."

Alex opened his mouth indignantly. "Down, youth!" snapped Nicor. "There is nothing in the rules covering pre-game festivities." He returned to midfield.

Another Sarennian pushed forward a great wheeled tank. "Ice cream," announced Ush Karuza grandly. "Help yoursselfss, my friendss!" As the Hokas threw themselves on it with besotted cries of glee, he pulled a book out of his pouch and gave it to the Professor. "And for you," he added, "a brand-new biography of Tyruss Cobb, sspecially prepared by the Ssarennian Sstate Department."

"Oh, boy!" The small, bespectacled Hoka sat down and began reading it at once. Ush Karuza oozed off with every appearance of satisfaction. Alex buried his face in his hands.

Nicor of Rishana spoke into his wrist microphone, and his voice boomed over the park: "Come, youths! My visualization demands that you now play ball!"

The spectators cheered. The band, somewhat confused, broke into *Auld Lang Syne.* The Toka Teddies wobbled out onto the field. Putzy sat up and muttered something about not feeling so good.

The Snakes, as visitors, were first up to bat. Their star hitter, Shimpur Sumis, wrapped his tentacles around his club and waved it gleefully. Lefty, the Teddy pitcher, found his way to the mound and began turning around to get his position. He kept on turning.

"Play ball, youth!" thundered the umpire. Shimpur Sumis yawned.

It seemed to infuriate Lefty. He sent his ball spinning in faster than Alex could follow. Either because he wasn't quite himself, or because he hadn't allowed for the greater reach of Sarennian tentacles, Shimpur Sumis connected with a solid hit. The ball smacked into left field. The monster dropped his bat and galumphed toward first base.

"Grab it, Professor!" screamed Alex.

The intellectual outfielder was too immersed in his new book to notice. The ball shot past him. His fans howled, "Wake up, ya bum! Grab dat ball!"

Shimpur Sumis rounded second.

A Hoka near Alex, clad in doublet and hose and feathered cap, leaped up, fitted an arrow to his longbow, and let fly. The Professor yelled as it pinked him, glared around, saw the ball, and loped after it. By a miracle, he got it back to the catcher just as Sumis went by third. The Sarennian retreated, grinning smugly.

The next one stepped up to bat. Lefty sent a whizzer past him. The ball smacked into the catcher's mitt.

"Ball one!" cried Nicor.

"Whaddaya mean, ball one?" squeaked Lefty, spinning around in a rage. "Dat wuz a strike if I ever seen one."

"A strike," said Nicor, glowering, "must pass between waist and shoulders."

"Yeah, but he ain't got any waist *or* any shoulders," protested Lefty.

"Hmmm, yes, so I see." Nicor pulled one of the fat volumes out of the bookcase beside him and consulted it. Then he took forth a transit and sighted on the batter. The crowd rumbled impatiently.

"The equivalent median line," said Nicor at last, "yields the incontrovertible result that the missile so injudiciously aimed was, indeed, ball one."

Alex shuddered. Putzy turned green under his fur.

The next ball met a hard-swinging bat. Again it zoomed by the immersed Professor. Again the archer fired. This time the Professor was ready. He plucked the arrow out of the air as it neared him and continued reading. Both Sarennians loped home. Their rooters set up a football-style cheer:

Hiss, hiss, hiss!
Who iss better than thiss?

Squirmy worm, destiny's germ
TEAM!!!

The next Sarennian went out on a pop fly just behind third. The one after that made it to first. But Lefty, even when pitching on hope and instinct, was not a hurler to be despised. The fifth Sarennian up to bat barely got a piece of the ball and both he and the Snake on base were put out in a wobbly double play.

The Teddies came to bat. They were uniformly ineffective with the single exception of mighty Casey, who, as Putzy was too sick to tell him not to, tried to fulfill a longstanding ambition to lay down a bunt, but only succeeded in bunting the ball over the left field fence. Score one run for the Teddies.

The next four innings were a rout. The regular Teddy team got even sicker and had to be taken out, and against the substitutes, the Sarennians made blissful scores. At the end of the first half of the fifth inning, the board read seven to one in favor of the Snakes.

By the second half of the fifth, the original team members were weak but recovered, and ready to take the field again with blood in their eyes, Casey was first up, and with a valiant return to his usual nonchalance, he put his hands in his pockets and sauntered toward the plate, a toothpick in his mouth and scorn in his eye. He whipped into his batting stance just as the Sarennian pitcher let go. There was a blur, a crack, and he was strolling off along the baseline, nodding graciously to his fans.

But for him it had been a poor and a weak hit. The Sarennian left fielder reached forth an interminable tentacle and nabbed it as it came smoking along the ground. He whirled and shot it back toward first base. Casey saw it coming and broke into a panting run. He thundered into first together with the ball.

"Out!" said Nicor, appearing at the bag.

"Out???" screamed Casey, skidding to a stop and coming back. "I wuz in dere ahead o' duh ball wit' enough time fer a nap."

"I say *out*," ruled Nicor. "Do not dispute with a superbrain—Time! Don't mention that word *time* to me!"

"Why, ya blind, bloody, concrete-skulled superbrain!"

Pop bottles began to fly from the stands, bursting to fragments in the air as the small robot-controlled anti-aircraft guns mounted on the right field fence went into action. Nicor ignored the bombardment and settled the discussion by flickering back into position behind the pitcher's mound.

The game continued. The Teddies were still a little weak and uncertain. The Hoka following Casey was caught out at shortstop and the next Hoka sent a high fly into right field where it was easily taken for the putout.

The Snakes came up to bat in the first half of the sixth inning. Lefty, turned white-hot with determination, retired the opposing side without gain by three straight strikeouts. The Hokas took over at the plate and the first six men up scored two men and loaded the bases. The score stood at seven to three with Casey yet to bat, and the Snakes called time out.

"What is the occasion, youth?" demanded Nicor of Ush Karuza.

The Sarennian smirked. "I find I musst invoke one of the handicapping ruless, ssir," he answered. "Article XLIII, Ssection 3, Paragraph 22-b. In effect, it iss that a certain gass iss necessary to our player'ss metabolissm. It being a mercaptan, completely non-toxic in small dosess ass you know, we may ssimply releasse it without sslowing the game down by wearing masskss and handicapping the Hokass."

"There are psychosomatic effects," objected Nicor. "I refer to the nauseous stench involved."

"I do not believe the ruless ssay anything about such side issuess," answered Karuza smugly.

Nicor went back to the books. At last he nodded. "I fear you are right," he added sadly. "But in the name of sportsmanship—"

Ush Karuza turned purple with rage and swelled up alarmingly. "Ssssir! How dare you!" he hissed. "Article CCXXXIL Amendment Number 546, paragraph 3-a, explissitly sstatess that Ssarennianss are incapable of the conssept of Ssportssmanship and sspessifically exemptss them from observing it."

"Oh." Nicor looked crestfallen. He checked. "True," he said bitterly.

Alex felt ill already. This looked like the end.

A great generator was wheeled into an upwind position on the field. It began to fume. Alex caught a whiff and felt his stomach rise in revolt. There could only be a few parts per million in the air, but it was enough!

"Oof!" groaned Putzy beside him. "Lemme outta here."

"You stay," said Alex desperately, grabbing him. "Play up, play up, and play the game!"

Nicor turned a delicate green. "My visualization of the cosmic all suggests I am going to be sick," he muttered.

Putzy opened a box of cigars and passed them around to his team. "Dis may help ya fer a little while," he said. "Now get in dere and fight!" Tears rose in his eyes. "Me aged grandmudder is sitting at home, boys, old and sick, laying dere amongst her roses and lavender waiting for yuh to bring home duh pennant. It'll kill duh sweet old lady if ya lose—"

"Ah, shaddap!" said his grandmother, leaning out of her place in the stands beside him and stuffing her knitting in his mouth.

Alex fumed away on his own cigaret, trying to drown the smell that curled around him. There must be *some* way to escape those salt mines!

With the mercaptan turning his stomach upside down on top of the effects of the drug, Casey still batted in the man on third on a sacrifice fly. The Hoka following him struck out. Retired, the Teddies lurched out onto the field and took another pasting. The score climbed against them—six Sarenn runs in the seventh, seven in the eighth, with the brief one-two-three interlude of the Teddies at bat hardly noticeable in the Snakes' slugging festival. When the Hokas came up again in the top of the eighth, they were trailing twenty to four.

Alex chewed his fingernails. There *must* be an answer to this! There must be some counter irritant, something which would get the Hoka back to the careless energy and childlike enthusiasm which served them so well . . . Counter-agents! The idea flared in his head.

He snatched at the water boy's arm. "Bring us something to drink!" he commanded. The little ursinoid sped away, to return with a slopping bucket which Alex knew very well did not contain water.

"Time out!" he yelled. "The Hokas request time out."

"What for, youth?" asked Nicor faintly.

"They need alcohol to protect themselves against the effects of the Sarennian gas. It's okay by the rule books, I'm sure."

Nicor brightened a little. "It does protect?" he inquired. "Then, youth, you may bring me some too."

Ush Karuza jittered about in a rage while the Teddies gathered weakly around the bucket and dipped their noses into it. Even by Hoka standards, they got it down fast. Nicor scowled at his complimentary beaker, sipped, winced and gasped. "*This* is necessary to them?" he cried. "I have seen halogen breathers, I have seen energy eaters, I have seen drinkers of molten lead, but here is the race that shall rule the sevagram!"

Casey lifted his dripping black snout. "Urp, he said. "Gotta toot'pick?"

"Play ball!" hollered Ush Karuza wrathfully.

The Babe waved casually at Putzy. "We'll get 'em," he said confidently, and connected with the first pitch for a clean single to left. The Professor came up with his book in one hand, stuck it under his arm just long enough to belt one out of the park, and walked home with his nose back in his book.

"Geez!" he muttered reverently. "Dat Cobb could sure play *ball!*"

Lefty stepped up to bat with an evil gleam in his eye. The Sarennian star pitcher launched a ferocious fast ball across the middle. Lefty let it go by. "Ooooof!" said the catcher.

"Strike one," said Nicor.

Time out to replace one catcher.

There was no second strike. Lefty bounced the next pitch off the right field wall for a stand-up triple.

Casey sneered and sauntered out to the plate. Grabbing the end of the Sarennian catcher's fourth tentacle, he began picking his teeth with it.

"Halt! Stop! Foul!" shrieked Karuza. "He *bit* my player!"

Some of Alex's hard-won baseball knowledge came to his aid. "Article XLI, Section 5, Paragraph 17-a: 'Players may take such nourishment as is required during the game,' " he flung back.

"But not off *my* players!" wailed Karuza.

Nicor weaved over to his books and consulted them. "I am afraid I can find nothing forbidding cannibalism," he announced. "It must never have occurred to the commission. Tsk, tsk."

The pitcher let fly. Casey set his bat end on the plate and jumped up to balance on it. "Strike one!" called Nicor.

"Nope," said Casey owlishly. "Yuh mean ball one, ump. Duh ball went under m'waist. Under m'feet, in fack!"

"So it did," agreed Nicor imperturbably "Ball one!"

"The ruless—" sputtered Ush Karuza.

"Nothing in the rules against balancing on top of a bat, youth." Nicor scratched his bulging head. "I do believe the commission will have to call a special meeting after this game."

The Sarennian pitcher wound up again. As the ball zoomed toward him, Casey swung the mightiest swing in Toka's history. The Snakes' second baseman saw the ball screaming at him and dropped to the ground in terror. A bolder monster in the outfield raised his glove and caught it. Or perhaps one should say it caught him—he was lifted off the ground described a beautiful arc, and landed three meters away. The ball went merrily on to cave in a section of the fence beyond.

Casey, who had been spinning on one heel unable to stop, came to a halt and staggered around the bases. He had plenty of time, because the Sarennians had to dig the ball out from between two planks.

Time out while the Snakes replaced one unconscious outfielder and one second baseman with a bad case of the shakes.

The rest of the Hokas followed the example of their star players and sailed twice completely through their lineup before being retired with a score of 19 to the Snakes' 20 at the end of the eighth. The crowd, including Alex, was going wild.

Shimpur Sumis came up to bat with a haughty look suggesting that he alone could settle the matter. Lefty, who was higher than a kite, threw him a ball so fast that it exploded on being struck. Nicor consulted his library for the rule on exploding balls, found none, and called it a strike . . . though he admitted that his visualization was not very complete today. Sumis' abused tentacles could not handle the bat well enough to keep him from being struck out.

Ush Karuza snarled and went over to the mercaptan generator and opened the valves wide. A thick, nearly visible stream of vapor rolled across the field to envelop the Hoka pitcher.

Lefty was too drunk to care. He sent off his famous curve. Then he gaped at it. So did the Snake batter. So did Alex. No—the ball couldn't possibly be where it was!

It landed in the catcher's mitt. "Strike one!" announced Nicor.

The next pitch was even more unbelievable than the last. It defied all known natural law and went in a sine curve. "Strike two!"

The batter flailed wildly the third time. Alex distinctly saw the club go through the ball, but nothing happened.

"Strike three!" said Nicor. "Youth, you are now external to the n-dimensional sociological hypersphere!"

"Huh?" asked Putzy.

"He means, 'You're out,' " translated Alex happily.

"Foul!" bawled Ush Karuza. "They're using black magic."

"There is nothing in the rules against magic," said Nicor.

"I just t'row a damn good coive, dat's all," said Lefty belligerently.

The next Sarennian fared no better. By that time Alex had figured out the situation. "The thick stream of mercaptan vapor has a refractive index appreciably different from air," he told Putzy. "No wonder it produces optical illusions. Hoist by their own petard!"

Putzy seemed dubious. "If dat least means what I t'ink it means," he said, "you shouldn't oughtta say it in front of me grandmudder."

The Teddies came to take their turn at bat. It was the last half of the ninth inning. The score stood at 19-20 with the Teddies trailing. The batting order at that moment stood: first The Babe, then the Professor, then Lefty, and then Casey. The Sarennians looked grim, but the Hokas in the stands, who had resorted to their potent pocket flasks while the team was getting their liquor from the water boy, were wildly jubilant. As The Babe picked up his bat and strode to the plate they began a cheer which finally died away to an awful silence as the whole crowd held its breath.

The Sarennian pitcher was clearly determined to let no hits be gotten off him. He wound up and let fly.

From the stands rose a mighty groan of horror, interspersed with shrill hoots of glee from the Sarennian section. For the stream of mercaptan vapor was still flowing past the pitcher *and all three balls wove a daisy chain past the plate!*

"Strike three!" cried Nicor. "Out!"

Sadly, The Babe came back. The stands were in an uproar. It looked as if open battle might break out between the Hoka and Sarennian fans. Alex cringed on his bench.

The Professor went up to the plate. The ball looped crazily by him. "Strike one!"

A long moan of agony went up from the Hokas.

"Strike two!"

The Professor braced himself. There was a wild, almost berserk gleam in his spectacles. The Sarennian pitcher writhed and twirled his tentacles with contemptuous confidence. The ball shot forward.

The Professor threw himself and his bat to meet it.

There was a tiny *tick*. The ball popped out of the vapor fog and trickled along the ground toward third base. There were only a few seconds of time before it was caught, but that was all the Professor's famous legs needed. There was a whiz, a blur, an explosion of dust, and the Hoka was safe at first.

The tying run was on, and there were two outs left to bring it home.

Lefty took his time selecting his bat. He swung it heavily a few times to test the balance and then slowly stalked up to the plate. The pitcher wound up. He threw. The stands groaned.

"Strike one!" thundered Nicor in a voice of doom.

The Sarennian catcher strolled out to return the ball to the pitcher. They conferred for a few seconds.

With the batter back in position, the pitcher wound up again. The ball snapped out of his mass of tentacles, flickered, and appeared in the catcher's mitt.

"Strike two!"

"Casey," said Putzy in a shaking tone, "get ready, boy."

Alex turned to look at the Teddies' mainstay. To his surprise, the little batter seemed cool and calm. "Relax, Putzy," Casey said. "It's in duh bag. All I gotta do is knock us bot' home."

"But dose pitches!" said Putzy.

"Lissen!" said Casey with some heat. "Lissen, ya don't t'ink I ever bodders to watch d' pitcher, do yuh? All I pays attention to is duh ball from duh time it gets to about two meters away from me. And duh ball gotta be straight den, or duh ump calls it a foul. Dey can't fool me none."

Slowly, hope began to dawn on Putzy's furry face. He was even smiling as Nicor called "Strike three!" and Lefty returned glumly from the plate.

Casey got to his feet and began his customary nonchalant stroll toward the batter's box. At first the crowd merely gaped at him in astonishment; but then, drawing courage from his apparent confidence, they raised a swelling cheer that rocked the stands. He doffed his cap and kissed his hand to the fans, waved, rubbed his hands in the dirt and took up his stance. Alex saw, through a vision blurred by tenseness, that the Sarennian pitcher was already losing heart at sight of this overweening opponent.

"Time out!" screamed Ush Karuza.

For a moment the park was held in agonized silence. Then a mounting growl like that of a Boomeringian sea-bear disturbed at its meal commenced and grew.

"For what reason, youth?" asked Nicor.

"Article XXXVI, Ssection 8, Paragraph 19-k," said Ush Karuza defiantly. "Any manager may encourage hiss team by verbal meanss."

Nicor checked. "Correct," he said. "You may proceed."

There was a scurry from the Sarennian dugout and a public address system was wheeled onto the field and its microphone set up before a small tape player. As the stands waited silently to see what this new move might portend, Ush Karuza switched it on. There was a hissing noise as the machine warmed up.

At the plate, Casey smiled indulgently.

And then the hissing stopped and a voice boomed over the park. It was not a Sarennian voice, but human; and the first words it uttered wiped the smile from Casey's lips and fell on the field like the hand of doom. For the voice was reciting, and the first words were:

> *It looked extremely rocky*
> *for the Mudville nine that day:*
> *The score stood two to four*
> *with but one inning left to play.*
> *So when Cooney died at second . . .*

"Oh, no!" wailed Putzy. "It's *it!*"

"What's it?" choked Alex.

"Dat pome—'*Casey At duh Bat*'—oooh, lookit poor Casey now—" The manager pointed a trembling finger at the Teddies' last hope, who was shaking with unbearable sobs as he stood at the plate.

"I protest!" screamed Alex, leaping from the bench and running wildly out to where Nicor stood.

"You have no right to protest," snapped the umpire, "You are merely a spectator."

"Den I pertest!" roared Putzy, skidding to a halt beside Alex. "Turn dat t'ing off!"

At the plate, Casey was melting down in his own tears as the tape swung into the fifth stanza.

Then from the gladdened
  multitude went up a joyous yell.
It rumbled in the mountaintops,
  it rattled in the dell,
It struck upon the hillside
  and rebounded on the flat.
For Casey, mighty Casey,
  was advancing to the bat

Casey was flat on the ground now, making feeble pawing motions as if he would dig his grave where he lay, crawl in, and die.

"Your protest is out of order," said Nicor.

Ush Karuza oozed oily sympathy. "I am afraid your batter iss not feeling well," he muttered.

. . . And when the writhing pitcher
  ground his ball into his hip,
Defiance gleamed in Casey's eye,
  a sneer curled Casey's lip. . . .

Abandoning the umpire, Putzy ran to his collapsed star and tried to lift him from the ground. "Fcr cripessake, Casey," he pleaded. "Stan' up. Just get us one little hit. Dat's all I ask."

"I can't," choked Casey. "Muh heart ain't in it no more. Dey trusted me in Mudville and I let 'em down."

The stillness over the park was broken only by his sobs and the inexorable recorded voice.

. . . Close by the sturdy batsman,
  the ball unheeded sped.

> *"That ain't my style," said Casey.*
> *"Strike one!" the umpire said. . . .*

Like a drowning man, Alex saw his whole life parade by him: Tanni, the children, Earth, Toka. It was not what he wanted. He wanted some way out of this inferno.

No other batter had a chance; the Teddies were too demoralized. But what to do, what to do? Surely he, Alexander Jones, had some means of helping, some talent—He gnawed trembling fingers as the poem tolled its way to its dreadful conclusion.

> *. . . And now the air is shattered*
> *with the force of Casey's blow!*

Damn all poets!

> *Oh, somewhere in this favored land*
> *the sun is shining bright,*
> *The band is playing somewhere*
> *and somewhere hearts are light,*
> *And somewhere men are laughing,*
> *and somewhere children shout,*
> *But there is no joy in Mudville—*

Poetry!

—MIGHTY CASEY HAS STRUCK OUT!

"Yipe!" said Alex.

There was one other outstanding ability which Ensign Alexander Jones had shown in the Guard besides hitting the dirt. And that was that when the occasion arose, he was very quick off the mark when there was something to be run to, or from. Therefore, just as some weeks earlier the promptitude with which he nosedived would have pleased his superiors, so now they would have joyed to see the speed with which he covered the distance between the umpire's post and the public address system. Even the Professor would have been pushed to match his velocity; and the way he stiff-armed the lone Sarennian guarding the recorder was a privilege to observe.

He snatched up the microphone and panted into it. "Go on, boss!" yelled Putzy, unsure what his adored plenipotentiary intended but ready to back him up.

"Pant, pant, pant," boomed Alex over the field.

Ush Karuza ran to stop him. "Hold, youth!" ordered Nicor. "He has a right to use the machine."

"Pant, pant," panted Alex, and began to improvise:

"But hold (pant), what strikes the umpire,
what causes him to glare
With fiery (pant, pant) look and awful eye
upon the pitcher there?
And Casey takes the catcher by the collar
with his hand,
He hales him to the (pant) umpire
and together there they stand."

Beside the plate, the Hoka Casey lifted his head in wonder, and wiping the tears from his eyes, stared openmouthed at Alex.

The human had had his dark suspicions the way Lefty was struck out last time. No chance to prove that, but he could weave it into his revenge.

'I bid you look,' cried Casey, 'I bid you
search him well.

For such as these our fine fair game
they soon would sound its knell—!' "

Alex hesitated, looking a trifle confused. "Dat's my plenipotentiary who said dat!" cried Putzy's grandmother; and thus heartened, he proceeded.

"The umpire checks them over
and the villains' faces fall
When out from each one's pocket he pulls
forth A HIDDEN BALL!
" 'Oh, shame!' cries out the Mudville crowd.
The echoes answer, 'Shame!'
'That such a dirty low-down trick should
blight our Casey's name.
The pitcher only faked his throw,
the catcher faked his catch.
The cowards knew that such as they
were never Casey's match.' "

"You untentacled mammal!" raged Ush Karuza. "You sslimeless, conformation of bone flesh!"

Alex had long ago discovered that mankind rarely reacts to insults couched in nonhuman terms. It did not offend him at all to be told that he was slimeless.

The Teddies' Casey was sitting up by the plate now and beaming. Alex took a deep breath and went on:

> " *'Now take your places once again.*
> *Once more!' the umpire cried.*
> *'And your next pitches will be fair*
> *or else I have your hide.*
> *Now take your places once again,*
> *to places one and all!'*
> *And as soon as they were ready,*
> *the umpire cried, 'Play ball!' "*

The Hoka Casey was up on his feet and clutching his bat. His eyes were riveted on Alex. And as the last two stanzas came out his little form hunched and twisted through the motions Alex described.

> *"And now the pitcher takes his stance,*
> *his face is black and grim*
> *And he starts his furious windup*
> *with a fearful verve and vim.*
> *And now he rocks back on his heel;*
> *and now he lets it fly.*
> *The ball comes sizzling forward*
> *watched by Casey's steely eye.*

> *"For Casey does not tremble,*
> *mighty Casey does not balk,*
> *Though it's clear the ball is high and wide,*
> *and they aim to make him walk.*
> *He steps forward in the batter's box,*
> *his bat's a lambent flame.*
> *Crack! Smash! The ball flies o'er the fence—*
> *AND CASEY WINS THE GAME!"*

The stands were going crazy. Hokas of all shapes, sizes, and descriptions came pouring down from their seats to mob and congratulate—

—Casey, of course.

Who else was responsible for the Mudville win?

To Hokan taste, it was almost an anticlimax after the glorious victory of the fictional Casey when the factual one playfully tapped a home run over the left field fence and won the Sector pennant.

In spite of custom, Alexander Jones did not preside over the wild festivities that night. He felt he deserved a quiet evening at home, alone with a tall drink and *quotation at the waterfront.*

Tanni would be coming back soon, and much as he longed to see her, he knew she would give him no chance to produce something really significant—some poem reflecting the realities of Life.

SAREN	2	1	1	1	2	0	6	7	0	20
TOKA	1	0	0	0	0	3	0	15	2	21

UNDIPLOMATIC IMMUNITY

I was born with a dull, sickening thud. Had I but known what an aching void yawned before me, I would never have started down that lonely road.

"Well—er—" said Alexander Jones, putting down the sheet of paper. "It's . . . um . . . interesting. But don't you think some of the phrases are a little, hm, hackneyed?"

"Of course," said the Hoka with the tweed coat and calabash pipe. He leaned back in his chair and cocked his feet up on the electrowriter: a meter or so tall, round-bellied, golden-furred, ursinoid, an outsize teddy bear with stubby hands and eager button eyes. His name was W. Shakespeare Marlowe. "Don't you see, it is precisely by the use of the hackneyed phrase, the integral unit of language itself, that I create the Myth."

Alex, who was a tall and lanky young human, sighed. That was what came of letting a Hoka read 20th-century criticism. "But why did you stop there?" he asked.

"I have to leave something to the reader's imagination," pointed out the writer. "That's the quintessence of art. Think how dull and prosaic it would have been if I had gone on to describe the rest of my life."

"Oh," said Alex weakly. "I see."

"Those are the same views intrinsic to my essay, *The Novel As An Art Form.* I have it here—" W. Shakespeare Marlowe produced another sheet from his pocket. "Observe, it says: '*The Novel As An Art Form,* by W. Shakespeare Marlowe. Paragraph. The novel *is* an art form. Period. The end.' Succinct, isn't it?"

"Very," said Alex.

"I knew you'd understand. I call it the new look in writing. Actually, it has its roots in Hemingway. But I refined it to its present form. You see, the trouble with writers has always been that they wrote too much. It cut down their production."

"Cut it down?" asked Alex uncertainly.

"Of course. Look at Twain, Dickens, Melville—a mere few dozen books. Whereas I often write a dozen novels in one day."

"Oh, no!" groaned Alex.

"Quite," said the Hoka, sticking his hands in his pockets and puffing complacently on his pipe.

They were alone in the outer office of the Tokan delegation's suite. A broad window revealed the spectacular towers of League City, spearing into the serene late-afternoon sky of New Zealand, Earth. A webwork of elevated mobilroads knitted the pinnacles together, from the soaring bulk of this official hostel to the immense hall where the Council of the Interbeing League met.

From the adjoining room came subdued squeaks of excitement. Alex wondered what the other Hokas were up to. So far he had kept them out of trouble, but . . .

W. Shakespeare Marlowe, his secretary, was a very mild case, having merely gone overboard for authorship. But the energy, enthusiasm, and literal-mindedness of Alex's charges could lead to their playing any role that struck their fancy with an almost hypnotized solemnity. It was fortunate that the Tokan business stood high on the agenda of the present Council session: the less time on Earth they had, the less chance for some disastrous escapade.

Alex glanced at the wall chrono. He was supposed to meet informally with Commissioner Parr in a few minutes, and had already dressed for the occasion in suitably dignified crimson tunic and green slacks. "We'd better be going, Marlowe," he said. The little Hoka stumped happily out with him.

Two slideways and a dropshaft brought them to a tasteful suite in which cocktails and canapés were laid out. Adalbert Parr, the Chief Cultural Commissioner, received them: a big, portly man with a florid face and wavy gray hair. He bowed stiffly, shook hands, and widened his eyes as Marlowe whipped out a pad and took notes. Then, with regulation heartiness, he waved at the others present.

"We were only to get acquainted, Plenipotentiary Jones," he said. "May I present the chief delegates from three planets in your sector? His Excellency, Representative His Highness Prince Idebar of Worben."

The Worbenites were from a fairly terrestroid planet, a highly civilized race, and Prince Idebar was known as one of the shrewdest diplomats in the Galaxy. He was tall, with sleek black hair, his face aged but still keen and aquiline, his carriage erect; indeed, to be completely human-looking he would only have had to trim his ears and remove his horns and spiked tail. The females of his species were less manlike. "Delighted, sir," he murmured.

"No more than I, sir," replied Alex with equal urbanity.

They bowed. Alex jumped back as the horns swept by his nose.

"Ahem!" said Parr. "May I present His Excellency, Tantho the Hairy, leader of the delegation from Porkelans."

This being was two meters high, barrelshaped, with enormous four-fingered hands at the end of short, muscular arms. He wore only a pocketed belt, but long blue fur covered his body. Two small eyes peered out of a face mostly hair, with just a suggestion of snout. "Most pleased," he rumbled in the official English of the League.

"Her Excellency, Miss Zuleika MacTavish of Bagdadburgh," intoned Parr.

As Her Excellency came into view around the bulk of Tantho, Alex had a sense of being hit with a perfumed blackjack. The Scottish-Arabic colony, founded by a rather puritanical group, had followed the usual law of reaction to interesting extremes. Zuleika MacTavish was tall and willowy, with flowing brown hair and great liquid eyes and a wide soft mouth and . . . well, the few wisps of colored translucency making up her native costume gave even an old married man like Alex a slight impulse to throw back his head and howl.

However, plenipotentiaries do not howl, or slaver, at beautiful representatives from neighboring planetary systems. Not if they want to stay on good terms with the Cultural Office of Earth Headquarters and—most particularly—their wives. So Alex goggled and sputtered in what he hoped was a suitably diplomatic manner, and scarcely noticed the dark, hawk-faced Colin MacHussein who was introduced as the delegate's special assistant.

"Please sit down, gentlebeings," said Parr. A servant offered a tray of drinks. Alex reached for an interesting-looking green one. Prince Idebar muttered an alarmed *"Garrasht!"* and caught his arm and warned:

"Excuse me, sir. That happens to be made from the jithna leaf of my planet. I believe it is chemically quite similar to poison ivy." Alex shuddered his thanks, and Idebar took the drink himself and sipped with practiced grace.

"Oh, His Highness has no reason to murder you," said Zuleika MacTavish acridly. She took a cigaret from her belt pouch and a long holder from her décolletage. Alex came out of a reverie in which he wished he could be—temporarily, of course—a cigaret holder, to hear Parr exclaim:

"Please! We save the, ah, disagreements for the agenda. This is merely a social gathering. My own concern is with Plenipotentiary Jones's planet, Toka, but I thought an exchange of views with his neighbors out in Sector Seven might be . . . enlightening. He is here to see about getting the autochthones upgraded."

Alex nodded. "The Hokas have met the requirements for Class C by establishing a planet-wide peace authority," he said—careful not to add a description of a meeting of teddy bears from nations modeled on the Wild West, Victorian England, the East Roman Empire, King Arthur's realm, and others. "Guiding them is, of course, my task, and I believe they are now ready for Class C." That was mostly a technicality, involving science scholarships for qualified natives, but an essential step on the path to full autonomy and membership in the Interbeing League.

The catch was, there were too many planets in process of becoming civilized, each a complicated special case. The League Council voted on their status, but in practice, of necessity, always followed the recommendation of the Commissioner. Which meant that Parr had to be convinced. Alex prayed that Worben, Porkelans, and Bagdadburgh had no objections to the upgrading. Quite apart from the Hokas themselves, it would mean a substantial raise in salary for him.

However, the little session was uneventful. The diplomats made polite noises and then returned happily to throwing courteous venom at each other. Alex got a distinct impression that there was trouble between Bagdadburgh on the one hand and Worben and Porkelans on the other. It was with some relief that he finally excused himself.

W. Shakespeare Marlowe followed him cheerily down the hall. "I can never thank you enough for bringing me along," he burbled. "I have notes for three new novels . . . sensational! The *haut monde,* wild, dissipated, the orgies as world-weary, cynical beings flog their jaded senses with ever new and more fantastic pleasures—"

"I thought they were rather dull," said Alex, with regret.

"It is the business of the artist to select and rearrange his material," said Marlowe firmly. "How else shall he portray the essence of Life?"

The main door to the Hoka suite opened before them and Alex trod in. He had left his delegates alone all day while he went through some necessary red tape, and had barely noticed that they sent out for some special items. Now, as he entered the living room, he stopped dead.

"Yipe!" he said.

Three Hokas sat around a table drinking tea. Two of them had adorned their rotund forms with archaic striped trousers and cutaway coats; top hats lay beside them. The third was completely muffled in a long black coat with its collar turned up, his beady eyes peering out from beneath a black slouch hat. They were being waited on by a fourth in chauffeur's uniform.

"What is this?" cried Alex. "Tharaxu—"

"The name," said one of the Hokas in cutaway, "is now Allenby. Foreign Office, don't y'know. Come join us in a spot of tea."

Alex's gaze roved wildly about the room. He saw numerous books from the hostel's extensive library. The authors were unfamiliar to him—Eric Ambler, E. Phillips Oppenheim, Sax Rohmer—they must be centuries old. The Hokas had apparently dialed for novels about the diplomatic service and—

He clenched his teeth and sat down. "I don't believe I've met the other gentlemen," he said in a hollow voice.

"Forgive me, old chap," said Allenby. "More tea, Bert."

The chauffeur poured.

"Who's Bert?" inquired Alex.

"Our chauffeur, of course," said Allenby. "Foreign Office has 'em, don't y'know." He bowed at the other cutaway. "Heinrichs."

"Heinrichs?"

"Code expert," said Allenby, gazing distantly at Heinrichs. "One of these efficient German types."

Heinrichs beamed. He had always been nearsighted and worn contact lenses; these he had now discarded for two monocles.

"Code?" choked Alex.

"Naturally," said Allenby. "My dear old chap (more tea, Bert. Thanks), surely you don't imagine we'd dare communicate with the home office except in code?"

"Oh," said Alex. Allenby sipped at his tea. Marlowe took notes. "And . . . er . . . this other gentleman?" said Alex when it became clear that the Hoka in the black hat was not going to be introduced.

Allenby looked around the room, leaned over the table, put a furry hand to his mouth, and whispered: "That's Z."

"Z?"

"Z," breathed Allenby. "You remember Z, of course. The chap who was so useful to us at the time of the Balkan crisis."

"Oh," said Alex.

He was too late. The Hokas were already off on their own path. He could only play along. "Well, gentlemen," he sighed, "you must not forget that this delegation has an important job to do—a very important job."

"Hear, hear," cheered Marlowe.

"The future of Toka depends on it," said Alex earnestly. "If we don't get upgraded this time, we can't apply again for twenty years."

"Roight!" said Bert.

"Bert!" said Allenby.

"Sorry, guv'nor," said Bert.

"We have to remember that we are on trial—"

"More tea, Bert," said Allenby.

"Yes, sir."

"On trial, I say. The future of Toka depends on our making a favorable impression. You must remember—"

"Knockout drops, Bert."

" 'Ere you are, sir."

Alex frowned, but was too busy explaining to inquire what was meant. "In most cases," he went on, "there is a delicate situation existing just under the surface of polite intercourse—"

"Let me give you a fresh cup of tea, old bean," said Allenby.

"Thanks," said Alex. "As I was saying, there are conflicts—" He took a swallow from his cup. "There can be situations that—"

The floor came up and hit him.

He struggled back to consciousness to find himself neatly laid out on a couch, and the suite empty. Two hours had passed; it was now 2030 o'clock. He felt like retreaded oatmeal.

After a while he managed to get to his feet, stagger to the bathroom, and gulp down an athetrine tablet. The pains vanished and his head cleared.

"Omigawd!" said Alex. "The Hokas!" He went out the door at full gallop.

Each floor of the hundred-story hostel—this was the 93d—had its own lounge. Alex burst into this room and found its comfortable chairs deserted, its robobar humming softly as it polished glasses . . . no sign of his charges. He was about to dash on, he knew not whither, when a glorious shape undulated through the rear entrance, paused, and sped forward. The soft eyes of Zuleika MacTavish fluttered incredible lashes at him and the soft hands with their luminous nail polish gripped his.

"Oh . . . Plenipotentiary Jones," she whispered "I was hoping I could find you alone."

"You were?' squeaked Alex.

"Please," she said. "I'm in desperate need of help."

Alex, who had been pawing at the floor in his eagerness to be off, began to paw a little more slowly. Not that the situation wasn't bad, with the Hokas on the loose; but after all, any gentleman who called himself a gentleman—

"Well, er, hruff!" he coughed. "If there's anything I can do—"

Zuleika leaned toward him, still several centimeters removed but slightly indenting his tunic. "It's not for myself, it's for Bagdadburgh," she pleaded. "There's so few of us, and those awful Worbenites and Porkelugians—" Suddenly her eyes were swimming with tears, and Alex put a fatherly arm around her.

"There, there," he began.

A shrill voice exploded behind him. "I say!"

Alex jerked free of the ambassadress and turned to confront the stem gaze of Allenby.

"Oh, er, good evening," he mumbled.

"Beg your pardon, old grapefruit," said the small Hoka frostily. "Your presence is required at the suite."

"Alex," breathed Zuleika, "I just have to talk with you."

"Yes, yes," said the man. "Later . . . to be sure, later—"

Zuleika gave him a thousand-watt smile through a mist of tears and walked slowly off. Alex stared after her, trying to recall the equations of simple harmonic motion. Allenby tugged at his sleeve. As they left, he found himself blushing, and the more angry he got on that account the more he blushed.

"Well, Allenby," he said gruffly.

"Well," repeated Allenby.

"Charming young lady," said Alex in a frantic tone.

"Yes. I rather imagine you feel like a father toward her."

"Why, of course. How did you know?"

"We," said the Hoka wisely, "know their methods."

"Methods?" asked Alex in bewilderment. "Whose methods?"

"You force me to be blunt, old parsnip," said Allenby. "The methods of beautiful spies. . . . Hist! Not another word till we're back. These walls have ears, don't y'know."

"Oh, no!" groaned Alex as he realized he had been cast in the role of Colonel Blimp.

"Play up, play up, and play the game!" said Allenby, patting him on the arm. "Stiff upper lip. Bite the bullet." With a courteous gesture, he produced a bullet from his cutaway and offered it.

"Play up yourself!" screamed Alex. "Now you listen to me—"

The slideway had borne them around a corner, and they saw Commissioner Parr's ponderous form on the opposite strip. He waved agitatedly at them and stepped onto the motionless central band. "Plenipotentiary Jones!" he barked. "What do you make of this?"

And he thrust under Alex's nose a large, ornate Oriental dagger.

"Found it stuck in my door," went on Parr. "Pinning down a note." He held out the message, and Alex read:

WHERE ARE THE SECRET PAPERS?

"Ulp," said Alex.

"Do you know whose idea of a joke this is?" rumbled Parr. He glared suspiciously at Allenby. "Have you seen this knife before?"

"I?" asked the Hoka. "Can't say I have, old cabbage." He helped himself to a pinch of snuff.

"Well . . . it's odd, to say the very least." Parr bowed stiffly, got back onto the westbound strip, and dwindled down the hall. Alex and Allenby continued east in a chilled silence.

The human found the suite in a state of hideous confusion. Its tables were heaped with paper of all sorts and varieties, and Heinrichs was busily examining these with a magnifying glass. Bert was making tea, Marlowe was writing, and Z sat muttering into his slouch hat.

"Ach!" said Heinrichs, looking up. "Vere vas der *hochwohlgeborene Bevollmächtigter* Jones?"

"With," said Allenby in tones of deepest deprecation, *"her."*

"Her?"

"Her, herself!"

"Now cut it out!" roared Alex. "Now listen to me! I won't have this—I positively forbid—" Suddenly and belatedly he realized from the happy expressions on the furry faces that he was once more sliding into the character they had determined he should play.

As he stood sputtering, Marlowe looked up and said eagerly: "What do you think of this, Jones? I'm making a new translation of the *Iliad.*"

"You are?" asked Alex blankly.

"Yes, indeed," beamed Marlowe. "I have chosen to represent the timeless spirit of Homer by using the metrical form most characteristic of our age, a rapid, mellifluous—well, hear for yourself." He cleared his throat and read:

"I sing of the wrath of Achilles,
which gave the Achaeans the willies.
Help me tell, O my muse,
how Troy got the goose
and of quarrels which really were dillies."

Alex was saved from making noises like a critic by the buzzing of the visiphone. He pressed the button and Parr's thunderous face popped into the screen. "Plenipotentiary Jones!" he said. "Would you come down to my apartment right away, please?"

Alex nodded and clicked off, wondering what had happened now.

"Z," said Allenby, "attend the Chief."

"Und better you take mine Luger," said Heinrichs, withdrawing a young cannon from his top hat.

"No!" cried Alex. But as he sped out, Z followed relentlessly.

It occurred to the human as he went down the corridor that he could at least get an explanation of what had been going on. "Z," he said firmly, "I want an explanation of what has been going on. In the first place, what was the idea of giving me knockout drops?"

"Policy, sir," said Z.

"Policy?" Alex snapped his mouth shut. Oh, no, he thought, he wasn't going to get into one of those brain-tangling discussions this time. "What about that dagger and note?" he demanded.

"Sir?" asked Z cautiously.

"Do you know anything about that?"

"What can one say?"

Alex stared at him, but he volunteered nothing further. "Well," asked the man finally, "what *can* one say?"

"Exactly," said Z mournfully.

"Exactly *what,* for the love of Saturn?" snarled Alex.

"Exactly nothing."

Alex choked. "All right," he said. "Tell me one thing. Just one thing. What's this all about? What's supposed to be going on?"

"Ah," said Z darkly. "Who can tell?"

"Can't you?"

"Sir!" cried Z reproachfully, drawing himself up. "I'm in the secret service. I never tell."

Before Alex could think of a reply, they were at the Commissioner's suite. Grouped around a table were Parr, Prince Idebar of Worben, Tantho the Hairy of Porkelans, and Zuleika MacTavish of Bagdadburgh. An air of tension prevailed.

"Oh, good evening, Jones," said Parr distantly. "Ah . . . this is one of your delegation?"

"Um, yes," said Alex. "Commissioner, Your Excellencies, Mr. Z."

"How do you do, Mr. Zee?" said Parr.

"One has one's methods," said Z mysteriously.

Parr looked a bit startled, but turned to Alex. "I asked you here because your delegation and Their Excellencies all have accommodations on the 93d floor, and no one else. Possibly we can throw some light on a, ah, very delicate and unfortunate situation. It seems that Their Excellencies have had their suites broken into and stripped of papers."

"Aha!" said Z.

They all stared at the Hoka. "What?" asked Tantho.

"Just aha," said Z. He pulled an Oriental dagger from his sleeve and began idly to clean his fingernails with its tip. Parr's eyes narrowed, but before he could speak, Zuleika flared:

"Can't you see, these, these *gentlebeings* were out to find what they could in my quarters, and just pretended to have their own broken into as well?"

"Your young Excellency," crackled Prince Idebar, "may I point out that a planet must resent slurs on its accredited representatives?"

"Please!" said Parr. "We only wish to get to the bottom of this. I suggest that the Interstellar Bureau of Investigation—"

"No!" snapped Tantho and Zuleika, while Idebar murmured: "I am afraid that is impossible."

"Ah—" began Z, but Alex hastily clapped a hand over his muzzle and babbled: "I'd better check my own place. I didn't notice any signs of burgling, but . . . I'll let you know—" With a sick grin, he hurried Z out.

"—and furthermore," stormed Alex when he was back in his suite, "breaking into the quarters of Council delegates is a territorial violation. I never saw anything like this! How did you—"

"Aow, naow," said Bert modestly.

"You, Bert?" whispered Alex.

"Of course, old onion," said Allenby proudly. "Bert is an ex-master criminal (now reformed, right, Bert?) and it was jolly old child's play for him, eh, what, what, what?"

"But those locks are finger-sensitive—pickproof!" said Alex.

"Simple, h'it were," said Bert. "H'I took me little h'ax—" He reached inside his uniform with a flourish and brought out an object like a giant jackknife with a hundred blades; from the body he snapped a small but wicked-looking axhead. "—then h'I took me little gouge"—he unfolded something like an icepick—"and me little jimmy, me little bryce and bit—"

Alex turned slightly green. "I see, I see," he groaned. "You needn't go into details."

"H'I picked those locks orl roight. H'I'd like ter see the lock h'I couldn't pick—"

"Bert!" reproved Allenby.

"Roight, guv'nor. Sorry, guv'nor." Bert lapsed into silence.

"—Anyway," said Alex after drawing a deep breath, "breaking into private offices and so forth . . . filling up our rooms with stuff like this—" He grabbed a handful of papers from under Heinrichs' magnifying glass. "What is this, anyhow? Here—

" *'Dear Miss MacTavish: This is to notify you that payment on your account for three black silk negligees, Size 12, and four pairs Upthrust brassieres, 107 cm. large, is now overdue—'* Hrump, we won't go into this. Hum." Alex cleared his throat and hastily shuffled the documents. "What's this, a private letter? Don't you know that one of the worst invasions of privacy is to read somebody's else's—um, I see the Worbenites have adopted English as their own international language— *'Dearest Iddykins—'* Good Lord, *Iddykins!* 'Dearest Iddykins, I had a dream last night and I dreamed you were speaking in the chamber of Earth but they had the ventilation turned up for the Chokgins representative. There you were, with nothing but your lightweight underwear on. For eighty years I've begged and prayed you to dress sensibly in your long woollies, you know you get the sniffles so easily, and I've tried to be a good wife to you but the moment you are out of my sight you cast caution to the winds—'* " Catching sight of the interested Hoka faces ringing him in, Alex broke off and cried wildly: "What do you want with this stuff?"

"Ve must decode," said Heinrichs.

"Ve must?" echoed Alex. "No . . . I mean—these aren't in code, dammit!"

"*Ja,* dey are."

"No, *no,* NO!"

"My dear old artichoke," said Allenby, "with all due respect, who is the code expert here, you or Heinrichs?"

"Heinrichs, of course!" roared Alex. "I mean—no, that's not what I mean. What I mean is— Now do don't get me off on *that!* The point is, this is a complete farce. There's nothing going on here"—the door chimed and Alex backed toward it, talking as he went—"that requires daggers in doors, burgling—come in—reading personal papers and so forth—come in, I said—and so on, and now that I have you here I'm going to show you that this business of intriguing is just something you've dreamed up—"

Becoming impatient, he opened the door manually. Leaning against the jamb, his face shaded by the tartan burnoose, was the silent and faintly sinister Colin MacHussein.

"Oh," said Alex. "What is it?"

To the Hokas' unbounded delight, MacHussein started to lean forward as if to whisper confidentially in his ear. The only problem was that he kept on leaning, further and further, until with a rush he ended face down on the carpet.

"MacHussein!" gasped Alex.

The Bagdadburgian did not reply. But for this seeming rudeness he had a good excuse. It consisted of a headgear the back of which was matted with blood.

Alex spun around and counted his Hokas. They were all present. He sat down and buried his face in his hands.

" 'Ere, sir," said Bert sympathetically. " 'Ave a nice 'ot cup of tea.

"Thank you," said Alex in a weak voice, accepting it. Then, cautiously: "No knockout drops, are there?"

"Aow, no, sir. Cream and sugar, two lumps."

"Thank you," repeated Alex and drank. "It's good."

"Thank you, sir. Bucks yer h'up h'in a tight spot, a bit of tea, don't it, sir?"

"Yes," said Alex. "Yes, indeed. When it's been a bad day ever since morning and when a man's been murd—" He leaped as if stung. "WHAT," he screamed, "AM I DOING SITTING HERE AND DRINKING TEA?"

"Thirsty, perhaps?" suggested Marlowe.

Alex slammed down the cup and saucer, shoving aside Z, who was about to search for secret papers. To the plenipotentiary's immense relief, the man was alive: it was the unpleasant but not grave effect of a powerful supersonic stun beam fired at short range.

"The body, of course, will have to be disposed of," said Z.

"No!" Alex began to function again. "Get out—all of you. Go get Parr, get a doctor, but for heaven's sake don't tell anyone what's happened. Get out!"

They got.

Left alone, Alex tried to remember his first-aid training. There wasn't much he could do except leave MacHussein undisturbed. The usual result of supersonic stunning was amnesia covering the past several hours. . . . He grew aware that this fumbling had gotten blood all over his tunic and slacks. Hastily he went to the bathroom, stripped off the clothes, washed his hands, and donned a robe. As he came out, the door chimed again. "Parr," he muttered, and aloud: "Come in."

Zuleika MacTavish sine-waved through, closing the door behind her. Deep, agitated breathing expanded her chest, which was not something Alex would have considered possible had he thought about it dispassionately. "Alex!" she said in a frantic whisper. "There's not a minute to lose. I have to talk to you!"

"Oh—" Alex jittered about. "Well, er, sit down, but—"

"This is no time to sit down." she followed him across the room, completely overlooking the corpse-like MacHussein. "This is the eleventh hour. Alex," she said, cornering him and seizing the lapel of his robe, "I know about you. I know your record. You have your heart in the right place."

"I do?" asked Alex feebly.

"Yes," said Zuleika. "Like me."

"Um . . . to be sure," mumbled Alex.

"You are the only man who can help me," cried Zuleika, throwing herself on his shoulder and bursting into tears.

"There, there," said Alex. He meant to pat her gently on the back, but somehow his hand slipped. "There, there, there." Getting no result from this, he disentangled himself, went to the brandy decanter, and poured out a stiff drink. She accepted it blindly and tossed it off at one gulp.

"It can't be that bad—" Alex was saying, when he was interrupted by a strangled, though ladylike, snort. Zuleika's finely molded face squeezed up, both hands flew to her throat, and she began to stagger around the room making ineffectual noises.

"What is it?" yelped Alex. Smitten with a horrible suspicion, he sniffed at the decanter. It was . . . yes, for his ambassadorial brandy the Hokas had substituted their native liquor, a 180-proof liquid dynamite which—"Omigawd! I'm sorry! Excuse me! 'Ere, 'ave a nice cup of 'ot—No, no, I mean, ice water—"

Zuleika downed it shakily, brushed aside his babbled apologies, and said with a new and fascinating huskiness in her voice: "No matter. Too much else to do. Prince Idebar and those awful Porkelugians—Goldfarb's Planet—you've got to help me! The whole future of Bagdadburgh depends on it!"

Alex found himself so busy unraveling her explanation that he forgot both MacHussein and the notoriously sudden wallop which Hoka brew delivers. Goldfarb's Planet was a terrestroid world out in Sector Seven; having no aborigines, it was open for colonization, but the award lay with the Council. Bagdadburgh, with a rapidly increasing population (if Zuleika was representative of its womenfolk, thought Alex, he could understand why they had a population problem), needed it badly, and would normally have been granted the title. Porkelans was also asking for it, but the reason was a mystery: their population was static. However, the Bagdadburgian intelligence service had discovered that Prince Idebar of Worben intended to support the Porkelugian claim—and his influence was so great that he was bound to get what he wanted unless he was blocked.

"But what's in it for Worben?" wondered Alex. "I know their present leaders belong to the Expansionist Party and they'd like more territory but they already have the legal limit of colonies."

"The Porkelugian government is corrupt," said Zuleika fiercely. "Tantho and his associates . . . bribed . . . betraying their own planet. Bribed by dirty Worbenite neodymium."

"Um . . . wait . . . you mean if Porkelans gets Goldfarb's Planet—"

"The Tantho gang would admit Worbenite settlers. In a few years, there'd be so many settlers they could vote for autonomy. But the Goldfarbian government would be a Worbenite puppet. We know it, I tell you. Tantho is selling out his planet for Worbenite neodymium. Would I touch their tainted money? I would not. You would not. But Tantho will. He does. He touches their tainted money every day. I'll bet he's sitting in his suite right now touching Worbenite money."

"But how do you know all this?"

"We got spies," hissed Zuleika. "We found out . . . Tantho an' Idebar got a written agreement about it. Don't trust even each other . . . got a regular contract . . . tainted money." She looked at him with vague, though lovely, brown eyes. "You wouldn't touch Worbenite money, would you?"

"N-no," said Alex. "I guess not. Not if it's tainted."

"Private contrac'. . . . would be proof we need to bust rotten con—conshpi—plot. Bust it wide open. Colin s'posed to steal contrac'. Special agent of ours. Where's Colin?" Zuleika peered about in a charming misty fashion. "Will you help me, Alesh?"

"I, well—"

"Oh, thank you, Alesh!" cried Zuleika, staggering a trifle. "Tha's y'r name, isn' nit? Oh, Alesh, hol'onna me, I feel a li'l dizzy—"

The door chimed.

"Hurray for Bagdadburgh!" whooped Zuleika. "Bagdadburgh, my ain planet! Would I stop at anything for Bagdadburgh?" she demanded of the empty air. "No!" she answered with a ringing cry, dramatically seizing the front of her wispy tunic and ripping it across. Then she stumbled over MacHussein, looked down, whitened, screamed, and fell into Alex's arms.

The door opened and Commissioner Parr strode in with several Hokas. He stopped dead.

Alex stared at him, dumbfounded. He could see no reason why the Commissioner should look at him with loathing. Then, glancing at a full-length mirror across the room, he reeled. In its crystal depths he saw a man in a dressing gown clutching a hiccoughing girl with torn tunic while at his feet another man lay weltering in blood and behind him two tables groaned under stolen papers.

"Commissioner!" bawled Alex in tones of anguish. "You don't think—you can't believe—Commissioner!"

"Please, Mr. Jones," said Parr loftily, withdrawing. "Don't paw me."

Alex had been protesting his innocence for a couple of minutes now. The Commissioner did not appear to be convinced. He stood in the middle of the room and stared coldly at Alex while MacHussein lay on the floor and Zuleika lolled in a chair. Even the Hokas were silent.

"But it's not what it looks like!" gibbered Alex.

"Hiccup!" said Zuleika.

"*I* didn't stun this man!" cried Alex. "I sent for you myself—"

"And the representative?" asked Parr scornfully. "I imagine she, too, fell through the door in her present condition?"

"No! She just took a drink, that's all."

"Which you gave her."

"Well, yes, but—"

"Ha!"

"I gave her the wrong thing."

"Indeed you did."

"Whoops!" said Zuleika faintly. "Porkelans, Worben—poke 'em inna nose. Throw'm to the bushcats."

"Now, Mr. Jones," said Parr, "you still have the status of your office and, therefore, diplomatic immunity. My hands are tied. But I shall, of course, make urgent recommendations to my superiors tomorrow to the effect that Toka badly needs a new plenipotentiary and, as the result of—to put it in as kindly a light as possible—your incompetence, the planet is not yet ready for advancement in grade."

If he had been perfectly fair, Alex might have agreed that Parr had a case. But it was his job, his reputation, and his Hokas that were at stake. He clutched at a straw. "You don't understand," he said. "I discovered there was an illegal conspiracy between the Worben and Porkelans delegates. Since the IBI can't act against diplomats, I had to use my own status to get the proof."

He flattered himself it was a good speech, but Parr gave him only the thinnest of smiles. "If such proof is forthcoming," said the Commissioner, "naturally I will reconsider. May I see it?"

"I—well—I haven't got all of it yet—"

"I thought not. It is my duty to inform Their Excellencies of the situation, and the aspersions you have cast on them must, of course, be taken into account in judging your case. Good evening, Mr. Jones." Parr bowed and went out.

Alex sat down and grabbed at the decanter. Before he could sort out his whirling thoughts, Marlowe trotted in with the hotel physician.

"Ah," said the doctor cheerily bending over MacHussein, "a stun beam. Tsk-tsk. But we're feeling much better now, aren't we?" Getting no response, he removed the burnoose and examined the injury.

Marlowe peered over his shoulder. "I am writing a novel about the medical profession," he squeaked. "Heroic, unselfish—"

The doctor reached for his stethoscope. It wasn't there. Z was peering into it for secret papers. "Hey!" said the doctor. Marlowe took busy notes as man and Hoka wrestled for the instrument. Winning the fight, the doctor checked his patient and prepared an athetrine injection. "This'll bring him around," he explained. "He should be all right when he wakes up."

"Aha!" said Z. "When he starts his drugged babbling—"

"Aren't you going to operate?" asked Marlowe, handing the physician a scalpel from his bag.

"For God's sake, no!"

"Not even a little operation?"

"No, I said! Get out of my way!"

"You have the soul of an editor," said Marlowe. "Instead of a novel, I think I shall write an exposé."

Somehow the doctor got MacHussein injected, bandaged, and laid out on a couch. He departed muttering.

Alex had recovered his wits enough to give Zuleika a soberpill. They stared grimly at each other.

"Well," said Alex, "I just hope you were right about that contract, and that we can find it. Otherwise—"

The girl nodded. "No less than four of our best secret agents learned of its existence just before I left for Earth," she said. "It'll be here somewhere—the Embassy Building Offices aren't private enough, and naturally it must remain secret to all but a few."

"But why did you—Damn it," protested Alex, " this is serious and I have to think. Will you *please* get another tunic?"

Zuleika looked down and blushed. She was, of course, wearing her Upthrust brassiere, 107 cm. large, but it was made of Sheerglo fabric, which happens to be perfectly transparent. Hastily she went to the closet and borrowed one of Alex's tunics. He was a reasonably athletic young man, but it was still a tight fit around the chest.

"Why did you drag me into this?" moaned Alex.

"I had to have someone," she pleaded. "You see, I was getting suspicious of Colin. He has been a secret agent of Bagdadburgh for years, but since we reached Earth I saw him too often talking with Idebar. I turned to you because you, well, you looked so strong and self-reliant and . . . oh, I'm *so* grateful to you—"

"Hrumf!" said Alex. "Never mind. Quite all right."

Zuleika swayed closer. "The whole future of my planet depends on finding that contract," she whispered. "I would do *anything* to get it—to get your help—"

"Now . . . now, wait . . . I've got a wife and . . . and children on Toka and—and—" Alex backed up. His collar felt tight. "Just take it easy."

"After that reception today, Colin disappeared," went on Zuleika. "I got desperate and came here. It was hard to believe anything wrong about him; he's worked with me for years, and always been such a perfect gentleman, though with his looks he could—Never mind." She sighed. "Of course, his being attacked like this proves I was mistaken." She laid her hands on Alex's shoulders and searched his eyes with her own. "But we still need your help."

"And I guess I need yours," agreed the man. "If we can find that contract, it'll clear us, but—"

"I'll be quite frank with you," said Zuleika. "We were going to burgle their apartments, but apparently your Hokas beat us to it, though how you knew even before I told you—" She regarded him worshipfully.

"Oh, well," said Alex with due modesty. "One has a knack—*Hey!*"

Zuleika jumped. This made her quiver. This in turn distracted Alex so much that he could not go on for a few seconds. Then he turned excitedly to the stolen papers. "But the contract must be *here!*" he shouted. "We're saved!"

"Whee!" said Bert, doing a swan dive into the nearest stack.

It took only a few minutes in spite of the Hokas' help. After that there were several more minutes of frantic re-searching. At the end, Hokas and humans regarded each other rather bleakly.

There was no contract. There was not even a protocol.

"I found a treaty on import quotas of rugglepthongs," said Allenby with an air of having done his best.

Colin MacHussein groaned and stirred. Zuleika went to the couch and sat down, laid his head on her breast and stroked his hair. "There, there," she crooned.

MacHussein blinked his eyes open. *"Garrasht!"* he mumbled. "What—oh—" He grew aware of them. "What happened?"

"Does it hurt much?" asked Zuleika softly. "Here, lie back and rest."

"No, I'm all right," said MacHussein crisply. He sat up. "But everything else is wrong. You haven't found that contract, have you?"

"No," said Alex. "What happened to you?"

"I don't know." MacHussein frowned, concentrating. "My memory stops several hours ago. Amnesiac effect, you know. But where did all this litter come from?"

Alex explained. "Apparently the contract isn't in this hotel after all," he finished.

MacHussein shook his head. "It would have to be, for their purposes. Have to be available for reference. But they knew we'd lift it if we could, so they must simply have hidden it better than we realized."

Bert bristled. "They couldn't 'ide nothink from me!"

"Afraid they did. We'll just have to try once more." Alex opened the door and peered out, to meet the unmistakable chilled-steel gaze of an IBI man. Others patrolled the slideways as far as he could see.

"Er . . . we don't need protection," said Alex weakly.

"No, sir," said the IBI agent. "You don't."

Alex closed the door.

"Hist!" said Z, at the window.

"Hist yourself," said Alex bitterly. "We *can't* get to their rooms now."

"There are," said Z, "other methods."

"What other methods?"

"I cannot tell," said Z.

However, he could act, for he opened the window. Alex went over and looked out. A meter below was a flange, some 20 centimeters wide, running around the tower for the benefit of the window-cleaning machines. Beneath, except for other flanges, was a good 400 meters of sky terminating in some very hard-looking pavement.

"Ulp!" said Alex.

"En avant, old turnip," said Allenby with revolting cheerfulness. Carefully he donned his top hat, put a fresh carnation in his buttonhole, stuck a rolled umbrella under one arm, and vaulted out onto the ledge.

MacHussein swallowed. "I'd better stay and hold the fort," he offered.

"No—" Alex gave up. There was no escape for him, unless he wanted the Hokas to go off with no one to control them. But he took some satisfaction in pushing MacHussein to the window. "Miss Mac-Tavish is the one to stay behind."

"Nonsense!" said Zuleika. "I told you I would do anything for my planet."

"Even on a window ledge?" asked Marlowe, interested.

"Even on a window ledge," she declared.

Alex got out into a fresh night wind that nipped his bare shanks but cooled his ears somewhat. Allenby was ahead of him; Bert, happily snapping and unsnapping tools from his instrument, came after; Zuleika, Z, MacHussein, and Marlowe followed.

Under better conditions Alex might have enjoyed the view. The great city sprawled for kilometers around, its arrogant pinnacles reaching for the stars, its roadways a faerie web of lights; far off, under a low moon, he could see the snowy heights of Mount Aorangi. But hugging a slick plastic wall with his heels sticking out over the edge of nothing—

"Naow 'ere, guv'nor," said Bert, "h'is the neatest bit of 'it h'all. See, h'I h'unfold this little drill, turn this little wheel, h'insert the nitro with this little 'ypodermic—clever, eh?" He nudged Alex knowingly in the ribs.

"Yipe!" said Alex.

There was a low wail behind him, Zuleika was shuffling along with her face to the wall. For her, though, this was not very practical.

"Turn me around, somebody!" she begged.

"Right-o," said Allenby gallantly. He reached past Alex and Bert with his umbrella. "Hold on to the end of this and step off the ledge; I'll swing you over to me. We Hokas are quite strong."

Alex assured her of this, and she obeyed. Then she vanished as the handle and the ferrule parted company. "Oh, piffle," said Allenby in an annoyed tone. "I forgot this was also a sword cane. Sorry, old girl."

Just in time, Bert grabbed her hair. This overbalanced Bert, who snatched at Alex. Alex clutched after Allenby, who also toppled but managed to throw his umbrella up for Z. The secret agent got it and went over the brink, dragging MacHussein along. Marlowe got MacHussein by the left foot and hooked his free elbow under the windowsill so he could take notes. Not till he had finished this did he use the really astonishing Hoka strength to draw himself back through the window and then haul in the rest. The most irritating part of it all was that as he pulled in the living rope, he piped forth a deep-sea chanty.

"Not making much progress, are we?" asked Allenby with undiminished good humor. His eye fell on Heinrichs, seated with paper and pencil. "Stop that and come along with us!"

"But I iss decoding!" protested Heinrichs.

"You can decode as we go," said Allenby sternly. He wheeled

about and went over the sill again. There was nothing to do but follow him.

This time the path was negotiated without incident. They rounded the corner of the building and saw ahead of them the windows of the Porkelugian and Worbenite suites. The former glowed with light; the latter, beyond them, were dark.

The windows were broad enough so that the whole party could stand looking in. The upper transoms were open, and words drifted out—conversation between Prince Idebar, Tantho the Hairy, and Commissioner Parr, who were sitting about with drinks and cigars.

"—most kind of you, sir, to warn us about those Hokas," said Tantho.

"Oh, just doing my duty," said Parr. "But I'm sorry I can't legally recover those papers for you until Jones has been fired."

"No matter," said Idebar, waving his tail airily. "I assure you we are not so foolish as to leave confidential documents where any unscrupulous hireling could find them. We have our methods."

This was too much for Z. He whipped out a dagger and tossed it expertly up, through the transom and across the room, to stick quivering in the wall before Tantho's sheepdog nose.

"What's that?" roared Parr, leaping to his feet.

Z pulled down his slouch hat and rubbed his hands. "We too have our methods," he said with a fiendish cackle.

It is disconcerting, to say the least, to be having a private chat on the 93d floor of an official building, and then suddenly to have daggers quivering in the wall and see five teddy bear noses flattened against your windowpane. When one nose is surmounted by a top hat, one by a black slouch, one by a chauffeur's cap, and one by two gleaming monocles, the effect is positively unnerving.

"What kind of place is this, anyway?" stormed Tantho with a not unjustifiable huffiness.

"Spies!" hissed Idebar, gliding forward.

"Spies yourself!" said Zuleika.

"Cut that out!" said Alex raggedly. "We've got to—"

Allenby was already scuttling down the flange to the Worbenite windows. The rest followed. Bert got to work cutting out the living-room pane. Behind them, Parr looked out, bellowing like a wounded bull. "Thieves! Barbarians! You'll get psychorevision for this, Jones! You—"

"Not so fast, please," squeaked Marlowe, busily taking notes.

"He iss schpeaking in ein zimple double-transposition cipher," decided Heinrichs, looking over Marlowe's shoulder.

"—and naow me little saw," said Bert, "and me little roll of tape, and me little—"

The pane gave way with a crash, and the burglars scrambled through. There was only the vaguest possible illumination from outdoors, but as he fumbled for the switch Alex could see MacHussein's shadowy form atremble. "Sunspots, what a day!" stammered the Bagdadburgian. "I need a drink—" He groped over to a barely visible decanter and put it to his lips and shuddered with relief.

Alex turned on the lights as the outer door opened. An IBI man looked in. Z sent a dagger whisking past him. The IBI man withdrew and Alex scurried about locking all the doors.

Feet thundered in the corridor. "Open up!" bawled Tantho.

Alex groaned. "We've got to find that contract fast," he chattered, staring at the wild disorder left by the previous Hoka visit . . . or visitation. "They'll break in—and for all we know, it's in the Porkelugian suite—"

Allenby glared at an inoffensive chair, broke off its tail-rest, and ripped the cushion with his sword cane. "Not here," he announced.

"Of course it isn't," said Z. "Don't you know secret documents are always left in plain sight?" His eyes glittered around. "Aha! I've found it!" He snatched a framed paper off the wall. Alex took it with shaking hands and read:

WHEREAS H. H. IDEBAR FANJ HURTHGL HAS SATISFACTORILY COMPLETED THE REQUIREMENTS FOR THE DEGREE OF MASTER OF ARTS IN THE FIELD OF GLOGSNORGLING, NOW THEREFORE BY AUTHORITY OF THE REGENTS . . .

"It vill haff to be decoded, of course," said Heinrichs.

The door glowed as someone turned a raybeam on it.

"Too late," said Alex dully.

The door fell, and Parr, Idebar, Tantho, and a dozen grim-faced IBI men rushed through. Alex stared down the muzzles of their Holmans and raised his hands.

"I've got you now, Jones!" raged Parr. "Diplomatic immunity or no, I'm going to have you locked away till—"

"We are not disposed to be malicious, Commissioner," said Idebar with his usual suavity. "Obviously Jones is a public menace, but we see no reason to press charges against the others."

"Aha!" said Z darkly.

"Guilty conscience, eh, what?" observed Allenby.

"To be sure," said Z. He tugged at Parr's sleeve. "Commissioner."

"What now?" demanded Parr, turning like a large elephant baited by a very small dog.

"Arrest that man," said Z, pointing to MacHussein.

"What for?" sputtered Parr.

"On suspicion."

"Suspicion of what? Who's suspicious of him?"

"I am," said Z with a sinister overtone.

"Now listen," screamed Parr, "that man was attacked himself—"

"Aha!" said Z. "That proves it."

"Proves what?"

"My suspicions."

"What suspicions?"

"None of your business," said Z, looking distrustfully at the Commissioner.

"My dear sir," broke in Idebar, "may I inquire what this is all about?"

Z turned to Allenby. "May he?"

"It should be referred to the home office," said Allenby. "But a field agent has to stick his neck out now and then, what? Damme, I *will* stick my neck out. He may."

"Go ahead, Your Excellency," bowed Z.

"I *was* going ahead," choked Idebar. "Mister . . . Mr. Jones, will you do something about these—these—"

"Allenby, what's the meaning of this?" gasped Alex.

The elegantly dressed Hoka extracted a handkerchief from his pocket and flicked invisible dust from his sleeve. "My dear old mangel-wurzel," he said, "must we do *all* the work? We have ransacked three suites, issued a mysterious warning, questioned eighteen members of the hostel staff, decoded thirty-four documents, and gathered everyone here for the dénouement. Having done this, we now sit back and wait for you to do what is yours to wit, reveal what is behind all this." He beamed, took a pinch of snuff, and added to MacHussein: "Sorry, old chap. You played the Great Game well."

The Bagdadburgian grinned and shrugged. "Let's get this over with, Commissioner," he suggested. "I could use some sleep."

Alex's brain leapfrogged. "Hey!" he cried.

"Arrest Jones," said Parr to the IBI agents. "I'll take the responsibility."

"Hold on there!" said Alex. He was still panting and shivering with the revelation that had burst on him. "Parr, I told you there was an illegal contract between Idebar and Tantho. That's the truth—and I now know where it is!"

"Oh, Alex," crooned Zuleika.

The man flung his arm dramatically out. The effect was somewhat

spoiled by his knocking over a floor lamp, and in any event it is difficult to cut a heroic figure in a bathrobe, but he pointed at MacHussein
and said with triumph: "You've got it!"

"You're raving!" said Idebar.

"Not very well trained in elocution, is he?" whispered Allenby to
Marlowe.

"No," agreed the Hoka writer. "The proper phrase is, of course:
'You're mad, I tell you—mad, mad!' "

Alex backed away, speaking fast, as the IBI men closed in.
"MacHussein isn't a human at all. He's a Worbenite. Do a little surgery
on a Worbenite, he'll look just like an Arab. I can prove it. When he
woke up, he used a Worbenite oath; I'd heard Idebar use it earlier.
Well, anyone could do that, of course, but it's one point. Then Zulei—
Her Excellency said he had been a perfect gentleman in all the years of
working closely with her. And she was holding his head in a very uh,
comfortable position—but he sat up immediately and said he felt fine.
Does that sound like a *human* male? Finally, when we broke in here
just now it was quite dark, but he went right to the decanter and drank
from it. How could he know it was brandy and not the jithna drink
which would poison a human? The answer is, he couldn't . . . and he
didn't care, because he's immune!"

"I really feel sorry for anyone in your mental state, Jones," purred
Idebar. "Why, MacHussein himself was stunned."

"Yes." Alex was backed into a corner now. He picked up the lamp
and used it to fend off the IBI agents. "That was to divert Zuleika's
growing suspicion from him and make us look bad to Parr. You must
have been alarmed when your suite was raided, and been fairly sure
the Hokas did it, so you wanted us under suspicion and therefore, you
hoped, immobilized. Actually, MacHussein was planted on Bagdadburgh years ago, to work his way up and be in a position to thwart—
Leggo there!" He wrested the lamp from an agent's hand and swatted
him.

"I shall file an official protest against your unbridled language,"
said Tantho with dignity.

Bert took out his giant burglar tool, joggled Prince Idebar's elbow,
and tried to interest the elder statesman in a lecture on lockpicking.

"You knew Zuleika's agents would be trying to get that docu-
ment," went on Alex. "You knew they might find it in any hiding place
or waylay anyone carrying it—except one person, their own trusted
comrade, MacHussein! He's carrying it right now!"

The dark-faced man sneered and turned to go. "I won't bother
answering that," he said. "Goodnight."

It was a mistake. Allenby made a beautiful flying tackle, shouting something about the playing fields of Eton. Bert picked him up by the ankles and shook him. And as he lay dazed, Z extracted the paper with a grand flourish and snapped it before Parr's eyes.

There was a long silence.

"Well?" said Parr when he had finished reading.

"Sleight-of-hand," blustered Tantho. "Planted on him."

Idebar nodded, elevating his brows. "There is also the matter of diplomatic immunity," he said in an ice-slick voice.

Parr reddened. "Yes," he said. "There is. I can't do anything to punish you—nobody can. But I can tell the Council what I saw. That will settle who gets Goldfarb's Planet." He bowed heavily at Alex. "My apologies, Plenipotentiary Jones. I shall file an account of this daring exploit in your already distinguished record and, of course, recommend Toka for upgrading. Good evening, gentlebeings."

He went out. His IBI troop followed. There was another silence, broken only by Alex's wheezing. This was choked off by a long and passionate kiss, after which it resumed somewhat more noisily.

Prince Idebar stalked up to him. "Congratulations," he said with a vitriolic note. "You have, ah—"

"—foiled me," suggested Marlowe.

"Thank you. You have foiled—"

"Perhaps 'checkmated'?"

"Checkmated me, then. Thank you!" gritted Prince Idebar.

"Quite all right," said Marlowe.

"Jones," said Idebar, "you have won. But I am not without influence, even now, and I shall certainly not let you continue your career unmolested."

Alex smiled sweetly. "I have diplomatic immunity," he said.

"If you think that will help—"

"I think it will . . . Iddykins."

The Worbenite started. "What?"

"Iddykins," said Alex. "There is the little matter of your winter underwear, Iddykins. Tell me, are you wearing it now? You have a very devoted wife, Iddykins, and I can think of several news services which would be happy to print a sample of her devotion . . . shall we say, a letter?"

"Um . . . yes." Idebar's aristocratic face purpled. "You do have the upper hand, it seems. Very well, sir." He stalked out, his tail lashing his ankles.

Tantho the Hairy started to follow. Alex grabbed his arm and pointed to the semiconscious MacHussein. "Better take him along," advised the human. "He's no more use to you, and might as well return to Worben. They can regenerate his normal appearance there."

Zuleika giggled. "I imagine," she said, "he'll be the first humanoid male in history who actually wanted to grow horns."

Alex blushed and led his Hokas out. Zuleika looked as if she might continue that line of thought, and he valued his own marriage.

FROM: Chief of Tokan Secret Service

TO: Operative X-7
Room 13
The Sign of the Cloak and Dagger
Mixumaxu, U.X.

CODE: 24-J-298-q

1. Your secret report on the Interbeing League, as described to the Hoka delegation, is now in my hands.

2. Good work, X-7. Stand by for further orders.

3. Further orders: It is the opinion of this department that one of the delegates to the Council of the Interbeing League on Earth is none other than the interstellar criminal and arch spy-ring master known only as Y.

4. You know what to do.

> (signed)
> *The Chief*

Hokas
Pokas!

Table of Contents

I.
Full Pack (Hokas Wild)

FULL PACK

When one is a regular ambassador to a civilized planet with full membership in the Interbeing League, it is quite sufficient to marry a girl who is only blond and beautiful. However, a plenipotentiary, guiding a backward world along the tortuous path to modern culture and full status, needs a wife who is also competent to handle the unexpected.

Alexander Jones had no reason to doubt that his Tanni met all the requirements of blondness, beauty, and competence. Neither did she. After a dozen years of Toka, he did not hesitate to leave her in charge while he took a native delegation to Earth and arranged for the planet's advancement in grade. And for a while things went smoothly—as smoothly, at least, as they can go on a world of eager, energetic teddy bears with imaginations active to the point of autohypnosis.

Picture her, then, on a sunny day shortly after lunch, walking through her official residence in the city Mixumaxu. Bright sunshine streamed through the glassite wall, revealing a pleasant view of cobbled streets, peaked roofs, and the grim towers of the Bastille. (This was annually erected by a self-appointed Roi Soleil, and torn down again by happy sans-culottes every July 14.) Tanni Jones' brief tunic and long golden hair were in the latest Bangkok fashion, even on this remote outpost, and her slim tanned figure would never be outmoded and she was comfortably aware of the fact. She had just checked the nursery, finding her two younger children safe at play. A newly arrived letter from her husband was tucked into her bosom. It announced in one sentence that his mission had been successful; thereafter several pages were devoted to more important matters, such as his imminent

return with a new fur coat and he wished he could have been in the
envelope and meanwhile he loved her madly, passionately, etc. She
was murmuring to herself. Let us listen.

"Damn and blast it to hell, anyway! Where *is* that little monster?"

As she passed the utility room, a small, round-bellied, yellow-
furred ursinoid popped out. This was Carruthers. His official title was
Secretary-in-Chief-to-the-Plenipotentiary, which meant whatever Carruthers decided it should mean. Tanni felt relieved that today he was
dressed merely in anachronistic trousers, spats, coat, and bowler hat,
umbrella furled beneath one arm, and spoke proper Oxford English.
Last week it had been a toga, and he had brought her messages written
in Latin with Greek characters; he had also buttonholed every passerby
with the information that she, Tanni, was above suspicion.

"The newsfax sheet, madam," he bowed. "Just came off the jolly
old printer, don't y'know."

"Oh. Thanks." She took the bulletin and swept her eyes down it.
Sensational tidings from Earth Headquarters: the delegates from Worben and Porkelans accused of conspiracy; Goldfarb's Planet awarded
to Bagdadburgh; a League-wide alert for a Starflash space yacht which
had been seen carrying the Tertiary Receptacle of Wisdom of Sanussi
and the as-yet-unidentified dastards who had kidnapped him from his
planet's Terrestrial embassy; commercial agreement governing the xis-
fthikl traffic signed between Jruthn and Ptrfsk—Tanni handed it back.
There were too many worlds for anyone to remember; none of the
names meant a thing to her.

"Have you seen young Alex?" she inquired.

Carruthers screwed a monocle into one beady black eye and
tapped his short muzzle with the umbrella handle. "Why, yes, I do
believe so, eh, what, what, what?"

"Well, where is he?"

"He asked me not to tell, madam." Carruthers eyed her reproachfully. "Couldn't peach on him, now could I? Old School Tie and all
that sort of bally old . . ."

Tanni stalked off with the secretary still bleating behind her. True,
she thought, her children did attend the same school which educated
the adult Hokas, but . . . Hah! In a way, it was too bad Alex was returning so soon. She had long felt that he didn't take a firm enough line
with his mercurial charges. He was too easily reduced to gibbering
bewilderment. Now she was made of sterner stuff, and—in a
Boadicean mood, she swept through a glassite passageway to the flitter
garage.

Yes, there was her oldest son, Alexander Braithwaite Jones, Jr., curled up on the front seat with his nose buried in an ancient but well-preserved folio volume. She much regretted giving it to him. Her idea had been that he could carry it under one arm and enjoy it between bouts of healthful outdoor play, rather than having to sit hunched over a microset; but all he did was read it, sneaking off to places like—

"Alexander!"

The boy, a nine-year-old, tanglehaired pocket edition of his father, started guiltily. "Oh, hello, Mom," he smiled. It quite melted her resolve.

"Now, Alex," said Tanni in a reasonable tone, "you know you ought to be out getting some exercise. You've already read those *Jungle Books* a dozen times."

"Aw, golly, Mom," protested the younger generation. "You give me a book and then you won't let me read it!"

"*Alexander!*" Boadicea had returned in full armor. "You know perfectly well what I mean. Now I told you to—"

"Madam," squeaked a voice, "the devil's to pay!"

Tanni yipped and jumped. Remembering herself, she turned in a suitably dignified manner to see Carruthers, hastily clad in pith helmet and fake walrus mustache.

"Message on the transtype just came," said the Hoka. "From Injah, don't y'know. Seems a bit urgent."

Tanni snatched the paper he extended and read:

FROM: Captain O'Neil of the Black Tyrone

TO: Rt. Hon. Plen. A. Jones

SUBJECT: UFO (Unidentified Flying Object) identified. Your Excellency:

While burying dead and bolting beef north of the Kathun road, received word from native scout of UFO crashed in jungle nearby, containing three beasts of unknown origin. Interesting, what?

> Yr. Humble & Obt. Svt., etc.,
> "Crook" O'Neil

For a moment Tanni had a dreamlike sense of unreality. Then, slowly, she translated the Hokaese. Yes . . . there were some Hokas from this northern hemisphere who had moved down to the sub-continent due south which the natives had gleefully rechristened India, and set themselves up as Imperialists. The Indians were quite happy to cooperate, since it meant that they could wear turbans and mysterious expressions. Vaguely she recalled Kipling's Ballad of Boh Da Thone. It dealt with Burma, to be sure, but if consistency is the virtue of little minds, then the Hokas were very large-minded indeed. India was mostly Kipling country, with portions here and there belonging to Clive, the Grand Mogul, and lesser lights.

The UFO must be a spaceship and the "beasts," of course, its crew, from some other planet. God alone knew what they would think if the Indians located them first and assumed they were—*what* would Hokas convinced they were Hindus, Pathans, and Britishers imagine alien space travelers to be?

"Carruthers!" said Tanni sharply. "Has there been any distress call on the radio?"

"No, madam, there has not. And damme, I don't like it. Don't like it at all. When I was with Her Majesty's Very Own Royal, Loyal, and Excessively Brave Fifth Fusiliers, I—"

Tanni's mind worked swiftly. This was just the sort of situation in which Alex, Sr., was always getting involved and coming off second best. It was her chance to show him how these matters ought to be handled.

"Carruthers," she snapped, "you and I will take the flitter and go to the rescue of these aliens. And I want it clearly understood that—"

"*Mom!* Can I go? Can I go, huh, Mom, can I?"

It was Alex, Jr., hopping up and down with excitement, his eyes shining.

"No," began Tanni. "You stay here and read your book and—" She checked herself, aware of the pitfall. Countermanding her own orders! Here was a heaven-sent opportunity to get the boy out of the house and interested in something new—like, for example, these castaways. They were clearly beings of authority or means, important beings, or they could not afford a private spaceship. There was no danger involved; Toka's India was a land of congenial climate, without any life-forms harmful to man.

"You can go," she told Alex severely, "if you'll do exactly as I say at all times. Now that means exactly."

"Yes, yes, yes. Sure, Mom, sure."

"All right, then," said Tanni. She ran back into the house, making hasty arrangements with the servants, while Carruthers set the flitter's autopilot to locating the British bivouac. In minutes, two humans and one Hoka were skyborne.

The camp proved to be a collection of tents set among fronded trees and tangled vines, drowsy under the late afternoon sun. A radio and a transtype were the only modern equipment, a reluctant concession to the plenipotentiary's program of technological education. They stood at the edge of the clearing, covered with jungle mold, while the Black Tyrone, a hundred strong, drilled with musket, fife, and drum.

Captain O'Neil was a grizzled, hard-bitten Hoka in shorts, tunic, and bandolier. He limped across the clearing, pith helmet in hand, as Tanni emerged from the flitter with Alex and Carruthers.

"Honored, ma'am," he bowed. "Pardon my one-sided gait, ma'am. Caught a slug in the ulnar bone recently." (Tanni knew very well he had not; there was no war on Toka, and anyway the ulnar bone is in the arm.) "Now a slug that is hammered from telegraph wire—ah, a book?"

His eyes lit up with characteristic enthusiasm, and Tanni, looking around, discovered the reason in her son's arms.

"Alex!" she said. "Did you bring that *Jungle Books* thing along?" His downcast face told her that he had. "I'm not going to bother with it any longer. You hand that right over to Captain O'Neil and let him keep it for you till we leave for home again."

"Awwwww, Mom!"

"Right now!"

"—is a thorn in the flesh and a rankling fire," murmured Captain O'Neil. "Ah, thank you, m'boy. Well, well, what have we here? The *Jungle Books*, by Rudyard Kipling himself! Never seen 'em before." Humming a little tune, he opened the volume.

"Now, where is that UFO?" demanded Tanni. "Have you rescued its crew yet?"

"No, ma'am," said the Captain, with his nose between the pages. "Going to go look for 'em this morning, but we were hanging Danny Deever and—" His voice trailed off into a mumble.

Tanni compressed her lips. "Well, we shall have to find them," she clipped. "Is it far? Should we go overland or take the flitter?"

"Er . . . yes, ma'am? Ha, hum," said O'Neil, closing the book reluctantly but marking the place with a furry forefinger. "Not far. Overland, I would recommend. You'd find landing difficult in our jungles here in the Seeonee Hills—"

"The what?"

"Er . . . I mean north of the Kathun road. A wolf . . . I mean, a native scout brought us the word. Perhaps you'd care to talk to him, ma'am?"

"I would," said Tanni. "Right away."

O'Neil shouted for Gunga Din and sent him off to look, then dove back into the volume. Presently another Hoka slouched from behind a tent. He was of the local race, which had fur of midnight black, but was otherwise indistinguishable from the portly northern variety. Unless, of course, you specified his costume: turban, baggy trousers, loose shirt, assorted cutlery thrust into a sash, and a flaming red false beard. He salaamed.

"What's your name?" asked Tanni.

"Mahbub Ali, memsahib," replied the newcomer. "Horse trader."

"You saw the ship land?"

"Yes, memsahib. I had stopped to patch my bridles and count my gear—whee, a book!"

"It's mine!" said O'Neil, pulling it away from him.

"Oh. Well, ah—" Mahbub Ali edged around so that he could read over the Captain's shoulder. "I, er, saw the thing flash through the air and went to see. I, um, glimpsed three beasts of a new sort coming out, but, um, they were back inside before I could . . . By that time the moon was shining into the cave where I lived and I said to myself, 'Augrh!' I said, 'it is time to hunt again—' "

"*Gentlebeings!*" cried Tanni. The book snapped shut and two fuzzy faces looked dreamily up at her. "I shall want the regiment to escort me to that ship tomorrow."

"Why, er, to be sure, ma'am," said O'Neil vaguely. "I'll tell the pack and we'll move out at dawn."

A couple of extra tents were set up in the clearing, and there was a supper at which the humans shared top honors with Danny Deaver. (A Hoka's muscles are so strong that hanging does not injure him.) When night fell, with subtropical swiftness, Alex crawled into one tent and Tanni into the other. She lay for a while, thinking cheerfully that her theories of management were bearing fruit. True, there had been some small waverings on the part of the autochthones, but she had kept things rolling firmly in the proper direction. Why in the Galaxy did her husband insist it was so difficult to . . .

The last thing she remembered as she drifted into sleep was the murmur of a voice from the campfire. "Crook" O'Neil had assembled his command and was reading to them. . . .

She blinked her eyes open to dazzling sunlight. Dawn was hours past, and a great stillness brooded over the clearing. More indignant than alarmed, she scrambled out of her sleeping bag, threw on tunic and shoes, and went into the open.

The camp was deserted. Uniforms and equipment were piled by the cold ashes of the fire, and a flying snake was opening a can of bully beef with its saw-edged beak. For a moment the world wavered before her.

"Alex!" she screamed.

Running from tent to tent, she found them all empty. She remembered wildly that she did not even have a raythrower along. Sobbing, she dashed toward the flitter—get an aerial view—

Bush crackled, and a round black-nosed head thrust cautiously forth. Tanni whirled, blinked, and recognized the gray-shot pelt of O'Neil.

"Captain!" she gasped. "What's happened? Come out this minute!"

The brush parted, and the Hoka trotted out on all fours, attired in nothing but his own fur.

"Captain O'Neil!" wailed Tanni. "What's the meaning of this?"

The native reached up, got the hem of her tunic between his jaws, and tugged. Then he let go and moved toward the canebrake, looking back at her.

"Captain," said Tanni helplessly. She followed him for a moment, but stopped. Her voice grew shrill. "I'm not moving another centimeter till you explain this—this outrageous—" The Hoka waddled back to her. "Well, speak up! Don't whine at me! Stand up and talk like a . . . like a . . . a Captain. *And stop licking my hand!*"

O'Neil headed into the jungle. Tanni gave up. Throttling her fears, she went after him. Colorful birds whistled overhead, and flowers drooped on long vines and snagged in her hair. Presently she found herself on a trail. It ran for some two kilometers, an uneventful trip except for the pounding of her heart and the Captain's tendency to dash off after small game.

At the end, they reached a meadow surrounding a large flat-topped rock. The Black Tyrone were there. Like their commander, they had stripped off their uniforms and now frisked about in the grass, tumbling like puppies and snarling between their teeth. She caught fragments of continuous conversation:

"—Sambhur belled, once, twice, and again . . . wash daily from nose-tip to tail-tip . . . the meat is very near the bone—" and other interesting though possibly irrelevant information.

Rolling about, Tanni's eyes found her son. He was seated on top of the rock, wearing only a wreath of flowers and a kitchen knife on a string about his neck. At his feet, equally nude and happy, sprawled Carruthers and the black-furred Mahbub Ali.

"Alex!" cried Tanni. She sped to the rock and stared up at her offspring, uncertain whether to kiss and cry over him or turn him across her knee. "What are you doing here?"

Captain O'Neil spoke for the first time. "Thy mother was doubtful about coming, Little Frog."

"Oh, so you *can* talk!" said Tanni, glaring at him.

"He can't talk to you, Mom," said Alex.

"What do you mean, he can't?"

"But that's wolf talk, Mom. You can't understand it. I'll have to translate for you."

"*Wolf?*"

"The Seeonee Pack," said Alex proudly. He nodded at O'Neil. "Thou hast done well, Akela."

"*Argh!*" said Mahbub Ali. "*I* run with no pack, Little Frog."

"By the Bull that bought me!" exclaimed Alex, contrite. "I forgot, Bagheera." He stroked the black head. "This is Bagheera, Mom, the Black Panther, you know." Pointing to the erstwhile Carruthers: "And this is Baloo the Bear. And I'm Mowgli. Isn't it terrific, Mom?"

"No, it isn't!" snapped Tanni. Now, if ever, was the time to take the strong line she believed in. "Captain O'Neil, will you stop being Akela this minute? I'm here to rescue some very important people, and—"

"What says thy mother Messua?" asked the Captain—or, rather, Akela—lolling out his tongue and looking at Mowgli-Alex.

The boy started gravely to translate.

"Alex, stop that!" Tanni found her voice wobbling. "Don't encourage him in this . . . this game!"

"But it isn't a game, Mom," protested her son. "It's real. Honest!"

"You know it isn't," scolded Tanni. "He's not really Akela at all. He should be sensible and go back to being himself."

"Himself?" murmured Baloo-Carruthers, forgetting in his surprise that he wasn't supposed to understand English.

"Captain O'Neil," explained Tanni, holding on to her patience with both hands. "Captain—"

"But he wasn't really Captain O'Neil either," pointed out Baloo.

On many occasions Tanni had listened sympathetically, but with a hidden sense of superiority, to her husband's description of his latest encounter with Hoka logic. She had never really believed in all the dizzy sensations he spoke of. Now she felt them. She gasped feebly and sat down in the grass.

"I wanted to let you know, Mom," chattered Alex. "The Pack's got Shere Khan treed a little ways from here. I wanted to know if it was all right for me to go call him a Lame Thief of the Waingunga. Can I, Mom, huh, can I?"

Tanni drew a long, shuddering breath. She remembered Alex, Sr.'s advice: 'Roll with the punches. Play along and watch for a chance to use their own logic on them.' There didn't seem to be anything else to do at the moment. "All right," she whispered.

Akela took the lead, yapping; Baloo and Bagheera closed in on either side of Alex; and the Pack followed. Brush crackled. It was not easy for a naturally bipedal species to go on all fours, and Tanni saw Akela walking erect when he thought she wasn't looking. He caught her eye, blushed under his fur, and crouched down again.

She decided that this new lunacy would prove rather unstable. It just wasn't practical to run around on your hands and try to bring down game with your teeth. But it would probably take days for the Hokas to weary of the sport and return to being the Black Tyrone, and meanwhile what was she to do?

"By the Broken Lock that freed me!" exclaimed Bagheera, coming to a halt. "One approaches—I mean approacheth."

"Two approach," corrected Baloo, sitting up on his haunches bearfashion. Being an ursinoid, he did this rather well.

Tanni looked ahead. Through a clump of bamboo-like plants emerged a black-haired form with a blunt snout under heavy brow ridges, the size of a man but stooped over, long arms dangling past bent knees. He wore a sadly stained and ragged suit. She recognized him as a native of the full-status planet Chakba. Behind him lifted the serpentine head of a being from some world unknown to her.

Akela bristled. "The Bandar-log!" he snarled.

"But see," pointed Baloo, "Kaa the Python follows him, and yet the shameless Bandar is not afraid." He scratched his head. "This is not supposed to be," he said plaintively.

The Chakban spotted Tanni and hurried toward her. "Ah, dear lady," he cried. His voice was high-pitched, but he spoke fluent English. "At last, a civilized face!" He bowed. "Permit me to introduce myself. I am Echpo of Doralik-Li, and my poor friend is named Seesis."

Tanni, glancing at the friend in question, was moved to agree that he was, indeed, poor. Seesis had come into full view now, revealing ten meters of snake body, limbless except for two delicate arms just under the big bald head. A pair of gold-rimmed pince-nez wobbled on his nose. He hissed dolefully and undulated toward the woman, wringing his small hands.

Tanni gave her name and asked: "Are you the beings who crashlanded here?"

"Yes, dear lady," said Echpo. "A most—"

Seesis tugged at the woman's tunic and began to scratch on the ground with his forefinger.

"What?" Tanni bent over to look.

"Poor chap, poor chap," said Echpo, shaking his head. "He doesn't speak English, you know. Moreover, the crash . . ." He revolved a finger near his own right temple and gave her a meaningful look.

"Oh, how terrible!" Tanni got to her feet in spite of Seesis' desperate efforts to hold her down and make her look at his dirt scratchings. "We'll have to get him to a doctor—Dr. Arrowsmith in Mixumaxu is really very good if I can drag him away from discovering bacteriophage—"

"That is not necessary, madam," said Echpo. "Seesis will recover naturally. I know his race. But if I may presume upon your kindness, we do need transportation."

The Hokas crowded around Seesis, addressing him as Kaa and asking him if he was casting his skin and obliterating his marks on the ground. The herpetoid seemed ready to burst into tears.

"But weren't there three of you?" asked Tanni.

"Yes, indeed," said Echpo. "But—well—I am afraid, dear lady, that your little friends do not seem to approve of our companion Heragli. They have, er, chased him up a tree."

"Why, how could they?" Gently, Tanni detached the fingers of Seesis from her skirt, patted him on his scaly head, and turned an accusing eye on Alex. "Young man, what do you know about this?"

The boy squirmed. "That must be Shere Khan." Defiantly: "He does look like a tiger too." He glared at Echpo. "Believe thou not the Bandar-log."

"These gentlebeings are no such thing!" snapped Tanni.

"Surely thy mother has been bitten by Tabaqui, the Jackal," said Baloo to Alex. "All the Jungle knows Shere Khan."

"This is *dewanee*, the madness," agreed Bagheera. "Heed thy old tutor who taught thee the Law, Little Frog."

"But—" began Alex. "But the hairy one dares say that—"

"Surely, Little Brother," interrupted Baloo, "thou hast learned by this time to take no notice of the Bandar-log. They have no Law. They are very many, evil, dirty, shameless, and they desire, if they have any fixed desire, to be noticed by the Jungle-People. But we do *not* notice them even when they throw nuts and filth on our heads."

"Oh!" groaned Echpo. "That I, an ex-cabinet minister of the Chakban Federation, B.A., M.S., Ph.D., LL.D., graduate of Hasolbath, Trmp, and the Sorbonne, should be accused of throwing nuts and filth on people's heads to attract attention!"

"I'm so sorry!" apologized Tanni. "It's the imagination these Hokas have. Please, please forgive them, sir!"

"Your slightest whim, dear lady, is my most solemn command and highest joy," bowed Echpo.

Tanni returned gallantly to the subject: "But how did you happen to be marooned here?"

"Ah . . . we were outward bound, madam, on a mission from Earth to the Rim Stars." Echpo produced a box of lozenges and politely

offered them around. "A cultural mission, headed by our poor friend
Seesis—is he bothering you, dear lady? Just slap his hands down. The
shock, you know . . . Ah . . . A most important and urgent mission, I
may say with all due modesty, undertaken to—pardon me, I cannot say
more. Our converter began giving trouble as we passed near this sun,
so we approached your planet—Toka, is that the name?—to get help.
We knew from the pilot's manual that it had civilization, though we
scarcely expected such delightful company as yours. At any rate, the
converter failed us completely as we were entering the atmosphere,
and though we glided down, the landing was still hard enough to
wreck our communications equipment. That was yesterday, and today
we were setting out in quest of help—we had seen from the air that
there is a city some fifty kilometers hence—when, ah, your Hokas
appeared and our poor friend Heragli—"

"Oh, dear!" said Tanni. "We'd better go get him right away. Can
you guide me?"

"I should be honored," said Echpo. "I know the very tree."

"Does thy mother hunt with the Bandar-log, O Mowgli?" inquired
Akela.

"Certainly not!" snapped Tanni, whirling on him. "You ought to
be ashamed of yourself, Captain."

"What says she?" asked Akela agreeably.

Alex repeated it for him.

"Oh!" said Tanni, stamping off.

"Ah . . . poor dear Seesis," murmured Echpo. "He should not be
left unguarded. He could hurt himself. Would your, ah, Hokas watch
him while we rescue Heragli?"

"Of course," said Tanni. "Alex, you stay here and see to it."

The boy protested, was *Alexander*'d down, and gave in and
announced importantly that he, the Man-Cub, wished the Pack to
remain with him and not let Kaa depart. Tanni and Echpo started into
the woods. Baloo and Bagheera followed.

"Hey, there!" said the woman. "Didn't Mowgli tell you to—"

"By the Broken Lock that freed me," squeaked Bagheera, slapping
his paunch with indignation, "dost thou take *us* for wolves?"

Tanni sighed and traded a glance with Echpo. As they went among
the trees, she calmed down enough to say: "I can fly you to Mixumaxu,
of course, and put you up; but it may take weeks before you can get off
the planet. Not many deep-space ships stop here."

"Oh, dear." The Chakban wrung hairy hands. "Our mission is so
vital. Could we not even get transportation to Gelkar?"

"Well . . ." Tanni considered. "Why, yes, it's only a few lightyears off. I can take you myself in our courier boat, and you can charter a ship there."

"Blessed damosel, my gratitude knows no limits," said Echpo.

Tanni preened herself. She was no snob, but certainly a favor done for beings as important as these would hurt no one's career.

Through the ruffling leaves, she heard a hoarse, angry bellow. "That must be your friend," she remarked brightly, or as brightly as possible when battling through a humid jungle with hair uncombed and no breakfast. "What did you say his name was?"

"Heragli. A Rowra of Drus. A most gentlemanly felino-centauroid, dear lady. I can't conceive why your Hokas insist on chasing him up trees."

A minute later the girl saw him, perched in the branches seven meters above ground. She had to admit that he was not unlike a tiger. The long, black-striped orange body was there, and the short yellow-eyed head, though a stumpy torso with two muscular arms was between. His whiskers were magnificent, and a couple of saber teeth did the resemblance no harm. Like Echpo, he wore the thorn-ripped tatters of a civilized business suit.

"Heragli, dear friend," called the Chakban, "I have found a most agreeable lady who has graciously promised to help us."

"Are those unprintables around?" floated down a bass rumble. "Every blanked time I set foot to earth, the thus-and-so's have gone for me."

"It's all right!" snapped Tanni. She was not, she told herself, a prude; but Heragli's language was scarcely what she had been led to expect from the Bandar's—oops!—from Echpo's description of him as a most gentlemanly felino-centauroid.

"Why, sputter dash censored!" rasped the alien. "I see two of 'em just behind you!"

"Oh, them?" said Tanni. "Never mind them. They're only a bear and a black panther."

"They're *what*?"

"They're . . . well . . . oh, never mind! Come on down."

Heragli descended, two meters of rippling muscle hot in the leaf-filtered sunlight. "Very well, very well," he grumbled. "But I don't trust 'em. Lick my weight in flaming wildcats, but these asterisk unmentionables wreck my nerves. Where's the snake?"

Echpo winced. "My dear fellow!" he protested delicately.

"All right, all right!" bawled the Rowra. "The herpetoid, then. Don't hold with these dashed euphemisms. Call an encarnadined spade a cursed spade is my way. Where is he?"

"We left him back at—"

"Should've knocked'm on the mucking head. Said so all along. Save all this deleted trouble."

Echpo flinched again. "The, ah, the Rowra is an old military felino-centauroid," he explained hastily. "Believes in curing shock with counter-shock. Isn't that right, Heragli?"

"What? What're you babbling about now? Oh . . . oh, yes. Your servant, ma'am," thundered the other. "Which bleeding way out, eh?"

"A rough exterior, dear lady," whispered Echpo in Tanni's ear, "but a heart of gold."

"That may be," answered the woman sharply, "but I'm going to have to ask him to moderate his voice and expurgate his language. What if the Hokas should hear him?"

"Blunderbore and killecrantz!" swore Heragli. "Let'm hear. I've had enough of this deifically anathematized tree climbing. Let'm show up once more and I'll gut 'em, I'll skin 'em, I'll—"

A chorus of falsetto wolfish howls interrupted him, and a second later the space around the tree was filled with leaping, yelling Hokas and the Rowra was up in the branches again.

"Come down, Striped Killer!" bawled Akela, bounding a good two meters up the trunk. "Come down ere I forget wolves cannot climb! I myself will tear thy heart out!"

"Sput! Meowr!" snarled Heragli, swiping a taloned paw at him. "Meeourl spss rowul rhnrrrr!"

"What's he saying?" demanded Tanni.

"Dear lady," replied Echpo with a shudder, "don't ask. General! General!—His old rank may snap him out of it—General, remember your duty!"

"LAME THIEF OF THE WAINGUNGA!" shouted Alex, bombarding him with fallen fruits.

Heragli closed his eyes and panted. "Oh, m'nerves!" he gasped above the roar of the Hokas. "All your fault, Echpo, you insisting on no sidearms. Of all the la-di-da conspir—"

"*General!*" cried the Chakban.

Tanni struggled around the Hokas and collared her son. "Alex," she said ominously, "I told you to keep them away."

"But they outvoted me, Mom," he answered. "They're the Free People, you know, and it's the full Pack—"

"FOR THE PACK, FOR THE FULL PACK, IT IS MET!" chorused the Hokas, leaping up and snapping at Heragli's tail.

Tanni put her hands over her ears and tried to think. It hurt her pride, but she sought desperately to imagine what Alex, Sr., would have done. Play along with them . . . use their own fantasy . . . yes and she had read the *Jungle Books* herself— Ah!

She snatched a nut from her boy just before he launched it and said sweetly: "Alex, dear, shouldn't the Pack be in bed now?"

"Huh, Mom?"

"Doesn't the Law of the Jungle say so? Ask Baloo."

"Indeed, Man-Cub," replied Baloo pontifically when Alex had repeated it, "the Law of the Jungle specifically states: 'And remember the night is for hunting, and forget not the day is for sleep.' Now that you remind me—thou remindest me, it is broad daylight and all the wolves ought to be in their lairs."

It took a little while to calm down the Hokas, but then they trotted obediently off into the forest. Tanni was a bit disconcerted to note that Baloo and Bagheera were still present. She racked her brains for something in the *Jungle Books* specifically dealing with the obligation of bears and black panthers also to go off and sleep in the daytime. Nothing, however, came to mind. And Heragli refused to climb down while—

Inspiration came. She turned to the last Hokas. "Aren't you thirsty?" she asked.

"What says thy mother, Little Frog?" demanded Bagheera, washing his nose with his hand and trying to purr.

"She asked if thou and Baloo were not thirsty," said Alex.

"Thirsty?" The two Hokas looked at each other. The extreme suggestibility of their race came into play. Two tongues reached out and licked two muzzles.

"Indeed, the Rains have been scant this year," agreed Bagheera.

"Perhaps I had better go shake the *mohwa* tree and check the petals that fall down," said Baloo.

"I hear," said the girl slyly, "that Hathi proclaimed the Water Truce last night."

"Oh . . . *ah?*" said Bagheera.

"And you know that according to the Law of the Jungle, that means all the animals must drink peaceably together," went on Tanni. "Tell them, Alex."

"Quite true," nodded Baloo sagely when the boy had translated. "Macmillan edition, 1933, page 68."

"So," said Tanni, springing her trap, "you'll have to take Shere Khan off and let him drink with you."

"*Wuh!*" said Baloo, sitting down on his haunches to consider the situation. "It is the Law," he decided at length.

"You can come down now," called Tanni to Heragli. "They won't hurt you."

"Blood and bones!" grumbled the Rowra, but descended and looked at the Hokas with a noticeable lack of enthusiasm. "Har d'ja do."

"Hello, Lame Thief," said Bagheera amiably.

"*Lame Thief?* Why—" Heragli began to roar, and Bagheera tried manfully to arch his back, which is not easy for a barrel-shaped Hoka.

"General! General!" interrupted Echpo. "It's the only way. Go off and have a drink with them, and as soon as you can, meet us here again."

"Oh, very well. Blank dash flaming etcetera." Heragli trotted off into the brush, accompanied by his foes. Their voices trailed back:

"Hast hunted recently, Striped Killer?"

"Eh? What? Hunted? Well, as a matter of fact, in England on Earth last month—the Quorn—Master of the Hunt told me—went to earth at—"

The jungle swallowed them up.

"And now, dear lady," said Echpo nervously, "I must presume still further upon your patience. Poor Seesis has been left unguarded all this time—"

"Oh, yes!" The woman's long slim legs broke into a trot, back toward the place where she had first met the herpetoid. Echpo lumbered beside her and Alex followed.

"Ah . . . it is a difficult situation," declared the Chakban. "I fear the concussion has made my valued friend Seesis, ah, distrust the General and myself. His closest comrades! Can you imagine? He has, I think, some strange delusion that we mean to harm him."

Tanni slowed down. She felt no great eagerness to confront a paranoid python.

"He won't get violent," reassured Echpo. "I just wanted to warn you to discount anything he may do. He might, for example, try to write messages . . . Ah, here we are!"

They looked around the trampled vegetation. "He must have slipped away," said Tanni. "But he can't have gone far."

"Oh, he can move rapidly when he chooses, gracious madam," said Echpo, rubbing his hands in an agitated fashion. "Normally, of course, he does not so choose. You see, his race places an almost fanatical emphasis on self-restraint. Dignity, honor, and the like . . . those are the important things. A code, dear lady, which"—Echpo's deep-set eyes took on an odd gleam—"renders them vulnerable to, er, manipulation by those alert enough to press the proper semantic keys. But one which also renders them quite unpredictable. We had better find him at once."

It was not a large area in which they stood, and it soon became apparent that they had not simply overlooked the presence of ten meters of snake-like alien. A shout from Alex brought them to a trail crushed into the soft green herbage, as if someone had dragged a barrel through it. "This," said the boy, "must be the road of Kaa."

"Excellent spotting, young man," said Echpo. "Let us follow it."

They went rapidly along the track for several minutes. Tanni brushed the tangled golden hair from her eyes and wished for a comb, breakfast, a hot bath and— She noticed that the trail suddenly bent northward and continued in a straight line, as if Kaa—Seesis, blast it!—had realized where he was and set off toward some definite goal.

Echpo stopped, frowning, his flat nostrils a-twitch. "Dear me," he murmured, "this is *most* distressing."

"Why—he's headed toward your ship, hasn't he?" asked Tanni. "He should be easy to find. Let's go!"

"Oh, no, no, no!" The Chakban shook his bat-eared head. "I wouldn't dream of letting you and your son—delightful boy, madam!—go any further. It is much too dangerous."

"Nonsense! There's nothing harmful here, and you said yourself he isn't violent."

"Please! Not another word!" The long hands waved her back. "No, dear lady, just return to the meeting place, if you will, and when Heragli gets there send him on to the ship. Meanwhile I will follow poor Seesis and, ah, do what I can."

Before Tanni could reply, Echpo had bounded off and the tall grasses hid him.

She stood for a moment, frowning. The Chakban was a curious and contradictory personality. Though his manners were impeccable, she had not felt herself warming to him. There was something, something almost . . . well, *Bandar-loggish* about him. *Ridiculous!* she told herself. *But why did he suddenly change his mind about having me along? Just because Seesis headed back toward the wrecked ship?*

"Shucks, Mom," pouted Alex, "everybody's gone. All the wolves are in bed—in their lairs, I mean, and Bagheera and Baloo gone off with Shere Khan, and the Bandar's gone to the Cold Lairs and we can't even watch Kaa fight him. Nobody lets me have any fun."

Decision came to Tanni. The demented Seesis might, after all, turn on Echpo. If she had any chance of preventing such a catastrophe, her duty was clear. In plain language, she felt an infernal curiosity. "Come along, Alex," she said.

They had not far to go. Breaking through a tall screen of pseudo-bamboo, they looked out on a meadow.

And in the center of that meadow rested a small, luxurious Starflash space rambler.

"Wait here, Alex," ordered Tanni. "If there seems to be any danger, run for help."

She crossed the ground to the open airlock. Strange, the ship was not even dented. Peering in, she saw the control room. No sign of Echpo or Seesis—maybe they were somewhere aft. She entered.

It struck her that the controls were in very good shape for a vessel that had landed hard enough to knock out its communication gear. On impulse, she went over to the visio and punched its buttons. The screen lit up . . . why, it was perfectly useable! She would call Mixumaxu and have a detachment of Hoka police flown here. The Private Eyes and Honest Cops could easily—

A thick, hairy arm shot past her and a long finger snapped the set off. Another arm like a great furry shackle pinned her into the chair she had taken.

"That," whispered Echpo, "was a mistake, dear lady."

For a second, instinctively and furiously, Tanni tried to break loose. A kitten might as well have tried to escape a gorilla. Echpo let her have it out while he closed the airlock by remote control. Then he eased his grip. She bounced from the chair. A hard hand grabbed her wrist and whirled her about.

"What is this?" she raged. "Let me *go!*" She kicked at Echpo's ankles. He slapped her so her head rang. Sobbing, she relaxed enough to stare at him through a blur of horror.

"I am afraid, dear Mrs. Jones, that you have penetrated our little deception," said the Chakban gently. "I had hoped we could abandon our ship here, since a description of it has unfortunately been broadcast on the subvisio. By posing as castaways, we could have used the transportation to Gelkar which you so graciously offered us, and hired another vessel there. But as it is—" He shrugged. "It seems best we stay with this one after all, using you, madam, as a hostage . . . much though it pains me, of course."

"You wouldn't dare!" gasped Tanni, unable to think of a more telling remark.

"Dare? Dear lady," said Echpo, smiling, "our poor friend Seesis is the Tertiary Receptacle of Wisdom of Sanussi. If we dared kidnap him, surely— Please hold still. It would deeply grieve me to have to bind you."

"Sanussi . . . I don't believe you," breathed the girl. "Why, you're unarmed and he must have twice your strength."

"Dear charmer," sighed Echpo, "how little you know of Sanussians. Their ethical code is *so* unreasonably strict. When Heragli and I entered Seesis' embassy office on Earth, all we had to do was threaten to fill an ancestral seltzer bottle we had previously . . . ah . . . borrowed, with soda pop. The dishonor would have compelled the next hundred generations of his family to spend an hour a day in ceremonial writhing and give up all public positions. We wrung his parole from him: he was not to speak to anyone or resist us with force until released."

"Not *speak* . . . oh, so that's why he was trying to write," said Tanni. A degree of steadiness was returning to her. She could not really believe this mincing dandy capable of harm. "And I suppose he slipped back here with some idea of calling our officials and showing them a written account of—"

"How quickly you grasp the facts, madam," bowed Echpo. "Naturally, I trailed him and, since he may not use his strength on me, dragged him into a stateroom aft and coiled him up. As long as Heragli and I abide by the Sanussian code—chiefly, to refrain from endangering others—he is bound by his promise. That is why we have no weapons; the General is so impulsive."

"But why have you kidnapped him?"

"Politics. A matter of pressure to get certain concessions from his planet. Don't trouble your pretty head about it, my lady. As soon as practical after we have reached our destination—surely not more than a year—you will be released with our heartfelt thanks for your invaluable assistance."

"But you don't need *me* for a hostage!" wailed Tanni. "You've got Seesis himself."

"Tut-tut. The Sanussian police are hot on our trail. Despite the size of interstellar space, they may quite possibly detect us and close in . . . after which, to wipe out the stain on *their* honor, they would cheerfully blow Seesis up with Heragli and myself. But their ethics will not permit them to harm an innocent bystander like you, so—" Echpo backed toward the airlock, half dragging the woman. His bulk filled the chamber, blocking off escape, as he opened the valves. "So, as soon as Heragli returns—and not finding me at the agreed rendezvous, he will surely come here—we depart."

His simian face broke into a grin as discordant noises floated nearer. "Why, here he is now. Heragli, dear friend, do hurry. We must leave this delightful planet immediately."

His voice carried to the Rowra, who had just emerged from the canebrake with Bagheera on one side and Baloo on the other. Staggering, Heragli sat down, licked one oversized paw, and began to wash his face. Peering past Echpo, Tanni saw that the General's swiping motions were rather unsteady.

"Heragli!" said the Chakban on a sharper note. "Pay attention!"

"Go sputz yourself," boomed the Rowra, and broke into song. "Oh, when I was twenty-one, when I was twenty-one, I never had lots of mvrouwing but I always had lots of fun. My basket days were over and my prowling days begun, on the very very rrnowing night when I was twenty-one—*Chorus!*" he roared, beating time with a wavering paw, and the two Hokas embraced him and chimed in: "*When we wash twenty-one—*"

"Heragli!" yelled Echpo. "What's wrong with you?"

Tanni could have told him. She realized suddenly, as she stood there with the Chakban's heavy grip on her wrist, that when she evoked thirst in Baloo and Bagheera, she had pointed them in one inevitable direction: the abandoned camp of the Black Tyrone. The phrase "take Shere Khan off and let him drink with you" could have only one meaning to a Hoka. Heragli, like many beings before him, had encountered the fiery Tokan liquor.

There are bigger, stronger, wiser races than the Hokas, but the Galaxy knows none with more capacity. Heragli was twice the size and eight times the weight of a Hoka, but his companions were just pleasantly high, while he was—no other word will do—potted. And Tanni was willing to bet that Baloo and Bagheera were each two bottles ahead of him.

The General rolled over on his back and waved his feet in the air. "Oh, that little ball of yarn—" he warbled.

"Heragli!" shrieked Echpo.

"Oh, those wild, wild kittens, those wild, wild kittens, they're making a wildcat of me!"

"*General!*"

"Old tomcats never die, they just fa-a-a-aade—huh? Whuzza matta wi' you, monkey?" demanded Heragli, still on his back, looking at the spaceship upside down from bloodshot eyes. "Stannin' onna head. Riddickerluss, ab-so-lute-ly . . . Oh, curse the city that stole muh Kitty, by dawn she'll— Le's havva nuther one, mnowrr, 'fore you leave me! Hell an' damnation," said Heragli, suddenly dropping from the peak of joyous camaraderie to the valley of bitter suspicion, "dirty work inna catagon. Passed over f' promotion, twishe. Classmate, too . . . Is this a ray gun that I see b'fore me, the handle toward muh hand? Come, lemme clutch thee. . . . Monkeys an' snakes. Gallopin' horrors, I call 'em. Never trus' a primate—" and he faded off into mutterings.

"General!" called Echpo, sternly. "Pull yourself together and come aboard. We're leaving."

"Huh? Awri', awri', awri'—" said Heragli in a bleared tone. He lurched to all four feet, focused with some effort on the ship, and wobbled in its general direction.

"Mom!" cried a boyish voice, and Alex broke into the meadow. "What's going on?" He spotted Tanni with Echpo's hand clutching her. "What're you doing to my mother?"

"Heragli!" yelped Echpo. "Stop that brat!"

The Rowra blinked. Whether he would have obeyed if he had been sober, or if he had not been brooding about other races and the general unfairness of life, is an open question. He was not a bad felino-centauroid at heart. But as it was, he saw Alex running toward the ship, growled the one word "*Primate!*" to himself, and crouched for a leap.

His first mistake had been getting drunk. His second was to ignore, or be unaware of, three facts. These were, in order:

1) A Hoka, though not warlike, enjoys a roughhouse.

2) A Hoka's tubby appearance is most deceptive; he is, for instance, more than a match for any human.

3) Baloo and Bagheera did not think Shere Khan should be allowed to harm the Man-Cub.

Heragli leaped. Baloo met him in mid-air, head to head. There was a loud, hollow *thonk*, and Heragli fell into a sitting position with a dazed look on his face while Baloo did a reeling sort of off-to-Buffalo. At that moment, Bagheera entered the wars. He would have been more effective had he not religiously adhered to the principle of fighting like a black panther, scrambling onto the Rowra's back, scratching and biting.

"Ouch!" howled Heragli, regaining full consciousness. "What the sputz? Get the snrrowl off me! Leggo, you illegitimate forsaken object of an origin which the compilers of Leviticus would not have approved! Wrowrrl!" And he made frantic efforts to reach over his shoulder.

"Striped Killer!" squeaked Bagheera joyously. "Hunter of helpless frogs! Lame Thief of the Waingunga! Take that! And that!"

"What're you talking about? Never ate a frog in m' life. Unhand me—gug!" Bagheera had wrapped both sturdy arms around Heragli's neck and started throttling him.

At the same time Baloo recovered sufficiently to stage a frontal attack. Fortunately, being in the role of a bear, he could fight like a bear, which is to say, very much like a Hoka. Accordingly, he landed a stiff one-two on Heragli's nose and then, as the Rowra reared up, wheezing, he fell into a clinch that made his enemy's ribs creak. Breaking cleanly, he landed a couple of hard punches in the midriff of

Heragli's torso, chopped him over the heart, sank his teeth into the right foreleg, was lifted off his feet by an anguished jerk, used the opportunity to deliver a double kick to the chin while flurrying a series of blows, and generally made himself useful.

"Run, Alex!" cried Tanni.

The boy paused, uncertain, as Rowra and Hokas tore up the sod a meter from him.

"Run! Do what Mother tells you! Get help!"

Reluctantly, Alex turned and sped for the woods. Tanni felt Echpo's grasp shift as he moved behind her. When he pulled a Holman raythrower from beneath his tunic, the blood seemed to drain out of her heart.

"Believe me, dear lady, I deplore this," said the Chakban. "I had hoped to keep my weapon unknown and untouched. But we cannot risk your son's warning the authorities too soon, can we? And then there are those Hokas." He pinned her against the wall and sighted on Alex. "You *do* understand my position, don't you?" he asked anxiously.

Struggling and screaming, Tanni clawed for his eyes. The brow ridges defeated her. She saw the gun muzzle steady—

—and there was a shock that threw her from Echpo's grip and out onto the ground.

Dazed, she scrambled to her feet with a wild notion of throwing herself in the path of the beam . . . But where *was* Echpo?

The airlock seemed to hold nothing but coil upon coil of Seesis. Only gradually, as her vision cleared, did Tanni make out a contorted face among those cable-thick bights. The Chakban was scarcely able to breathe, let alone move.

"Sssssso!" Seesis adjusted his pince-nez and regarded his prisoner censoriously. "So you lied to me. You were prepared to commit violence after all. I am shocked and grieved. I thought you shared my abhorrence of bloodshed. I see that you must be gently but firmly educated until you understand the error of your ways and repent and enter the gentle brotherhood of beings. Lie still, now, or I will break your back."

"I—" gasped Echpo. "I . . . had . . . my duty—"

"And I," answered Seesis, swaying above him, "have my honor."

Alex fell into his mother's arms. She was not too full of thanksgiving to pick up the fallen gun. Across the meadow, Baloo and Bagheera stood triumphant over a semi-conscious Heragli and beamed at their snaky ally.

The Cold Lairs were taken. The Man-Cub had been rescued from Bandar-log and Lame Thief. Kaa's Hunting was finished.

II.
The Napoleon Crime

THE NAPOLEON CRIME

Be it understood at the outset, the disaster was in no way the fault of Tanni Hostrup Jones. Afterward she blamed herself bitterly, but most unfairly. She was overburdened with other matters, hence unable to concentrate on this one. She had no reason whatsoever to suspect evil of Leopold Ormen; after all, he was a Dane like herself, as well as being a famous journalist. Furthermore, while Tanni was chaste, she was a full-blooded woman, her husband had been gone for days and might not return for weeks, and Ormen had a great deal of masculine charm.

Having arrived on Toka by private spacecraft and settled into the Mixumaxu Hilton, he made an appointment to see her and at the time agreed on arrived at the plenipotentiary's residence. The day was beautiful and the walk through the quaint streets a delight. Native Hokas swarmed about, their exuberance often becoming deference when they saw the human. He smiled benignly and patted an occasional cub on the head. The adults looked just as cuddly: rather like bipedal, meter-tall teddy bears with golden fur and stubby hands, attired in a wild variety of costumes, everything from a barbarian's leather and iron to the elegant gray doublet and hose of his little companion, as well as Roman, Mandarin, cowboy, and other garb. Yet with few exceptions the squeaky voices chattered in English.

Thus, when he reached his destination, Ormen was not unduly surprised to be greeted at the door by a Hoka wearing coarse medieval-like clothes, hobnailed boots, a yellow hood, and a long white false beard tucked into a broad belt from which hung a geologist's hammer, a coil of rope, and a lantern. "Hello," the man said, and gave his name. "Mrs. Jones is expecting me."

The Hoka bowed, careful to do so in a fashion that showed he was not accustomed to bowing. "Gimli the dwarf, at your service," he replied, as gruffly as his larynx allowed. "Welcome to Rivendell. The Lady Galadriel did indeed make known to me that— Ah, ha! Hold!" Both his hands shot out and seized Ormen's left.

"What off Earth?" exclaimed the journalist.

"Begging your pardon, but that ring you're wearing. You'll have to check it before you go in."

"Why?" Ormen stared down at the gold band and its synthetic diamond. "It's only an ornament."

"I doubt not your faith, good sir," declared Gimli, "but you may conceivably have been tricked. This *could* be the One Ring under a false seeming—you not even invisible. Can't be too careful in these darkling times, right? You'll get it back when you leave."

Ormen tried to pull free, but the native was too strong. Suppressing an oath, the visitor yielded. Gimli turned the ring over to an elderly Hoka who had shown up, also whitebearded but attired in a blue robe and pointed hat and bearing a staff. Thereafter the self-styled dwarf ceremoniously conducted Ormen through the door. The entry-room beyond had been hung with tapestries that appeared to have been very hastily woven; colored tissue glued on the windowpanes imitated stained glass, while candlelight relieved the dimness. Elsewhere the house remained a normal Terrestrial-type place, divided between living quarters and offices.

Tanni Jones received the newcomer graciously in her parlor. She was tall, blond, and comely, as was he, and eager to see anybody from the home planet. "Please sit down, Mr. Ormen," she invited. "Would you care for coffee, tea, or perhaps something alcoholic?"

"Well, I've heard about the liquor they make here, and confess to being curious," he said.

She shuddered a bit. "I don't recommend you investigate. What about a Scotch and soda?" When he accepted, she rang for a servant, who appeared with churchwarden pipe in hand and bare feet on which the hair had been combed upward. "We'll have the happy hour usual, Gamgee," she said. "*Scotch* Scotch, mind you."

The humans began to talk in earnest. "What's happening?" Ormen inquired. "I mean, well, isn't your staff acting rather oddly?"

Tanni sighed. "They've discovered *The Lord of the Rings*. I can only hope they get over it before the fashion spreads further. Not that it would upset Alex—my husband, that is, the plenipotentiary—to be hailed as the rightful King when he returns. He's used to that sort of thing, after all our years in this post. But meanwhile—oh, for example, we get visitors from other worlds, nonhumans, and many of them are important—officials of the League, representatives of firms whose cooperation we need to modernize Toka, and so on." She shuddered again. "I can just imagine the Hokas deciding some such party must be orcs or trolls or Ring-Wraiths."

"I sympathize. You inhabit a powder keg, don't you?"

"M-m, not really. The Hokas do take on any role that strikes their fancy, and act it out—live it—with an uncompromising literal-mindedness. But they're not insane. They've never yet gotten violent, for instance; and they continue to work, meet their responsibilities, even if it is in some fantasy style. In fact," said Tanni anxiously, "their reputation for craziness is quite undeserved. It's going to handicap my husband on his mission. I suppose you know he's gone to Earth to negotiate an upgrading in status for Toka. If he doesn't succeed in convincing the authorities our wards are ready for that, we may never in our lifetimes see them become full members of the Interbeing League; and that is our dearest dream."

Leopold Ormen nodded. "I do know all this, Mrs. Jones, and I believe I can help." He leaned forward, though he resisted the temptation to stroke her hand. "Not that I'm an altruist. I have my own living to make, and I think there's a tremendous documentary to be done about this planet. But if it conveys the truth, in depth, to civilized viewers throughout the galaxy—yes, and readers too, because I'd also like to write a book—public opinion should change. Wouldn't that be good for your cause?"

Tanni glowed. "It certainly would!"

Ormen leaned back. She was hooked, he knew; now he must play his line so carefully that she remained unaware of the fact. "I can't do it unless I have complete freedom," he stated. "I realize your husband's duty requires him to impose various restrictions on outsiders, who might otherwise cause terrible trouble. But I hope you—in his absence, you are the acting plenipotentiary, aren't you?—I hope you'll authorize me to go anywhere, see anything and anybody, for as long as I'll need to get the whole story. I warn you, that may take quite a while, and I'll be setting my aircar down in places where the Hokas aren't accustomed to such a sight."

As said, Tanni cannot be blamed. She did not rush into her decision. In the course of the following week, she had several meetings with him, including a couple of dinners where he was a fascinating, impeccably courteous guest. She inquired among the local folk, who all spoke well of him. She studied recordings of his previous work from the data file, and found it excellent. When at last she did give him *carte blanche,* she expected to keep track of what he was doing, and call a halt if a blunder seemed imminent. Besides, Alex should be back presently, to apply the sixth sense he had perforce developed for problems abrew.

That none of these reasonable considerations worked out was simply in the nature of Hoka things.

First she was kept busy distracting the natives, lest a Tolkien craze sweep through thousands of them. That was less difficult than it might have been elsewhere on the globe. Most of the human-derived societies were still rather isolated and naive. This was a result of policy on Alex's part. Not only did he fear the unforeseeable consequences of cross-fertilization—suppose, for example, that the Vikings came into close contact with the Bedouins—but a set of ongoing, albeit uncontrolled psychohistorical experiments gave him hints about what was best for the race as a whole. Nevertheless, it did leave those cultures vulnerable to any new influence that happened by.

As the seat of the plenipotentiary and therefore, in effect, the capital city of the planet, Mixumaxu was cosmopolitan. Its residents and those of its hinterland were, so to speak, immunized. This did not mean that any individual stuck to any given role throughout his life. On the contrary, he was prone to overnight changes. But by the same token, these made no fundamental difference to him; and therefore the Jones household continued to function well in a bewildering succession of guises.

Soon after she had headed off the War of the Rings, Tanni got caught up in the *Jungle Books* affair. Since that involved beings of status, and a scandal which must not become common knowledge lest the tranquility of the galaxy be disturbed, the sequel kept her occupied for weeks. She handled her end of the business with a competence which caused the Grand Theocrat of Sanussi, in an elaborate honors ceremony years later, to award her a cast-off skin of his.

Meanwhile a cruel disappointment arrived, in the form of a letter from Alex. Complications had developed; the delegation from Kratch was, for some reason known only to their nasty little selves, using every parliamentary trick to delay the upgrading of Toka; he must stay and fight the matter through to a successful conclusion; he didn't know how long it would take; he missed her immeasurably, and enclosed one of his poems to prove it.

Tanni refrained from weeping in front of their children. She did utter a few swear words. Afterward she plunged into work. Suddenly there seemed to be a great deal of it. Information-gathering facilities were stretched thin at best, so that she was seldom fully apprised of events on other continents; but such reports as came in were increasingly ominous. They told of unrest, strange new ideas, revolutionary changes—

No wonder that she lacked time to follow what Leopold Ormen was about. Events moved far too fast. All at once she saw catastrophe looming before her. The single thing she could think to do was send a frantic, although enciphered, message to her husband; and indeed, this was the single thing she could have done.

An airbus took Alexander Jones from League headquarters in New Zealand to the spaceport on Campbell Island. There he walked past sleek, gleaming starships to the far end of the field, where sat a craft larger than most, but battered and corrosion-pocked. Its bulbous lines proclaimed it to be of nonhuman manufacture, and its registration emblem to be a tramp freighter. Beneath the name etched on the bows was a translation into the English of the spaceways: *Thousand-Year Bird*. Alex mounted the movable ramp that led to the main personnel lock and pressed the buzzer button.

A gentle, if mechanical voice sounded from the speaker grille: "Is someone present? The valve isn't secured. Come in, do, and make yourself at home."

Alex pushed on the metal. Nothing happened. "Brob, it's me, Alexander Jones," he said into the intercom. "It won't open. The valve won't, I mean."

"Oh, dear, I *am* sorry. I forgot I had left it on manual. One moment, please. I beg your pardon for the inconvenience."

Something like a minor earthquake shivered through hull and ramp. The valve swung aside, revealing an oversized airlock chamber and the being who had the strength to move so ponderous an object. "How pleasant to see you again, dear fellow," said the transponder hanging from his neck. Meanwhile his real voice, which the device rendered into frequencies a human could hear, vibrated subsonically out of his feet and up into the man's bones. "Welcome to my humble vessel. Come in, let me make you a cup of tea, tell me how I may serve you."

The 'sponder likewise converted Alex's tones into impulses Brob sensed through his skin. On their airless world, his species had never developed ears. "I've got a hell of a request to make, and you don't really know me well enough, but I'm desperate and you seem to be my only possible help."

Eyes that were soft and brown, despite their lack of moisture, looked thirty centimeters downward to Alex's lanky height. "Sir, it has been a pleasure and an enlightenment making your acquaintance. Furthermore, I feel certain that your purpose is not selfish, but for some public good. If so, whatever small assistance I can perhaps render will earn me merit, which I sorely need. Therefore it shall be I who enter into your debt. Now do come in and tell me about this."

Brob led the way, moving gracefully despite his bulk; but then, Earth gravity was a mere one-third of his planet's. For that matter, had he been short like a Hoka, he would have been considered even more cute. He too possessed a pair of arms, his thicker than a gorilla's and terminating in enormous four-fingered hands, and a pair of stout legs, ending in feet that were a meter long and half as wide; their soles enclosed the tympani with which his race listened and spoke. The torso was so rotund as to be almost globular. The head was equally round; though it naturally lacked a nose, it had a blunt snout whose lipless mouth was shaped into a permanent smile. All in all, he suggested a harp seal puppy. Baby-blue fur covered him, save on the hands and feet; there it was white, which gave him an appearance of wearing mittens and booties. His actual clothing consisted of the 'sponder and a belt with pockets full of assorted tools.

The saloon of the ship whose owner, captain, and crew he was seemed less alien than might have been expected, considering how unlike Earth was the planet which humans called Brobdingnag. That world had begun as a body more massive than Jupiter. A nearby supernova had blown away its gas and deposited vast quantities of heavy elements over the solidifying core. They included radioactives. Somehow life had evolved, making use of this source of energy rather than the feeble red sun. Plants concentrated isotopes which animals then ate. Brob, as Alex dubbed him for lack of ability to pronounce his real name, did not live by oxidizing organic materials like most creatures in known space, but by fissioning nuclei. His physical strength was corresponding.

The metabolism posed no hazard to anyone else. The fission process worked at a far lower level than in a powerplant, and whatever radiation it gave off was absorbed by the dense tissues around the "stomach." Brobdingnagians traveling abroad needed merely take certain precautions in disposal of their body wastes. Regardless, many beings feared and shunned them. Having delivered a cargo to Earth, Brob found himself unable to get another, and the waiting time while his broker searched for one grew lonely as well as long. Chancing to meet Alex in a Christchurch pub, where he had gone in hopes that somebody would talk to him, he was pathetically grateful when the man not only did, but pursued the acquaintance afterward.

For his part, Alex enjoyed Brob's tales of distant worlds. Sometimes he grew bored, because the alien had fallen in love with Japanese culture and would drone on for hours about calligraphy, flower arranging, and other such arts. Yet even that was better than sitting around yearning for Tanni and his children, cursing the abominable Kratch, and wondering how many more weeks it would take to complete his business.

Brob did his best to bow as he gestured his visitor to sit down on a tatami mat, politely ignoring the shoes that the human had not removed. He left Alex to meditate upon a lily and a stone, placed in a bowl of water beneath a scroll depicting Mount Fuji, while he occupied himself preparing for a tea ceremony. This was necessarily modified, since as he sipped the aqueous substance, it turned to steam. Serenely, he contemplated the white clouds swirling out of his mouth, before at last he inquired what he could do for his friend.

Alex had learned not to be boorishly direct in Brob's presence. "Let me review the situation, though you do know why I'm stuck here on Earth," he said. "The Chief Cultural Commissioner had approved Toka's advancement, the vote looked like being a pure formality, and then the Kratch delegation objected. They couldn't just be voted down, because they levelled charges of misgovernment. Nothing as simple as tyranny or corruption. I could easily have disproved that. No, they claim my entire policy has been wrong and is bound to cause disaster."

Brob nodded gravely. "You have explained to me," he replied; the teapot and cups trembled. "I have admired your restraint in not dwelling upon it in conversation."

Alex shrugged. "What use would that be? The fact is, I've often had to do things on Toka that, well, played kind of fast and loose with the letter of the law. I had no choice. The Hokas are like that. You know; I've told you a bundle about them. Ordinarily no one sees anything wrong in a plenipotentiary exercising broad discretion. After all, every planet is unique. Nothing really counts except results, and I pride myself that mine have been good. But how can I argue against the claim that I've created the *potential* for calamity?"

"I should think a look at your record, and a modicum of common sense, would suffice to make the legislators decide in your favor."

"Oh, yes. But you see, after they'd raised this issue, the Kratch promptly raised a host of others, and got mine postponed. It's blatant obstruction on their part. Most of the delegates recognize that and are as disgusted as I am. But the Constitution forces them to go through the motions—and forces me to sit idle, waiting for whatever instant it will be that the case of Toka is opened to debate.

"It's enough to make a paranoid out of a saint," Alex sighed. "One set of villains after another, year after year—the Slissii, the Pornians, the Sarennians, the Worbenites, the Chakbans—my wife wrote me about those—conspiring and conniving. I've really begun to wonder if some evil masterminds aren't at work behind the scenes, and I wouldn't be surprised but what they're Kratch." He sighed again. "It's either believe that, or else believe we're only characters in a series of stories being written by a couple of hacks who need the money."

"It may be sheer accident," Brob suggested. "Mortal fallibility. There is a great deal of wisdom in the universe; unfortunately, it is divided up among individuals."

Alex ran a hand through his already rumpled brown hair. His snub-nosed countenance grew stark. "Okay," he said, "what I've come to you about is a . . . a sort of dreadful climax. I've received a letter from my wife and—Toka really is about to explode. I've got to get back at once and see if I can do anything to save the situation."

"Well, yes, I should imagine that that would be indicated," Brob murmured and rumbled. "Can you describe the problem a little more fully?"

Alex pulled the letter out of his tunic. "She sent it by message torpedo; it's that urgent. It's coded, too, but by now the words are burned into my brain. Let me give you a sample." He read aloud:

" 'Somehow, our policy of keeping the different Hoka societies relatively isolated has broken down. Suddenly, they had been introduced to concepts of each other. And this hasn't been in the casual way of individuals traveling around, like that sweet little Viking you met when you'd been press-ganged onto that eighteenth-century British frigate. We've always allowed for that degree of contact. No, what's happened this time must have been deliberately caused. Besides, ideas totally new to the planet, dangerous ideas, have been appearing. I've had agents in the field collecting books, video tapes—but the damage has already been done, and the Hokas themselves don't know or care how it happened. A fire like that is fatally easy to start; then it spreads of itself.

" 'For instance, right on the plains of this continent, the Wild West has been introduced to the biography of Genghis Khan. Of course the cowboys promptly went overboard for being ferocious Mongols—' Er, Tanni ordinarily handles her figures of speech better than that; but anyway— 'So far it's been harmless. The Mongols ride around to every cow town demanding it surrender to the will of the Kha Khan, and explaining that they don't stutter but "Kha Khan" really is his title. The town is always happy to yield, because they make this the occasion of a drunken party. As one mayor said to me when I flew there to question him, it's better to bottle a place than sack it. But the potential is terrifying, because the cowboys out Montana way have decided they're European knights who must resist any heathen who invade their country.

" 'And the Russian Hokas are no longer content to sit around strumming balalaikas and singing sad songs; they have elected a Czar and babble about the Third Rome. Over in the United States, Abolitionists are feverishly looking for slaves to set free—and beginning to get volunteer Uncle Tom types—while the Virginia Gentlemen talk of secession. In the South Sea, a King Kamehameha has appeared, and war clubs are replacing ukuleles, and I'm afraid they'll see use. It goes on and on around the globe, this sort of dangerous nonsense.

" 'What frightens me worst, and causes me to write this, is Napoleon.' " Alex cleared his throat. "You realize, Brob, that a Hoka can be perfectly sane and still claim he is Napoleon. Um-m. . . . 'He has displaced the King of France. He is organizing and equipping his Grand Army. Even after my experience of Hoka energy and enthusiasm, I am surprised at how fast the workshops in their country are producing weapons.

" 'Inevitably, those eighteenth-century British have gotten alarmed and are arming too. Their island is right across a strait from that continent, you remember. I might have been able to calm them down, except that lengthy biographies of humans who lived in that period have been circulating to inflame their imaginations. I was in London, trying to argue them out of it, and threatening to expose them to the ridicule of the galaxy. I couldn't think what else to do. The Hoka who calls himself the Duke of Wellington drew himself up to his full height, fixed me with a steel eye, and barked, "Publish and be damned!"

" 'Oh, darling, I'm afraid! I think these playacting prophecies of wars to come will soon fulfill themselves. And once Hokas actually start getting maimed and killed—well, I believe you'll agree that they'll go berserk, as bad as ever our species was in the past, and the whole planet will be drenched in blood.

" 'Alex, could you possibly return?' "

The man's voice broke. He stuffed the letter back into his pocket and dabbed at his eyes. "You see I've got to go," he said.

"Do you expect that you can accomplish anything?" Brob asked, as softly as he was able.

Alex gulped. "I've got to try."

"But you are compelled to remain here on Earth, waiting for the unpredictable moment at which you will be called upon to justify your actions as plenipotentiary and urge the upgrading of your wards."

"That's no good if meanwhile everything else I'm responsible for goes down the drain. In fact, a horror like that would throw the whole system of guidance for backward worlds into question. It could open the way for old-fashioned imperialism and exploitation of them."

"If you departed for Toka," Brob said, "the Kratch would doubtless seize that opportunity to bring up the matter of your stewardship—when you are not present to defend yourself—and win custody of the planet for one of their own, who could then work toward the end of discrediting the present protective laws, as you suggest." He made a sign. "If this hypothesis maligns the motives of the Kratch, I apologize and abase myself."

"You needn't, I'm sure." Alex leaned forward. His index finger prodded Brob's mountainous chest. "I've been collecting information about them. Their government is totalitarian, and has expansionist ambitions. It's been engaged in all sorts of shenanigans—which have been hushed up by nice-nelly types in the League who hope that if you ignore a villain he'll go away. This whole thing on Toka can't be simple coincidence. It's too well orchestrated. The likelihood of war arises precisely when I can't be on hand— Do you see?"

"What then do you propose?" asked Brob, calm as ever.

"Why, this," Alex said. "Look. Toka's a backwater. No passenger liners call there. If I left on my official ship, it would be known; I need clearance for departure, and the Kratch must have somebody keeping watch on this port. They'd immediately move to get their accusations onto the floor, and probably have their agents do their best to hasten the debacle on Toka. But if they don't *know* I've gone—if they assume I'm hanging around waiting and drinking too much as I have been— they'll let matters continue to ripen while they continue to stall. And maybe I can do something about the whole miserable affair. Do you see?"

Brob nodded. "I believe I do," he answered. "You wish me to furnish clandestine transportation."

"I don't know who else can," Alex pleaded. "As for payment, well, I have discretionary funds in my exchequer, and if I can get this mess straightened out—"

Brob swept an arm in a grand gesture which smashed the tea table. "Oh, dear," he murmured— and then, almost briskly: "Say no more. We need not discuss crass cash. I will tell my broker that I have lost patience and am departing empty. Your task will be to smuggle yourself and your rations aboard. Do you not prefer ham sandwiches?"

* * *

Despite its down-at-heels appearance, the *Thousand-Year Bird* was a speedster, power-plant equal to a dreadnaught's and superlight drive as finely tuned as an express courier's. It made the passage from Sol to Brackney's Star in scarcely more than a week. Alex supposed that Brobdingnagians had an innate talent for that kind of engineering; or maybe it was just that they could work on a nuclear reactor as casually as a human could tinker with an aircar engine, and thus acquired a knack for it.

Quite aside from the crisis, Alex had reason to be glad of such a high pseudovelocity. It wasn't so much that Brob, profusely apologizing, kept the artificial gravity at that of his home world. His health required a spell of this, in between his long stay on Earth and his prospective stay on Toka. Given a daily dose of baryol, Alex could tolerate the condition for a while, though soon his lean frame grew stiff and sore under its weight of 240 kilos and he spent most of the time stretched out on an enormous bunk. The real trouble was that Brob, having little else to do under way, spent most of same time keeping him company and trying to cheer him up; and Brob's bedside manner left something to be desired.

The alien's intentions were of the kindliest. His race had no natural enemies even on its own planet; if he chose, he could have pulled apart the collapsed metal armor of a warcraft, rather like a man ripping a newsfax sheet in half. Hence he had no reason not to be full of love for all life forms, and—while he knew from experience that it was not always true—his tendency was to assume that all of them felt likewise.

After a few sermons on the moral necessity of giving the Kratch the benefit of the doubt, since they were probably only misguided, Alex lost his temper. "You'll find out different when they bring an end to a hundred years of peace!" he yelled. "Let me alone about it, will you?"

An apologetic quiver went through the hull. "Forgive me," Brob said. "I am sorry. I didn't mean to raise thoughts you must find painful. Shall we discuss flower arrangements?"

"Oh, no, not that again! Tell me about some more of your adventures."

The 'sponder burbled, which perhaps corresponded to a sigh. "Actually, I have had few. For the most part I have simply plodded among the stars, returning home to my little wife and our young ones, where we cultivate our garden and engage in various activities for civic betterment. Of course, I have seen remarkable sights on my travels, but you don't appreciate how outstanding among them are those of Earth.

Why, in Kyoto I found a garden which absolutely inspired me. I am certain my wife will agree that we must remodel ours along similar lines. And an arrangement of our very own glowbranch, ion weed, and lightning blossoms would—" Brob was off afresh on his favorite subject.

Alex composed his soul in patience. The Hokas had given him plenty of practice at that.

The ship set down on Mixumaxu spaceport, Brob turned off the interior fields, and suddenly Alex was under blessed Terrestrial-like weight again. Whooping, he sprang from his bunk, landed on the deck, and collapsed as if his legs had turned to boiled spaghetti.

"Dear me," said his companion. "Your system must be more exhausted than we realized. How I regret the necessity I was under. Let me offer you assistance." Reaching down, he took a fold of the man's tunic between thumb and forefinger, lifted him daintily, and bore him off to the airlock, not noticing that Alex's feet dangled several centimeters in the air.

After taking parking orbit around the planet, he had radioed for permission to land. He had mentioned that the plenipotentiary was aboard, but forgotten to say anything about himself; and nobody on Toka had heard about his race, whose trade lanes did not bring them into this sector. Thus the ground crew who had brought the ramp, and Tanni who had sped from her home, were treated to the sight of their man feebly asprawl in the grip of a leering, blue-furred ogre.

A native security guard whipped out a pistol. "Hold still, sir!" he squeaked. "I'll kill that monster for you."

"No, no, don't shoot," Alex managed to croak.

"Why not?"

"Well, in the first place," said Alex, making his tone as reasonable as possible under the circumstances, "he wouldn't notice. But mainly, he's a good person, and—and— Hi, there, honey."

The ramp, which had not been constructed for the likes of Brob, shivered and buckled as he descended, but somehow he made it safely. Meanwhile Alex thought the poison must have spread far and deep, if a Hoka—in sophisticated Mixumaxu, at that—was so quick to resort to a lethal weapon.

Tanni's passionate embrace proved remarkably restorative. He wished they could go home, just the two of them, at once, before the children got back from school. However, politeness required that they invite Brob to come along, and when they were at the house, Alex's fears resurged and he demanded an account of the latest developments.

Woe clouded Tanni's loveliness. "Worse every day," she answered. "Especially in Europe—our Europe, I mean," she added to Brob, "though don't confuse it with that Europe that the ex-cowboys in what used to be Montana have— Never mind." She drew breath and started over:

"Napoleon's filled the French Hokas with dreams of *la gloire*, and the German Hokas are flocking to become his grenadiers—except in Prussia, where I've heard about a General Blücher—and three days ago, the Grand Army invaded Spain. You see, Napoleon wants to give the Spanish throne to his cousin Claud. That's caused the British Hokas—the British circa 1800 A.D., that is—thank God, so far the Victorian British on their own island have kept their senses, maybe because of Sherlock Holmes—anyway, yesterday they declared war, and are raising a fleet and an army of their own for a Peninsular campaign. And we won't even be able to handle the matter discreetly. I got hold of Leopold Ormen by phone and begged him to clear his stories with me, but he refused—insisted on his right of a free press, and in such a gloating way, too. . . . I'd taken him for a nice man, but—" Her voice broke. She huddled down in her chair and covered her face.

"Leopold Ormen? The journalist?" inquired Alex. "What's this?"

Tanni explained, adding that the man had since gone elsewhere, quite out of contact.

Alex cursed. "As if we didn't have troubles enough!" Suspicion struck fangs into his spirit. "Could his presence here be simple coincidence? I wonder. I wonder very much."

"Do you imply that Mr. Ormen may have stirred up this imbroglio?" asked Brob, appalled. "If so, and if you are correct, I fear he is no gentlebeing."

Alex sprang from his seat and paced. "Well, he can scarcely have accomplished everything alone," he thought aloud. "But he can sure have helped a lot to get it started, flitting freely around with the prestige of being a human, and that glib manner I recall from his broadcasts. . . . Don't cry, darling."

"I shan't," Brob said. "My species does not produce tears. However, I am deeply moved by your expression of affection."

Tanni had not begun sobbing. That was not her way. Grimly, she raised her glance and said, "Okay, he tricked me. At least, we've sufficient grounds for suspicion to order his arrest. Though he has his own flyer and could be anywhere on the planet."

Alex continued to prowl the carpet. "I doubt that that would be any use at this stage," he responded. "Arresting him, I mean. Unless we had absolute proof that he was engaged in subversion, which we don't, we'd lay ourselves open to countercharges of suppression. Besides, our first duty is not to save our reputations, but to prevent bloodshed."

He struck fist in palm, again and again. "How *could* matters have gotten so out of hand, so fast?" he wondered. "Even for Hokas, this is extreme, and it's happened damn near overnight. Around the globe, too, you tell me; the Napoleon business is just the most immediate danger. Somebody, some group, must be at work, propagandizing, offering evil advice. They wouldn't have to be humans, either. Hokas would be ready to believe whatever they heard from members of any technologically advanced society. In fact, humans have gotten to be rather old hat. Somebody different, exotic, would have more glamour, and find it easier to mislead them."

"Yes, I've thought along the same lines, dear," Tanni said. "Naturally, I forbade the French to mobilize, but the only reply I got was something about the Old Guard dies, it does not surrender. The British—well, they ignored my countermanding of their declaration of war, but I don't think they have been directly subverted. They're simply reacting as one would expect them to."

Alex nodded. "That sounds likely. The enemy can't have agents everywhere. That'd be too conspicuous, and give too many chances for something to go wrong. A few operatives, in key areas, are better."

He stopped in midstride, tugged his chin, rumpled his hair, and decided: "Britain is the place to start, then. I'm off to see what I can do. After all, I am their plenipotentiary, whom they've known for years, and if I appear in person, they'll at least listen to me."

"Shall I accompany you?" offered Brob. "On Toka I am, if not glamorous, surely exotic. Thus my presence may lend weight."

"It will that!" Alex agreed. He supposed his aircar could lift the other being.

Numerous Georgian houses graced the city renamed London. Though the Hokas could not afford to replace every older building at once, they had decorated many a wall with fake pilasters, put dummy dormers onto round roofs, and cut fanlights into doors. Tophatted, tailcoated Regency bucks swaggered through the streets, escorting ladies in muslin; seeing Alex and Brob, such males would raise their quizzing glasses for a closer look. Inspired by Hogarth, the commoners who swarmed about were more vocal at sight of the newcomers. Luckily, the dinosaurian animals hitched to wagons and carriages were not as excitable as Terrestrial horses. In general, this place was more safe and sanitary than its model had been; Alex had managed to bring that about in every society that his wards adopted.

Thus far. Today he saw a high proportion of redcoated soldiers who shouldered muskets with bayonets attached. He overheard a plaintive voice through a tavern window: "Please, matey, do resist us like a good lad. 'Ow can we be a proper press gang h'if h'everybody *volunteers?*"

Proceeding afoot, since Brob would have broken the axles of any local vehicle, Alex and his companion reached Whitehall. There a guard of Royal Marines saluted and led them to the First Lord of the Admiralty. The man had called ahead for this appointment; even the most archaic-minded Hokas maintained essential modern equipment in their more important offices, although in the present case the visiphone was disguised as a Chippendale cabinet. The native behind the desk rose. He had attired his portly form in brown smallclothes and set a wig on his head. It didn't fit well, and rather distracted from the fine old-world courtesy of his bow, by slipping down over his muzzle.

"A pleasure to meet you again, my dear fellow, 'pon my word it is," he said in calm, clipped accents while he readjusted the wig. "And to make your acquaintance, sir," he added to Brob, "as I trust I shall have the honor of doing. Be seated and take refreshment." He tinkled a bell. The staff were prepared, for a liveried servant entered immediately, bearing a tray with three glasses and a dusty bottle. "Fine port, this, if I do say so myself." Indignantly: "To think that Boney would cut us off from the source of supply! Infernal bounder, eh, what? Well, damme, he'll whistle a different tune, and out of a dry throat, when we've put him on St. Helena."

Alex settled down and took a cautious sip from his goblet. The drink was the same fiery distillation that was known as claret, sherry, brandy, rum, whisky, or whatever else a role might call for. "I am afraid, Lord Oakheart, that Bonaparte has no intention of going to St. Helena," he replied. "Instead—" He broke off, because the Hoka's jaw had dropped. Turning about to see what was wrong, he spied Brob. The giant spacefarer, careful to remain standing, had politely swallowed the drink given him. Blue flames gushed out of his mouth.

"Er, this is my associate, from Brobdingnag," Alex explained.

"From where?" asked Oakheart. "I mean to say, that Swift chap does have several interesting ideas, but I wasn't aware anybody had put 'em into effect . . . yet." Recovering his British aplomb, he took a pinch of snuff.

Alex braced himself. "Milord," he said, "you know why we've come. Armed conflict cannot be allowed. The differences between the governments of His Majesty and the Emperor shall have to be negotiated peacefully. To that end, my good offices are available, and I must insist they be accepted. The first step is for you people to take, namely, cancelling your expedition to Spain."

"Impossible, sir, impossible," huffed the Hoka. "Lord Nelson sails from Plymouth tomorrow. True, at present he has only the Home Fleet under his command, but dispatches are on their way to the colonies, summoning all our strength afloat to join him at Trafalgar. How can we stop 'em, eh? No, the British Lion is off to crush the knavish Frogs."

Alex thought fast. A leaderless armada, milling about, would have still more potential for causing disaster than one which was assembled under its respected admiral. "Wait a minute," he said. "It'll take two or three weeks for those windjammers to reach the rendezvous, whereas Spain's only two or three days' sail from here. Why is Nelson leaving this early?"

Oakheart confirmed his guess: "A reconnaissance, sir, a reconnaissance in force, to gather intelligence on the enemy's movements and chivvy him wherever he shows his cowardly face with fewer ships than ours."

"In that case, suppose I ride along. I could, well, maybe give Lord Nelson some helpful advice. More importantly, being on the scene, I could attempt to open negotiations with the French."

Oakheart frowned. "Most irregular. Danger of violation of the Absolutely Extreme Secrets Act. I am afraid I cannot countenance—"

Alex had learned how to turn Hoka logic against itself. "See here, milord, I am the accredited representative of a sovereign state with which your own has treaties and trade relations. I am sure His Majesty's government will accord me the usual diplomatic courtesies."

"Well . . . ah . . . but if you must talk to that Bonaparte rascal, why don't you simply fly to his camp, eh?"

Alex stiffened and replied coldly: "Sir, I am shocked to hear you propose that His Majesty's government should have no part in a vital proceeding like this."

Oakheart capitulated. "I beg your pardon, sir! No such intention, I assure you. Roger me if there was. Here, I'll give you a letter of introduction to the admiral, in my own hand, by Jove!" He reached for a goosequill, imported at considerable expense from Earth. As he wrote, he grew visibly more and more eager. Alex wished he could see what was going down on the paper, but no gentleman would read someone else's mail.

The human had excellent reasons—he hoped—for taking this course. While the Hoka Napoleon himself was doubtless well-intentioned, whatever persons had inflated his vainglory until he was red for war were, just as doubtless, not. They would be prepared for the contingency of a direct approach by a League authority. A blaster could shoot his aircar down as it neared, or he could be assassinated or kidnapped after he landed, and the Hokas led to believe he had been the victim of a tragic accident.

Traveling with Nelson, he had a better chance of getting to the Emperor, unbeknownst to the conspirators. Whether or not he succeeded in that, he expected to gather more information about how matters actually stood than he could in any other fashion.

Tanni would never let him take the risk. If nothing else, she'd fly out in her own car and snatch him right off the ship. Reluctantly, he decided to tell her, when he phoned, that he was engaged in delicate business which would keep him away for an indefinite time.

Since their ancient Slissii rivals departed, Hokas had had no need of military or naval forces, except to provide colorful uniforms and ceremonies. Hence the Home Fleet gathered at Plymouth was unimpressive. There were about a dozen Coast Guard cutters, hitherto employed in marine rescue work. There were half as many commandeered merchant ships, though these, being squareriggers of the Regency period, naturally bore cannon. There were three minor warcraft, the pinnace *Fore*, the bark *Umbrageous*, and the frigate *Falcon*. And finally there was a line-of-battle ship, the admiral's pennant at its masthead and the name *Victory* on its bows.

Leaving Brob ashore, lest the gangplank break beneath him, Alex boarded the latter. Two sailors who noticed him whipped fifes out of their jackets and played a tune, as befitted a visitor of his rank. This caused crewmen elsewhere on deck to break into a hornpipe. A Hoka in blue coat and cocked hat, telescope tucked beneath his left arm, hurried across the tarry-smelling planks.

"Welcome, Your Excellency, welcome," he said, and gave Alex a firm handshake. "Bligh's the name, Captain William Bligh, sir, at your service."

"What? I thought—"

"Well, H.M.S. *Bounty* is being careened, and besides, Lord Nelson required a sterner master in wartime than Captain Cook. Aye, a great seaman, Cook, but far too easy with the cat. What can I do for Your Excellency?"

Alex realized that a fleet admiral would not occupy himself with the ordinary duties of a skipper on his flagship. "I must see His Lordship. I have an important message for him."

Bligh looked embarrassed. He shuffled his feet. "His Lordship is resting in his stateroom, sir. Indisposed. Frail health, you know, after the rigors of Egypt."

Alex knew full well. Horatio Lord Nelson's public appearances were few and short. The nuisance of having to wear an eyepatch and keep his right arm inside his coat was too much.

Bligh recovered his spirit. He lowered his voice. "Although I'd say, myself, Lady Hamilton's had a bit to do with his weariness. You understand, sir." He gave Alex a wink, a leer, and a nudge in the ribs that sent the human staggering.

Instantly contrite, he offered to convey the letter. Alex gave him the sealed envelope, wishing again that he knew just what Oakheart had written. Hoka helpfulness often took strange forms. Bligh trotted aft. Alex spent the time arranging for his luggage to be fetched from his aircar. He saw Brob standing near it on the dock, surrounded by curious townsfolk, and wondered how he could do the same for his friend.

Bligh returned, twice as excited as before. "We shall have the honor of dining with His Lordship this evening," he announced. "Meanwhile, the squadron must be off on the afternoon tide. But we've time for a tot of rum in my cabin, Commodore, to welcome you into our company."

"Commodore? Huh?" Alex asked.

Bligh winked anew, though he kept his thumb to himself and, instead, took the man's elbow. "Ah, yes, I know full well. Ashore, the walls have ears. Mustn't let the Frenchies learn Commodore Hornblower is on a secret mission in disguise, damme, no. When we're safe at sea, I'll inform the men, by your leave, sir. Brace 'em up for certain, the news will, scurvy lot though they be." Walking along, he shrilled right and left at the crew: "Avast, ye lubbers! Look lively there! Flogging's too good for the likes o' ye! Keelhauling, aye, scuttle my bones if I don't keelhaul the first mutinous dog who soldiers on the job! Marines excepted, of course," he added more quietly.

In his quarters he poured, proposed the health of the King and the damnation of Boney, and fell into a long jeremiad about his lack of able officers. "The weak, piping times of peace, that's what's done it, Commodore." Alex listened with half an ear. If Oakheart's fantasy had appointed him Hornblower, maybe he could turn the situation to his advantage. Hornblower certainly rated more respect from Hoka mariners than any mere plenipotentiary—

A knock sounded on the door. "Come in, if ye've proper business," Bligh barked. "If not, beware! That's all I say, beware."

The door opened. A sailor in the usual striped shirt, bell-bottomed trousers, and straw hat saluted. A truncheon hung from his belt. "Bosun Bush, sir, press gang, reporting," he said. "We've caught us a big 'un. Does the captain want to see him?"

"Aye, what else?" Bligh snapped. "Got to set these pressed men right from the start, eh, Commo—eh, Your Excellency?"

The boatswain beckoned. Flanked by a couple of redcoated marines, Brob's enormous form made the deck creak and tremble as he approached. "What the hell?" burst from Alex. "How did they ever get you aboard?"

"They rigged a derrick," Brob answered. "Most kind of them, no? I had not even requested it when suddenly there they were, instructing me in what to do."

"Stout fella, this, hey, sir?" beamed the boatswain.

Captain Bligh peered dubiously at the acquisition. "He does look strong—" His ebullience returned to him. "Nevertheless, he'll soon find that aboard a King's ship is no life of ease." To Brob: "You'll work 'round the clock, me hearty, swab the planks, climb the ratlines, fist canvas along with the rest of 'em, or you'll hang from a yardarm. D'ye understand?"

Alex had a horrible vision of what would happen to the *Victory* if Brob tried to climb its rigging. His memory came to the rescue. Once he too had been impressed onto a ship out of this very England.

"Here's the first mate you said you lack, Captain Bligh," he declared in haste.

"What?" The skipper blinked at him.

"Pressed man always appointed first mate," said Alex, "in spite of his well-known sympathy for the crew."

"Of course, sir, of course," Bush chimed in happily.

"Well—" Bligh scratched his head. "Far be it from a simple old seaman like me to question the wisdom of Commodore Hornblower—"

"Commodore Hornblower!" The boatswain's eyes grew large. He tugged his forelock, or rather the fur where a human would have had a forelock. "Begging your pardon, sir, I didn't recognize you, but that's a clever disguise you're wearing, shiver me timbers if it ain't."

Bristling, Bligh turned his attention to Brob. "Well?" he snarled. "What're you waiting for, Mr. Christian? Turn out the crew. Put 'em to work like a proper bucko mate. We've the tide to make, and a fair wind for Spain."

"But, but I don't know how," Brob stammered.

"Don't try to cozen me with your sly ways, Fletcher Christian!" Bligh shouted. "Out on deck with you and get us moving!"

"Excuse me," Alex said. "I know this man of old, Captain. I can explain." He stepped forth, drew Brob aside, and whispered:

"Listen, this is typical Hoka dramatics. The crew are perfectly competent. They don't expect anything but a show out of the officers, as far as actual seamanship goes. You need only stand around, look impressive, and issue an occasional order—any order that comes to mind. They'll interpret it as being a command to do the right thing. Meanwhile I'll handle the details for both of us." Luckily, he reflected, that need not include rations. He could eat Tokan food, though it was preferable to supplement it with a few Terrestrial vitamin pills from his kit. He always carried some on his person. Brob had eaten before they left Mixumaxu, and one of his nuclear meals kept him fueled for weeks.

Bemused, the alien wandered off after Bosun Bush, rather like an ocean liner behind a small tugboat. Alex was taken to a vacant cabin and installed. It was reasonably comfortable, except that a human given a Hoka bed must sleep sitting up. One by one, the ships warped from the docks, set sail, and caught the breeze. When Alex re-emerged, *Victory* was rolling along over chill greenish waters, under a cloud of canvas like those that elsewhere covered the sea. Air sang in the rigging and carried a tang of salt. Crewmen went about their tasks—which included, ominously, the polishing of cannon as heavy as Brob himself—or, off watch, sat around telling each other how French blood would redden the ocean. Land was already low on the northern horizon.

Alex didn't stay topside long. He had had a difficult time of late, and faced a dinner with Lord Nelson, Captain Bligh, and heaven knew who else, in his role as Hornblower. Let him get some rest while he was able.

Shouts, trumpet calls, drumbeats, the thud of running feet roused him from an uneasy night's sleep. He stumbled forth in his pajamas. Pandemonium reigned, Hokas scurrying everywhere to and fro. Aloft, a lookout cried, "Thar she blows—I mean to say, Frogs ahead, two p'ints t' starboard!"

"Stand by to engage!" yelled Captain Bligh from the quarterdeck.

Alex scrambled up the ladder to join him. Nelson was there already, the empty sleeve of his dressing gown aflap in the wind, a telescope clapped to his patchless eye. "We've the weather gauge of them," he said. "They'll not escape us, I trow. Run up the signal flags: England expects every man will do his duty."

Aghast, Alex stared forward, past the bowsprit and across the whitecaps. Dawnlight showed him three large sailing vessels on the rim of sight. Despite the distance, he identified the Tricolor proudly flying at each staff. Louis XIV had built a navy too. (The Hoka France had never had a Revolution, merely an annual Bastille Day fête. At the most recent of these, Napoleon had taken advantage of the usual chaos to depose the king, who cooperated because it would be more fun being a field marshal. The excitement delighted the whole nation and charged it with enthusiasm. Only in Africa was this ignored, the Foreign Legion preferring to stay in its romantic, if desolate, outposts.)

"No danger of their escape, milord." Bligh rubbed his hands. "See, they're coming about. They mean to meet us. We outnumber 'em, aye, but those are three capital ships. Ah, a jolly little fight it'll be."

Down on the main deck, and on the gun decks below, sailors were readying their armament. The sardonic old prayer drifted thence to Alex's ears: "For that which we are about to receive, Lord, make us duly grateful." Marine sharpshooters swarmed into the masts. He shuddered. Like children at play, the Hokas had no idea what shot and shell would inflict on them. They would find out, once the broadsides began, but then it would be too late. Nor would they recoil. He knew well how much courage dwelt in them.

Feeling ill, he mumbled, "Admiral, wouldn't it be best if we— er—avoided commitment in favor of proceeding on our mission? Preserve the King's property, you know."

Nelson was shocked. "Commodore Hornblower! Do you imagine British seamen would turn tail like a . . . like a . . . like a crew of tail-turners? Egad, no! Britannia rules the waves! Westminster Abbey or victory!"

Captain Bligh smiled. "I'm sure the Commodore is no craven, but has some ruse in mind," he said cunningly. "What is it, sir?"

"I—well, I—" Desperate, Alex looked downward from the rail which his white-knuckled hands gripped. Brob stood like a rock in a surf of Hokas. "Can you do anything, anything at all?" the human wailed to him.

"As a matter of fact," Brob responded diffidently, "I believe I may see a perhaps useful course of action."

"Then for mercy's sake, do it! Though . . . we can't take French lives either, do you realize?"

"I would never dream of it." Brob fanned himself, as if the very thought made him feel faint. "You shall have to lower me over the side." He looked around him. "Possibly with one of those—er—spars to keep me afloat."

"Do you hear that?" Alex exclaimed to Nelson and Bligh. "Brob—

uh, Mr. Christian can save the day." They stared blankly at him. He saw he must give them an impression of total calm, complete mastery of the situation. Somehow, he grinned and winked. "Gentlemen, I do indeed have a ruse, but there isn't time now to explain it. Please ready a cargo boom and drop the mate overboard."

Nelson grew distressed. "I do not recall, sir, that any precedent exists in the annals of war for jettisoning the mate. If we should be defeated, it would count heavily against us at our courts martial."

Bligh was quicker-witted. "Not if he's mutinied," he said. "Do you follow me, Christian, you treacherous scoundrel? Don't just stand there. Do something mutinous."

"Well, er—" With a mighty effort, against his every inclination, Brob raised a cable-thick middle finger in the air. "Up yours, sir. A rusty grapnel, sir, sideways. I do require a grapnel."

"Ah, hah! D'ye hear what he was plotting? Next thing we knew, we'd be adrift in an open boat 4000 miles from Timor. Overboard he goes!" bellowed Bligh in his shrill soprano.

A work detail was promptly organized. To the sound of a lusty chanty, Brob, a spar firmly lashed to his massive body and carrying his implement, went on high, swung above the gunwale, and dropped into the waves. An enormous splash followed. Fearful of the outcome, yet intensely curious himself, Alex watched his friend swim off to meet the French.

They were still well out of gunshot range. Windjammers can't maneuver fast. The sight of the monster nearing them alarmed the crews, who opened fire on him. Two of the cannonballs struck, but bounced harmlessly off.

Coming to the nearest vessel, Brob trod water while he whirled his hook at the end of a long chain. He let fly. It bit hard into a mast and snugged itself against a yard. Brob dived and began to haul. Drawn by the chain, the ship canted over—and over—and over—the sea rushed in through gunports and hatches.

Brob came back to the surface. A deft yank on the chain dislodged the grapnel and brought it to him again, along with a portion of the mast that he had snapped across. The warcraft wallowed low. It was not sinking, quite, and nobody had been hurt, but its powder was drenched, leaving it helpless.

Brob gave a similar treatment to the next. The third showed a clean pair of heels, followed by hoots of British derision.

Brob returned to the *Victory*, where his sailors winched him on deck to the tune of "Way, hey, and up he rises, ear-lie in the morning." Lord Nelson magnanimously issued him a pardon for his insubordinate conduct and Captain Bligh ordered an extra ration of grog for everybody.

Indeed, beneath their boasting, the Hokas seemed glad to have avoided combat. That gave Alex a faint hope.

Whether or not the entire naval strength available to France in these parts at this time had been routed, none was on hand when the flotilla from England dropped anchor two days afterward. Sunset light streamed over a hush broken only by the mildest of breezes and the squeals of leathery-winged seafowl. The bay here was wide and calm. Above it loomed the Iberian peninsula. Like its namesake on Earth, this land was rugged, though lushly green. A village, whitewashed walls and red tile roofs, nestled behind a wharf where fishing boats lay moored.

Also red were the coats of marines ashore. They had occupied the place as a precaution against anyone going off to inform the enemy of their arrival. It turned out that there was no danger of that. These isolated local folk were unconcerned about politics. Rather, they were overjoyed to have another set of foreign visitors. They had already seen Napoleon's Grand Army pass through.

Indeed, that host was encamped about ten kilometers off, beyond a high ridge to the southeast, alongside a river which emptied into the bay. Alex supposed the Emperor had chosen that site in order to be safe from surprise attack and bombardment out of the sea. He saw the smoke of campfires drift above trees, into the cool evening air.

Standing on the quarterdeck between Nelson and Bligh, he said fervently, "Gentlemen, I thank you for your cooperation in this secret mission of mine. Tonight I'll go ashore, alone, to, er, get the cut of the Frenchman's jib. Kindly remain while I'm gone, and please refrain from any untoward action that might warn him."

His plan was to steal into yonder camp, find Napoleon, identify himself, and demand a ceasefire (not that firing had begun, except for target practice, but the principle was the same). It should be less risky than an outsider would think. Hokas would scarcely shoot at a human, especially one whom various among them would recognize as the plenipotentiary. Instead, they would take him to their leader, who if nothing else would respect his person and let him go after they had talked.

This was the more likely because he had had the sailmaker sew him an impressive set of clothes. Gold braid covered his tunic, gold stripes went down his trousers, his boots bore spurs and his belt a saber. From the cocked hat on his head blossomed fake ostrich plumes.

From his shoulders, unfastened, swung a coat reaching halfway down his calves, whose elbow-deep pockets sported huge brass buttons. Borrowed medals jingled across his left breast.

The main hazard was that the subversives would discover his presence before he had had his meeting. To minimize this chance, he meant to sneak as far as he could.

He might actually make it undetected to the Emperor's tent. On such short notice as they had had, even fast-learning Hokas could not have developed a very effective military tradition. Sentries would tend to doze at their posts, or join each other for a swig of *ordinaire* and a conversation about the exploits of Brigadier Gerard.

Nelson frowned around his eyepatch. "Chancy," he said. "Were it anybody but you, milord, I'd forbid it, I would. Still, I expect Your Grace knows what he's about."

"My Grace?" Alex asked, bewildered. "But I haven't been made a lord yet—that is, I'm plain Commodore Hornblower—" Seeing the look on the two furry faces, he gulped. "I am. Am I not?"

Captain Bligh chuckled. "Ah, milord, you're more than the bluff soldier they think of when they say 'Wellington.' That's clear. You couldn't have routed 'em as you did—as you're going to do, here in the Peninsula and so on till Waterloo—you couldn't do that if your mind weren't shrewd."

Admiration shone in Nelson's eyes. "I'll wager the playing fields of Eton had somewhat to do with that," he said. "Have no fears, Your Grace. Your secret is safe with us, until you've completed your task of gathering intelligence and are ready to take command of your troops."

"Scum of the earth, they are," Bligh muttered. "Just like my sailors. But we'll show those Frenchies what Britons are worth, eh, milord?"

Alex clutched his temples. "Omigawd, no!" He stifled further groans. Whether Oakheart had included the assertion in his letter, or whether these officers had concluded on their own account, now that he was going ashore in his gaudy uniform, that he must really be the Duke of Wellington, traveling under the alias of Horatio Hornblower—did it make any difference?

To be sure, somewhere in England, a Hoka bore the same name. Tanni had mentioned him. That mattered naught, in his absence, to the elastic imaginations of the natives.

Alex struggled to remember something, anything, concerning the original Wellington. Little came to him. He had only read casually about the Napoleonic period, never studied it, for it was not an era whose re-enactment he would have allowed on Toka, if he had had any say in the matter. At one time, Alex recalled, somebody had tried to blackmail the great man, threatening to publish an account of his involvement with a woman not his wife. Drawing himself up to his full height and fixing the blackmailer with a steely eye, the Iron Duke had snapped, "Publish and be damned!" It seemed rather a useless piece of information now, especially for a happily married man who cherished no desire for illicit affairs.

Alex blanched at the prospect of being swept along by events until he in fact commanded the British army in outright combat. That would certainly put an end to his career, and earn him a long prison sentence as well.

He rallied his resolution. The thing must not happen. Wasn't that his entire purpose? Why else would he be dressed like this?

Having reassured an anxious Brob, he went ashore in a dinghy rowed by two marines, and struck off inland. Night fell as he strode, but a moon and a half illuminated the dirt road for him. Apart from the warmth and scratchiness of his clothes, the uphill walk was no hardship; he was still young, and had always been athletic—formerly a champion in both track and basketball.

Loneliness did begin to oppress him. Save for farmsteads scattered over the landscape the coziness of whose lamplit windows reminded him far too much of home, he walked among trees and through pastures. Shadows bulked, menacing. He almost wished he had brought a firearm. But no, that might be construed as a threat, and generate resistance to his arguments. Persuasion seemed his solitary hope.

In due course he entered a forest, but soon he welcomed its darkness, when he stood looking down into a valley ablaze with campfires. Campaigning or not, Hokas liked to keep late hours. Tents, more or less in rows, lined the riverbanks; he saw fieldpieces gleam, the bulks of the "horses" that drew them, a large and flag-topped pavilion which must house Napoleon; he heard a murmur of movement down there, and occasional snatches of song. While this Grand Army did not compare with the original, it must number thousands.

Having picked a route, Alex began the stealthy part of his trip. His pulse was loud in his ears, but his feet were silent. The stalking and photographing of wild animals had long been a sport he followed.

Eventually he passed a couple of pickets, who were too busy comparing amorous notes to observe him. His limited French gave him the impression that Madeleine was quite a female—unless she was a pure fiction, which was not unlikely. Farther on, he belly-crawled around fires where soldiers sat tossing dice or singing ballads that all seemed to have the refrain *"Rataplan! Rataplan!"* Lanes between tents offered better concealment yet.

And thus he did, indeed, come to the out-size shelter at the heart of the encampment. From its centerpole a flag fluttered in the night wind, bearing a golden *N* within a wreath. Moonlight sheened off the muskets and bayonets of half a dozen sentries who stood, in blue uniforms and high shakos, before the entrance. A brighter glow spilled from inside, out of an opened windowflap at the rear. Alex decided to peek through it before he declared himself.

He did—and drew a gasp of amazement.

Luxuriously furnished, the pavilion held a table on which lay the remnants of a dinner (it seemed to have been an attempt at turning a native flying reptiloid into chicken Marengo) and several empty bottles. Perhaps this was the reason why a rather small and stout Hoka kept a hand thrust inside his epauletted coat. He stood at another table, covered with maps and notes, around which four spectacularly uniformed officers of his race were gathered. It was the alien squatting on top, next to the oil lamp, who shocked Alex.

Had he straightened on his grasshopper-like legs, that being would not have reached a Hoka chin. His two arms were long and skinny, his torso a mere lump which his black, silver-ornamented clothes did nothing to make impressive. Gray-skinned and hairless, his head was a caricature of a man's—batwing ears, beady eyes, needle-sharp teeth, and a nose ten centimeters long, that waggled as he spoke in a voice suggestive of fingernails scratching a blackboard.

He was employing English, the most widespread language on Toka as it was throughout the spaceways. Probably he knew less French than Alex did, whereas Napoleon and his staff would have had abundant contact with humanity before they assumed their present identities.

"You must seize the moment, sire," he urged. "Audacity, always audacity! What have we done hitherto, we and the Spanish troops, but march and countermarch? Not a single shot fired in anger. Madness! We must seek them out, attack and destroy them, at once. Else we will have them at our backs when the English, that nation of shopkeepers, arrive in force."

The Hoka Napoleon gestured with his free hand. "But we don't want to hurt the Spaniards," he objected. "After all, they are supposed to become my loyal subjects, under my cousin. *Du sublime au ridicule il n'y a qu'un pas,* as my distinguished predecessor put it, after the retreat from Moscow."

"Nonetheless," hissed the alien, "we must take decisive action or else undergo an even worse disaster than that same retreat. What is the use of your military genius, my Emperor, if you won't exercise it?" He turned to another Hoka, whose fur was red rather than golden. "Marshal Ney, you've talked enough about your wish to lead gallant cavalry charges. Do you never propose to get out there and do it?"

"*Oui, Monsieur* Snith," replied that one, "although I had, um-m, seen myself as an avenger, or better yet a defender, and the Spanish haven't done us any actual harm."

So, thought Alex, the alien's name was Snith. He had already recognized whence the being hailed. As he had suspected, this was a member of the Kratch. Now he knew, beyond doubt, that the Universal Nationalist Party which held power on their world had begun actively to undermine the wardship system and thus weaken the entire Interbeing League. Out of discord among the stars could come war; out of war, chaos; out of chaos, hegemony for those who had anticipated events.

"Hear me," the Krat was saying. "Has not my counsel put you on the way to power and glory? Do you not want to bring your species under a single rule, and so prepare it to deal equally with those that now dominate space? Then you must be prepared to follow my plans to the end." He lowered his voice. "Else, my Emperor, I fear that my government must terminate its altruistic efforts on your behalf, and I go home, leaving you to your fate."

The Hokas exchanged glances, somewhat daunted. Clearly, Snith had instigated their grandiosity, and continued to inspire and guide it. For his part, Alex felt sickened. Well, he thought, he'd wait till the conference was over and Snith had sought his quarters, then rouse Napoleon and set forth a quite different point of view.

A bayonet pricked his rump. "Yipe!" escaped from him. Turning, he confronted the sentries. They must have heard his heavy breathing and come to investigate.

"*Qui va là?*" demanded their corporal.

Alex mastered dismay. If the Hokas were reluctant to attack their fellow planetarians, they would be still more careful of a human. A face-to-face showdown with Snith might even change their minds. "Show some respect, *poilu*!" he rapped. "Don't you see who I am?"

"*Je ne suis pas—Monsieur,* I am not a *poilu*, I am an old *moustache*," said the corporal, offended. "And 'ere by my side is Karl Schmitt, a German grenadier lately returned from captivity in Russia—"

Alex's whirling thought was that these French could not have

studied their Napoleonic history very closely either. The Emperor himself interrupted the discussion, by stumping over to the opening. *"Mon
Dieu!"* he exclaimed. *"Mais c'est Monsieur Le Plenipotentiaire* Jones!
Sir, is this not irregular? The use of diplomatic channels is more in
accord with the dignity of governments."

Snith reacted fast. "Ah, ha!" he shrilled. "There you see, my
Emperor, how the Earthlings who have so long oppressed your world
despise you. Avenge this insult to the honor of France."

Alex reacted just as fast, although he was operating mainly on
intuition. "Nonsense," he said. "In point of fact, I'm being—I mean I
am none less than the Duke of Wellington, dispatched by none less
than the Prince Regent, the Prime Minister, the First Lord of the Admiralty, Lord Nelson, and Commodore Hornblower, on a special mission
to negotiate peace between our countries."

He drew himself up to his full height and did his best to fix Snith
with a steely eye.

"Hein?" Napoleon gripped his stomach harder than before. "Now
I am confused, me. Quick, a carafe of Courvoisier."

Snith jittered about on the table. "Where is your diplomatic
accreditation, miserable Earthling?" he squealed, waving his tiny fists.
"How will we be sure you are not a spy, or an assassin, or a—a—"

"A shopkeeper," suggested Marshal Ney.

"Thank you. A shopkeeper. My Emperor," said Snith more calmly,
"a British ship must have brought him. Else he would have flown in
like an honest plenipotentiary. Therefore he must be in collusion with
perfidious Albion. Arrest him, sire, confine him, until we can discover
what new threat lies in wait for you."

Under the gaze of his marshals, Napoleon could not but be strict.
"Indeed," he said regretfully. *"Monsieur le Duc*, if such you are and if
your intentions are sincere, you shall have a formal apology. Meanwhile, you will understand the necessity of detaining you. It shall be
an honorable detention, whether or not we must afterward place you
before a firing squad." To the soldiers: *"Enfermez-il, mes enfants."*

In a kind of dull consternation, Alex realized that his image
required him to go off, a prisoner, too stoic to utter any protest.

First Napoleon took custody of his sword, and under Snith's waspish
direction he was searched for hidden weapons, communications
devices, and anything else of possible use. If only he had had a
portable radio transceiver along, he could have called Brob at the
instant things went awry. The giant could gently but firmly have freed
him. Why didn't he think of simple precautions like that beforehand?

A fine secret agent he was! The excuse that he wasn't supposed to be a secret agent, and moreover had had a good deal else on his mind, rang false.

The squad conducted him to a nearby farmhouse. They turned the family out, but those didn't object, since the Emperor had ordered they be well paid for the inconvenience. Alex had often thought that the Hokas were basically a sweeter species than humankind. Perhaps a theologian would suppose they were without original sin. The trouble was, they had too much originality of other sorts.

The house was humble, actually a cottage. A door at either end gave on a living room, which doubled as the dining room, a kitchen and scullery, and two bedrooms, all in a row along a narrow hall. The floor was clay, the furnishings few and mostly homemade. When the windows had been shuttered and barred on the outside, Alex's sole light would be from some candles in wooden holders.

"I give myself, me, ze honor to stand first watch outside ze south door," said the squad leader. "Corporal Sans-Souci, at Your Lordship's service. Karl, *mon brave*, I reward your *esprit* and command of English by posting you at ze north end."

"*Viel Danke, mein tapfere Korporal,*" replied the little German grenadier. "If *der Herzog* Vellington vould like to discuss de military sciences vit' me, please chust to open de door."

Jealousy made Sans-Souci bristle. "*Monsieur le Duc* is a man of ze most virile, *non?*" he countered. "If it should please 'im to describe 'is conquests in ze fields of love, and 'ear about mine, my door shall stand open too."

"No, thanks, to you both," Alex muttered, stumbled on into the cottage, and personally closed it up. He knew that, while either trooper would happily chatter for hours, exit would remain forbidden. Despite their size, Hokas were stronger than humans, and these must have a stubborn sense of duty.

Alex sank down onto a stool, put elbows on knees and face in hands. What a ghastly mess! Outnumbered as they were, the British could do nothing to rescue him. If they tried, they would be slaughtered, which was precisely what Snith wanted. Brob— No, Alex's idea about that being had been mistaken. Cannon and bullets meant nothing to Brob, but Snith undoubtedly had energy weapons against which not even the spacefarer could stand.

Could he, Alex, talk Napoleon into releasing him? Quite likely he could—for example, by an appeal to the Emperor's concern for the diplomatic niceties—except, again, for the everdamned Snith. The Krat had the edge; he could outargue the man, whose position was, after all, a bit dubious in the eyes of the French (and in his own eyes, for that matter). Thus, if Alex was not actually shot, he would at least languish captive for weeks, probably after being moved to a secret locale. Meanwhile Snith would have egged Napoleon into an attack on the Spanish army, and shortly thereafter Nelson's assembled fleet would begin raiding the coasts and landing British troops, and before the League could do anything to prevent it, there would have been wholesale death and devastation. No doubt it would also occur elsewhere on Toka. Snith might be the leading Kratch agent, but obviously he had others doing the same kind of dirty work in chosen societies around the planet.

Wearily and drearily, Alex decided he might as well go to bed. In truth, that was his best course. Sometimes in the past, when he slept on a problem, his subconscious mind, uninhibited by the rationality of his waking self, had thrown up a solution crazy enough to work. The trouble now was, he doubted he could sleep.

He rose to his feet, and stopped cold. His glance had encountered an object hanging on the wall. It was a small leather bag, stoppered and bulging. This being a Spanish home, it must be a *bota*, and that word translated as "wineskin."

Alex snatched it to him, opened it and his mouth, and squeezed. A jet of raw, potent liquor laved his throat.

A deep buzz wakened him. Something brushed his nose. Blindly, aware mainly of a headache and a raging thirst, he swatted. The something bumbled away. Its drone continued. Soon it was back. Alex unlidded a bleary eye. Light trickled in through cracks and warps in the shutters across his bedroom window. A creature the size of his thumb fluttered clumsily, ever closer to him. Multiple legs brushed his skin again. *"Damn,"* he mumbled, and once more made futile swatting motions.

The insectoid was as persistent as a Terrestrial fly. Maybe an odor of booze on his breath attracted it. Alex would get no more rest while it was loose.

He forced himself to alertness. Craftily, he waited. The huge brown bug hummed nearer. Alex remained motionless. His tormentor drew within centimeters of him. He kept himself quiet while he studied its flying pattern. Back and forth it went, on spatulate wings. Uzz, uzz, uzz it went. Alex mentally rehearsed his move. Then, pantherlike, his hand pounced. Fingers closed on the creature. "Gotcha!" he rasped. A sorry triumph, no doubt, but better than no triumph at all.

The bug fluttered in his grip. He was about to crush it, but stopped.

Poor thing, it had meant him no harm. Why must he add even this bit to the sum of tragedy that would soon engulf Toka? (What a metaphor! But he was hung over, as well as oppressed by the doom he foresaw.) At the same time, he was jolly well not going to let it disturb his sleep any more.

He could carry it to a door, have that door swung aside, and release *his* prisoner. But then the sentinel would be eager to talk to his prisoner, and that was just too much to face at this hour.

Alex swung his nude body out of bed. A chamber pot stood nearby. He raised the lid, thrust the bug inside, and dropped the lid back in place. The bug flew about. Resonance made the vessel boom hollowly. Alex realized he had not done the most intelligent thing possible, unless the house contained another chamber pot.

He looked around him. Daylight must be very new, at sunrise or before, since it was weak and gray. In a while someone would bring him breakfast. He hoped it would include plenty of strong black coffee. Afterward he would insist on a hot bath. Damnation, here he was, unwashed, uncombed, unshaven, confined in a peasant's hovel. Was that any way to treat the Duke of Wellington?

As abruptly as the night before, Alex froze. Now his gaze did not stop at a leather flask, which in any case lay flaccid and empty. Figuratively, his vision pierced the wall and soared over valley and hills to the sea. Inspiration had, indeed, come to him.

It might be sheer lunacy. The chances were that it was. He had no time for Hamlet-like hesitation. Nor did he have much to lose. Seizing the pot, he hurried out of the room and down the hall to the north end of the cottage. He had changed his mind about conversation with his guards.

None the worse for a sleepless night, Karl flung wide the door when Alex knocked, though his muscular little form continued to block any way out. Mist had drenched his uniform, and as yet blurred view of the camp below this farmstead, but reveilles had begun to sound through the chill air.

"*Gut Morgen, gut Morgen!*" the grenadier greeted. "Did de noble captiff shlumber vell? Mine duty ends soon, but I vill be glad to shtay and enchoy discourse *am Krieg*—"

He broke off, surprised. M-m-uzzz, oom, oom went the jar that Alex held in the crook of an arm.

"Mine lord," Karl said after a moment, in a tone of awe, "you iss a powerful man, t'rough and t'rough. I vill be honored to empty dot for you."

"No need." Alex took the lid off and tilted the vessel forward. The bug blundered forth. As it rose higher, sunrise light from behind the fog made it gleam like metal. Karl's astounded stare followed it till it was out of sight.

Thereafter he scratched his head with his bayonet and murmured, "I haff heard dey feed dem terrible on de English ships, but *vot* vas *dot?*"

Alex smiled smugly, laid a finger alongside his nose, and replied in a mysterious voice, "I'm afraid I can't tell you that, old chap. Military secrets, don't y'know."

Karl's eyes grew round. "*Mein Herr?* Zecrets? But ve gafe you a zearch last night."

"Ah, well, we humans—for I am human, you realize, as well as being the Duke of Wellington—we have our little tricks," Alex answered. He assumed a confidential manner. "You're familiar with the idea of carrier pigeons. Before you became a German grenadier, you may have heard about our Terrestrial technology—miniaturization, transistors—but I may say no more. Except this, because you're stout and true, Karl, whether or not you're on the wrong side in this war. No matter what happens later today, never blame yourself. You could not possibly have known."

He closed the door on the shaken Hoka, set the mug aside, and sought the south end of the house.

"*Bonjour, monsieur,*" hailed Sans-Souci. I 'ope ze noble lord 'as slept well?"

"Frankly, no," said Alex. "I'm sure you can guess why."

The soldier cocked his ears beneath his shako. "*Eh, bien,* ze gentleman, 'e 'as been lonely, *n'est-ce pas?*"

Alex winked, leered, and dug a thumb into the other's ribs. "We're men of the world, you and I, corporal. The difference in our stations makes no difference. . . . Uh, I mean a man's a man's for a' that, and— Anyhow, if I'm to be detained, don't you agree I should have . . . companionship?"

Sans-Souci grew ill at ease. " 'Ow true, 'ow sad. But Your Lordship, 'e is not of our species—"

Alex drew himself up to his full height. "What do you think I am?" he snapped. "I have nothing in mind but a lady of my race."

"Zat will not be so easy, I fear."

"Perhaps easier than you think, corporal. This is what I want you to do for me. When you're relieved, pass the word on to your lieutenant that, if the Emperor is virile enough to understand, which he undoubtedly is, why, then the Emperor will order a search for a nice, strapping wench. There are a number of humans on Toka, you recall—League personnel, scientists, journalists, lately even an occasional tourist. I happen to know that some are right in this area. It should not be difficult to contact them and— Well, corporal, if this works out, you'll find me not ungrateful."

Sans-Souci slapped his breast. "Ah, *monsieur*," he cried, "to 'elp love blossom, zat will be its own reward!"

A couple of new soldiers appeared out of the fog and announced that they were the next guards. Sans-Souci barely took time to introduce them to the distinguished detainee—a stolid, though hard-drinking private from Normandy and a dashing Gascon sergeant of Zouaves—before hastening off. Alex heard a clatter from behind the house as Karl departed equally fast.

Returning inside, the man busied himself in preparations for that which he hoped would transpire. Whatever did, he should not have long to wait. Any collection of Hokas was an incredible rumor mill. What the sentries had to relate should be known to the whole Grand Army within the hour.

Excitement coursed through his blood and drove the pain out of his head. Win, lose, or draw, by gosh and by golly, he was back in action!

He estimated that a mere thirty minutes had passed when the door to the main room opened again, from outside. At first he assumed a trooper was bringing his breakfast, then he remembered that English aristocrats slept notoriously late and Napoleon would not want his guest disturbed without need. Then a being stepped through, closed the door behind him, and glared.

It was Snith.

"What's this?" the Krat screamed. The volume of the sound was slight, out of his minuscule lungs.

"What's what?" asked Alex, careful to move slowly. Though he towered a full meter above the alien, and probably outmassed him tenfold, Snith carried a dart gun at his belt; and his race was more excitable, impatient, irascible than most.

"You know what's what, you wretch. That communication device of yours, and that camp of your abominable co-humans somewhere close by. Thought you'd sneak one over on me, did you? Ha! I'm sharper than you guessed, Jones. Already scouts have brought back word of those English in the bay and the village. We'll move on them this very day. But first I want to know what else to expect, Jones, and you'll tell me. Immediately!"

"Let's be reasonable," Alex temporized. While he had expected Snith to arrive alone, lest the Hokas learn too much, he could not predict the exact course of events—merely devise a set of contingency plans. "Don't you realize what harm you're doing on this planet? Not only to it, either. If ever word gets out about your government's part in this, you can be sure the rest of the League will move to have it replaced."

The Krat sneered upward at the human's naked height. "They won't know till far too late, those milksop pacifists. By then, Universal Nationalism will dominate a coalition so powerful that— Stand back, you! Not a centimeter closer, or I shoot." He touched the gun in its holster.

"What use would that be to you?" Alex argued. "Dead men tell no tales."

"Ah but you wouldn't be dead, Jones. The venom in these darts doesn't kill unless they strike near the heart. In a leg, say, they'll make you feel as though you're burning alive. Oh, you'll talk, you'll talk," responded Snith, obviously enjoying his own ruthlessness. "Why not save yourself the agony? But you'd better tell the truth, or else, afterward, you'll wish you had. How you'll wish you had!"

"Well, uh, well— Look, excuse me, I have to take a moment for nature. How can I concentrate unless I do?"

"Hurry up, then," Snith ordered.

Alex went to the chamber pot. He bent down as if to remove its lid. Both his hands closed on its body. Faster than when he had captured the bug, he hurled it. As a youth in the Naval Academy, he had been a basketball star. The old reflexes were still there. The lid fell free as the mug soared. Upside down, it descended on Snith. Too astonished to have moved, the Krat buckled beneath that impact. Alex made a flying tackle, landed on the pot and held it secure.

Snith banged on it from within, boomlay, boomlay, boomlay, boom. "What's the meaning of this outrage?" came his muffled shriek. "Let me go, you fiend!"

"Heh, heh, heh," taunted Alex. He dragged the container over the floor to a chair whereon lay strips of cloth torn off garments left by the dwellers here. Reaching beneath, he hauled Snith out. Before the Krat could draw weapon, he was helpless in the grasp of a far stronger being. Alex disarmed him, folded him with knees below jaws, and began tying him.

"Help, murder, treason!" Snith cried. As expected, his thin tones did not penetrate the door.

He regained a measure of self-control. "You're mad, insane," he gabbled. "How do you imagine you can escape? What will Napoleon do if you've harmed his . . . his Talleyrand? Stop this, Jones, and we can reach some *modus vivendi.*"

"Yeah, sure," grunted Alex. He gagged his captive and left him trussed on the floor.

Heart pounding, the man spread out the disguise he had improvised from raiment and bedding. Thus far his plan had succeeded better than he dared hope, but now it would depend on his years of practice at playing out roles before Hokas, for the costume would never have gotten by a human.

First he donned his Wellingtonian greatcoat. Into a capacious pocket he stuffed the weakly struggling Snith. Thereafter he wrapped his hips in a blanket, which simulated a skirt long enough to hide the boots he donned, and his upper body in a dress which had belonged to the housewife and which on him became a sort of blouse. Over all he pinned another blanket, to be a cloak with a cowl, and from that hood he hung a cheesecloth veil.

Here goes nothing, he thought, and minced daintily, for practice, through the cottage to the farther door. It opened at his knock. An astonished Sergeant Le Galant gaped at the spectacle which confronted him. He hefted his musket. *"Qui va là?"* he demanded in a slightly stunned voice.

Alex waved a languid hand. "Oh, sir," he answered falsetto, "please let me by. I'm so tired. His Grace the Duke is a . . . a most vigorous gentleman. Oh, dear, and to think I forgot to bring my smelling salts."

The Hoka's suspicions dissolved in a burst of romanticism. Naturally, he took for granted that the lady had entered from the side opposite. *"Ah, ma belle petite,"* he burbled, while he kissed Alex's hand, "zis is a service you 'ave done not only for *Monsieur le Duc,* but for France. We 'ave our reputation to maintain, *non? Mille remerciments. Adieu, et au revoir.*"

Sighing, he watched Alex sway off.

The mists had lifted, and everywhere Hoka soldiers stared at the strange figure, whispered, nudged each other, and nodded knowingly. A number of them blew kisses. Beneath his finery, Alex sweated. He must not move fast, or they would start to wonder; yet he must get clear soon, before word reached Napoleon and made *him* wonder.

His freedom was less important than the prisoner he carried, and had been set at double hazard for that exact reason. This, maybe, was the salvation of Toka. Maybe.

When he had climbed the ridge and entered the forest, Alex shouted for joy. Henceforward he, as a woodsman, would undertake to elude any pursuit. He cast the female garb from him. Attired in greatcoat and boots, the plenipotentiary of the Interbeing League marched onward to the sea.

At his insistence, the flotilla recalled its marines and sought open water before the French arrived. Nelson grumbled that retreat was not British, but the human mollified him by describing the move as a strategic withdrawal for purposes of consolidation.

In Alex's cabin, he and Brob confronted Snith. The diminutive Krat did not lack courage. He crouched on the bunk and spat defiance. "Never will I betray the cause! Do your worst! And afterward, try to explain away my mangled body to your lily-livered superiors."

"Torture is, needless to say, unthinkable," Brob agreed. "Nevertheless, we must obtain the information that will enable us to thwart your plot against the peace. Would you consider a large bribe?"

Alex fingered his newly smooth chin and scowled. The ship heeled to the wind. Sunlight scythed through ports to glow on panels. He heard waves rumble and whoosh, timbers creak, a cheerful sound of music and dance from the deck; he caught a whiff of fresh salt air; not far off, if he flew, were Tanni and the kids. . . . Yes, he thought, this was a lovely world in a splendid universe, and must be kept that way.

"Bribe?" Snith was retorting indignantly. "The bribe does not exist which can buy a true Universal Nationalist. No, you are doomed, you decadent libertarians. You may have kidnapped me, but elsewhere the sacred cause progresses apace. Soon the rest of this planet will explode, and blow you onto the ash heap of history."

Alex nodded to himself. A nap had done wonders for him akin to those which had happened ashore. Pieces of the puzzle clicked together, almost audibly.

Conspirators were active in unknown places around the globe. They must be rather few, though; Snith appeared to have managed the entire Napoleonic phase by himself. They must, also, have some means of communication, a code; and they must be ready at any time to meet for consultation, in case of emergency. Yes. The basic problem was how to summon them. Snith knew the code and the recognition signals, but Snith wasn't telling. However, if you took into account the feverish Kratch temperament. . . .

A slow grin spread across Alex's face. "Brob," he murmured, "we have an extra stateroom for our guest. But he should not be left to pine in isolation, should he? That would be cruel. I think I can get the captain to release you from your duties as mate, in order that you can stay full time with Mr. Snith."

"What for?" asked the spacefarer, surprised.

Alex rubbed his hands together. "Oh, to try persuasion," he said. "You're a good, kind soul, Brob. If anybody can convince Mr. Snith of the error of his ways, it's you. Keep him company. Talk to him. You might, for instance, tell him about flower arrangements."

The planet had barely rotated through another of its 24.35-hour days when Snith, trembling and blubbering, yielded.

It was necessary to choose the rendezvous with care. The conspirators weren't stupid. Upon receiving their enciphered messages, which bore Snith's name and declared that unforeseen circumstances required an immediate conference, they would look at their maps. They would check records of whatever intelligence they had concerning human movements and capabilities at the designated spot. If anything appeared suspicious, they would stay away. Even if nothing did, they would fly in with such instruments as metal detectors wide open, alert for any indications of a trap.

Accordingly, Alex had made primitive arrangements. After picking up a long-range transmitter in Plymouth, he directed *Victory* alone—to an isolated Cornish cove, whence he issued his call. Inland lay nothing but a few small, widely scattered farms. Interstellar agents would think naught of a single windjammer anchored offshore, nor imagine that marines and bluejackets lurked around the field where they were supposed to land—when those Hokas were armed simply with truncheons and belaying pins.

Night fell. All three moons were aloft. Frost rings surrounded them. Trees hemmed in an expanse of several hectares, whereon haystacks rested hoar; the nearest dwelling was kilometers off. Silence prevailed, save when wildfowl hooted. Alex shivered where he crouched in the woods. Twigs prickled him. He wanted a drink.

Ashimmer beneath moons and stars, a teardrop shape descended, the first of the enemy vehicles. It grounded on a whisper of forcefield, but did not open at once. Whoever was inside must be satisfying himself that nothing of menace was here.

A haystack scuttled forward. It had been glued around Brob. Before anybody in the car could have reacted, he was there. His right fist smashed through its fuselage to the radio equipment. His left hand peeled back the metal around the engine and put that out of commission.

"At 'em, boys!" Alex yelled. His followers swarmed forth to make the arrest. They were scarcely necessary. Brob had been quick to disarm and secure the two beings within.

Afterward he tucked the car out of sight under a tree and returned to being a haystack, while Alex and the Hokas concealed themselves again.

In this wise, during the course of the night, they collected thirty prisoners, the entire ring. Its members were not all Kratch. Among them were two Slissii, a Pornian, a Sarennian, a Worbenite, three Chakbans; but the Kratch were preponderant, and had clearly been the leaders.

A glorious victory! Alex thought about the administrative details ahead of him, and moaned aloud.

Two weeks later, though, at home, rested and refreshed, he confronted Napoleon. The Empire was his most pressing problem. Mongols, Aztecs, Crusaders, and other troublesome types were rapidly reverting to an approximation of normal, now that the sources of their inspiration had been exposed and discredited. But Imperial France not only had a firmer base, it had the unrelenting hostility of Georgian Britain. The Peace of Amiens, which Alex had patched together, was fragile indeed.

Tanni was a gracious hostess and a marvelous cook. The plenipotentiary's household staff, and his children, were on their best behavior. Candlelight, polished silver, snowy linen, soft music had their mellowing effect. At the same time, the awesome presence of Brob reminded the Emperor—who was, after all, sane in his Hoka fashion—that other worlds were concerned about this one. The trick was to provide him and his followers an alternative to the excitement they had been enjoying.

"Messire," Alex urged over the cognac and cigars, "as a man of vision, you surely realize with especial clarity that the future is different from the past. You yourself, a mover and shaker, have shown us that the old ways can never be the same again, but instead we must move on to new things, new opportunities—*la carrière ouverte aux talents*, as your illustrious namesake phrased it. If you will pardon my accent."

Napoleon shifted in his chair and clutched his stomach. "Yes, *mais oui*, I realize this in principle," he answered unhappily. "I have some knowledge of history, myself. Forty centuries look down upon us. But you must realize in your turn, *Monsieur le Plenipotentiaire*, that a vast outpouring of energy has been released in France. The people will not return to their placid lives under the *ancien régime*. They have tasted adventure. They will always desire it."

Alex wagged his forefinger. Tanni's glance reminded him that this might not be the perfect gesture to make at the Emperor, and he hastily took up his drink. "Ah, but messire," he said, "think further, I beg you. You ask what will engage the interest of your populace, should the Grand Army be disbanded. Why, what else but the natural successor to the Empire? The Republic!"

"Qu'est-ce que vous dites?" asked Napoleon, and pricked up his ears.

"I comprehend, messire," Alex said. "Cares of state have kept you from studying what happened to Terrestrial France beyond your own period. Well, I have a number of books which I will gladly copy off for your perusal. I am sure you will find that French party politics can be more intricate and engaging than the most far-ranging military campaign." He paused. "In fact, messire, if you should choose to abdicate and stand for elective office, you would find the challenge greater than any you might have encountered at Austerlitz. Should you win your election, you will find matters more complicated than ever at Berezina or Waterloo. But go forward, indomitable, *mon petit caporal!*" he cried. *"Toujours l'audace!"*

Napoleon leaned over the table, breathing heavily. Moisture glistened on his black nose. Alex saw that he had him hooked.

At Mixumaxu spaceport, the Joneses bade Brob an affectionate farewell. "Do come back and see us," Tanni invited. "You're an old darling, did anybody ever tell you?" When he stooped to hug her, she kissed him full on his slightly radioactive mouth.

The couple returned to their residence in a less pleasant mood. Leopold Ormen had appeared at the city and applied for clearance to depart in his private spaceship.

Tanni begged to be excused from meeting him again. She felt too embarrassed. Alex insisted that she had made no mistake which he would not have made himself under the circumstances, but she refused anyway. Instead, she proposed, let her spend the time preparing a sumptuous dinner for the family; and then, after the children had gone to bed—

Thus Alex sat alone behind his desk when the journalist entered at the appointed hour. Ormen seemed to have lost none of his cockiness. "Well, Jones," he said, as he lowered himself into a chair and lit a cigarette, "why do I have to see you before I leave?"

"We've stuff to discuss," Alex answered, "like your involvement in the Kratch conspiracy."

Ormen gestured airily. "What are you talking about?" he laughed. "Me? I'm nothing but a reporter—and if perchance you get paranoid about me, that's a fact which I'll report."

"Oh, I have no proof," Alex admitted. "The League investigation and the trials of the obviously guilty will drag on for years, I suppose. Meanwhile you'll come under the statute of limitations, damn it. But just between us, you were part and parcel of the thing, weren't you? Your job was to prepare the way for the Kratch, and afterward it would've been to write and televise the stories which would have brought our whole system down."

Ormen narrowed his eyes. "Those are pretty serious charges, Jones," he lipped thinly. "I wouldn't like your noising them around, even in private conversation. They could hurt me; and I don't sit still for being hurt. No, sir."

He straightened. "All right," he said, "let's be frank. You've found indications, not legal proof but indications, that would cause many of my audience and my readers to stop trusting me. But on my side— Jones, I've seen plenty on this planet. Maybe somehow you did pull your chestnuts out of the fire. But the incredible, left-handed way that you did it—not to mention the data I've gotten on your crazy, half-legal improvisations in the past— Let me warn you, Jones. If you don't keep quiet about me, I'll publish stories that will destroy you."

From his scalp to his toes, a great, tingling warmth rushed through Alex. He had nothing to fear. True, in the course of his duties he had often fallen into ridiculous positions, but this had taught him indifference to ridicule. As for his record of accomplishment, it spoke for itself. Nobody could have bettered it. Nobody in his right mind would want to try. Until such time as he had brought them to full autonomy, Alexander Jones was the indispensable man among the Hokas.

He could not resist. Rising behind the desk, be drew himself to his full height, fixed Leopold Ormen with a steely eye, and rapped out: *"Publish and be damned!"*

III.
Star Prince Charlie

PROLOGUE

Seen from Earth, the sun of the planet which men have named New Lemuria lies in the southern constellation of Toucan. Of course, it is not seen from Earth except through powerful telescopes, for it lies more than 200 light-years away. A Sol-type star is nowhere near bright enough to reach the naked eye across such a distance.

Nevertheless, New Lemuria is especially interesting to humans, not only because the world is quite similar to Earth, but because its natives are quite similar to them. It was only natural for the Interbeing League to make humans its agents for the guidance of this race. Although the League was organized for the mutual benefit of all starfaring creatures, one must admit that—for example—an eight-tentacled Zaggerak, breathing hydrogen at minus 100 degrees, would be at somewhat of a disadvantage here.

And guidance, education, development have long been recognized as a duty which the civilized owe to the primitive. Glamorous though a preindustrial society may look, it is nearly always overburdened with handicaps and horrors which modern science and technology can eliminate. Furthermore, every new planet which joins the League is one more contributor to its strength and prosperity.

At the same time, the greatest care is essential. Development must not go too fast. Only imagine atomic bombs in the possession of Stone Age savages! More seriously, imagine natives becoming dependent on the products of an industry which they are unable to operate themselves. Still more seriously, consider the chaos and heartbreak that a sudden breakdown of ancient institutions always causes. Finally, by far the most important, is the right of every people to freely choose their own destiny.

Thus guidance may not be thrust on a race. It may only be offered. If the offer is accepted, the agents of the League must operate with extreme care, never letting their actions run ahead of their knowledge. They must enforce severe restrictions both on themselves and on any visitors from space. Often the natives will object to such a policy of making haste slowly. But it is for their own long-range good.

At first the case of New Lemuria looked fairly typical. League representatives contacted the leaders of its most advanced society. To be exact, they contacted the rulers of the Kingdom of Talyina, the largest, strongest, and most influential country on the planet. It had reached an Iron Age level of development. Socially it was backward, being a kind of feudal monarchy. But the Talyinan lords were willing to let the League establish a base, if only for the sake of the trade goods this would bring in.

From the League viewpoint, that was just a means to an end—the gradual introduction of the ideas and ideals of civilization. It would take generations, perhaps centuries before New Lemuria was ready for full status and membership in the commonalty of the starfaring worlds. But the program looked straightforward.

Until, early in this particular game—

WILLIAM RUPERT,
New Lemuria: A Study of the Random Factor,
thesis submitted in partial fulfillment of the
requirements for a master's degree in socio-
technics at the University of Bagdadburgh.

1
THE INNOCENT VOYAGE

For once the Honorable Athelstan Pomfrey, Plenipotentiary of the Interbeing League to the Kingdom of Talyina and (in theory) the planet of New Lemuria, had met somebody more pompous than himself.

"But," he sputtered, "but I am not convinced you understand, yes, comprehend the situation. The, ah, exigencies. Underdeveloped autochthons of warlike thought patterns, having lately undergone political upheaval—"

"Quite," interrupted Bertram Cecil Featherstone Smyth-Cholmondoley.

So far he had replied to Pomfrey's booming pronouncements, admonitions, and citations with fourteen "quites" and eight "indeeds." As he stood aside, Charlie Stuart found himself enjoying the spectacle. He began to feel hopes of getting some fun, as well as instruction, out of his daily sessions with Bertram.

Not that he wasn't fond of his tutor. But why had bad luck decreed that the Hoka would seize on the one particular model he did? Surely the cosmos held more colorful possibilities than an Oxford don.

Now his father was chuckling, too. That made Charlie happier still. Dad had seemed glum for quite a while, and Charlie knew the reason. Malcolm Stuart, captain of the space freighter *Highland Lass*, was worried about his only son. Charlie felt it but didn't know what to do about it. Somehow, in the last few years, an invisible wall had risen between them. Each realized how much the other wanted to break through, but neither was able.

"You will be well beyond the treaty zone where League police may travel," Pomfrey was saying for about the twentieth time. "If you get into trouble, we can't send a rescue party after you. Can try to negotiate, but if that fails, my hands are tied."

"Quite," said Bertram Smyth-Cholmondoley.

The two of them were worth traveling far to watch, Charlie thought. They stood with their rotund stomachs almost touching; the paunch of the human Plenipotentiary overhung the middle bulge of the Hoka. Pomfrey was balding and jowly. He gained little from his fashionable purple jacket, lacy white shirt, yellow bell-bottom trousers, and red slippers. They simply added to his respectability.

Bertram's quieter garb gave a wild contrast. For one thing, it was hundreds of years out of date, belonging to the nineteenth or early twentieth century on Earth. Faultless morning coat, old school tie over starched linen, striped trousers, spats, top hat, and monocle in one eye—which didn't actually need any help—would have been suitable in a museum. They most certainly were not suitable on a living teddy bear whose round head reached to the chest of an adult human.

"Oh, your persons should be safe," Pomfrey intoned. "I wouldn't let you go at all if they weren't used to visitors in Grushka and if the local baron didn't keep this entire island well pacified."

"Indeed," said Bertram in his shrill voice and clipped accent. He waved a languid hand which, except for the stubbiness of the fingers, was very humanlike. The rest of him was less so. His moon face, crowned by upstanding semicircular ears, consisted of two beady black eyes and a blunt muzzle with a moist black nose. Though he walked erect on two legs, those were short and thick, even in proportion to his tubby body. Soft golden fur covered his skin.

"My apprehensions principally concern unpredictable effects you yourselves may have on the citizenry," Pomfrey declared. "Remember, they underwent a revolution a few years ago. Unrest is prevalent. Banditry is on the increase through most of the kingdom. It is not inconceivable that some random influence may touch a nerve, spark an explosion."

"Quite," said Bertram.

"Should adverse effects ensue, you would be liable to punishment," Pomfrey continued. "We, the fully civilized, are responsible for the welfare of our underdeveloped brothers, or at a minimum for not provoking unnecessary trouble among them. Indeed—"

Bertram gave him a mildly indignant look, as if to accuse him of stealing that word.

Charlie's gaze wandered. How long must this argument go on?

The Commission dwelled in a walled compound. The buildings were prefabricated on Earth, therefore uninteresting to a visitor who had spent most of his eighteen years on that planet. The flower beds between them did hold gorgeous, strangely colored and shaped native blossoms, whose perfumes blended with the sea salt in a gentle breeze. Above one side of the compound towered the spaceship he had come in. But his eyes went from that metal spear to treetops glimpsed across the stockade. Their green was subtly different from any he had ever seen back home. They rustled and shimmered beneath a few white clouds which walked through a dazzling day.

How he longed to be off!

"I frankly wish you and young Mr. Stuart had not taken an electronic cram in the Talyinan language," Pomfrey was droning. "A number of islanders, including your guide, speak English. If you, with only the sketchiest knowledge of the psychopolitical situation, of this entire culture and its mores, if you should ignorantly say something which disturbs one of those turbulent warriors—"

Bertram must have been getting impatient too, for he was finally stirred to a new reply. "Tut-tut!" he said, and tapped Pomfrey in the stomach.

"What?" The Plenipotentiary gaped at him.

Bertram reached up, hooked Pomfrey's elbow, and pulled the human down toward him till their heads were at a confidential distance. He did this without effort. In spite of being short and chubby, Bertram, like any Hoka, had astounding strength and speed. He would have been more than a match for three or four full-grown men in good shape, let alone an aging and overweight diplomat. Casually, he yanked the other down so that the chief representative of the Interbeing League was forced to stand on one foot and flail his free arm to keep balance.

"Yonder lad," said Bertram kindly, "is, as you have observed, my pupil. I've been engaged to tutor him during his travels. He must be prepared to enter college when we return. *Ergo*, in the absence of his father, Captain Stuart, I stand *in loco parentis* to Master Charles Edward. On this little jaunt of ours into the hinterland, I myself shall be responsible. Hence you may set your mind at rest. *Quod erat demonstrandum.*" After a second he added, "Your mind is at rest, isn't it?"

"Guk!" gargled Pomfrey, striving to escape from the iron grip upon him, regain his lost balance, and reassert his dignity. "It is! It is!"

Bertram released him. He gasped and wiped sweaty brow.

"Then pip-pip, old chap." The Hoka beamed. "Best we be off now, if we're to make Grushka by nightfall, eh, what? I've studied those jolly old maps of yours." He bowed to the space skipper. "Sir, I feel confident our junket will prove most educational for my charge." In a whisper that could be heard for meters: "Enlightening. Psychologically salutary. Right?" To Charlie: "Come, my young friend, say your farewells in proper style and let's be gone. We've already kept our chauffeur waiting an unconscionable time. Mustn't abuse the lower classes."

Charlie first offered Pomfrey a polite, formal, good-bye. The Plenipotentiary wasn't a bad man. He seemed too fussy and rule-bound, perhaps not the ideal choice for a medievallike country. But he had been hospitable enough and had actually raised no serious objection to the proposed tour. To shake his father's hand was more difficult for Charlie. Except for red hair, blue eyes, and freckled, sharply cut features, they hadn't a great deal in common. Both wished it were otherwise. Captain Stuart was tall and rawboned, hearty of manner, as intelligent as a space officer must be, but fonder of sports than study. Charlie would never match his father's height. In plain blue tunic and trousers, his frame showed wiry rather than muscular.

"So long, Dad," he said, in a low voice.

"Take care," Captain Stuart answered softly. Louder: "A good orbit to you! Enjoy yourself!"

"Th-thanks." Charlie turned about fast and hurried off with Bertram.

Captain Stuart stared after them till they were out of sight. Pomfrey cleared his throat. "Ah-hum!" said the Plenipotentiary. "I hope my cautionings don't have you worried. Simply my duty, to reinforce proper procedures in their minds. They should encounter no hazard whatsoever. And it's merely for a week."

In fact, the jaunt was scheduled for less than that, since New Lemuria rotates in twenty hours.

The tall man shook himself. "Oh. Sure," he said.

"Merely a trip to Grushka, to inspect native architecture, folkways, historic sites, et cetera," Pomfrey continued. "Scores of people have made it, mostly spacehands but not infrequently passengers, when a vessel which called here has had to layover like yours. The inhabitants are used to tourists."

Stuart nodded absently. He had reviewed the situation in detail before he gave his own permission.

His ship had brought a consignment of off-planet wares and was supposed to pick up local products in exchange—dried seafood, vegetable oils, exotic furs, and handicrafts. Because of the current troubles, these goods were not waiting for him, but delivery was promised soon. In such cases, the rule was that a freighter delayed liftoff. Native merchandise was seldom especially valuable to a far-flung civilization. But the encouragement of those natives to deal with that civilization was important.

The Kingdom of Talyina occupied no continent, but rather a group of islands. Shverkadi was neither the greatest nor the least of these. It lay near the western edge of the archipelago. The League Commission wanted to remain a little off side, so as not to get too closely involved with a monarchy that was often oppressive. It established its base at the thinly populated north end of Shverkadi. The harbor town of Grushka was at the south end.

"I would have avoided the lecturing altogether," Pomfrey said— Stuart privately doubted that—"except for the recent political unrest, which may not be finished yet. But given reasonable discretion, no outsiders should meet serious problems."

"Anyhow," the captain replied in a rough tone, "you can't keep a young fellow tied down forever. You've got to let him try his wings, never mind the risk."

Pomfrey stroked a double chin. "The, ah, circumstances do appear a trifle unusual," he remarked.

Stuart couldn't help blurting, "Maybe not. Spacemen spend long stretches away from home. It makes for strains in the family."

"You wish to, ah, become closer to your son, and therefore took him along on this trip?"

"Yes. He's always been . . . well, bookish. Too much by himself, I think; living too much in his imagination, not the real universe. Oh, don't get me wrong. I'm all for learning. If Charlie becomes an artist or a scientist or whatever, that's fine. But hang it, he ought to live more. Finally my wife and I agreed he should come on a voyage with me. A swing through the frontier worlds might stimulate him to be more active, more sociable. That's why I haven't opposed, have even pushed, his idea of visiting Grushka. And I'm deliberately sending no one along except Bertram. Let's start Charlie coping with things by himself, instead of daydreaming while somebody else manages for him."

Pomfrey raised his eyebrows. "I must say, Captain, that sophont who accompanies him is, mmm, unique."

Stuart relaxed a bit and laughed. "Isn't he!"

Pomfrey grimaced. "A Hoka, did you call him?"

"Yes. Native of the planet Toka. I'm surprised you haven't heard of it. It's still under guidance, but moving fast toward full status. A good many individuals of that race already have jobs or scholarships that keep them on other worlds. Bertram studied in Great Britain. It's affected him."

"It certainly has!" Pomfrey huffed. "Though why he should imitate a classical rather than a modern Englishman is beyond me."

Stuart laughed again. "That's the Hoka character. They're extremely bright and quick to learn. But they have absolutely overriding imaginations. Any role that strikes a Hoka's fancy he'll play to the hilt, till he hits on a different one that he likes better." He paused. "Or is 'play' the right word? 'Live' might be more accurate. Oh, a Hoka doesn't get confused about identity or anything like that. But apparently he's so single-minded, so thoroughgoing, that his new personality *becomes* the true one, for him or for his entire society. I've been on Toka myself and seen complete replicas of the Wild West, Camelot, the French Foreign Legion—things Earth forgot long ago, but the Hokas found in books or tapes. Somehow, our Bertram decided to be an old-time Oxford don."

"And still you hired him for a tutor?" Pomfrey asked.

"By and large, I'm well pleased. Bertram may slouch about smoking a foul old pipe and quoting tag ends of Latin. But he knows what he's supposed to know, and he gets the information into Charlie's head. I can't even guess how much miscellaneous learning he carries around besides. And then he's physically powerful. We might someday be glad he is."

Pomfrey winced at that reminder. Stuart saw, and decided to be gentle to his host. "Why not come aboard ship?" he invited. "I've stuff you haven't seen yet, from any number of planets, that ought to interest you. Frankly, I admire you for sticking it out in this backwater where nothing important ever happens."

2
STRANGER IN A STRANGE LAND

As he left the compound, Charlie lost what sadness he had felt at bidding his father good-bye. He was off for adventure! He all but pranced in sheer glee. Gravity on New Lemuria is 90 percent that of Earth—no great difference, but he could feel that he was several kilos lighter than at home. And the sun stood at early morning; wind whooped off the sea and brawled in the trees; overhead soared winged creatures that were snowy against a sapphire sky.

The vehicle in which he and Bertram were to ride stood beyond the main gate. Its driver lifted his right arm in salute.

He was a typical New Lemurian of this region, which is to say he looked rather like a man whose legs were a trifle too long for the stocky torso. In fact, all his proportions were noticeably though not extremely nonhuman. His hands bore six fingers apiece. On his blocky head, the eyes were large and green, with no whites showing; the nose flat; the ears pointed and movable. His blue hair grew in a crest over the top of his scalp. His skin was bright yellow. He had no beard but, being a male, sported catlike whiskers, which he had dyed red.

For clothes he wore a bolero jacket of scaly leather, green trousers tucked into floppy boots, a scarlet sash, and a pouch. Sheathed at one hip was a knife, at the other a curved sword.

"Greeting!" he hailed in English. The shape of his speech organs added an indescribable overtone to his Talyinan accent. "I am Toreg, your friendly guide. Please to go aboard."

While Charlie had seen a yachina before, this was his first chance to travel in one. It ought to be an unusual experience, to say the least. The conveyance vaguely resembled a wooden Ferris wheel. Around its rim were six platforms. On each of these stood a yachi—the chief beast of burden on New Lemuria, suggestive of a giant kangaroo, though with a larger head and a blue pelt. The yachis were tethered, not harnessed, in place. At the hub of the double wheel hung a gimbal-mounted open box with benches inside.

Toreg helped carry their baggage up one of the spokes. These were also ladders, being twinned and having rungs between their halves. After stowing the gear, the three took their places, Charlie on the rear bench, the two others side by side in front. "Please to hang on tight till we have speed," warned the native. "I, Toreg, require this." He took a long whip from a socket and cracked it behind the yachi directly ahead of him.

Well trained, the beast leaped upward. Obedient to the third law of motion, the yachina began rolling forward. The next yachi bounded likewise, and the next, until they were all rhythmically hopping. Six gongs of varying tones, beaten by a cam-driven arrangement, directed them.

At first progress was in shuddering jerks. But as the yachina accelerated, the ride became smoother. Soon they moved at what Charlie estimated was an even ten kilometers per hour. It seemed like an utterly mad design for a vehicle, before he reflected that New Lemuria had no horses, oxen, or indeed any large and steady-gaited domestic animals.

Feet thumped on planks; gongs resounded; gravel in the dirt road rattled; the whole structure creaked and groaned. Above the noise, Toreg said, "We stop at village called Push for lunch and change team. Next we push on. Is joke. Is to go ha-ha."

"Well, actually, old egg," replied Bertram in fluent Talyinan, "considering the meaning of 'Push' "—which was the name of a variety of seafowl—"I am forced to admit that your otherwise miserable pun includes winged words."

"Hai!" exclaimed Toreg in the same language. "You talk good Peoplespeak!"

Bertram's nose rose slightly in the air. "Come, come, my dear fellow," he said, in English so he could employ certain technical terms. "I speak not good but perfect Talyinan. You will find Master Stuart equally proficient. True, we did not acquire a bally native lingo just for the sake of a week's touring. It was to initiate my pupil in the use of the electronic language inductor."

Toreg's crest and whiskers bristled. His lips curled back, revealing formidable teeth. "Seek you to make fun of me?" he growled in his own tongue. "If so, declare it like an honest male, that we may duel and I cut you in half."

"Oh, piffle." Bertram adjusted his monocle. "I couldn't allow that. Not when I'm responsible for the scion of the Stuart house. Fine sort of guardian I'd look, cut in half. Eh, what? No offense intended, I assure you. Here, have a drop of sherry and let us revel in the good old rustic scene, what, what, what?" From beneath his coat he produced a silver hip flask uncapped and offered it.

Toreg took the container and sniffed. A broad grin made his mustache tips quiver. No doubt his threat had not been seriously meant, Charlie decided. In a violent culture, a male of warrior stock had to be touchy or at any rate act like it.

Charlie turned his attention from Toreg to the landscape about them. And indeed the landscape was delightful. Tall feather-leaved trees, full of rich fragrance, bright-winged insects and caroling birds, confronted a grassy slope which led down to sparkling sea waters. Afar he glimpsed a fishing boat, high-prowed beneath a red fore-and-aft sail.

Of course, he thought, he probably should avoid words like "insect," "bird," or "grass." Though life on New Lemuria had close parallels to that on Earth, any biologist could point out innumerable differences. However, for ordinary purposes it was easiest to use unscientific language—for instance, to say "fish" instead of "ichthyoid."

"Ho!" Toreg was exclaiming happily. "Shmiriz!"

"No—" Bertram began. He was too late. Toreg put the flask to his mouth and poured down a healthy swig of the contents. Then he choked. He dropped the liquor and clutched at his throat.

"Ee-ee-aa-aaroo-ooh!" he howled. "I burn! I am on fire! Poisoned! Help!"

Bertram caught the flask in midair and turned around to Charlie. "Now there, young Stuart," he said gravely, "let that be a lesson to you. Note well the effects of a limited education. This disgraceful hullaballoo over a simple drop of sherry."

"That's what you call it," Charlie retorted. "It's really that awful rotgut nobody but a Hoka can drink without ruining himself inside."

"Tut-tut," said Bertram. "I see I must coach you in logic. A gentleman drinks sherry. I am a gentleman. Therefore, what I drink is sherry."

Meanwhile Toreg's wails had diminished to grunts, which gradually developed a pleased note. At last he paused, looked at Bertram, and licked his lips. "More sherry?" he asked.

"Within strict limits, old chap," said the Hoka. "You must remain fit to drive, what? And you're accustomed to nothing stronger than that, ah, shmiriz you mentioned." The metabolism of his own race gave him an incredible capacity for alcohol before he was much affected by it.

"Ha, little you know!" Toreg grabbed the flask and took a more careful gulp. "I am a warrior—a household trooper of Lord Dzenko of Roshchak—as mighty at the flowing bowl and the steaming trencher as I am on the field of battle."

Bertram grew interested. "Say on, old bean," he urged.

For an alarmed instant, Charlie wondered if his tutor might decide to switch roles and become a barbaric Talyinan. But no, that would scarcely happen. However volatile on the surface, Hokas kept steadfast in what counted. Besides, they usually adopted characters from human history or literature.

A warrior's life had always tempted Charlie. Everyone seemed to like him well enough, but he had no close friends and often felt lonesome. He would then imagine himself with a wholly changed personality—a man of action, who led other men on great feats of derring-do. . . .

He came back to reality with a start. He must have been day-dreaming for quite a while. Toreg had been nipping and talking and had gotten maudlin.

"I *was* a warrior, a household trooper of Lord Dzenko, mighty at the laden board and on the clanging battlefield. Today I am but a servant of the humans."

"Dear me." Bertram clicked his tongue in sympathy. "Cashiered, eh? Drumhead court-martial, no doubt. Stripped your buttons off."

"Huh? What're you hooting about? I was sent away in honor, I was. My good Lord Dzenko—may he live prodigiously—had to reduce the size of his guard. He had to let me go, 'mong a lot of others. But he didn't want to." Toreg waggled a forefinger. "As a matter of fact, fuzzy one, my good Lord Dzenko pers'nally found me the job I've got. He knows the Plenipotentiary. I've heard him more'n once, asking the Plenipotentiary to help us here in his province. He could, you know—the Plenipotentiary, I mean. He could whistle up flying ships and, uh, guns and everything, and make an end of Olaghi. But no, he won't. Keeps quacking about, uhn, noninterference . . . the law of the League—"

"Well, why did Lord Dzenko have to dismiss most of his fighters?" Bertram asked. "High cost of living, perhaps?"

"No," Toreg growled. "Olaghi made him. Olaghi the accursed."

Charlie listened, fascinated, while Bertram got the story. It took hours. Not only was Toreg a little incoherent by now, but centuries of history needed explaining.

However, basically the past of Talyina paralleled many countries on Earth. A conquering warlord had created the kingdom by bringing less powerful chieftains under him, throughout the islands. But while those magnates had to swear service to the king, they kept a great deal of local authority and their own troops of warriors. These they used against bandits, pirates, and foreign enemies. Occasionally this feudal system broke down, but hitherto order had always been restored after a period of chaos.

At last few bandits or pirates were left, and no foreign enemies within ready sailing distance. About that time the League established its Commission. Pomfrey hoped for social progress, the gradual evolution of barons into squires and their councils into a true, democratic Parliament. But he was only allowed to encourage that, not take any direct hand in affairs.

Several years ago, the last head of the old royal house died without heirs. Pomfrey had been preparing for this, urging the barons to elect a new king but limit his powers. Unfortunately, a strong noble, Olaghi, had been preparing, too. With the help of several of his fellows, he seized the capital and proclaimed himself the ruler. After some fighting, the lords of the islands yielded.

Olaghi thereupon proceeded to make social changes of his own. He replaced as many barons as he was able with his favorites. He forced the remainder to reduce their private troops to mere guardian corps. Besides collecting tribute from them, he imposed high new taxes directly on the common people.

Yet Talyina did not revolt. Apart from the fact that Olaghi had taken care to make a successful revolution look impossible, there was the fact that no Talyinan could really imagine doing without a king. And he was on the throne, however dubious his claim to it.

"Bad to worse, bad to worse," Toreg mumbled. "Time indeed for the Prince of the Prophecy to arrive, if ever he does. . . ."

Sad though the tale was, Charlie didn't let it spoil his enjoyment. The countryside was picturesque, and the natives he saw didn't look unhappy. When he pointed this out, Toreg insisted it had a double cause. First, Shverkadi Island was in the fief of Lord Dzenko, who managed to protect his subjects somewhat, especially since the capital was far from here. Second, more important, the League outpost was on Shverkadi, and Olaghi was too cunning to let the representatives of the stars see daily wretchedness.

What Charlie spied seemed prosperous in a primitive fashion. After a stretch of forest, broken by an occasional camp of charcoal burners, cultivated clearings began to appear. South of Push, the coastal land was nothing but farms.

The stop at the village was a diverting spectacle. Toreg pulled on a brake lever with one hand while he disconnected the gongs with the other. Lacking a beat to guide them, the yachis jumped out of phase, until they stopped altogether. Thus the wheel jerked to a halt. Charlie and Bertram nearly lost their seats. This was at the inn, a long thatch-roofed wooden house near the waterfront. Behind it, a few similar buildings sprawled along dusty irregular streets, where animals wandered about among females, who nearly all carried heavy burdens of one sort or another. In front lay the dock. Most boats were out fishing. Most males not aboard them were in the fields, toiling with hoes and spades. Charlie had thought the Middle Ages atmosphere romantic, but now he started to see why the League felt that everybody had a right to modern machinery as soon as he could safely use it.

In the dirt-floored common room stood a plank table and benches. The travelers sat down and had lunch, paying for it in brass coins of the kingdom, of which they had an ample supply. They were served by the landlord's wife and daughters. New Lemurian females lacked the cat whiskers of the males and indeed looked still more human except for being completely bald. Their customary dress was a one-piece gown, ankle-length, ornamented with tie-dyeing or beadwork, caught at the waist by a belt from which dangled small tools for their endless tasks.

The food was coarse black bread, cheese, meat, and fruits, accompanied by ale or milk. Again he realized he was using English words for things which were never of Earth. Everything had a taste, smell, and texture alien to him, usually flavorful but strange—like the milk, which reminded him of nutmeg and dill pickles. The basic bio-chemistries were so similar that a human or a Hoka could eat most New Lemurian dishes and get ample nourishment. Yet the variations were such that no native germ could live in their bodies. The Talyinans had barely begun to learn about sanitation—one of Pomfrey's more successful programs—but Charlie and Bertram need not fear getting sick on this planet.

The landlord's sons released the tired yachis. When the moment came to put a fresh team on the wheel, Toreg did the job himself. Charlie soon saw why. It took special skill.

Apparently yachis were not very sharp-witted. Their normal reaction upon being startled or displeased was to leap three or four meters straight up. Twice Charlie had the entertainment of seeing Toreg carried along, clinging to a tether and swearing a blue streak till he thumped back down, rolled over, and sprang erect.

Under the circumstances, it was surprising how kindly he treated the animals. Aside from sulfurous language, he did not force but coaxed them onto their platforms, working the monster wheel forward so as to bring each position near the ground. In spite of Toreg's bloodthirsty talk about his military prowess, Charlie decided the Talyinans could not be as simple or as brutal as they might appear.

The yachina got going again and rolled south. The road was broader and better. Traffic increased. Regular wagons trundled their loads, drawn by their owners or hirelings. Charlie also saw a few mules at work, another benefit of interstellar trade. An occasional rider bounded by on his yachi, cloak flapping off his shoulders, midriff tightly swathed, and jaws bandaged shut against the continual jolting. Peasants in the grainfields, children herding tame fowl or meat animals, unimpressed when they saw a human go by, gawked at sight of the Hoka. Slowly on the left, at the edge of the sea horizon, grew the dim vision of a neighbor island, and in the channel between, trawlers dragged their nets.

At midsummer in Talyina the days are long. Yet the sun had dropped low when Charlie reached Grushka and his destiny.

3
A NIGHT AT AN INN,

This town had a population of a few thousand. As at Push, they lived in thatched timber houses, gaudily painted. But these narrow, twisty, littered and evil-smelling streets were cobbled, which made the last part of the yachina ride teeth-rattling, and the docks accommodated quite a number of boats and small ships. The hostel which Toreg had chosen fronted on a market square. Opposite stood the League's gift to a combustible community, a fire station, with horse-drawn wagons and hand-operated water pumps. At their present stage, the Talyinans would have gotten little good from motorized equipment. Where would they find energy charges, replacement parts, or skilled mechanics?

A plump landlord bustled out to greet the arrivals. When he saw Charlie, he rubbed his hands together. The youth suspected that prices went up a hundred percent for a "rich Earthling." The landlord wasn't too surprised by Bertram; a few nonhuman spacefarers had already visited New Lemuria.

"Ah," he burbled in English, "welcome, lovely folk, to your every-modern-convenience lodgings at the Sign of the Ritz! Immediate reservations. A gong boy will bring your baggage. Wash off the stench of travel while my wives prepare delicious dainties for your gorging and swilling. How eager are we to listen to your boasts! How few our bedbugs! How silent our fowl in the dawn!"

Inside was a wainscoted rough-raftered taproom, fronds strewn on its clay floor, dimly lit by sconced candles and the flames on the hearth. A chimney conducted away most smoke, another innovation from the stars. The rest of the "modern conveniences" amounted to a compartment where guests were required to check lethal weapons, a bath whose cold-water shower was fed by a cistern, and a couple of overstuffed leather armchairs beside the central table and its benches. Upstairs were bedrooms, on whose straw pallets visitors usually spread their own sleeping bags.

Having cleaned himself, Charlie joined Bertram and Toreg at dinner. This was a thick stew, plus abundant drink served in carved wooden flagons. Word of the newcomers was getting around, and townsmen were coming in to meet them. The landlord beamed at the extra trade. Charlie was hard put to answer the questions which poured over him. With scant organized entertainment, and most of them illiterate, these people were happy to meet outsiders. Charlie's opinion of the Middle Ages went down another notch.

He was tired, however. It had been a lengthy and exciting day. After his meal he curled into one of the big chairs. Nobody followed him. They clustered around Bertram, who was the real novelty as well as the inexhaustible talker. Charlie was glad of that. He decided he'd just sit and listen for a bit, then go to bed.

The sight before him was exotic, he thought: rude chamber, leaping, sputtering flames and weaving shadows, Talyinan males crowded on benches or squatting on the floor. Bertram sat at the end of the table across from Toreg. His short golden-furred form, now clad in a tuxedo, seemed appealingly helpless among these burly fishers and artisans.

"More sherry?" he invited.

The guide, who had already had some of it, shook his head. "No. You try shmiriz." He thumped a pot of the local brew down onto the planks.

"Tut-tut," reproved Bertram. "A gentleman prefers sherry." He stopped to think. "Or should it be port, at this hour? Yes, by Jove, port. Forgetful of me. Must make a note." His monocle caught a fire gleam as he took forth a penstyl and scribbled on his cuff. "Right-o. Would you care for a spot of port, my good fellow?"

"No," growled Toreg. "You try our shmiriz. Not to insult us."

"Oh, very well," agreed the Hoka. He emptied the pot into his flagon.

"Shmiriz got power," Toreg bragged. "Turns your ears purple."

A gasp of awe rose from the crowd when Bertram drained his huge cup in a single swallow.

"Nonsense," he said. "Do my ears look purple?"

Toreg squinted blearily. "Too much fur on them to tell," he complained.

Charlie's eyelids drooped. . . .

A racket brought him awake. Through the door swaggered half a dozen more Talyinans. They made the rest appear meek. Above their trousers and boots they wore coats of jingling ring mail. Above their scarred faces rode spiked conical helmets with noseguards and chain coifs. Over their backs were slung round shields on which the emblem of a fire-breathing snake had been painted. Besides their swords, two carried battle axes, two crossbows, two pikes whose butts they stamped on the ground. Every belt held at least four knives.

The leader bulked enormous, a full two meters in height. His shoulders filled the doorway. His whiskers, each dyed a separate color, reached nearly as wide.

Toreg stared, leaped to his feet, and shouted in joy, "Mishka! My dear old boss!"

"Toreg!" bawled the giant. "Why, you flop-eared flap-tongue, welcome back!" His green glance fell on Bertram; Charlie, off in the shadows, escaped notice. "Hai! Doom and hurricanes, what pretty doll have you fetched us?"

The group tossed their weapons a-clatter toward the checkroom, for the landlord's family to pick up. When Mishka strode to the table, Charlie felt the earth quiver a bit. Bertram rose. "Lemme . . . innerdooshe you." Toreg hiccupped. "Uh, Bertram Smyth-Chum-Chum . . . Chum-m-m . . . from, uh, where's it you said? Meet muh former boss." He got control over his tongue. "Mishka, Sergeant in Chief of Household Guards to Dzenko, dread Lord of Roshchak! Mishka, first warrior of the West, equal to forty in combat, man of unquenchable thirst and appetite!"

" 'D'je do," said Bertram politely.

"Let's shake hands like humans," Mishka proposed, not to be outdone in courtesy. Or did he wish to test strength? Muscles rippled and knotted; he must be squeezing hard. Bertram smiled and squeezed back. Astonishment came over Mishka's countenance. He let go at once. His left hand surreptitiously fingered the right.

Still, he held no grudge, simply regarded the Hoka with sudden respect. "Drink!" he clamored while he shucked his helmet. Civilians on the benches scrambled to make room before the warriors should pitch them off.

"And what brings you here, Sergeant, if I may ask?" Bertram inquired.

"Oh, patrol against bandits," Mishka said. "Didn't find any. Plague and shipwreck, what a dull tour! Going home tomorrow. Rather hear about you, fuzzy sir."

Charlie's lids fell down again. . . .

He must have slept for a couple of hours. A roar wakened him.

Blinking, he saw that the fire had guttered low and most of the guests had departed. Their work started at sunrise, after all. Mishka's squad and Toreg snored on the floor or, heads on arms, across a table shiny from spilled liquor. Only their outsized chief and the small Hoka had stayed the course, and both of them were finally showing its effects.

"Olaghi!" Mishka trumpeted. He crashed his flagon down. "I'll tell you 'bout King Olaghi, may the Great Ghost eat his liver! Olaghi the Tyrant! Olaghi the Cruel! Olaghi the Meat-Stingy! Woe to the world, that Olaghi rules over Talyina!"

"Not the best sort, I take it?" Bertram asked.

"*Best?* Worst—worst usurper—"

"Usurper?" Bertram's ears pricked up. According to Toreg's account during the day, Olaghi had as much hereditary right to the throne as anybody, little though that might be.

"Usurper!" Mishka snarled, and pointed his own ears forward like horns. "Not is he from Bolgorka, the capital, whence th' ol' royal house sprang. He's bloody foreigner—from Nyekh. Not really part of Talyina. Just got dual monarchy with us. And now they've shoved their man onto our backs!"

"Ah." The Hoka nodded. "Of course. I understand. Rather like the first Georges."

"The whats?"

"Quite. Kings of England on Earth. In the eighteenth century of our reckoning, but not English—a Hanoverian line—"

Bertram went on to relate the history. Carried away by it—and, no doubt, liters of shmiriz—he waxed more and more indignant at the wrongs inflicted by the Hanoverian kings, especially on Scotland, after that brave country had risen to restore the rightful dynasty—the Stuart dynasty, from which in fact his own companion could claim descent. . . .

Charlie dozed off. . . .

When next he woke, it was to the sound of singing. Bertram stood on the table. Gone were his monocle, bow tie, and coat. Rolling his r's in an accent which had nothing of Oxford about it, he bellowed, in his reedy voice, a Jacobite song hastily translated into Talyinan.

"Charlie is my darling, my darling, my darling—"

Down on the bench, Mishka regarded him glassy-eyed and open-mouthed.

"—The young Chevalier!" finished Bertram, and added a few steps of the Highland fling. Bouncing back to his seat, he refilled both cups. "Beautiful, is it no? Aye, beautiful!"

Since the translation had necessarily involved phrases like "the

young yachi rider," the present Charles Edward Stuart felt doubts
about that. Mishka didn't.

"Beautiful." The guardsman wiped a tear from an eye. "Reminds
me—you listen now." He began to chant rather than sing:

Woe is the world, when for Talyina's weal
Reigns no true ruler, but only a rascal.
Sorrow and sadness make sour the shmiriz.
Weary are Westfolk who wobble 'neath burdens—

"Wobble? I dinna ken the trope, lad," Bertram said, or the native
equivalent thereof.

"Shut up," Mishka grunted. "You listen. This is the Holy Prophecy.
Hun'erds o' years old."

He went on at some length, describing a period during which a
murrain was on the yachis and eggfowl, cooking pots stood empty
everywhere, and the hearts of warriors were grieved, for a false king
had brought down the anger of the gods upon the realm. But then—his
basso rose in volume, causing a few of the sleepers to stir and mutter—
then came hope.

When all feel forsaken, and fell is the hour,
Wildly and welcome from out of the west,
Royally red-haired, and riding in leaps,
The Prince of the people comes pounding
     to save them—

"Red hair, aye, aye!" shouted Bertram. "Like my ain young
Chevalier yonder!"

Charlie shook his head in bewilderment. The entire scene had
taken on an eerie, dreamlike character.

Mishka chanted relentlessly:

Five are the Feats that his followers wait for.
Many will meet then to marvel and join him,
The wonders he worked having proven him worthy.
Hear, under heaven, the hero's five doings!

It took concentration to sort out, from interminable verses loaded
with elaborate figures of speech, just what was supposed to happen.
But Charlie gathered that this prince would establish his identity by
accomplishing five things impossible for anybody else.

First, with a crossbow, in a fog and at fifty paces, he would shoot a bellfruit off the head of his best friend. Next, he would slay something unspecified but dreadful known as the Sorrow of Avilyogh. Thereafter he would sail ("Singing and swigging while other lie scasick") to Belogh, where he would fight and overcome three invincible warriors, brothers, whom that town maintained. His fourth deed, on the island of Lyovka, was of a more intellectual type. It seemed that three Priests of a certain god dwelled there, who challenged all comers to answer three riddles. Those who tried and failed, as everyone did, were cast into a fiery furnace. But the prince gave the correct replies with scornful ease. His last feat was to enter the Grotto of Kroshch, wait out the high tide which completely submerged it, and emerge unharmed—even playing his horpil, whatever that might be.

When he had thus proved himself, warriors would flock to his standard. Mishka concluded triumphantly:

In terror, the tyrant who caused all the trouble,
The false king, goes fleeing, unfollowed, in shame.
Tall over Talyina towers the mighty.
Righteous, the red-haired one rules us forever!

He slammed his flagon back down on the table. It broke, while a fountain of shmiriz leaped up over him. He didn't notice. The landlord did and made a notation on his score.

"There!" Mishka exclaimed, thick-voiced. "Wha'd 'you say to that, hai?"

The equally befuddled Hoka leaped to the floor and struck a pose, right arm flung outward, left hand clutching breast. "I say rise for the Young Prince!" he piped. "Ride, mon! Ride, and carry the wor-r-rd that Bonnie Prince Charlie has come back to his ain!"

With a whoop that shook the rafters, Mishka also sprang erect. "I go! Take rowboat . . . cross channel . . . rouse m'Lord Dzenko—for freedom!" He snatched his helmet off the table. The padded lining was still within the outer coif of mail, and he clapped the whole unit over his head. Unfortunately, he clapped it on backwards and spent a minute choking and blundering about until he got it right.

Enthusiasm undimmed, he grabbed a sword from the checkroom and staggered off into the night. His war calls echoed among the darkened houses.

Bertram was not much steadier on his feet as he approached Charlie. "Hoot, mon," he said in English, "are ye awake the noo?"

"I—gosh, I don't know," Charlie faltered.

"Aweel, 'tis time ye waur abed." The Hoka scooped him up in strong but gentle arms and bore him away, while crooning:

Speed, bonnie boat, like a bird on the wing.
"Onward!" the sailors cry.
Carry the lad who is born to be king
Over the sea to Skye. . . .

4
KIDNAPPED

Charlie woke late and alone. Having donned undergarments, tunic, trousers, and stout shoes, he went downstairs in search of breakfast. Toreg sat brooding over the remnants of his. "Good morning," the human said in Talyinan. "I'm sorry I overslept."

"Oversleep all you want," mumbled his guide. "Oo-ooh, my head! Worst is, that fuzzy demon was up at dawn—*cheerful.*"

"Where is Bertram?" As Charlie seated himself, a wife of the landlord brought him a dish of scrambled native eggs (they had green yolks) and a cup of hot herb tea.

"I know not," Toreg answered. "He asked me where to find a tailor and a swordsmith and bounced off. Never did I get back to sleep."

"That's too bad," Charlie said. "Uh, we will go for that ride you mentioned yesterday, won't we?" Toreg had promised a trip into the hills behind town, to see their forests and wildlife.

The guide nodded. Immediately he clutched his brow and groaned.

The fresh cup of tea seemed to make him feel a trifle better. When Charlie had eaten, they went outside. Hitched to a rail stood three saddled horses. "I didn't know there were any of these here, except for the fire department," said Charlie.

"It rents them to tourists," Toreg explained.

"What? But suppose a fire broke out!"

"Which is more important, some smelly fishermen's cabins or the mayor's treasury?"

Charlie's view of the Middle Ages sank still further. To be sure, he thought, these simple wooden houses probably weren't too hard to replace, while off-planet money could buy modern tools and materials of improvement. But did the mayor spend it on his community? Nothing in sight suggested that he did.

"Gr-r-reeting, my Prince!" resounded behind him.

Charlie jumped at the unexpected, squeaky burr. Turning, he saw Bertram. The Hoka was not dressed in the outdoor clothes he had brought along, tweed jacket, plus-fours, deerstalker cap, and so forth. Instead, he must have commissioned the tailor and smith he found to do hurry-up jobs for him.

Upon his head was a flat tam-o'-shanter sort of cap with a long feather in it. From his shoes, heavy stockings of native wool rose to his knees. Upon his body he wore a great piece of coarse red-green-and-black plaid cloth, pleated, folded, bunched, and belted to form a kilt whose end draped across torso and left shoulder. Below his stomach dangled a furry pouch. Various sizes of daggers were thrust under belt or stocking tops. Slung scabbarded over his back was a broadsword nearly as long as he was tall. This type was not unknown in Talyina, though curved sabers were generally preferred, but he had added to it a basket hilt.

"Bertram!" Charlie cried.

"Bertram?" said the Hoka. "Nay, Hieness, nae Sassenach I, but your ain Hector MacGregor—a rough, untutored Hieland mon, 'tis true, but loyal to my Prince, aye, loyal to the last wee drappie o' bluid. Ah, Charlie, 'tis lang and lang we've awaited your coming, lad."

Struck by a dreadful suspicion, Charlie tried to bring the Hoka back to his senses. "Bertram Cecil Featherstone Smyth-Cholmondoley," he said in as stern a tone as possible, "you were supposed to come along on this trip in case of trouble—"

"Aye!" With a bloodcurdling yell, the little being whipped out his sword and whirled it till the air whistled. "Let any dar-r-re lay hand on my Pr-r-rince, and the claymore o' Hector MacGregor wull cleave him for the corbies!"

Charlie leaped back. The blade had almost taken his nose off. Toreg was unimpressed and still in a sour mood. "Come along, if we're to finish our ride ere nightfall," he grumbled. "Or like you the thought of riding in the dark when ilnyas prowl?"

The Hoka sheathed his weapon and scrambled to the saddle, whose stirrups had been adjusted for him. "Aye, come, my Prince," he chirped. "And ne'er fear for your back whilst Hector MacGregor rides to guard it."

Numbly, Charlie mounted too. Toreg did likewise, doubtless glad in his present condition to be on a horse instead of a jolting yachi.

Hooves clopped on cobblestones, and the group rode out of town, followed by the stares of passersby.

It was another beautiful day, breezes full of the scents of green growth, brilliant sunlight, warbling birds. The road through the countryside soon became a mere trail, left farmsteads behind, and wound into ever steeper, wooded hills. From these Charlie had magnificent views across the island and the blue-glittering strait to its neighbor. On a headland there he spied the walls and towers of a castle. That must be Roshchak, the seat of Lord Dzenko.

As he rode, Charlie figured out what had happened to his companion. Inspired by warlike company and that curious folk poem which Mishka rendered, the typical Hoka imagination had flared up. It had seized on the coincidence of Charlie's name—well, not entirely coincidence. Captain Malcolm Stuart was of Scots descent and he named his son after the Bonnie Charlie of romantic memory, the prince whose Highland followers had tried to restore the Stuarts to the throne. The soldiers of Hanoverian King George defeated them, and Charles Stuart was forced into exile. His supporters—Jacobites, they were called— could do little more than compose sentimental songs about their Prince.

Yes, of course that part would appeal to a Hoka. Away with dull old Bertram! Up with the wild clansman Hector MacGregor!

No appeal to common sense would reverse Bertram's change. The Hoka knew perfectly well that this wasn't the eighteenth century or even the planet Earth.

Charles Edward Stuart decided not to waste breath denying his royalty. Let him play along with Bertram's—no, Hector's—fancy. It could do no harm, he supposed, and might even be fun. When they got back to the ship, his father could doubtless find some way to straighten matters out.

He had spent a couple of hours in these meditations while the horses plodded onward, Toreg nursed his hangover, and Hector recited endless border ballads. The gloomier they were, the happier the Hoka got. Charlie had almost settled down to enjoy his outing, when they met the warriors of Dzenko.

They were passing through a ravine. Its brush-covered walls blocked off vision away from the trail. Rounding a bend, the travelers confronted half a dozen armed New Lemurians.

Charlie recognized the patrol from last night. Now they were yachi-mounted. The horses shied when a couple of the kangaroolike chargers bounded past them, to cut off retreat.

"Good day. May all your enemies welter in gore," Sergeant Mishka said in conventional politeness. "How pleasant to meet you here."

Toreg, who knew them, snapped, "Belike not by chance. Methinks you waited for us, having asked in Grushka about our plans."

"Well, yes, after I returned from Roshchak before dawn and shook my squad awake," Mishka admitted. He smiled at Charlie. "When my lord Dzenko heard of you, who are red-haired and a prince—"

"I'm not really."

"Aye, Bonnie Prince Charlie and none ither!" cried Hector. "And who are ye to question the Royal Per-r-rson?"

"I question him not," Mishka replied. "I do but bear word that my lord would be honored did his Highness pay a call."

"Why, uh, I, I meant to," Charlie stammered. He did not like the way these armored males crowded near or the set expressions on their faces. "Later."

"Today," Mishka said. "We have a boat ready."

"Thanks," Charlie said. "but I'd rather—"

"I must insist."

Hector sprang from the saddle. Down on the ground, he put one foot on a boulder which protruded from the soil, drew his sword, and swung it in whining arcs. The nearby yachis edged away.

"Inseest, do ye? Nae mon shall force the Prince tae any place whaur he doesna weesh tae gae, ne'er whilst Hector MacGregor lives."

Mishka growled. His own sword flew free. His men lifted weapons.

"Hold it!" Charlie screamed. "I—I do want to see Lord Dzenko. Very much. I can't wait." To Hector he added, "Take it easy, clansman. I, uh, I will honor Lord Dzenko with my presence."

"Weel, weel," muttered the Hoka as he sheathed his blade. "But 'tis nae true Scots name, yon Dzenko."

"Oh, he's a Lowlander, I'm sure," Charlie improvised.

"Lowlander?" For a second the Hoka frowned, as if he were about to be Bertram and declare that Dzenko was not a name from anywhere on Earth. Luckily, however, he recalled that he was Hector, who didn't know any better. "Aye, nae doot, syne your Hieness says so."

The Talyinans relaxed. "Come," snapped Mishka. "We ride."

An hour's stiff travel downhill brought them to a cove, a notch in the wilderness where nobody dwelled. A large rowboat or small galley lay beached. They shoved it off and climbed aboard. One soldier stayed to tend to the animals. These were seldom transported across water; yachis bounced too much.

Mishka had spoken little. Now he ordered Charlie and Bertram into the cabin. The boy knew the reason. It explained his having been accosted in the ravine, rather than openly in town. Lord Dzenko must want everything kept secret.

Oars creaked and splashed. The boat drove forward at a good pace. Charlie wished he could look out, but the cabin had no portholes. "Ah," said Hector shrewdly, "noo I see! Yon laird be a closet Jacobite, and ye're aboot tae conspire wi' him against the usurper." He sighed. "If ainly I'd wits tae help ye twa plot! I'm nobbut a rough, unlettered Hielander, though, wi' naught tae offer save his steel and bluid." He fumbled in his pouch. "And, aye, my sporran holds money, and a sandwich, and"—he drew out his flask—"a wee bit whisky, should my prince hae hunger or thirst."

"No, thanks," Charlie whispered.

The boat docked at a village below the castle. Mishka gave hooded cloaks to the human and the Hoka, and his guardsmen surrounded them closely while they went up the path to the stronghold.

In spite of his worries, Charlie was gripped by what he saw. Here was no medieval ruin or restored museum piece. This was a working fortress.

Gray stone blocks were mortared together to form a high wall. On its parapets tramped men-at-arms in mail, archers in leather jerkins. At intervals rose turrets. From flagpoles on their tops blew banners which were not merely ornamental, but which told who the owner and his chief officers were and identified battle stations for each member of the garrison.

Behind a main gate of heavy timbers and strap iron, a flagged courtyard reached among several stone buildings. Greatest of these was the keep, a darkling pile whose windows were mere slits. Wooden lean-tos edged the curtain wall, wherein the manifold workaday activities of the castle went on.

Porters carried loads; grooms tended yachis; blacksmiths and carpenters made the air clamorous; bakers and brewers filled it with odors which blended with woodsmoke and the smell of unwashed bodies. Females and children were present, too, as well as small domestic animals and fowl walking freely and messily about. Everybody seemed to have a task, though nobody seemed in a hurry about it. Voices chattered, laughed, swore, shouted, sang snatches of song; wooden shoes thumped on stones.

Mishka dismissed his troopers at the entrance to the keep and himself conducted Charlie, Hector, and Toreg inside. The walls of an entry room bore tapestries and hunting trophies. The floor was carpeted with broad-leaved plants, whose sweetness relieved the reek of smoke from a gigantic feasting chamber where an ox-sized carcass was roasting.

By the dim interior light, Mishka pointed to a spiral staircase off the entry. "Follow that, if it please you."

At the fourth-floor landing, he received the salutes of two guards and opened the door. "Come," he said, "and meet my lord Dzenko."

5
THE REDHEADED
LEAGUE

Within, the stone of a fair sized room was relieved by rugs and by plastered walls whose frescoes depicted battle scenes. The scarlet pigment used for blood did much to brighten things, for otherwise there was only a shaft of sunlight through a narrow window. A few carved chairs were placed at irregular intervals. In one of them, sat a gaunt middle-aged New Lemurian, his face deeply lined, the blue of his crest sprinkled with gray. He wore a flowing rainbow-striped robe and silver necklace, and his whiskers were gilded.

Mishka clicked heels. "Lord Dzenko, here have brought you, unbeknownst to others as you bade, the fiery-topped person who may be the Deliverer of the Prophecy. Also, for good measure, his guide—my lord will remember Toreg—and, er—"

"Sir Hector MacGregor," said Charlie in haste, before the Hoka could declare himself a commoner. It might be protection against indignities.

Hector was quick to pick up the cue. "Aye," he declaimed, striking a pose, "an ancestor o' mine was ennobled after the Battle o' Otterburn. Let me tell ye. 'It fell aboot the Lammas tide, when the muirmen win their hay—' "

Charlie shushed him, "My name is Charles Edward Stuart. My father is captain of the ship which lately flew in from the stars. He expects me back soon."

Dzenko smiled. "I trust we can oblige him. Pity that the strange law of your folk—or perhaps their weakness—binds him from coming after you in force."

Charlie gulped. Living so close to the League's enclave, this baron must be more sophisticated about it than most.

"But do be at ease," Dzenko urged. "My only wish is to welcome you, the Prince of the Prophecy, our rescuer from oppression."

"Huh?" exploded from Toreg. "But, but, Lord—him? Why, he's not even one of our kind!"

"Does the Prophecy anywhere say he must be?" Dzenko purred. "Indeed, have you ever heard of a dweller on our world who has red hair?"

"N-no, Lord," Toreg admitted. Excitement seized him. "Could it really be? Could Olaghi in truth be overthrown, and I get my rightful job back?"

"The councils of the mighty are not for common ears," Dzenko said. "You may go, Toreg, and greet your old comrades." The guide bowed and rushed out. "You stay, Mishka," continued the baron. The gigantic guardsman placed himself at parade rest in a corner.

"You know I'm nothing of the sort," Charlie protested. "This is only a, a coincidence."

"Conceivably. Though a wise saw has it that 'Chance is the hand of heaven which hauls us.' " Dzenko rose, to take the human's arm in a confidential manner and lead him across the room. "Upon receiving the news, I, ah, did feel it my duty to investigate further. If nothing else, your presence might cause unrest among the populace."

"Maybe," Charlie admitted. "I suppose I'd better go straight back to the compound."

Dzenko's grasp tightened on his elbow. "On the other hand, perhaps you had better not."

To and fro they paced. Hector stumped behind them. "See you," Dzenko went on, low-voiced, "I say no word against our beloved King Olaghi. He would demand my head on a pikeshaft did I call him aught but a good ruler. Yet is any ruler ever as good as he might be? There are even some who call him a tyrant. Mind you, I say this not myself, but some do. When rumors start flying, a prudent man wants to know whether or not they hold the truth, so he can advise the people who are dependent on him. Now naturally, I don't imagine there's aught to this talk about your being the young Prince who'll perform the Five Feats and dethrone the wicked ruler of legend, but still, at the same time—"

He talked in that vein for several minutes. Charlie got the impression he was really stalling. Meanwhile, a clamor grew below them, shouts, running feet, occasional blasts on the crooked Talyinan trumpets.

"Mishka!" said Dzenko at last. "See what that noise is about and shut them up."

Though sharply spoken, the order had a false sound in Charlie's ears, as if rehearsed well in advance. But the guardsman clattered out at once and down the stone steps.

"The commoners are quite impetuous, you know." The baron sighed. "Get them overheated, and bloodshed is apt to follow."

Mishka reappeared, hustling Toreg along in front of him. The racket from below pursued them, louder than ever, hardly muffled when the door closed.

"Well, Sergeant, what goes on?" Dzenko demanded.

"This clown here went right out and told them the Prince has come," Mishka snarled. He gave Toreg a shake.

"What?" Dzenko's anger seemed more deliberate than genuine, but the guide quailed.

"Y-you didn't tell me not to, lord," he stammered.

"I *didn't?*"

"Did you? I, I—"

"Stupid lout!"

"Yes, my lord." Toreg cowered.

"Be quiet!" barked Dzenko. He turned on Mishka. "What do they want? And make sure you get things straight."

Stung in his pride, the officer flushed and responded stiffly, "I hope my lord does not confuse me with this yachi-brain."

"Fry and sizzle you, numbwit!" roared Dzenko. "Will you answer a simple question or will you not?"

"Yes, my lord," said Mishka, sulkier yet. "They want to see the Prince shoot the bellfruit off the head of his friend."

Dzenko relaxed. "Well, well," he said. "I was afraid of something like this. That's why I was anxious to handle matters discreetly, Charles. Take an old legend, and the commoners will believe every word of it. Now what is our wisest course?"

"If you sent me away—" Charlie began.

Dzenko shook his head. "No, I fear that won't do."

"Won't do?" asked Charlie, dismayed.

"Won't do," Dzenko emphasized. "I appreciate your not wanting to have any truck with a foolish folk tale. But I have my people to think of. They're wildly agitated. Nought will calm them down again until they see you shoot at the bellfruit. I hate to ask you—"

"I hate to refuse—" Charlie tried.

"But, as I was saying," proceeded Dzenko, "if you do it not, they'll suppose it's because you are an impostor, and the custom around here is to roast impostors over a slow fire. Of course, my guard and I would do our best to defend you. But on Olaghi's orders, they are so few these days that I much fear the peasantry would overwhelm them and take you from us. And really, it's not such a stiff request, is it? All you are asked to do is shoot a bellfruit off the head of your best friend, using a crossbow, in the fog at fifty paces."

Charlie's stomach felt queasy. He seized after an excuse. "But my best friend isn't here! He's far off on Earth."

"Come, come," chided Dzenko. "We see your best friend, right at your back. I'm sure he'll be willing to help. What say you, Sir Hector?"

The Hoka's bearlike head nodded vigorously. "What mon dares say Hector MacGregor doesna trust the aim o' his ain true Prince?" he snorted. "Aye—I'll stand target wi' a bellfruit, or an apple, or a walnut, where noo sits my bonnet."

"Tell me, my lord," Charlie asked. "As long as I try to do it, will that satisfy them? I mean, even if I miss?"

"Oh, yes. Should you miss, they will indeed be saddened, to know you are not the Deliverer after all. But none can fairly say you refused to try. What few complainers remain will not be too many for my guardsmen to handle."

"And . . . once I've taken this shot, Sir Hector and I are free to leave? Go back to the compound if we want?"

"My dear boy! Leave? Go back? After shooting the bellfruit off your best friend's head? Certainly not! You must continue to do the other four Feats and liberate the kingdom."

"Sure, sure," said Charlie. "But that's if I shoot the way the legend tells. Suppose I miss."

Dzenko waved his hand. "Why, then you can go wherever you like, do whatever you wish," he replied airily. "Except for their disappointment, it won't matter much to anyone."

"Okay, I'll do it."

"Good!" Dzenko beamed. "I knew we could count on you."

It was necessary to wait for the evening mists to blow in off the sea, in order that every condition of the poem be fulfilled. Charlie and Hector were kept in the upstairs room meanwhile, under guard of Mishka. But servants brought them a sumptuous lunch. And to his surprise, Charlie found that the sergeant was, in his way, both intelligent and decent. He actually apologized for the trouble he had caused.

"In a tide of shmiriz, I roused my lord from slumber," he explained. "Later I bethought me how foolish I had been. Think of my astonishment when I got orders to bring you hither. As my lord's sworn man, I must needs obey." He sighed. "Ah, 'twould be wondrous were you in truth he who shall cast the yoke off us. But though you deny it, I wish you well."

"Dzenko doesn't seem to take the legend seriously," Charlie said. "So why did he want me brought here in the first place?"

"He told you 'twas to make certain matters will not get out of hand."

"Is that the whole truth?" Charlie asked, thinking how calculated the scene this afternoon had appeared.

"Well, he's a deep one, my lord is," Mishka admitted.

"We've need o' craftiness, if we're to avenge Culloden," Hector declared. Charlie knew he referred to the battle in 1746, when the last Jacobite force was defeated, but it seemed late to do anything about that.

Near sunset, an honor guard fetched them. They tramped out of the castle through an awed silence. Every native in the neighborhood had gotten the word and come to watch—close-packed lines of amber-skinned beings in mostly drab clothes, held back by armed troopers in ring mail or jerkins. The procession went to the north shore of the island, where a course had been marked on the beach.

Surf boomed, nearly invisible in a chill, thick fog which tolled over the waters. That mist smelled of salt and seaweed, but the low sun turned it golden. Solemnly, Lord Dzenko removed Hector's cap and placed on the furry round head a purple fruit the size of a clenched fist. The Hoka stood unflinching, nothing but love and encouragement in his beady gaze. Mishka took Charlie's arm and, just as gravely, strode fifty huge paces over the sand before he stopped and turned.

A few trusted warriors accompanied them. Nobody was allowed near Hector and Dzenko. Spectators along the strand were dim blurs in the mist.

"May the gods guide your aim," said Mishka as he put a cocked crossbow in Charlie's hands.

Another soldier whispered, "How sure our baron is of the Prophecy's fulfillment, that he stands right beside the target!" For at this distance, both of them were lost to sight.

Charlie hefted the weapon. Its wooden frame was cold and damp. He was astonished at the weight. The cord that powered it had been wound tight. The short quarrel rested in a groove in the stock. Its razor-sharp steel head would go clear through Hector if it struck him.

The human hesitated. Mishka was standing close, able to see what he did entirely too well. Charlie tried moving the crossbow around, but these warriors were made of stern stuff. Although the deadly quarrel swung past their noses, none of them blinked.

Abruptly a gust of wind brought a streamer of fog which turned everything hazy. Charlie swung the weapon to his shoulder. He had to miss but dared not be obvious about it. Yes, he thought, this must be the right aim, to put his shot safely out into the waves. He squeezed the trigger. The crossbow twanged, banged, and slammed back against him.

For a moment, only the surf spoke. Then to his stupefaction, cheers began to lift from the crowd he could barely see.

"Struck! Struck fair and square! . . . Cloven through the core! . . . A wondrous firing, nay, incredible, miraculous! He is the Prince of the People! Rejoice, rejoice!"

Through the fog loomed the lean figure of Dzenko and the stocky one of Hector. The baron held in his left hand the halves of a bellfruit, in his right a crossbow quarrel.

"Congratulations, my Prince!" he shouted.

"We didna doot ye for a meenute," Hector added.

Night brought clear air and a nearly full moon. The moon of New Lemuria is smaller than that of Earth, but also closer. It shows larger and brighter in the sky and raises higher tides.

Charlie looked out the window of the upstairs room, upon a castle turned to silver and shadows. The hush of night contrasted with the din of evening's celebrations. Charlie was alone with Dzenko.

The nobleman sat near a brazier which glowed to fight off the chill. He toyed with a knife such as every Talyinan carried. Candle flames made the blade shimmer against gloom.

"You faked that test," Charlie accused him. "You knew I'd aim wide and out to sea. You arranged for nobody to be near enough to see what happened. As soon as you heard my bow go off, you palmed the bellfruit on Hector's head and let a split one fall from your sleeve, along with a quarrel."

Dzenko smiled. "Sir Hector believes you struck truly, Prince," he answered.

"A Hoka will believe anything, if it suits his fancy!" The adulation lavished on Charlie the past hours had emboldened him. "Why did you do it? You've visited the League compound often. You know I'm not allowed to meddle in your politics."

"But you are allowed to travel," Dzenko pointed out. "If the natives choose to interpret your actions in special ways, that's scarcely your fault, is it?"

"Do you really mean for me to do those silly Feats—or rig them for me the way you did this one?"

Dzenko stroked his whiskers. "We can but try."

"I *won't!*"

"I fear you must." Dzenko's tones stayed low and smooth. "The whole of Roshchak has the news. Already boats must be bearing it elsewhere. I warned you what the reaction would be to an impostor. Well, what of the reaction when hopes are blasted? Besides your own life, Charles, think of the other lives that would be lost, as people rose in rebellion and, lacking proper military guidance, got cut down by Olaghi's army. No, face the fact: You have a destiny."

"To do what?"

"To help overthrow a cruel tyrant. I know you Earthlings want to see more freedom in this world. Well, for years Olaghi has been taking away what there was."

"I, well, I have heard—from Toreg and Mishka—some complaining about you barons having to pay heavy tribute and reduce the size of your armed forces. But that's just your class and the professional warriors who feel hurt."

Dzenko shook his head sadly. "Prince, consider. Where can we barons get the means to pay off Olaghi, except out of our commoners? And in addition, his tax gatherers squeeze them directly—heartlessly. Those who are ruined by it must go either into beggary or into Olaghi's immediate service. I suspect that is the real purpose behind the new taxes, not any need of the kingdom. And as for whittling down the household troops of the barons, it does more than make them unable to revolt. It means they can no longer patrol their fiefs well. Thus bandits and pirates are again rising up to prey on the people." He lifted his knife. "Prince," he said, and his voice rang, "by this, my steel, I charge you to help me right these grievous wrongs. If your spirit be true, you cannot refuse."

Charlie understood that he had no real choice. Unless he could somehow give Dzenko the slip, he was in the baron's power. If he didn't cooperate, he could be quietly murdered—or maybe tortured till he yielded.

Yet was Dzenko's cause an evil one? Charlie harked back to various unhappy remarks which Pomfrey had let drop. The Plenipotentiary frankly wished that Olaghi had never been born.

Suppose he, Charles Edward Stuart, did play out this charade of the Five Feats. As clever a leader as Dzenko would find ways to make them come out right. Afterward, Dzenko could be left in charge of the kingdom. He was said to govern his own province effectively, and he should be far more agreeable to suggestions from the League than Olaghi was.

As for Charlie, he saw himself as a liberator, a man on a white horse—no, yachi—riding down the streets of Bolgorka, capital of

Talyina, while crowds cheered and threw flowers. Later they would erect statues to him. . . .

"My father will be frantic," Charlie protested weakly.

"I will send him a message that you have decided to accept my offer of a guided tour through the whole realm," Dzenko answered. "He can proceed on his voyage. I have League funds available, to buy passage home for you and your companion after you have completed your mission."

"My father will be furious," Charlie said, but without force. When he heard the facts, Captain Stuart would have to admit that his son could not have behaved otherwise.

6
SONGS OF EXPERIENCE: THE TIGER

For the sake of discretion and, he said, the youth's personal safety, Dzenko sent Charlie off before dawn, in care of Mishka, to a hunting lodge he owned in the woods. There the two of them spent four days. Mishka taught his charge the rudiments of the knightly arts—yachi riding, the use of weapons, the correct forms for boasting of one's own prowess. Charlie declined to study shmiriz guzzling.

In the evenings they talked. Far from being an ignorant roughneck, Mishka was widely traveled and had many stories to tell. He had been born in another province to a poor fisher family. After an adventurous career as a sailor, he enlisted in Dzenko's guard largely because he wanted to be near the League compound and learn more about the strangers from the stars. In a few years he had risen to the top. He had been saving his pay and hoped before long to retire to his birthplace and marry.

He in his turn asked eager questions. When Charlie remarked that he must be exceptional, Mishka said not. Though most Talyinans were illiterate, respect for learning was ingrained in the peasantry, as well as the aristocracy.

"Then you can't believe this nonsense about my being the Prince," Charlie said.

"M-m, I don't know," the trooper responded. "My father always taught me the Prophecy was a direct revelation from one of the gods. You wouldn't want me disrespectful of my father, would you? Of course, maybe *you're* not the Prince."

"I know I'm not."

"Do you? Nothing in the Prophecy says he'll be aware of it himself till after the Five Feats have been performed, any more than it says he'll've been born on this world. We just took for granted he would be. Let's wait and see how things go, hai?"

Charlie almost blurted forth how the first deed had been faked but stopped himself in time. Mishka's code of honor would not let him admit his lord might have acted less than ethically—not without much better proof than was available here. Such an accusation would only lose Charlie his friendship, and the human felt very alone.

Hector could have come along but had elected to stay behind and supervise some craftsmen in the construction of a set of bagpipes. In addition, he had weavers prepare an ample supply of cloth in different tartans.

At the end of the waiting period, Toreg arrived to fetch Charlie and Mishka. The human asked about the message to the League compound, and Toreg said he wasn't supposed to deliver that till the end of the week's absence originally planned. For the same reason, they would travel by night to Avilyogh. That was a tricky stretch of water, where no master of a sailing vessel dared move after dark, but Dzenko was commandeering a motor ferry.

The motor, Charlie discovered, was a treadmill in a well amidships of the big craft, geared to a pair of paddle wheels. Ordinarily, it was powered by steerage passengers, while the wellborn took their ease topside. Now Dzenko put to work the members of his retinue. These were a couple of dozen soldiers, a personal servant or two, and a court minstrel named Hasprot, whose duty would be to commemorate Charlie's actions in a suitable epic poem. The baron's grown sons were left on the separate islands which he had given them the administration of. It would not have been wise to go in a large, conspicuous company. The king might hear of that and look into the matter.

Despite his excitement, Charlie slept well in the bunk assigned him. Soon after dawn, they entered the harbor of Vask, chief town on the steeply rising, thickly forested island of Avilyogh.

The community resembled Grushka in both size and architecture, except for being dominated by a huge circular building of rough stone. Dzenko said that was the Councilhouse, where the adult males met to consider public business. It was also the home of Igorsh, baron of this province, who presided over meetings, though he could vote only in case of a tie. "Why, that sounds kind of, uh, democratic," Charlie said.

"Avilyogh is backward," Dzenko answered. "Its lords never have managed to put the commoners in their place and run things efficiently."

Startled, Charlie gave the master of Roshchak a long stare. But events moved too fast for him to ponder. In minutes the party had docked, disembarked, and were trampling through the streets. Females and children stared; some cheered, probably because newcomers broke the monotony. Few males were about. Dzenko had sent word ahead to Igorsh that he had a vital matter for discussion. So most of the local electorate were assembled to hear it.

At the center of the Councilhouse was a great circular chamber, its flagstone floor surrounded by tiers of benches. Above, a ring of windows admitted light and drew off some of the smells which the crowd of seated fishermen and farmers bore with them even when they were dressed in their dull-colored best. Nevertheless, wealthier males held burning sticks of incense.

Lord Igorsh occupied a massive chair in the middle. It was mounted on a revolving platform, so that his guardsmen could turn him to face anyone speaking from the benches. He was a stout person, who, instead of a robe like Dzenko, wore ordinary jacket and trousers. His sole finery was a shabby red cloak and a gold chain of office.

Local courtesy did not require him to rise. Instead, he lifted an arm and boomed, "Greeting, excellent colleague. As head of the Grand Council of Avilyogh, I welcome you and your folk to our sacred gathering place. We are honored by your visit—" Having run out of set, formal phrases and being as bewildered as his people—who had uttered a gasp when Charlie and Hector appeared—he began to flounder. "But I must say this is . . . is rather sudden and . . . um . . . mysterious? Yes, mysterious. My lord of Roshchak must forgive us that we have had no time to prepare a reception suitable to his dignity."

Dzenko laid his hand on the hilt of the sword he bore, raised the other palm, and posed with knees bent, right foot forward. It looked ridiculous to Charlie, but evidently had a solemn meaning in Talyinan culture. The buzz of talk among the encircling commoners died out.

"What says the ancient wisdom?" belled Dzenko. " 'Haste is a weapon to harry foes home. He who moves swiftly escapes the springing of traps.' "

"True, true," replied Igorsh. "Well is it written: 'Wise are the words of the war-skilled among us.' "

Dzenko twitched his whiskers and waggled his ears in acknowledgment of the compliment. "But also," he said, not to be outdone either in urbanity or learning, " 'Knowing is he who draws nigh to good neighbors.' "

"Indeed." The other nodded. " 'Friends are the fiercest of weapons 'gainst foemen.' "

" 'Alliance is bound to be better than battle.' "

"Yet 'Shunned is the ilnya by all other animals.' "

"However, 'Causes in common make curious partners.' "

" 'Greatest are gains that in goodwill are shared.' "

" 'The first and the foremost of profits is fame.' "

"Well, well," said Igorsh, rubbing his hands together, "if that's settled, no doubt we can work out the details at leisure. Ah . . . your message hinted at a possible arrangement between our fiefs, for mutual benefit . . . something warlike, you implied?"

"Yes," Dzenko drew his sword and waved it flashing aloft. He pointed to Charlie. "Behold our Deliverer, the Prince of the Prophecy!"

Another gasp turned into a roar. Igorsh himself needed a few minutes to recover from amazement and shout for order. He had no gavel, but his guardsmen beat weapons on shields until at length there was silence again.

Dzenko told the story with skilled oratory, taking a good half hour about it. Part of that was due to interruptions. The members of this parliament behaved—to Charlie's mind—like large-sized children, jumping up and down at dramatic moments, howling forth proverbs, slogans, and deep-sea oaths. But doggedly, Dzenko made his point clear. He emphasized the presence of many witnesses when the first of the Feats had been performed.

Charlie felt guilty at going along with the fraud. But the enthusiasm of the Avilyoghans was genuine. Why should they take the risks and make the sacrifices of rebelling against Olaghi, were the king not in truth a despot who ought to be overthrown?

Finally—"Well told, Lord Dzenko!" cried Igorsh, and rose to flourish his own blade. "I think I may speak for a general consensus, that this land will fully support the Prince once he has done us the honor of slaying that curse under which we have suffered since time immemorial, the Sorrow of Avilyogh!"

Cheers thundered between the walls. Charlie forgot how tired his feet were from standing. It struck him that he had no idea what he was supposed to do.

"What says the Council?" called Igorsh, sweeping his gaze around the benches. "Would three days hence be a good time to hold the slaying?"

The males applauded. But Dzenko raised his blade to call for attention.

"May I remind the distinguished Council of the reason for my own speed in coming hither?" he said. "It were well for the Prince and those who follow him that they be far from here long before the tyrant Olaghi learns about the miracle. He will not sit idle, you know."

"True," said Igorsh doubtfully. "Still, anything less than three days is rather short notice. After all, the town will want to raise the head tax on people coming in to see the slaying. Our food vendors will want to lay in extra supplies to sell. Besides the inns, many private households will want to prepare rooms for rent. Not to mention manufacturers of souvenirs—"

"I propose for your consideration," said Dzenko, "that the advantages of such activities be weighed against the possibility of Olaghi sailing into Vask Harbor with his battle fleet and reducing the town to ashes."

"Hm, yes, there is that," agreed the Council chief. "Day after tomorrow, then?"

"This afternoon," said Dzenko firmly.

"But really, my dear colleague—"

Dzenko nudged Charlie. Since the baron of Roshchak must have some plan, the human could only pipe up, "Today. I've got to do it my own way, don't I?"

Igorsh sighed. "Ah, well. A sad thing it is, to think upon the many folk who would wish to see this event and meanwhile enjoy the sights and cooking of our town. But if they must miss it, they must. Tell me, O Prince, how do you mean to slay our Sorrow?"

"Why, uh, that is—" Charlie stuttered.

"The Deliverer keeps his own counsel," Dzenko said smoothly.

"He can use my boat!" cried a voice from the stands.

"No," shouted others. "Mine! . . . Mine! My boat, I say—"

A barrel-chested individual in leather clothes stood up and roared hoarsely, "What need has the Prince for a boat? Can a boat fare on dry land?"

Another large person, whose knitted garments smelled of fish, bounced to his feet and retorted, "Dry land? Show me dry land at the bottom of Grimsa Deep!"

"Grimsa Deep? Who said anything about Grimsa Deep?"

"Where else?" demanded the second male. "Do you suppose the great decapod—the gods rot his tentacles for the nets he has torn and the catches he has stolen—do you suppose he lives anyplace else?"

"What babble is this?" bawled his opponent. "Dare you pretend some mere sea monster is the Sorrow of Avilyogh? Nay, what can it be save the Rookery of Tetch?" He directed his words at Charlie. "From those unclimbable heights descend huge flocks of xorxa birds to ravish the grainfields of every farmer for three days' journey around. What could be sadder?"

"Decapod! Xorxa birds!" A plump male in a fur-trimmed robe stood erect. "Have you lost your wits, men, to even hear such maunderings? What was ever the Sorrow of Avilyogh but the bandits who lurk in the Hills of Nitchy, robbing the caravans till no honest merchant can send a consignment overland from one end of our island to another? Know you how exorbitant sea freight has become?"

The clamor grew with more candidates offered. Just before people came to blows, Igorsh had shields beaten again. And Dzenko's voice cut through, crying, "Hold! Hold! I speak for the Deliverer!" until the assembly was seated and quiet.

"Enough of this," said the baron scornfully. "Did you think the Prince himself knows not what is the Sorrow of Avilyogh?"

He paused for effect. "Well, what is it?" Igorsh asked at length.

"Why!" Dzenko spread his arms wide. "What but the Giant Demon Ilnya which has prowled your hills throughout the centuries? What but its accursed existence has spoiled your luck and brought these other misfortunes on you? Now no more! Today the Prince will seek out the Demon and slay him, and a golden age will come to Avilyogh!"

Males stared at each other. Charlie caught some of the puzzled murmurs: "Demon? . . . Giant Ilnya? . . . I never heard . . . Well, at least it isn't that decapod. 'Tisn't your fool Rookery, either. . . ."

Meanwhile Igorsh inquired plaintively, "But where is this creature? I, ah, I must admit my own memory is somewhat hazy on the subject. It's, ah, not ordinarily discussed."

"Of course it isn't," Dzenko said. "Doesn't that prove how cunning the Demon is? But fear no more. In the interests of expediting things, esteemed colleague, I took the liberty of dispatching huntsmen of my own to your island. They landed secretly and, armed with magical knowledge given them by the Prince, scouted out the lair of the ogre. I have a map they made. According to it, the Prince should be able to get there in a mere few hours."

Many people shuddered to think the fiend had been so near them for lifetimes, and they never aware of it. They drew signs against evil. There was no further argument.

It wasn't that New Lemurians were stupid, Charlie thought . . . they were by nature as intelligent as humans. But they were brought up in an environment where countless superstitions were believed. Nobody had ever taught them to ask for scientific evidence before accepting a story.

If any did suspect this was being staged, they must be keeping quiet for the sake of getting rid of the hated King Olaghi.

A party left Vask before noon. It consisted of Dzenko's following, plus Igorsh and some of the more prominent citizens of his barony. Conversation was impossible while bouncing along on a yachi, and Charlie had much time to brood. He hardly noticed the woodland scenery as he climbed the heights of the island.

When they stopped for lunch, he drew Dzenko aside into a thicket; a nearby waterfall helped cover their low words. The noble had beckoned a certain member of the troop to come along. This was a weather-beaten sly-eyed male who, while equipped like a soldier, was actually the huntmaster of Roshchak.

"Hadn't you better tell me what's what?" Charlie proposed.

"You do need instructions," Dzenko agreed. "Boraz, are you sure everything is in order?"

"As of yesterday morning, it was, Lord," the hunter replied. To Charlie he added, "I stayed behind when the rest of my gang returned, to care for the ilnya, and got back barely in time to catch the ferry."

"Care . . . for . . . the ilnya?" Charlie spoke in a daze.

Through his mind passed what he had heard about beasts of that kind. An ilnya was a carnivore, the size of a tiger and not unlike one in appearance, save for blue fur, short tail, and enormous hind legs which helped it run down its prey. The distribution of such species throughout the islands meant there had been land bridges in the past.

Fear chilled him. "I don't know anything about ilnya hunting," he said thinly.

"You need not," Boraz said. "My men and I captured this brute and chained him in a cave. You will go in alone. How declares the Prophecy? 'Swiftly, then, merrily, swinging his swordblade, Slays he the scarer called Sorrow of Avilyogh.' All you have to do is stand out of reach and hack away. When he's dead, cut off his head to slip the chain free, and bury it. The chain, I mean; you'll need the head to show."

The time grew unbearably long as they traveled on—and then, when they dismounted at mid afternoon, it was as if no time had passed whatsoever.

Nothing appeared real to Charlie. He felt his own trembling and smelled his own sweat. The sunlit greenness around him seemed infinitely far away.

Boraz pointed. Uphill from the animal trail which they had been following, barely visible between trunks and leafy boughs, a cave mouth gaped black in a bluff. "Yonder lairs the Demon," said the hunter. "Can you not smell his nearness?" Indeed a rank odor lay beneath the forest fragrances.

Awed, the natives stood mute. Mishka drew blade. "Take you my sword," he bade Charlie, "and would that I might be with you!"

"The Prince fares alone to his destiny," Dzenko said fast.

"What's this?" exclaimed Hector. "Alone? Ne'er whilst breath moves a MacGregor breast!"

All eyes went to the Hoka. He planted his feet firmly and glowered defiance. Small though his teddy bear form was amid the big New Lemurians, they were too shaken to attempt force on him. "Whaur Bonnie Prince Charlie fights, there fight I," he told them.

"Order him to stay," Dzenko snapped.

It was the wrong tone to take. "Why should I?" Charlie flared. "I am the Prince. Remember?"

"But," said Igorsh reasonably, "*you* must slay the Sorrow of Avilyogh. You're not supposed to have assistance."

The wily Dzenko saw a way out. "Our Deliverer's faithful servant can leave his steel behind," he said. "And . . . ah . . . things may happen when one is dealing with a demon, things not fit to be related in public. You will keep silence about whatever you witness, will you not, Sir Hector?"

"If the lad asks it, I wull." The Hoka nodded.

Dzenko gave Charlie a meaningful glance. "Silence may be to your best advantage, Prince," he reminded.

"Yes," whispered Charlie. "Please, Hector."

"I swear, then, by the honor o' my clan, nae wor-r-rd s'all e'er pass my lips," promised the Hoka. "Aye, twill not e'en get as far as my teeth."

Quickly he divested himself of sword and miscellaneous knives. He kept his bagpipes, maintaining that these were a military necessity. Igorsh was dubious; bagpipes were completely unknown in Talyina, and this might be a weapon of some kind. Hector defied him to find any sharp edges in the apparatus, and he gave way.

Mishka wrung Charlie's hand and clapped his shoulder. No one had words. Boy and Hoka trudged uphill to the cave.

Quietness hung heavy. Shivering, Charlie entered. For a second he stood blind in damp, strong-smelling gloom. Then his eyes adapted and he could see.

The cave was about ten meters deep. Its floor was soft dirt, easily movable to hide the chain, collar, and staple that held the ilnya captive. When first he made out the beast, at the far end, Charlie strangled on a cry. It was truly a giant.

But it lay so quietly. He decided it was asleep. Step by step he moved closer, until he realized that this was an old animal—oh, very old. Its great body was bone-thin, its coat faded and in many patches fallen out. As he watched, it began to snore. The mouth curled back, and he saw that the fangs were snags or altogether gone. Once it had been proud and beautiful, but now—no wonder Boraz's men had been able to lay nets and ropes around it and drag it here to await its death!

"Och," said Hector eagerly, "ye've nobbut to stab whilst yon cat snarks, and your second Feat is done."

Dread washed out of Charlie, leaving only a huge compassion. "I, I can't," he protested. "That'd be like shooting somebody's old pet dog."

"Pet? I dinna think yon claws are for decoration, laddie." Hector considered. "Aweel, gi'en the size o' him, I doot one stab wad sairve anyhoo. So, if you wish, I'll rouse him." He tucked the bag under his arm, put one of the pipes to his muzzle, and blew. The bag inflated.

A grisly vision rose before Charlie—the butchery he was supposed to carry out. It might take hours to end the torment.

"No!" he cried. "Stop! I won't! I don't care what they do to me—"
He was too late. Hector had begun playing.

A screech such as New Lemuria had never heard before erupted in the cave. Echoes blasted Charlie's eardrums and rattled around in his skull. The ilnya came awake. By sheer reflex, it bounded upward. Its head struck the roof. It fell with an earthshaking thud and lay still.

Slowly, in eerie wails and moans, the bagpipes deflated. Hector goggled through the dusk. "What . . . what— 'Tis dead!"

Charlie took his courage in both hands and approached the ilnya. He knelt, prodded it, felt for any breath. There was none. "Yes," he said.

"What happened?" Hector asked.

Charlie rose. "I think," he said in a hushed voice, "I'll never know for sure, but I think— It was so old and feeble, and it could never have heard anything like that racket of yours before. I really think it died of a heart attack. Thank God for His mercy."

"A heart attack?" For an instant, Hector was dumbfounded. Then he brightened. "Ah, the bra' notes o' Hieland music! Ever hae Caledonia's foes withered and fallen awa' at the pure and powerful sound o' it!"

7
MAN AND SUPERMAN

Now Charlie must remove the head of the ilnya and hide the evidence. "I hate being dishonest like this," he said.

"Statecraft, lad," Hector reassured him. "Turning his ain guile again' the Sassenach." He inflated his instrument once more. "Yet 'twas a gallant beast here, desairving o' meelitary honors." And while Charlie did the job, the Hoka skirled forth a coronach.

Thus Charlie emerged from the cave with his ears numb and ringing. Mishka whooped and sobbed for joy as he ran to embrace the human. "Why, where've the others gone?" Charlie wondered.

"They fled from the Demon's shrieks and roars," Mishka answered. "I can't really blame them, either. 'Twas all I could do to stand my ground while those gruesome noises shook my very liver."

"Shrieks?" Hector tilted his bonnet in order to scratch his head. "Roars? I heard naught. Naught the least. Did ye, lad?" He snapped his fingers. "Och, but o' coorse, I was playing the pipes. Naught could reach me but yon sweet melodies."

And, Charlie realized, those were precisely what had stampeded the Talyinans. Mishka didn't draw that conclusion, fortunately—or unfortunately, since the tears on the guardsman's cheeks made the human feel guiltier than ever. He got no chance to think further about that. The sergeant lifted a horn slung at his side and winded it to summon the rest of the party. They hadn't gone far and made their yachis take huge leaps while they shouted forth their happiness.

Charlie couldn't resist twitting Dzenko: "I never thought you would flee from a being you understood so well."

The baron looked embarrassed. "It was . . . unexpected . . . that noise. I almost thought the Prophecy spoke truth—" He caught himself. "That is," he snapped, "my men were departing, and naturally they needed me to lead them."

Entering the cave, the Talyinans murmured in awe. Charlie wondered why. Admittedly the ilnya was of uncommon size, but weren't the signs plain that it had also been of uncommon age? Besides, they had never had a legend about an ogre in such a shape till Dzenko invented it for them this morning. Yet they solemnly offered prayers and poured shmiriz on the ground to the gods before they began skinning the animal. The carcass they would leave for a sacrifice, the head they would mount in the Councilhouse, but the hide they would cut up into tiny squares for distribution among the folk as prized relics.

Hasprot, minstrel of Roshchak, took the word after they started home. He was a short and skinny male, his gray crest of hair dyed with the blue juice of berries and his whiskers waxed to keep them from drooping. He affected polka-dotted trousers, bells on his boots, and a jacket not of leather but of fluorescent pink neolon from Earth. However, he did have a good voice, and he was among the few who could speak—not needing his jaws tied shut—while bouncing along on a yachi. He could even play a horpil as he rode. That was an instrument not dissimilar to an ancient Greek lyre, except that it was tuned to a different scale and had a rattle built into the frame which was shaken at suitable points in a recital.

> *Hark* [he intoned] *to the tale that I have*
> *of the hero,*
> *The Prince of Prophecy prancing among us—*

Charlie listened in amazement. The part about the shooting of the bellfruit was fairly straightforward, if a trifle florid. ("Piercingly peering through fog stood the Prince.") You couldn't blame Hasprot for having been taken in by Dzenko's trick. But when he came to the Sorrow of Avilyogh, the minstrel gave his imagination free rein. For example, there was the moment in the fight when the Demon had turned itself into a raging fire and threatened to burn them all to a crisp. Still more outrageous, Charlie thought, were the forty-seven Demon kittens which had been about to rush from the cave and lay waste the whole province when the sight of the valiant lords Dzenko and Igorsh sent them wailing back belowground. Hasprot's diplomatic narration extended to the rest of the group. According to him, they had not fled. No.

Raging, they ran where they reckoned the foe
Starkly might strike, did he stretch the Prince dead.

This section of the epic chanced to be composed during a rest stop, and Charlie saw heads nod and heard self-satisfied voices rumble, "Ah, yes. . . . Just so. . . . Indeed, indeed. . . . How well he captures the essence. . . . Hasprot, would you mind repeating that bit about how I personally challenged the Demon?"

Because their lives were hard and usually dull when not disastrous, these people needed brightly colored visions. When suddenly it seemed that these might become real, they were bound to seize on that hope and to gloss over any flaws in the evidence—not even aware that they were doing so. Likewise, they unconsciously edited their eyewitness memories in order to save their pride.

The same thing had happened over and over on Earth.

Charlie glanced at Hector. Was that kilted teddy bear really very different from the natives . . . or from man?

He was too tired to think further. When they reached Vask, well after sunset, he stumbled directly to bed. Hector had to be restrained from playing him a lullaby on the pipes.

With a fair wind to fill gaily striped sails, two dozen ships plowed eastward. They included not only the combined naval forces of Roshchak and Avilyogh, but volunteers that had arrived after Dzenko's couriers, and ordinary folk in boats, had spread the news of the Prince through the western islands. Charlie found it fantastic that he should be aboard the flagship of a war fleet, a mere three days after he landed.

The vessels varied in size and appearance. But a typical fighting ship was about thirty meters long, broad in the beam, high in prow and stern, gaudily painted, and decorated with a fierce-looking figurehead. The two masts were square-rigged, apart from a fore-and-aft mizzen sail. The steersman used a wheel to control a central rudder and a primitive magnetic compass for guidance. Down on the main deck, a few peculiar cannon poked their snouts through the bulwarks on either side. However, the principal armament was catapults and mangonels. A hundred males were crowded aboard. Few were professional warriors, just ordinary fishers, farmers, laborers, or sailors, who had no armor except perhaps a shield or a kettle helmet and whose weapons had been in their families for generations.

The sea danced and sparkled. Foam went lacelike over the sapphire and emerald of its waves. They whooshed when they made the ships rock. From horizon to horizon, islets were scattered green—here and there a cottage or village visible—as if a jewel box had burst open. Surf broke upon reefs in a blinding purity of white. The sun was warm, but the wind was cool and brisk; it smelled of freshness and distance. Seafowl cruised and cried against an enormous heaven.

From the staff of the lead ship flew a tartan banner which Hector had supplied. Charlie and Dzenko stood alone on the foredeck, gazing down across a mass of crewmen and fighters. It was a conference which the human had demanded. He was tired of being put off with vague promises or distracted with sports and excursions, while the baron handled everything that mattered.

"Have no fears," Dzenko said. "Our cause advances as if the gods had greased it. We proceed openly now, because the king is bound in any case to get word soon of what's happening. But he will need time to investigate and still more time to gather in his strength, from those provinces whose masters support him. Meanwhile, the rest will be flocking to us. Especially after you have accomplished the third of the Feats."

"Yes, what about that?" Charlie fretted. "To fight the Three Brothers of Belogh—" He regarded his own slight frame.

Dzenko twirled a whisker. "Have no fears," he repeated. "All is arranged. I've not been idle since the first we met."

"But do the Brothers—well, I mean, suppose they admit afterward that they threw the fight with me."

"They won't," Dzenko promised, "because they are quite sincere. My agents went to a good deal of trouble there.

"See you, young friend, in olden years—when the Prophecy was composed—the city-state of Belogh was powerful. And ever it maintained three of its doughtiest fighters, who were supposed to be brothers, as champions. They took the lead in battle, and they represented the city in trials by combat.

"When Belogh was brought into the kingdom, this custom died out. But it was never officially abolished, and traditions about it survive. The task of my agents was to find three, ah, suitable brothers and persuade them and the local government that they be proclaimed heirs to the post. These three believe it's strictly honorary, a credit to their family and, ah, an assertion of Beloghan spirit in our era of despotism. When you land and challenge them, they will have to accept. But I trust they will get no advance warning. If they knew who you are, they might decline the engagement, and then how could you prove your identity?"

He stared at the main deck. "Yes," he continued, "we must always be careful."

His glance fell on Hector, who stood in earnest talk with Mishka. "For instance," he mused, "that associate of yours has seen a shade too much and may let slip information best kept from the public. It would not be overly distressing, would it, if he . . . ah . . . suffered an accident?"

Horror smote Charlie. "What?" he yelped.

"Oh, nothing cruel," Dzenko pledged. "Brawls will happen, you know, when armed males are crammed together. If several of them simultaneously took offense at something he said— Do you follow me?"

"No!" Charlie shouted. "If, if anything . . . like that—well, if you want my help, you'd better keep Hector safe! Otherwise," he choked forth, "you may as well kill me too . . . because I'll be your enemy!"

"Hush," urged Dzenko. Eyes were turning forward, attracted by the noise. "If it will make you happy, I hereby swear that"—he grimaced—"that creature will be safe as far as I am concerned. Are you satisfied? Perhaps we ought not to talk further this day." In a swirl of his robe, he strode off.

Charlie took a while to calm down before he also descended the ladder. Hector and Mishka met him. "Prince," the sergeant declared, "we have discussed your forthcoming ordeal—"

"Aye, hear him oot, lad," said the Hoka.

"And we have decided—" Mishka went on.

"He has wisdom in his words," Hector stated.

"That you should get instruction in yakavarsh—" Mishka said.

"E'en though he be nae Hielander," Hector added.

"Which is the art of unarmed combat—" Mishka continued.

"So leesten to him most closely," Hector advised.

"Whereby the wrestler may turn the opponent's own strength against him," Mishka said, and waited for the next interruption. When there was none, he waxed enthusiastic. "Not only is yakavarsh an excellent means of self-defense, Prince; it is in truth an art, yes, a philosophy, a way of life. Consider the lovely curve as a body soars through the air! Create an infinity symbol when you elegantly dislocate his arm! See a gateway to eternity in the angle of his broken neck!"

Charlie was willing and spent some hours trying to learn Talyinan judo. He failed. New Lemurians are proportioned too unlike humans for any of the holds to work very well for him. But at least the open-air exercise kept him from growing queasy when the wind stiffened and a chop set the ship rolling. That might not have been a problem in itself, had the Prophecy not said he would cross the water "Singing and swigging while others lie seasick." The warriors kept bringing him rich food and drink and then expected him to give an a capella concert.

8
SOLDIERS THREE

After Belogh had lost its independence, it dwindled to a small fishing port. The great stone amphitheater had stood unused for generations. Though Dzenko's following was added to the townspeople and farmers, the audience filled less than half the available space. When Charlie left the room given him to arm in and trod out into the arena, his feet scuffed up clouds of fine white dust.

The day was bright and hot. He sweated in the underpadding of the ring mail coat which had been hastily altered to fit him. Still more did he sweat in the conical noseguarded helmet, for it needed twice as much lining as it was meant to have, were it not to cover his head like a candle snuffer. A drop ran into one eye and stung. The smell and taste of the dust were acrid. The round shield hung heavy on his left arm.

He looked about. Spectators made splashes of subdued color on gray tiers. He sensed their excitement before they started shouting. Dzenko had forbidden his men to breathe any word of Charlie's identity. The newcomer had been introduced cloaked, cowled, and masked by a scarf, as a noble faring incognito, who had heard the institution of the Three Brothers was being revived, disapproved of it, and challenged them to fight the matter out with him. Nevertheless, the circumstances were bound to start talk buzzing among those who knew the Prophecy, and now everybody could see that the stranger was human.

Hector, his second, patted Charlie on the back. "Guid luck to ye, lad," he breathed. "Stand steady and strike hard. Remember Otterburn. Remember Bannockburn. And Killiecrankie. And the Scots wha hae wi' Wallace bled. Noo I maun be off." Likewise armored, his tubby form tramped to where a yachi stood tethered for him, a lance beside it. The observer for the Brothers was already mounted, a husky person in full warlike panoply. Afoot, Hasprot, the minstrel, strummed his horpil and doubtless composed in advance many of the lines which would describe this event.

Charlie's glance searched after Dzenko. It found him in a box favorably positioned for viewing, along with Igorsh of Avilyogh, the lord mayor of Belogh and his family, and other dignitaries. The baron threw the boy a stark smile. More heartening was Mishka, who rose and clapped vigorously at sight of his friend.

A roar lifted from the crowd. Out of their own door came the Three Brothers.

Charlie swallowed. He hadn't expected them to be so *big*. They towered close to two meters. He hoped some of that impression was due to the plumed and visored helmets and the plate armor rather than ring mail which they wore. The sheen off the metal hurt his eyes. He prayed the billowing dust would soon dull it.

As per instructions, they clanked and Charlie jingled across the arena to stand beneath the official box. The lord mayor blinked at them. He was an aged, wrinkled, shaky male whose best clothes, seen at close range, bore countless darnings and patches.

"Ah . . . greeting, greeting, gentlemen," he quavered. "Obedient to the, ah, the ancient law of Belogh . . . looked it up yesterday evening in the archives, I did, while everybody else was reveling . . . hard to concentrate in that racket, but I persisted, I did, and . . ." His voice trailed off. "Where was I? Oh, yes. The ancient law of a challenge—I think—bugs have eaten a lot of it—I think in case of a challenge, I have to try and make peace before it's fought." He stared at Charlie. "Surely you, a—did I hear somebody say 'Prince'?—well, I regret I have no more daughters to offer in marriage—"

"I should hope not," snapped a stout middle-aged female in his party, "seeing I'm the youngest and it's been twenty-three years—"

"Ah, yes." The mayor nodded. "Granddaughters, I meant to say. I'm completely out of marriageable granddaughters, my dear Prince, so I'm afraid—but perhaps—"

Under Dzenko's warning scowl, Charlie replied as boldly as he was able: "Sir, I came here not to marry but to fight."

"Eh? What? Well, well. But why not? Not much difference anyway."

Impatiently, Dzenko plucked the lord mayor's sleeve and hissed in his ear. "Very well, very well, let the combat begin," agreed the latter.

"I believe you're supposed to salute me. And it really would be quite nice if you saluted each other. On your honor, gentlemen, begin."

The Brothers lifted swords above shields. Charlie did the same, while taking the chance to study the others. Their armor fitted as poorly as his helmet. Doubtless it was a set of heirlooms.

Yet when all were back in the center of the arena and politely raised blades, and a trumpet sounded, and they strode forward to the encounter, Charlie's pulse fluttered. His three opponents were like remorseless robots grinding down on him.

They ground very slowly, however. Meanwhile, their second started to bounce his yachi around and around the contestants. This inspired Hector to imitation. Dust fountained up. The Earthling heard Hasprot chant:

> *The bugle has blown and the battle will start*
> *The south is the side of the city combatants.*
> *Towering, totaling more than a ton,*
> *Brutally armed are the Brothers of Belogh—*

The minstrel had to compete with Hector, who was singing "Charlie Is My Darling" at the top of his own lungs.

The dust was getting thick as a seafog, a dry mist which clogged nostrils and throat. He could barely make out his rivals a few meters off. Why in the name of sanity did that yokel have to create such a cloud?

Wait! Could it be that he wanted to hide the engagement so that nobody could see how easily the local team was overcome?

The fact was, Dzenko had told the human, his agents had taken care to pick the three oldest brothers of acceptable ancestry that they could find and persuade these to set up as the Warriors Advocate of former times. (The appeal had been to their civic spirit. Besides asserting its cultural identity, if Belogh revived picturesque customs, it might attract tourists, especially starfarers.) The agents had assured Dzenko that the group consisted of dodderers like the lord mayor. Charlie should be able to wear them out and make them surrender with no danger to himself or any need to harm them.

What was that terrible clangor which broke loose in the whirring grayness? It gave believability to Hasprot:

> *Heavily hewing, the heroes are met.*
> *Singing, the sword of the Prince now descends*
> *In a left to the head that would lay most men low,*
> *And a right to the ribs that rocks his foe back—*

Perhaps his imagination compensated the audience for its inability to see what went on, though Charlie did hear boos.

A shape loomed out of chaos. The human recognized the yachi-mounted native in bare time to jump aside from the lance aimed at him.

"Wait!" he screamed. "Hey, wait! You're not supposed to—" The yachi bounded past, stopped, spun around. The rider dropped his spear, drew his sword, and chopped downward. Somehow Charlie caught the blow on his shield, but it staggered him. In sick terror, he knew that the dust had been raised not to blur view of the defeat of the Brothers but to hide his own murder by their second. Afterward the trio would claim they had legitimately slain him. "Honor" demanded that they win.

Though how honorable, really, were Dzenko's wiles?

Again the sword smote from above. Charlie's blade met it, and was nearly torn from his grasp. Hasprot declaimed:

> *I chant of a champion's challenge anew.*
> *Sir Hector will have quite a hand in the fight.*
> *Calm and courageous, he couches his lance—*

The Hoka must have guessed what was going on. Ablaze with indignation, he bounced into sight on his own yachi. "Defend y', blackguard!" He squeaked.

Charlie thought he saw contempt on the face of the hulking Beloghan as that rider turned to meet the little alien. But Hector's first blow nearly cast him from his saddle. Smiting, they disappeared into the dust. "Crimson the field is, as carnage grows common," reported Hasprot.

Charlie felt dizzy with relief. Yet he dared not stop. He groped his way ahead. The frightful noises of battle he had heard were silenced. Instead, as he neared his opponents, he caught sounds of—what?—yes, wheezing and panting.

Vaguely before him appeared the Three Brothers. They leaned on each other for support. "No, Moach," one said in a high-pitched, thready voice, "I can't whang my shield any longer, no more than you or Chekko can. I must have a rest."

"What's the matter with that grandson of yours?" the second demanded of the third. "He should have taken care of that . . . that upstart . . . by now . . . shouldn't he?"

In grim glee, Charlie entered their view. "He didn't," he announced, and lifted his blade.

Unable to move their own weapons, the Brothers wailed, "Mercy! Mercy! We yield! Only get us out of these confounded bake ovens—" One of them fell backward in a great clatter and lay feebly waving his arms and legs like an overturned insect.

Charlie heard Hasprot:

Blow-struck and bleeding his body, the Prince
Waits what may well be the wound that
 will slay him.
Skyward goes soaring the sword of a Brother.
Down the edge drops—

But the dust did not settle. The minstrel saw Charlie stand triumphant and, not missing a beat, continued:

And disarms the Brothers.
Yare are the Three to yield to the youth,
Who graciously gives them their lives as a gift,
Though fully well able to flick them to flitches—

Across the arena, Charlie saw Hector stand above a prostrate warrior who himself pleaded to be spared.

He had won! He was safe! In the glory of that, Charlie knew he would, indeed, show pity on his antagonists, not only let them go but forbear to tell of their plot. After all, whispered a part of his mind, his own role in this wouldn't bear the closest examination.

"Prince of the Prophecy," Dzenko shouted, "reveal yourself!"

As Charlie bared his red head to a cooling breeze, the crowd went wild.

Belogh was under the sway of a baron who dwelled at the far end of Vletska, the large island on which this town stood. That powerful but cautious lord had hung back from making a commitment to the revolution. Dzenko sent new messengers to him. The word they bore was that the Prince had truly come; that already he had performed three of the Five Feats, and the rest were mere technicalities; that therefore everyone who loved freedom—and, it was added, wanted to be on the winning side—should immediately join the cause.

"I am certain he will," Dzenko told Charlie, "but he'll take a few days yet to make up his mind. In the meantime we must lodge here, before we go on to Lyovka." The island where the Riddling Priests lived was more strategically placed for fighters to rendezvous who came from all over the kingdom.

Belogh had few accommodations. Most of the travelers had to sleep outdoors or on shipboard. Charlie and his entourage would actually have preferred that to the lord mayor's drafty palace. But etiquette demanded they accept the proffered hospitality.

"Good show, good show," the elderly leader had congratulated the boy. "Yes, good show, Garamaz—er, I mean—whatever your name is—oh, yes, Prince. Ah . . . I told you I was all out of marriageable granddaughters. But I've since been reminded that a, ah, third cousin's child is just about your age, and I ought to mention her to you. Take my advice, though, and don't have anything to do with her. Temper like an ilnya's—eh, what?"

He broke off as a buxom female jerked at his arm and whispered in his ear.

"No, I am not talking out of turn!" said the lord mayor crossly. "I believe in calling a spade a spade. No more than that. Give a man fair warning. I simply stated she has a temper like— Oh, very well." He allowed himself to be led away.

Charlie had been astounded that the subject was ever brought up. Didn't these Beloghans understand that humans and New Lemurians were different species? There was no possibility of such a couple having children. Perhaps they were anxious enough to make the alliance that they didn't mind too much.

Not that Charlie dreamed of going along with them. No doubt someday he would get married. But that would be to a proper girl, not a bald, misshapen female of a barbarian race!

Thinking about the matter later on, he grew ashamed of himself. He had no right to feel superior. He looked just as peculiar to the New Lemurians as they did to him. And as for culture, they knew less science and engineering, true. But only a short time ago, historically speaking, no country on Earth had been further along. And how much did the Talyinans know—arts, trades, crafts, traditions, the ways of nature—of which he was totally ignorant?

Really, it was incredible that these people were even friendly to him, let alone idolized him as their Prince. Few nations in the past of Earth would have been so broad-minded.

He found that being a legendary hero is a full-time job. Everybody wanted to tell him his troubles, enlist his aid in his pet projects, give him his advice, build himself up in hopes of winning his favor, or beg him to heal him of sickness by his surely magical touch. After two days of this, he felt he had to get out or explode.

Dzenko raised no objection. In fact, the baron made a public speech explaining that the Prince must depart for a while from his worshipful followers, in order to plan the next move in his campaign, and that their cooperation in not disturbing him was essential. Charlie suspected Dzenko was glad to get rid of him; he knew his questions annoyed the Lord of Roshchak.

Thus Charlie came to be driving along the north coast of the island, accompanied only by Hector. That was an uninhabited stretch, treeless, begrown with stiff gray-green bushes, beset by a chill wind under a leaden overcast. He thought it desolate. The Hoka waxed eloquent about the bonnie heather o' the muirs.

This time they had a real wagon. Inspired by thirdhand accounts of human piston engines, some local genius had adapted the principle to yachi-drawn transportation. Four animals on either side of a long tongue leaped in a rhythmic succession which, with the help of a spring coupling, gave a fairly smooth ride. They were timed by a device cogged to the front axle, which snapped a whip behind the ears of each one in turn.

Charlie gazed across the sea rolling gunmetal on his left. "What I hate most," he said, "is the idea of war. Is Olaghi so bad that overthrowing him is worth hurting and killing people?"

"Freedom is aye dearly bought, lad."

"And what about the League law?" Charlie fretted. "I'm afraid I *am* violating the noninterference rule. Maybe Mr. Pomfrey will believe I had to do it to save my life. But maybe he'll decide I didn't make enough of an effort to— What's that?"

The wagon jolted and jerked as the yachis got out of step. Hector snatched the reins and halted them. Jumping to the ground, he hunched down to examine the whip-timing device.

"Aye," he nodded sagely, " 'tis the distreebutor."

"The distributor?" Charlie asked, climbing down to join him.

"Aye. Dinna ye ken, lad, we Scots are a' engineers? Look here." A stubby yellow-furred finger pointed. "A nut on yon bolt has been replaced wi' anither a wee bit too large, which has noo worked its way doon the shank. Hm-m-m, I think the rate could hae been estimated, so we must aye break doon richt hereaboots. . . ."

He began to tinker. His work ended in less than a minute.

From the crest of a nearby hill where they had lain in wait, five large New Lemurians, armed and armored, came dashing. Hector went after the sword and shield he had along. The newcomers halted in a semicircle, a few meters from the wagon, and Charlie saw wound-up crossbows leveled at him.

His palms prickled. His stomach revolved. "Hold it, Hector," he said dully. "They've got the drop on us."

A tough scar-faced warrior called in a sarcastic tone, "Greeting, Prince. I have the honor to invite you aboard the flagship of his Majesty Olaghi, High King of Talyina."

"What?" croaked Charlie.

"His fleet lies out to sea," the officer explained. "We have a swift shallop to transport you thither, beached a short walk hence. You will accept, will you not?"

Charlie looked again at the crossbows, gulped, and nodded.

"No, Captain Stuart," said Athelstan Pomfrey, "I much regret the necessity, but I cannot let you or any of your spacemen leave this compound. Not unless and until you leave this system altogether, under appropriate escort."

"You've got to be joking," exploded Charlie's father, "and this is no damn time for it!"

"I am not," said the Plenipotentiary. "I am doing my duty." He tried to soften the atmosphere. "Since you have obtained permission from your owners to wait for the return of your son, you are entirely welcome to stay. I will endeavor to make the time pleasant."

"While he's disappeared—and we keep hearing about some kind of trouble brewing out there, maybe a civil war—*pleasant?*" Stuart struggled for self-control. "I never believed that message from Duke Whosis over on the next island. Running off like that just isn't Charlie's style. Something's rotten for sure. All I want is to take a few men and rayguns in an aircar and go fetch him back from wherever he is."

"Would you use violence if you could not recover him peacefully?"

"Of course I would! He's my son!"

"I deeply sympathize," Pomfrey said. "However, such actions would constitute interference and imperialism within the meaning of the act. The principle must always be that we venture beyond our treaty zones at our own risk, while remaining bound to respect the rights of natives." He paused. "You may use my subspace radio to appeal this ruling to headquarters, though I guarantee you it will be upheld. For safety's sake, I must restrict you and your men to the compound." He paused anew. "You realize, I trust, that I have the personnel and weapons at my disposal to enforce this."

Captain Stuart shook his head, dazedly. "You mean we're under arrest?" he whispered.

"If you insist on so regarding it," Pomfrey replied, "you are."

9
A MIDSUMMER
NIGHT'S DREAM

Several hours' sail to the north was an islet, high and steep, its barren slopes populated only by seabirds. Behind it lay anchored the ships of Olaghi. Their presence was unlikely to be discovered; should a fishing vessel chance by, it could be captured. The flotilla was no larger than that which Dzenko had led to Belogh. The bulk of the king's far-flung navy must still be on its way to join him here.

His flagship was twice as big, complex, and formidable as any other vessel Charlie had seen on New Lemuria. Besides sails, it boasted a treadmill motor, which turned not paddle wheels but a propeller. Cannon muzzles bristled from double rows of ports. The main deck was broad and unencumbered, with the two masts set far forward and aft. Thus a wheelhouse on the poop overlooked a wide flat surface where six curious objects rested. Though their wicker bodies were almost hidden by furled fabric, Charlie decided they must be lighter-than-air flying craft. He got that idea from a captive balloon bobbing astern at the end of a long Jacob's ladder, a sphere with a basket where a lookout kept watch.

As he climbed aboard, disguised in a hooded cloak, he encountered warriors. They mostly resembled Dzenko's force, scantily equipped commoners. Very few could have been volunteers, to judge from the way their officers cursed, struck, and kicked them for the least reason. The sailors fared still worse. Most of those wore merely loincloths, and Charlie saw marks of the lash on more than one back. He witnessed a mate club a pair with a belaying pin when they stopped work for a moment's wonder at sight of Hector.

"Are they really forced into service?" he asked the chief of his kidnappers.

"Yes, scum that they are," the other replied. "Would you believe, instead of being grateful for a chance to die for our beloved Olaghi, they'll often as not try to hide from his recruiters? Caught, they'll whine about their families going hungry without them to bring in food. Liars, every last wretch of them. I've personally ransacked the cottages of some and found stuff that could be sold to buy groceries for months. Good, warm clothing, well-made tools, dishes, furniture, things like that. My wife's going to rejoice."

"You mean the king's men rob his own people?"

"Watch your language," huffed the native. "Fines, that's what we collect, fines levied on a bunch of draft dodgers." He glowered. "Not that we'd have had to draft many, if your gang of traitors hadn't started this trouble. March along."

Hector bristled to see Charlie hustled sternward. The boy frantically signaled the Hoka to keep quiet. They were surrounded by sharpened steel.

A door in the poop led to a guarded entry room. Beyond, across a hall, another door gave on a cabin whose spaciousness, broad glass windows, and luxurious outfitting could only be regal. A female strummed a horpil and sang for the male who sat there otherwise alone. He made a rugged contrast. His big frame was clad simply, apart from golden necklace and bracelets. His face, while battlescarred and weather-beaten, looked fairly young. Charlie strove not to cringe beneath his hard stare. This must be Olaghi.

He jerked a thumb at the female. The speed with which she left the chamber showed how frightened she was of him. The officer saluted him and announced, "Your Majesty, we bring you the Earthling who claims to be the Prince of the Prophecy, and his, um, er, co-conspirator."

"So you've told me," Olaghi said in a deep, hoarse voice. On the way here, Charlie had seen his catcher use a miniaturized sun-battery-powered radio transceiver, and he noticed a similar unit on a table here. "Don't repeat yourself. Get back and see about the other rebel leaders."

The officer was obviously surprised that the king wished to be alone with two enemies, but saluted, and the door closed behind him and his men.

Charlie was even more astounded when Olaghi smiled and invited, "Sit down, you two. Let's talk."

"Sir?" Charlie whispered. He was quick to obey, because suddenly his knees wouldn't hold him up. Hector took a stance, arms folded, behind his chair.

"You have nothing to fear if you cooperate, that is. Of course, if you're stubborn—" Olaghi touched the knife at his waist. Yet he smiled on. "Nothing personal, understand."

"I— I—" Charlie's tongue felt drier than in the arena.

"Frankly," Olaghi drawled, "I'm more curious about this funny little attendant of yours than I am about you. I'll want details on what you've been doing, but I know the general pattern already." He drew breath. "You see, I'm not at all the kind of reactionary your Pomfrey thinks. No, I'm the most progressive ruler Talyina's had since the Founder. Look how I've been reforming our institutions—breaking down feudalism, building an up-to-date absolute monarchy. And I'm interested in modernizing material things, too. I've gotten scientific books from other planets, and my engineers are designing cannon, shrapnel, aerial fighter-bombers, motorships that can take our armies clear across the ocean for making conquests. Yes, I mean to go down in history as the Great Civilizer." He scowled. "It'd be easier if the League would sell us what we need. As is, I've only managed to get some radio sets like this one, which was smuggled out. I've put secret agents, radio-equipped, in the less trustworthy provinces. They keep me alerted on what's happening and carry out jobs for me. Dzenko counts on weeks, while couriers go back and forth to rally my loyal supporters. In fact, they're already bound my way. Tell me," he asked chattily, "what do we suggest we do with Dzenko? I favor bronzing him—alive, of course—to keep with my children's baby shoes."

Charlie shivered. While Olaghi was brilliant in his fashion, he remained a lord of the wild marches of Nyekh, whose career grew from fighting tribesmen as savage as himself, until he concentrated his power and seized the throne.

"But don't be afraid," he repeated. "I'm aware you were only Dzenko's tools, you two. You owe him nothing. Besides, I'd much rather have the goodwill of your League than irritate it by harming you . . . unnecessarily, that is." He waved at a carafe and some crystal goblets. "Would you care for a slug of shmiriz while we talk? Or I can send after fruit juice if you want."

Heartened, Charlie related the entire tale of what had happened since he left the compound. Olaghi listened intently, often asking a shrewd question. In an hour, the king had a full grasp of the situation.

"A-a-ah," he rumbled at last. "As I thought. Dzenko's been restless for years. I'd have done him in a long time ago, if there hadn't always been trouble elsewhere. Now he's been quick to use the happenstance that you fit the Prophecy, or, rather, he made it fit you. He's a smart devil, no denying that. But he's overreached himself. Without you for a sign to them, his followers will melt away like dawn dew. Panic, you see, when their godling fails. I shouldn't need more strength than I've already got here, to destroy the few who try to fight.

"So all we need to do, Charles Stuart, is keep you aboard for a six-day or two. Afterward I'll personally convey you home; might as well collect whatever reward may be offered. And you, why, you'll be clear as far as your League law is concerned. How's that sound? Good, ha?"

Charlie nodded. He ought to be jubilant. He was out of danger, freed of a role he had never wanted; his parents' anxieties about him would soon be relieved; meanwhile, he could relax in better quarters than any he had yet enjoyed on this ill-starred trip.

Then why did he feel miserable? Why did he keep thinking of people like Mishka, Toreg, and the impressed soldiers and sailors around him?

Olaghi did not want his men reminded of the Prophecy, which they also cherished. He decided Charlie must be confined to a cabin near his own, a comfortable one to which attendants would bring meals. Just outside its door, a companionway led from the hall up to the poop deck. That was officer country. The prisoner could visit it if he kept his red hair well covered and was accompanied by a guard.

Hector, who amused Olaghi, at first got the freedom of the ship, "provided," the king warned, "you breathe no hint of your master's identity. I'd soon know if you did, and neither of you would like what came next. Remember, I don't *have* to keep you alive."

"I'll be the dourest Scot ye e'er did meet," snapped the Hoka, "commencing wi' ye."

Offended or perhaps ultra-cautious, Olaghi clapped down restrictions. Hector would sleep in the forecastle, and he and Charlie must never be together.

As he stood at a rail next morning and looked across the flight deck, Charlie saw his friend pass beneath in company with a petty officer, talking. He heard: "—nay, I canna tell ye what we're aboot, save that 'tis a matter o' state secrets on the soomit level—" The Hoka broke off for a moment to shout upward in English, "Courage, lad! Stout hearts and true remain to save ye!"

Charlie didn't venture to reply. Undramatic practical politics wouldn't suit Hector MacGregor's taste. But the fact was, no matter how ruthless, Olaghi would lean backward *not* to harm them. He had too much to gain by returning such a distressed traveler—including a chance at more of the technology which fascinated him.

Certainly the royal engineers had accomplished marvels on the basis of what scant information they had been able to get about advanced machinery. Their most ambitious, if not quite their most successful, work thus far was the cannon. Charlie had observed the same devices aboard a few of Dzenko's craft, but in negligible numbers. Olaghi's flagship carried a full battery of them.

The League forbade the sale of explosives to warlike societies, and the Talyinan islands had no sulfur deposits for the manufacture of gunpowder, should anyone learn the formula. Hence Olaghi, early in his reign, had commissioned the development of artillery fired by compressed air. The missiles were necessarily light—thin-walled globes full of oil ignited by a fuse or glass balls which broke on impact into showers of "shrapnel." Considering their inaccuracy and feebleness, their medieval types of counterparts remained more effective. But Olaghi hoped for gradual improvement. Charlie had watched crews at practice, ten males at once on a long lever, pumping up a gun while they sang:

What'll we do with a leaky air tank?
What'll we do with a leaky air tank?
What'll we do with a leaky air tank,
When the order's for a broadside?
Way, hay, the gauge is rising—

Both lyrics and melody suggested that somebody had once heard a visiting human translate an old Earth sea chantey.

No matter how ludicrous these efforts, they showed New Lemurians to possess intelligence. What might these people accomplish if they were free to work for peaceful progress rather than a belligerent tyrant?

Moonlight faded in the cabin windows as Charlie tossed and drifted into sleep. He was slow to rouse when a soft, high-pitched voice called him. Struggling through layers of dreaming he wondered if he hadn't begun a fresh nightmare. Moonbeams struck level through shadow to pick out a figure, cloaked and cowled, beside his bunk. The garment was of a kind worn by females; there were a few aboard to serve and entertain Olaghi and his higher-ups. But this wench was so tall—

"Hist, laddie," she whispered. "Busk yoursel' and come!"

She? No. . . . The cloak dropped off to reveal Hector on the shoulders of his petty officer acquaintance. The Hoka's left hand gripped his steed by the throat; his right hand held a knife under the Talyinan's jaw.

"What?" Charlie mumbled in his daze.

"Surely ye recall Flora Macdonald, laddie," said Hector, "the fair daughter o' Clan Ranald in the Hebrides, wha aided ye to evade the English guards on Benbecula whaur ye'd ta'en refuge after Culloden. What mon o' true heart can e'er fail tae hauld sacred the memory o' Flora, wha saved her Bonnie Prince Charlie?"

"Huh?"

"O' coorse, we've nae such aboord here, and I maun eemprovise," said Hector regretfully. "I snaffled a mantle frae ane o' the lassies and later tauld this loon tae meet me in a dark place whaur he wad hear what was to his advantage. I'd sounded him oot afore and knew him for greedy. So I swarmed up his coat, seized his dirk, and stifled his yawp, the while I tauld him the steel wad dirl in his gullet did he gie trouble. Covered o'er, we walked past the sentries, who're sleepy at this hour and anyhoo could scarcely see mair in the gloom than a female on some errand. They've nobbut contempt for females and didna think tae question her, yon barbarians, wha ken naught o' Flora Macdonald."

His fist smote the base of the Talyinan's skull. The officer crumpled, not seriously hurt—his breath rattled where he lay—but switched off for a goodly time. Hector hopped clear, stuck the confiscated knife in his belt, and urged, "Noo, Prince, quick, ere they grow suspeecious."

Charlie kicked off his blanket. Bewilderment rocked his mind. Chill sidled around his bare legs. Against it, he wore a nightshirt Olaghi had given him.

"Ah, guid," Hector approved, "ye're clad as a Prince should be when escaping, namely, like Flora's maidsairvant, Betsy Burke. But let's awa'!" He swept the other up across one shoulder.

Charlie writhed, to no avail. Hector held him easily while opening the door and bounded on into the hall. No guard stood outside; a watch in the entry and one on the poop deck were deemed sufficient.

Meteoric, the Hoka traversed the companionway. Charlie glimpsed wheelhouse, waters a-sheen beneath a sinking moon, stars still bright though the east was paling. Light glimmered off the helmet and pike of an armed lookout. That male never had a chance. Before he knew anybody had arrived, Hector leaped, with a karate kick to the belly. Air whoofed from the Talyinan. He folded over. The Hoka continued on course.

"But—but wait—" Charlie stammered. Wholly awake at last, he realized in horror that he was being rescued. The ship dwindled below him as Hector shot up the rope rungs between the parallel cables which anchored the observation balloon.

The person in its basket saw what was making it bob. He bellowed an alarm. Charlie heard shouts respond from below.

A warrior on balloon duty saved weight by leaving behind armor and weapons which could be of no use, or so it had been supposed until Hector arrived. "Yo-heave-ho?" chortled the Hoka, and threw the Talyinan overside.

"Stop!" Charlie wailed. "You don't understand—"

He was too late. Hector had already cast loose the tethers. With a jerk and a sway, the balloon floated northward.

"Harroo!" exulted the Hoka. "We're on our wa', lad. Fair stands the wind for Belogh."

10
WIND, SAND,
AND STARS

"You fool!" Charlie yelled. "What've you done?"

In the pale light, he saw the Hoka's puzzlement. "Wha hae I done?" Hector replied. "Why, wha but spring ye frae the grip o' your grim and treacherous enemy, tae bring ye again amang them wha love ye and wad win for ye' your richtful crown?"

"But they can't! I mean, I, I— It isn't my crown, none of this is any of our business, here we were finally safe and, and guaranteed a ride back where we belong, and you had to come spoil it—b-b-because it didn't fit that dream world of yours—you interfering idiot!"

"Is it really so, laddie?" whispered the Hoka.

Charlie turned his back on him.

Through mumble of wind and creak of rigging, he heard a thin, heartbroken voice choke forth: "Aweel, then, syne I hae been o' such dissairvice to my Prince, best I lay me doon and dee. God send ye better followers, but He canna find any wha'll care more for ye than did your puir auld thickheaded Hector MacGregor."

Charlie spun around, barely in time to see his companion leap out of the basket.

"Stop!" he screamed, but he was too late. "Hector. . . . Bertram . . . Hector, I never meant—I—oh, if only—Hector, I'd never say anything against you, I'd be anything you wanted—"

At which point he saw a hand clasp the wickerwork, and another, and he noticed how the carrier was tilted in that direction. The Hoka chinned himself till he could climb inboard. Full of good cheer, he said, "I thocht ye might change your mind, laddie—that 'twas nobbut weariness wha spake, and never Bonnie Charlie. So I clung to a sand-bag hanging there for ballast, till ye came back to your senses." He laid a finger beside his black nose and winked. "Ah, rough I be, and nane too bricht, but we Scots are by defineetion unco canny."

Charlie, still in a state of shock, gave the kilted figure a very sharp look. No matter how thoroughly he acted out a part, the Hoka never seemed to let go of a certain basic shrewdness.

A few minutes later they examined their surroundings, by the light of moon, stars, and oncoming dawn. Secured at the middle of the basket was a sheet-iron stove, vented to the mouth of the bag so that the heat of a fire would expand the air inside and give lift. A supply of charcoal seemed alarmingly low. Charlie shoveled in more and peered across the glimmering waters. The desert isle lay behind him, but as yet he could not make out Vletska, the land on which Belogh stood. The wind wasn't moving at all fast. If they ran out of fuel far from shore, he and Hector might well drown.

Thus he had trouble hiding his relief from his companion soon after sunrise. Out of the north were bound six flying objects, crimson cigar shapes. They had to be Olaghi's blimps, in pursuit. Wonderful! They'd overhaul this motorless balloon, bring the prisoners back— And Charlie realized the king would doubtless order the Hoka's execution.

He *had* to prevent that. No matter the early-morning chill, sweat prickled him. How could he threaten or bribe or wheedle Olaghi into granting a pardon? No believable method came to mind. It didn't help his thinking that he grew ever more hungry and thirsty.

At last he forced himself to raise the subject. "And don't just say you'll go to your death with a stiff upper lip," he finished.

"Never," Hector agreed. "I'm nae bluidy Englishman. A firm lower jaw is for me."

"I don't want you dead, not any old way!" Charlie saw how to put it. "If I should be recaptured, I'd need you alive to help me get free again."

"Aye, there's that, and I dinna mind confessing the preenciple gies me a wee sense of relief." Hector pondered. "If we can make shore or swimming distance of it, we can descend till I can go doon by a rope. They'll na bother wi' me, when ye're the true prize." He pointed to a smudge on the southern horizon. "Yonder's Vletska. Mony a weary mile to gang."

Through a crude telescope, Charlie studied the nearest of his pursuers. Beneath a long hot-air container, a wicker gondola accommodated nine males. Four of them rode bicyclelike devices which turned propellers; two adjusted control surfaces for direction; three stood by what must be weapons of some sort.

Only slowly were those awkward, underpowered machines closing the gap. From their bearing, Charlie deduced that a shift in airflow
had forced them to maneuver crosswind, which was difficult for them.
That gave him an idea. He knew wind direction often varies with alti-
tude. Vletska Island was a big target, and he needn't care where he hit
it.

Experimenting, he found he could sink by opening a valve in the
fabric and dampening the fire. To rise, he could stoke up, or better, in
view of the fuel shortage, he could discard sandbags. Gleeful, he
caught a differently aimed breeze and watched the blimps fall behind.
They fought their way to favorable conditions and once more
approached him. But that took time, during which the hills of Vletska
grew clearer to the sight.

He let the Olaghists draw so nigh that he heard warriors swear
when he repeated his evasion. With their greater volume, the blimps
could not match the speed of the balloon where it came to vertical
movement.

But winds were dying down as the sun climbed and the warmth of
day equalized temperatures. Charlie recalled the flat calms frequent
around noon. His heart sank. His stomach, less loyal, growled.

A shout startled him. "Look, laddie, look! Deleeverance!"

Charlie's gaze swept past the Hoka's forefinger. Toylike at its distance, a ship which was a smaller version of the king's was bound from
the island. Behind followed half a dozen more conventional craft. And
off that flight deck rose one cigar shape after the next.

Hector danced for joy. Rigging complained and the basket wobbled dangerously. " 'Tis the fleet o' the Vletska laird!" he caroled.
"What else could it be? They've gane o'er to the side o' truth and reason . . . and noo, having spied what they surely ken is the royal air
force, they're headed oot tae see what's afoot. . . . Och, lad, we're
safe!"

"Not yet." Charlie moistened his lips. The baron's fliers numbered
three; Olaghi's six were a lot closer.

In the near-breathless hush that had fallen, the blimps moved more
readily than before. The balloon could dodge them only by bobbing up
and down like an elevator. Charlie could not bring himself to protest
when Hector dumped still-burning contents of the stove overboard,
then refilled it soon afterward. They had expended their ballast. And it
was a sinister sight, a gondola full of warriors gliding within meters,
warriors who shook their fists and howled curses.

The time was actually about half an hour, but felt like a piece of
eternity, while the balloonists labored to stay free. It ended abruptly.

The baronial blimps arrived, and Charlie and Hector found themselves in the middle of a dogfight.

Furiously, crewmen pedaled and backpedaled, hauled on ropes which led to control surfaces, manned their armaments. Even in a calm, their vehicles were so clumsy that the difference in numbers between the two sides didn't much matter. A pair of opponents might lumber around for minutes to get within range of each other, and then the least lazy breeze pushed them apart again.

Arrows and crossbow quarrels flew between them. But the minor leaks these made in gas bags were not too dangerous, when amply fueled stoves supplied abundant heat to keep the fabric inflated. Telescoping lances and shears didn't work, in spite of valiant efforts, nor did water pumps, intended to douse an enemy's fire. An equal failure was every attempt to ram or to lay alongside, grapple fast, and board.

The typical encounter consisted of two blimps gradually working inward, passing near at last while crews struggled to inflict damage and captains exchanged abuse through megaphones, before they drifted elsewhere. The vessels would then try to come about for a fresh attempt. This went more and more slowly; the pedalers were growing exhausted.

Charlie stared as if hypnotized—until he became aware that the combat was now above him. Or rather, he saw with a gasp, he was below it. His supply of charcoal was gone. As the balloon cooled, contracted, and made shuddering noises, it sank.

"What can we do?" he cried.

"Swim," said Hector doughtily. He prepared a bundle of kilt, stockings, and shoes, to tie on his head. "Let me hae your sark, Hieness," he requested. "They'll be glad when I donate it to the Edinburgh Museum."

They might have gained time by jettisoning the stove. But it was still too hot to touch. When the basket struck, a cloud of steam hissed up. The bag followed, spread across a wide area. The passengers had to dive and go for some distance below the surface not to be dragged along as the whole apparatus sank.

The sea was cool. It tasted less salty than a terrestrial ocean. Sunlight skipped across waves. Charlie and Hector trod water while the ship bore down on them.

A glance aloft showed the battle finished. Olaghi's aeronauts knew they had no chance to complete their mission and returned while they were able. The Vletskans trailed them at a cautious distance, to see where the foe had come from.

Their carrier lowered a lifeboat, which hauled in the escapers.

Naked, chilled, starved, worn out, Charlie was just barely able to climb a ladder let down the ship's side. Warriors crowded the flight deck. Led by Mishka, they cheered him till his head rang.

Dzenko was also on hand. His robes billowed with his haste to greet the arrivals. "Congratulations, Charles," he said, low-voiced beneath the shouts. "We must confer at once. I managed to keep your disappearance quiet after we found your abandoned wagon—yes, even after we saw those aircraft from afar and I guessed what the case must be—but now let's plan how to get maximum propaganda value out of the episode. This can double your prestige, you know."

"Uh-huh," said Charlie, and fainted.

The last thing he saw before the darkness took him was Dzenko's face. It bore an expression of scorn.

11
THE SOCIAL CONTRACT

From his spies, as well as what had lately happened, Olaghi had to know that the augmented revolutionaries outnumbered his support. Blimpmen reported to Dzenko and his council that the king's flotilla had been quick to hoist sail and beat northeastward. Given such a head start, it couldn't be run down, and nobody tried.

"But won't he collect a huge force and come back?" Charlie worried.

"He will gather what he can," Dzenko replied. coolly. "I look for at least as much to rally to us at Lyovka."

They were bound there. Earthling and baron stood on the quarterdeck below the flagship's poop. It was beautiful weather. Whitecaps marched before a fresh breeze which sang in tackle, filled out sails, and drove the fleet swiftly in the direction of sunrise. Everywhere Charlie looked, he saw vessels. Warcraft were far fewer than tubby merchantmen or humble fishing smacks. Truly the common people of Talyina seemed eager to follow the Prince.

Recovered from his weakness of day before yesterday, Charlie should have rejoiced. But several things spoiled the time for him. Minor among them was the racket from the bows, where Hector was playing his pipes. They had been recovered with everything else in the wagon, which the kidnappers hadn't stopped to loot. Talyinans quickly acquired a taste for Highland music. A large group of off-duty enthusiasts crowded around the Hoka.

Worse matters plagued Charlie. He was back in the dangerous role of folk hero. The more he thought about a civil war, the more he hated the prospect, because of the suffering it must cause. And suppose his side did win, which looked nowhere near as certain as Dzenko claimed—suppose that, what afterward? He couldn't settle down to reign over this crazy kingdom! Yet could he in good conscience walk out on it? What chaos might not follow?

He cleared his throat. "Uh, Dzenko," he said. "Lyovka. Isn't that where the . . . the Riddling Priests live?"

"Yes. Don't fret about them."

"But I'm scheduled to— Well, how have you rigged things there?"

"I haven't. Remember, I have only a few men who are both cunning and trusty. And we must act fast. They could make detailed preparations for us in the first two instances. But every other place was too far off. Better to use them to spread the word about you as widely as possible, persuade the chieftains and rouse the rabble."

Charlie gulped. "So what about those Priests?"

"Don't fret," Dzenko repeated. "Actually, they're like the Brothers of Belogh: meant something once, but not anymore. The riddles were part of the ceremony when New Lemurian sacrifices were made to the god—mm, what's his name?—Klashk, I think. Nothing like that has happened for centuries. True, the cult still exists, in a fashion. But nobody seeks its temples, unless a scattering of beggars and grannies. The Three Priests would have to find honest work, or starve, did they not receive a pittance from public funds, inasmuch as this is reckoned a branch of the Lyovkan state church."

"Oh," said Charlie, somehow less relieved than might have been expected. "Then all I have to do is visit them and go through the motions."

Dzenko frowned. "No. You will stay well clear of them."

"What? Why?"

"Because you could fail their test. The riddles are secret. A man of mine sought to bribe the Priests to reveal them, but the pious witlings refused. Quite indignant, they were." Dzenko gave Charlie a meaningful glance. "If you attempt it, they might well fire up the old furnace."

"How do we handle the matter?"

Dzenko shrugged. "It's of petty consequence. See you, I judge I have crossed a threshold. We needed the inspiration of the Prince in the beginning. But the way recruits are now flocking to our standard, the sheer growth of our power will by itself attract more. Success breeds success. The wish to overthrow Olaghi, the hope of a share in plunder or other advancement, the simple stampede to join any popular cause—motivations such as these will suffice."

"Still, we can't ignore the original promise, can we?" In a sudden wild hope: "Or can we? Could you smuggle me straight back to the compound?"

Dzenko shook his head. "No. That would be a disaster, as our ene-mies knew when they seized you. You must remain in our vanguard till victory. But as for the Riddling Priests, set your mind at ease. You are not required to seek them out at any particular moment. Upon arrival we'll explain that the time is not ripe for it. In due course we'll announce that it has taken place and naturally you triumphed. Given general tumult, nobody will pause to question our communiqué."

"The Priests will!"

"Belike. And perhaps a few others. Have no fears, Charles. My men will scout most carefully beforehand. They will know exactly what throats to slit, and when and where, and what 'explanation' we should offer for the disappearances—"

"No!" yelled Charlie, aghast.

Dzenko rolled a sardonic green eye in his direction. "Ah, yes. I had forgotten what odd prejudices you humans have."

Charlie smote his fist on the rail. "I won't let you. I, I—if those murders happen, I'll . . . tell everybody the truth." He glared at the New Lemurian. Between his anger and the fact that they both stood in plain view of scores of warriors who adored him, he felt no fear, though he trembled with emotion.

"Well, well," said Dzenko soothingly. "Be calm. If you insist, I'll work something else out. Preventive detention, for example, until we've firm control of the kingdom. It'll not be as easy as assassination and for any problem, I prefer the most elegant solution. But an alterna-tive can no doubt be arranged."

Fiery-faced, Charlie plowed ahead:

"What you wanted to do, that's, well, typical of what's wrong in this country. There's no law except strength which offers little to the powerless. If a baron treats his commoners well, that's just because he happens to be halfway decent, or he knows that's how he can get more work and taxes out of them. They have no protection against the next baron being a monster—or the next king, like Olaghi."

Dzenko's whiskers bristled. "Full well do I know what Pomfrey and those liberals wish to happen in Talyina," he clipped. "Have you never thought, you infant, a . . . republic, do they call it? . . . a republic would deprive us nobles of our own rights? We have well earned them: aforetime when our ancestors took the lead against sea rovers and sav-ages; in this day, when we keep the peace in unruly provinces, and manage estates large enough to be properly productive, and try cases, and conduct olden usage and ceremony which hold society together, and support learning and religion, and deal with foreigners—oh, everything needful to maintain what order and progress the realm enjoys. It's damnably hard work, I tell you. You have no idea how the other half lives."

"Well, maybe your class was necessary at first," Charlie argued. "But Talyina isn't a wild frontier any longer. It hasn't got any further use for warlords, including the biggest one who calls himself the king. You're overdue for something better."

Seeing the thunderclouds gather on Dzenko's brow, he added hastily, "Look, I'm not being hostile to you. I mean, of course we won't throw you nobles off your lands, or strip you of your titles, or any such thing. That'd be way too long a step. And actually, your class can, well, it can still supply a lot of leaders. It's just that we're ready for the common people to have a chance at leadership, too, and freedom in their private lives, and a better break all around."

"What do you mean, 'we,' Earthman?" Dzenko growled, clasping the hilt of his sword.

Charlie braced himself. "What's the point of this whole project if it doesn't lead to a real improvement?" he demanded. "Otherwise we'd only trade one despot for another. Oh, sure, I—you—whoever it was, he'd prob'ly be a, uh, benevolent despot. He'd do some worthwhile things. But what about those after him? And the people would still be tied down. Listen, I am the Prince of the Prophecy, and if we win, I'll want to see a lot of reforms made!"

For an instant, fear tinged him. Dzenko seemed angry enough to attack. But piece by piece, the baron mastered himself. His countenance turned into a smiling mask.

"Now, now, we can hardly afford squabbles among our ranks," he said. "You may in your youth be overhasty. Yet I'll not deny, I could be overslow. See you, from my experience of statecraft, I can foretell endless practical difficulties in carrying out what you propose. Nonetheless, you have at your beck knowledge of a longer history than Talyina's. And if naught else, certain changes might bring the League to loosen restrictions on what off-world traders may sell us." He paused. "You will agree, responsible leaders cannot enact far-reaching measures without long and prayerful consideration. Let us retire to mull over what has been said. Later we will hold many conferences, you and I and what wise advisers we can find. Does that sound reasonable?"

"Y-yes," Charlie whispered.

Dzenko bowed and departed. Charlie stayed.

He felt briefly dizzy, as if he were about to faint again, and then exhausted, wrung out. Had he really stood up to that Machiavellian veteran? It didn't seem like anything which shy Charles Edward Stuart would ever dream of doing. . . . Well, yes, he would dream of it. But here he had done it. And he'd even made his point—won as good a compromise as could be hoped for at this stage—incredible!

Charlie breathed the salt air. Strength flowed back into his heart.

A heavy tread, and a long shadow across him, brought his attention back from the sea. Mishka had come to his side. As head of guards to the chief noble in the Prince's retinue, he rated access to the quarterdeck.

"Why, hello," said Charlie.

"Greeting. I saw you by yourself and wondered if you'd like some company." Diffidence sounded peculiar in a rumbling basso, out of so towering a body. Mishka wore nothing today except a loincloth; beneath his golden skin, the muscles rippled.

"I would!"

"You seemed to be having quite an argument with my lord of Roshchak." Charlie nodded, and Mishka continued: "Watch out for him, Prince. Most nobles can't think. They never felt any need to learn how. Fighting, feasting, hunting, ordering the lowborn around, that's nigh all they know. During my wanderfoot days, I watched many a one drowse off where he sat to try a lawsuit or preside over a folkmoot. Often as not, 'tis a hireling clerk who runs the real business of the province, and commoners live out their lives in their villages, seldom seeing more than the tax collector. Dzenko's different."

Charlie nodded thoughtfully. He had a similar impression. In that respect, he had overstated his case. Doubtless more aristocrats could be accused of laxity than tyranny. That didn't have to be an altogether bad thing. On the contrary, it caused people to get experience in self-government. The fact remained, though, the people were always too limited in what decisions they could make. A seed of democracy appeared to exist in Talyina, but it would never flower without roots.

"You're too solemn for a youth, Charlie," Mishka said.

"Well, I'm supposed to be the Prince." He forced a smile.

"Supposed to be? You are." In spite of his words, the giant spoke warmly, even familiarly. Like most of his kind, he accepted the supernatural as part of daily life. Charlie had a destiny, yes, but that didn't mean the two of them couldn't be friends.

"And you need more ease than has of late been granted you," Mishka went on. "D'you happen to remember, I'm from Lyovka myself? I plan to go visit my kin as soon as may be after we've landed. Would you care to come along? We can sneak off, the two of us. No fear of abduction this time. Nor fear of a great fuss being made over you; I'll see to that. Naught but a pleasant day's outing, and home cooking, and a chance to meet a few very ordinary folk."

"Thanks," Charlie said. "I'd enjoy it a lot."

Mad though his mission was, he could no longer feel sincerely regretful that he had been dragooned back into it.

12
THE RETURN OF
THE NATIVE

Glats, principal town on Lyovka, was the largest Charlie had seen thus far. It enjoyed a spectacular setting on a great semicircular bay, whose waters could shelter hundreds of ships at once. The land rose steeply behind, first the famous Seven Hills of Glats—among them the one on which most temples were located—and then higher and higher until the horizon was walled off by low green mountains, and distantly beyond them snow peaks seemed to float in heaven.

Word had run ahead of him in a speedy sloop. The news, not only of his latest Feat, but of his capture and escape, confirmed citizens' belief that he was their true Prince. He suspected certain leaders privately doubted it but were willing to pretend. After he had landed on a jam-packed wharf and ridden in a parade walled by cheering throngs, he was received in the palace with overwhelming pomp and circumstance.

It got on his nerves. Besides his dislike for living a lie, his single steady companion was Hector, and he grew lonesome. Worse, he grew bored. Flattery and kowtowing were no substitute for fellowship. Every waking moment he must be on view, watch his behavior, wear clothes which, however gorgeous, were hot, heavy, and hampering. Every meal was a state occasion. He had to meet a seeming infinity of people and either remember their names or fake it. Still more than in Belogh, he must listen politely to hours-long pitches for persons and causes of no interest to him. Twice the local nobles escorted him off the grounds. The first time was to review troops and give a speech. The second time was to dedicate a new aqueduct and give a speech.

He might have been absorbed by the confidential councils of Dzenko and other Talyinan magnates who had come here. But the baron always gave some reason why Charlie hadn't been notified of the most recent such meeting. He considered insisting on his right to attend, then decided not to. If they really didn't want him present, they'd put on a dull charade and hold their important conferences elsewhere in secrecy.

At least the harbor was filling up at an encouraging rate. Every day vessels arrived, until no berths remained and ships anchored in the bay. That brought good business for ferrymen and, ashore, for innkeepers. Hector went out nightly to roister in streets turbulent with warriors, fishers, farmers, woodcutters, sailors, hunters, traders, artisans, tinkers, laborers come to fight for the Prince. The next morning Charlie would listen wistfully to the Hoka's account of the fun he had had.

Thus, after a week, his heart jumped when Mishka got him aside and they plotted their excursion.

Charlie announced that he wished to spend a day or two alone in his rooms, to meditate. Nobody objected; Dzenko seemed awed. As the head of the Prince's guards, Mishka had chosen males whom he knew he could trust to stand watch in the hours before dawn. Hector must stay behind; he was too conspicuous, and besides, somebody had to make sure no one snooped. But wrapped in a cloak and cowl, trailing along like a servant behind Mishka's hugeness, Charlie left the area unnoticed. In an isolated starlit alley waited two yachis.

By sunrise they were far into the countryside. A thinly trafficked dirt road followed a scenic coast. When the travelers stopped for breakfast, in an enormous dewy quietness, the plain bread and cheese seemed like the best food Charlie had ever eaten.

After three hours' journey, he came to Mishka's home. This was his first look at a rural community, such as the immense majority of Talyinans spent their lives in. He was astonished at the contrast with the towns. A small population could and did cope with problems, like cleanliness, which were too much when thousands of people crowded together under primitive conditions.

This place reminded him of ancient Japanese pictures. Perhaps twenty houses and buildings like sheds or a smithy reached back from a pier where nets on poles dried in the sun. Roofs curved high above low wooden walls, their beam ends delicately carved. At every corner hung a pot for catching rainwater; the colorful fired clay made Charlie think of Christmas trees. Through open doors and broad unglazed windows whose shutters had been thrown back, he glimpsed interiors which were sparsely furnished but airy, sunny, and immaculate. The whole village had a scrubbed appearance; the dock had no smell of fish, only tar. Some wives were sweeping the streets outside their dwellings. Others were spinning, weaving, sewing, cooking, or preserving. Each was done with a care that betokened love and created beauty. Most carried babies on their backs. Infants who could walk were in the charge of children just a little bigger than themselves.

The rest of the youngsters were hard at work, according to age and ability. Charlie spied a number of them out herding fowl or animals on a common pasture or hoeing in grainfields behind the settlement. Those fields were terraced; they rose gradually up the hillsides toward the forested mountains, intensely green, a lovely sight; but Charlie winced to think how much patient, backbreaking toil had gone into them, and still did.

Cries of excitement lifted when the riders bounded into sight, and of welcome when Mishka was recognized. Yet nobody ran to crowd around, as townsfolk did. Charlie asked why.

"It is the custom," said Mishka. "All know that first my kindred and I wish to be alone with our joy, before we share it."

He drew rein and sprang off. Two males waited outside a house. They expected this visit since Mishka had sent word in advance. So they wore their best robes, faded, darned, freshly washed. One was powerful, middle-aged, his features scored and darkened and his crest bleached by a lifetime of weathers. The other was big too, but full of years, bald, toothless, and blind. Besides the usual knife he bore a sword.

Mishka took his hands first, and bowed deeply "Foremost among my honored," the guardsman said, "your grandson asks for your blessing."

Gnarled fingers felt across his arms, shoulders, face, and came to rest cradling his cheeks. "This is indeed you," the old male whispered. "And whole and hale; I feel strength shine from you. Whatever god has been your friend, be he thanked. As for my blessing, that have you always borne."

He released Mishka, who turned to the other, likewise clasped hands and bowed, and said, "Father, your son has come home and asks for your blessing."

Wordless, but his lips not altogether steady, his parent touched him on breast, mouth, and brow. Then they hugged each other.

Charlie had dismounted and thrown back his cowl. His red hair blazed in the sun. Mishka bowed next to him. "Prince," said the Talyinan, "behold my grandfather, Vorka, and my father, Ruzan." To them: "Sires, behold the Prince of the Prophecy and my dear comrade, Charles Edward Stuart."

Ruzan went on his knees, palms together, but Vorka drew his

sword hissing from the sheath and brought its deadly brightness aloft in a soldier's salute.

"I—I'm glad to meet you," Charlie fumbled. Mishka had told him to expect ceremoniousness but to be at ease because no one awaited similar actions from a foreign guest. Nonetheless, this dignity made the Earthling feel dwindled and awkward.

Ruzan rose. "We thank you for the honor you bring us," he said.

"And for our freedom!" Vorka's tone rang. Sightless, he scabbarded his blade in a single snap.

Mishka went inside. Charlie started to follow. "I pray you, Prince," Ruzan said, "We give him a short while to greet his mother. It is the custom."

"Oh . . . yes." The human shifted from foot to foot. "Uh, he's told me a lot about you, sir. You're a fisherman, you and your younger sons?"

"No more them," Ruzan said quietly. "Kyraz drowned last year when a storm capsized our boat." Now Charlie recalled Mishka's stoical mention of that and flushed. "Arko has gone to Glats to enlist under your banner, Prince. I would too, but someone must troll our living from the sea."

Charlie tried to express sympathy. Vorka gripped Ruzan's shoulder and said, "A proud blood flows in my son, Prince. He has not chosen the easiest way."

"Your blood," Ruzan said low. To Charlie he explained: "My father was the guardian of our village aforetime. That was when the succession to the barony of Lyovka fell into dispute, and for years fighting went up and down this island. There were no patrols, and folk grown desperate after their steadings had been looted would often join the bandits that began to swarm. The village then chose Vorka, who had served in the troops and knew swordplay, to guard it. No more than a single such man could the village support. But throughout the evil years he watched, and fought, and slew, himself more than once wounded, seldom given a full night's rest, and the village lived, unplundered, unburned, its sons safe from death and its daughters from shame, until peace came back upon the land."

Charlie had heard the tale before. He would sooner have cut his tongue out than interrupt Ruzan's recital of it.

Presently Mishka emerged, to bid them enter. His mother, his married sister, and the children of the latter knelt on the reed mats in homage to their Prince. His brother-in-law had joined the fighting force.

Seated on low stools, Charlie and the family partook of tea.

Mishka told the boy it was customary to refrain from eating at the reunion of kinfolk until ancestral rites had been performed at the temple.

Villagers hailed the party in soft voices as it proceeded to the halidom. This was little more than a roof over a shrine, inside a wooden fence where many-colored flowery vines climbed. The shrine held an altar, a granite block. On top of this was a blackened bowl-shaped hole. Its sides were chiseled with symbols of sun, moon, stars, sea, land, wind, and life. Otherwise the area was raked white gravel, carefully spaced and tended shrubs, and knee-high stone slabs which stood well apart, a different sign carved into every one.

The priest waited in sky-blue robes. He was also the community's master carpenter. His workscarred right hand held a blossom with great, flaring petals, his left a smoldering stick whose smoke perfumed the salty air. The visitors bowed to him, and he to them.

Mishka whispered in Charlie's ear, "A family keeps its own stone—" Then they were at his.

Again they bowed. Charlie found himself doing it. Vorka spoke: "Ancestors and beloved, you who are departed, rejoice with us this day, that a son of the house has come home. And beside him goes the Prince of the Prophecy, who shall deliver us from wrong and harm. Oh, but he builds on the work of your lives, which you left for us when you went down in darkness. Return now! May the Flower Flame call you back; may your spirits share our gladness."

Mishka went to the priest and received the bloom. He laid it in the altar bowl. With the incense stick he set it alight. A clear brilliance consumed it, and meanwhile the family knelt and said their prayers. Charlie knelt, too.

Afterward, shyly, the priest said, "Prince, my abode is but a few steps hence. If you could spare some pulsebeats, you may be interested—"

What he showed Charlie was a collection of books, preserved in fragrant wooden boxes. Their bindings were ivory, intricately carved. Parchment sheets bore illuminated texts. To create such a thing must have taken man-years, somehow stolen from toil for survival in the course of generations.

"There is much wisdom stored here," said the priest. "Very much wisdom for a small village like ours. Counsels from the gods; deeds of our forebears; poetry; music; and, yes, the workaday truths by which men endure, seasons, tides, the ways of water and of soil, what simples may help in what sicknesses— Well, my Prince knows. Now I will begin a new page for the latest of our chronicles, to tell how you came and knelt before Mishka's ancestors and how you guested at this house and held these books."

"Yes. . . ." Charlie felt utterly inadequate. An idea occurred to him. Though he wore plain Talyinan traveling clothes, he had at his belt a purse of money. From this he drew a fistful of gold and silver, a fortune by commoner standards. "Will you, uh, will you accept a donation?"

"I thank you, Lord, no." Gently, the priest closed Charlie's fingers back over the precious metal. "It is for our honor that we give what little we may, to the Prince who gives us our freedom."

"True," rumbled Ruzan. "Come, we must go make ready." To the priest, "We begin when the sun stands at noon."

"I wait in happiness," replied he.

The way back from here led within sight of the beach. There lay an overturned hull on which several males used tools. Seeing Mishka, whose bulk hid Charlie from them, they waved and shouted.

"Why, yonder's Dolgo," the warrior said. "And Avan and—" He moved to go join his former shipmates.

His father stopped him. "No, son. You'll meet them at the feast. Disturb them not before then."

"Right, sire." Mishka rejoined his relatives.

"Why shouldn't he?" Charlie asked.

"It would delay them in their work," Ruzan answered. "You see what a big boat that is. We can ill do without it, for though every crew markets its own catch, it gives a tithe of what it gets to our treasury, for the care of the poor and to keep us all alive in years of bad weather. So we offered thanks when this boat drifted ashore after a hurricane not long ago, however much we mourned the ten men who did not return with it. Most of our fishers are out to sea. These must go back too, as soon as they can." He sighed. "I feel almost guilty myself that I stayed behind today."

Mishka squeezed his hand.

The revel was a communal affair. Every villager brought food or drink to a tree-shaded green. Lanterns, wind bells, and flags had been strung around to make the place festive.

For no matter how important the occasion, it was not solemn. In fact, Charlie had never been at a jollier party. The table was loaded, the shmiriz flowed unstinted, drums and wooden flutes rollicked to set feet a-bouncing, jokes crackled, and nobody talked politics. Charlie wasn't put on a pedestal; he was invited to join the songs and dances. Young and in top condition, he soon found the females could whirl him breathless.

And there Mishka capered with a New Lemurian girl who Charlie suddenly saw was quite pretty; and there the priest and his wife leaped by; and old blind Vorka joined the chanters as they roared forth the measure:

Swing your lady swiftly.
Sweep her in your arms, lad.
Do a dosey-do now,
Then double back and circle. . . .

Somewhere amid the noise and laughter, a part of Charlie wondered how many folk on Earth knew how to have this good a time.

When the foe might appear at any moment, unbeknownst before an aircraft or picket boat saw his masts on the horizon and beat home to report it, no leave could be for more than a day. Late in the afternoon, the celebration ended. Charlie stayed outside, making what conversation he was able, while Mishka bade his family a private farewell.

Thereafter the two of them saddled their yachis and headed back to town.

Mishka was about one and a half sheets in the wind. Jaws bandaged to save his teeth and tongue while he rode, he couldn't bawl out songs, but he hummed them as loudly as possible. No fears touched him. Maybe he would never see his kin again. But maybe he would. The coming of the Prince made that the more likely, in his eyes. And regardless of what some hostile god might do, he *had* seen them. He savored the memory.

Charlie, who had stuck to plain fruit juice, felt otherwise. He'd enjoyed his excursion, mostly, but that same fact got him brooding.

At a rest stop, he said, "They're so . . . so real, your people."

"Hoy?" Mishka responded. "Of course they're real."

"I mean, well, compared to the Olaghis and, yes, the Dzenkos and—" Charlie stared across a sea turned golden by evening. "And me."

Mishka blinked. "What are you talking about, Prince?"

That I'm *not real!* Charlie wanted to shout. *That I'm a liar, a puppet, a*—but he must keep silence.

"You seem gloomy," Mishka said. "Are you troubled by the morrow? Never be that. You are the morrow." He sat quiet for a while, before he asked almost casually, "By the way, when do you plan to take on the Riddling Priests? And is there any chance I could watch?"

It was as if someone else used Charlie's throat: "Why not tonight?"

13
FAHRENHEIT 451

That Klashk the Omniscient had been a great god early in the history of this island was evident from the site of his temple, near the top of Holy Hill. But these days the building was in ruinous condition. The roof leaked, the unpainted walls sagged, the fluting of the wooden colonnade was long lost to the knives of idlers, and most of the rooms were thick with dust and choked with junk that nobody had got around to throwing out. Charlie and Mishka did get a superb view from the porch, downward across the town and outward across the bay, which glowed beneath a lustrous sunset. But they were too intent on their purpose to give it much heed.

Charlie didn't think he was being reckless, anyhow, no more reckless than he had to be for the sake of his own self-respect. He couldn't force himself to tell Mishka's kind of person, later on, that at some point he had confronted the Riddling Priests, when in fact he had not. If Dzenko knew his purpose beforehand, the baron would find a way to stop him, quite likely murderous. Therefore he came unannounced.

But he thought he could hold his own in a battle of wits. At school on Earth he had always been the best of his class where it came to riddles. If he should be stumped here, he'd pull the trick of giving an answer that didn't make sense and then claiming the riddle he had been asked was only part of a larger one, which he should be clever enough to make up on the spot. Come what may, he didn't suppose the clergy of so impoverished a parish would really dare harm the Prince of the Prophecy.

Passersby stared when a giant warrior and a slight figure muffled in cloak and cowl tethered their yachis and strode through the temple door. Several trailed after them.

They entered a dark vestibule. As they approached an inner archway, an elderly male stepped from it. He was wrinkled and squinting, his green robe ragged and soiled, but a golden chain hung around his neck, carrying a pendant like an X superimposed on an O.

"Hai!" he shrilled. "What impiety is this? Weapons stay out here. That includes knives, younkers."

"Are you one of the Riddling Priests?" Charlie asked.

"Yes, yes," was the irritable reply. "What'd you think I was? The Hierophant of Druguz?" The New Lemurian thrust his bald pate forward. "Something funny about you, the short fellow. Not built right, you aren't."

Charlie threw back his hood. "I am not of your race . . . uh . . . your reverence," he said. Louder: "I am the Prince of the Prophecy, come to join issue with you!"

The curiosity seekers, homebound laborers from the look of them, gasped. It disturbed Charlie that the Priest didn't seem much impressed.

"Well," he only said. "About time. Needed a while to get up your nerve, did you? Very well, very well. When had you in mind?"

"Now."

"Hai? What? See here, I don't care who you claim to be, I'll have no levity in the House of Klashk."

This wasn't going the way Charlie had expected. He braced his feet, close to Mishka's comforting bulk, and declared as stoutly as he was able, "Sir, I do not joke. I insist. At once. This hour."

"But that's ridiculous!" sputtered the Priest. "First Riddling in . . . in . . . three hundred and fifty-seven years, is that right? Yes, three hundred and fifty-seven years. Milestone occasion. Needs days of advance arrangement. Temple swept and garnished. Magnates invited. Choirboys recruited. Vestments cleaned. Ceremonies planned and rehearsed. Yes, a six-day at least. Better a twelve-day."

"We will do it immediately," Charlie retorted, "or not at all. Remember what an impetuous young hero the Prophecy says I am." He added a flick of malice: "Or are you nervous about the outcome?"

"Certainly not," snapped the oldster. "It's a mere question of due respect, and—well, come on in and we'll talk about it." He raised his fist. "Leave your weapons here, I told you!"

Charlie and Mishka obeyed and followed him into the main chamber. It was pathetically bare. A few cheap rushlights flickered far apart along the walk, leaving the room full of murk. The stone floor was naked save for dirt and litter. A handful of worshipers (more accurately, perhaps, contemplators) squatted before an altar at the far end.

They typified the tiny congregation Dzenko had described: decrepit females, males younger but still seedier. Behind the altar was a huge double door.

While Charlie and Mishka took this in and the slum dwellers gaped at them, the Priest tottered off to locate his colleagues. They lived on the premises and arrived in a couple of minutes with him. They too were getting along in years, attired in worn-out robes but splendid pectorals. It was obvious that they had donned these canonicals rather hastily, for one was still wiping sleep from his eyes and the other grease from his mouth.

The first Priest beckoned to the newcomers. "Over here," he ordered them. "Stop that babble of yours, and let's agree on a date that makes sense."

His associates were quick to become alert. "Yes," another said, "if you are indeed the Prince of the Prophecy—"

Low noises rose from the onlookers. Charlie had felt the amazement and tension grow in them as they stared. Now their guess was confirmed. He glimpsed two or three leaving, no doubt to fetch their friends. . . . Wait! Possibly someone would go to the palace and tell the nobles, in hopes of reward. He did have to keep things moving.

The Priest who had spoken last was still doing so. "—an extraordinary event." He leaned near and whispered, "Think of the converts, the donations, the glory of Klashk, and the honor of his servants."

Charlie wished he could inform them that delay might cost them their lives. Instead, he could merely say, "Tonight or never. I do have other business, you know, and it won't wait."

The first Priest gave him a stare of pure hatred. "As you will, then." Raising his voice till echoes flew spookily through the gloom: "Who volunteers to stoke the sacred furnace?"

Charlie was astounded and Mishka growled, when half a dozen males sprang forward. The boy turned to the Priests. "After all," he said, "it's just a matter of form. You know I'm going to win."

"We know nothing of the sort," answered the third of them.

"What?" roared Mishka. "The Prophecy says—"

"The Prophecy," interrupted the Priest, "is supposed to have been inspired by the god Bullak. It is no work of great Klashk, who indeed, once when they disputed in heaven, called Bullak a deceiver. Therefore the Prophecy is heretical, and we are the chosen instruments of Klashk to prove its falsity."

Charlie met his eyes and knew in a sudden chill that he had encountered three fanatics.

They bustled about, supervising the workers and making preparations themselves. Charlie and Mishka stood aside, nearly ignored. "This doesn't look too good, my friend," the guardsman muttered.

"No, m-maybe not." Charlie's glance followed the eager paupers. More were beginning to pour in. He thought of a discreet departure, but saw the exit so crowded that there'd be no chance.

The chamber brightened after the rear doors were swung wide. They gave on a walled courtyard where a sandstone idol loomed, eroded well-nigh to shapelessness. Before it lay a great rusty iron caldron with a lid. That must be the furnace, Charlie decided. Under a Priest's guidance, the people fetched wood from a shed in the corner and stacked it high.

"But why," Charlie whispered in despair, "why will they help . . . against the Prince who's supposed to set them free?"

"They are the very poor," Mishka said, "outcasts, beggars, starvelings. They come to old Klashk because every other god has forsaken them. What difference would freedom make in their lives? Whereas, if Klashk consumes you—well, King Olaghi might be happy enough about it to scatter some gold pieces around."

Then Charlie knew there is more to politics than a simple opposition of good and evil. A democratic government ought in time to help these folk, but how could he make them believe this, when they snarled and spat in his direction as they went by?

He gulped and husked, "I guess I'd better win."

"If you don't . . . hmm," Mishka murmured calmly. His trained gaze searched about. "One of those scrawny bodies, swung by the ankles, should clear a pretty wide circle. First I'll boost you out this window here. You go after help. I expect I can stand the mob off, meanwhile. If not—" He shrugged. "That's the risk my grandfather took."

Charlie swallowed tears. Mishka must not be torn apart or roasted alive if they bore him down! Yet his rescue, or his avenging, would involve the massacre by armored soldiers of these miserable ignoramuses.

He prayed for word soon to reach Dzenko. The baron would undoubtedly hasten here, a platoon at his heels, and break this affair up before it went beyond control.

Flames caught in kindling. Above the idol, the sky turned deep violet, and the evening star winked forth. The Priests got the people settled down on their haunches in the nave. A hundred pairs of eyes glimmered out of shadow. Solemnly, the Riddling Three bowed, chanted, lifted hands, and genuflected.

Everything had taken time. If Dzenko or anyone in authority were coming from the palace, he would have arrived already. Sweat ran down Charlie's ribs. His knees felt like rubber, his lips like sandpaper, his tongue like a block of wood.

"You who would win to wisdom, tread forward!" intoned the Priests.

Mishka nudged Charlie. "That's you, lad," he whispered. "Get in there and fight. Remember, if it comes to a real scrap, keep hold of my belt so they can't drag you from me, and I'll slug our way to the window."

He followed Charlie as the Earthling went to stand before the altar. Behind it, the three Priests were faceless in the dark against the fire which leaped and crackled around their furnace. An absolute hush had fallen upon the watchers.

"Know, seeker of wisdom," the Priests declared, "Klashk the Omniscient bestows it freely, but on none save those who prove themselves worthy. The rest he—"

"Gives lodging," said one of them. "Takes unto himself," said a second. "No, 'gives lodging,' that's right," said the third.

They glared at each other. " 'Gives lodging.' . . . 'Takes unto himself.' . . . Wait a pulse-beat, I seem to recall something like 'transfigures'—" The mumbled conference trailed off.

"Confound you, boy," cried a voice, "I *told* you we needed time to rehearse! But no, you wouldn't listen. You knew better."

A grim laugh escaped from Mishka. That sound was a draft of courage to Charlie. "No matter," he said, and was faintly surprised to hear how steady his voice, how clear and lightning-quick his mind had become. "The Prince of the Prophecy doesn't stand on ceremony. Ask me the first of the Riddles."

The Priests went into a huddle. Charlie waited.

It occurred to him that probably in former times the prospective sacrifices were quizzed in secret, lest the next victims be forewarned. That the present-day ministers had let this contest become public was a measure of their own confusion. Well, forget about culture shock and the rest. Some ethnic folkways deserved wiping out.

A Priest laid fingertips on altar. "Prepare your soul," he said. "The first of the Riddles: 'Why does an eggfowl cross the highroad?' "

"Huh?" choked the human. "That old chestnut?" Before he could stop to think what subtleties might be here, impulse had spoken. "To get to the other side."

A buzz of wonder arose at his back. The three dim shapes before him staggered. After a moment they went into a fresh huddle.

"The proper answer—" said the questioner at length.

Mishka growled and bristled his whiskers. He was very big.

"The full and proper answer," said the Priest, "is 'To get whither she would go upon the farther side.' " A stir and an undertone went through the audience. They weren't interested in hairsplitting technicalities. He must have foreseen this, because he continued: "Yet since your response holds the essence of truth, and Klashk is the most generous of gods, we rule you are correct."

It sighed through the high, dark nave.

"Besides," said the second Priest, "there is the next of the Riddles." He paused for dramatic effect. "How long ought the legs of a man to be?" Strictly speaking, an English translation would have to be "New Lemurian." But the natives naturally thought of themselves as the norm of creation.

Charlie kept mute while suspense mounted. He wasn't trying to develop his reply or even put on a good show. He was busy clarifying matters to himself.

As humanlike as these beings were, it was no surprise that they would invent essentially the same brain teasers. But on Earth those were schoolboy jokes. Here they were mortally serious. Why?

Well, when communications were slow, limited, and often disrupted, a new idea might never travel far. And if it happened to acquire a sacred character—yes, maybe riddles were a ritual in Talyina, not an everyday amusement—he must ask Mishka about that—

"I await your response, youth," said the second of the Priests, "or else your calefaction."

"Huh? Oh." Charlie shook himself. "Sorry. My mind wandered. How long ought the legs of a man to be? Why, 'Long enough to reach the ground.' "

This time a roar arose. Here and there he caught shouts like "He really is the Prince! The Prophecy really is true!" Meanwhile, the Priests conferred again.

On a sound of triumph, the third of them stepped forth to say, "Hearken well. For this is the Riddle that none has solved since first the world began, a dewdrop out of the Mists of Dream. 'What fares without legs in the dawn, on two legs by day, and on eight after nightfall?' Answer, or enter the furnace."

Blackness was fast gathering above the courtyard. The flames whirled higher. The paupers who fed them were tatterdemalion troll shapes. The caldron would soon glow red.

Charlie's heart stuttered. What was this?

It had started like the classic Earthly enigma, that the sphinx of myth had posed: "What goes on four legs in the morning, two at noon, and three at evening?" The response, of course, was: "Man. He crawls on all fours in the morning of his life, walks upright on his two legs in the noon of his manhood, and in evening must needs use a cane, making three legs together."

But this—

Silence descended, and grew and grew, save for the noise of the fire.

It burst upon Charlie. At least, what had he to lose? He said aloud, "Man."

The third Priest fainted.

The assembly screamed, sprang about, groveled on the floor before the Prince of the Prophecy.

An hour later, when things had quieted down and the temple been cleared, Charlie and Mishka sat with the three old males in the room which they shared. Their repentance had been so contrite that he couldn't bring himself to refuse their offer of a cup of tea.

Candles were too expensive for them. A wick floated in oil which a stone lamp held. The flame stank. Its dullness hardly mattered; there was little more to see than three straw pallets and three wooden stools. The visitors had two of these, while the Priests took the floor.

"Lord, how did you read the Final Secret?" asked the third of them meekly.

"Simple." Charlie felt he had earned the right to boast a bit. "As a baby, a man is carried around by his mother. Grown, he uses his two feet. Dead, he is borne to his grave by four pallbearers."

They covered their faces.

Charlie couldn't but feel sorry for them. They'd been ready to burn him, yes, but all their lives they had been told that this was proper and, indeed, the god made the victims welcome in heaven. Reflecting on past Earth history, he dared not be self-righteous. And here he had come and knocked their faith out from under them, the only comfort their lives had ever known.

He ought to do something. "Uh, look," he said. "You were mistaken about the Prophecy, but that doesn't mean you were about everything. As a matter of fact, I happen to know that the will of Klashk has gotten much misunderstood over the centuries. It would please him no end if you set matters straight. That's why I'm here, to help right wrongs—including wrong theology."

Three haggard visages lifted toward his.

He improvised fast: "It's simply not true that Klashk and . . . and the other god you mentioned earlier are at loggerheads. That's just a lie put out by an evil immortal named Satan, who wants to stir up trouble.

Actually, Klashk himself made some excellent suggestions while the Prophecy was being composed."

The Priests shuddered and moaned with hope.

"However," Charlie said sternly, wagging a forefinger, "this business of live sacrifices has got to stop. It may have been all right for your primitive ancestors, but people know better today. Why do you think the worship of Klashk has nearly died out? Because his ministers weren't keeping up with the times, that's why. Get rid of that furnace tomorrow morning. In return, I'll issue a bulletin thanking Klashk for his hospitality and urging people to come pay him their respects. And I'll see about having your stipend increased."

It was heady to command such power.

Two of the Priests blubbered their gratitude. He who had first met Charlie kept a certain independence of spirit. "Lord," he said, "this shall be as you wish. Yet the service of Klashk has ever required the testing of wits. Is it not written, 'He shall require of them knowledge, that he may return unto them wisdom'? The Riddles were at the core of the faith. Now any street-bred fool can say them."

Charlie frowned. "I told you, those sacrifices—"

"No, no, Lord! We agree. Effective immediately, Klashk wants no more than flowers. He wasn't getting more anyway, these past three hundred fifty-seven years. Still, the duty of a Priest is to know at least one arcane conundrum. It needn't be used, except as a part of elevating novices to full rank. But, Lord, I pray you, in your understanding and mercy, give us a new Riddle."

"Well," Charlie said, "well, if you put it that way."

He pondered. Breathless, they leaned forward to catch every syllable he might utter.

"Okay," Charlie said. "You may or may not know this already, but let's see." He spoke the question weightily: "What is purple and dangerous?"

The Priests stared at him, and at each other, and back again. They whispered together. Mishka ran fingers through his crest, as puzzled as they.

"Lord," said the boldest of the three at length, "we yield. What is purple and dangerous?" Charlie rose. "A bellfruit with a crossbow," he told them, and he and Mishka left them to their marvel and delight.

Hubbub reigned in the palace. Lanterns bobbed around the grounds; inside, candles glowed from every holder; courtiers, military officers, servants scurried through rooms and along corridors, yelling.

Charlie's first concern was to return to his suite, unnoticed. In the chaos, that wasn't hard. Hector sat there, honing what he called his claymore.

"Weel, laddie," greeted the Hoka, "hae ye had a guid day amang the puir crofters?"

"Wow," said Charlie faintly. He had begun to feel how tired he was. "Let me tell you—"

" 'Twas a wise idea to gang oot, mingle wi' the plain folk, and eat the halesome parritch, chief of Scotia's food. Ye grand ones need aye tae be reminded that a man's a man for a' that."

Noise from the hall reminded Charlie of something else: the strange fact that nobody had come to fetch him at the temple, though the news of his latest exploit must have spread through town like a gale. "Where are the nobles?" he asked. "What's going on?"

Hector's black button eyes widened. "Hae ye no heard, laddie? They're off tae whup their respective units into some kind o' readiness. Nae easy task on such short notice." He perceived Charlie's bewilderment. "Aye, not long before sunset the word came. Olaghi's fleet has been sighted, bearing doon on this isle, far sooner and larger than awaited. Nae doot his unmanly radios hae let his forces gather thus swiftly. Tomorrow we fight, Prince, we fight."

14
BEAT TO QUARTERS

Paradoxically, at first Charlie's latest success hampered the preparations of his side. By morning most able-bodied males in town and environs had heard about it and hastened to join the navy. From the quarterdeck of their flagship, he and Dzenko watched turmoil cover the docks.

"I . . . didn't expect this," he said, abashed.

"No." The baron's cold reply was barely audible above the shouts, foot thuds, and metal clangor. "It would not occur to you to consult me before setting our whole enterprise at hazard."

"Hold on, there, master," said Mishka, who stood behind. "You know as well as I do, we've gained, not lost. We've ample time to square things away; the tide won't let us pull out for hours yet. And those're some good fighters yonder—amateurs, but so are the king's pressed crews, and ours are here of their own wish."

Dzenko glared at him and snapped, "Speak to your liege lord with more respect."

The sergeant answered in a level tone, "I will, when he speaks thus to my Prince."

Dzenko stalked off. Charlie's uneasiness was soon lost in the excitement of watching the preparations. It was true that the commoners showed poorly at first glance, compared to the armored and well-drilled professionals among them. Not only did they mill about, but they looked as if they had outfitted themselves at a junkyard. But that mightn't make too great a difference. Judging by remarks and reminiscences Mishka had voiced during the journey, a medieval style of battle had little to do with close maneuvers under tight leadership. It was more like an armed brawl.

To be sure, a sea engagement required control, up to the moment when ships grappled together and crews fought hand to hand. Mishka gave Charlie a running commentary as they watched arrangements being made. The core of the fleet was the warships, and whatever civilian craft carried naval officers aboard. The rest—that wildly assorted, ragtag majority of freighters, smacks, luggers, lighters, jollyboats, practically anything which would float—were to steer wide of this cadre, on either side. The hope was that they could execute a pincer movement, get in among Olaghi's ships, and if nothing else, harass the foe.

"From what the scouts tell," Mishka said, "the enemy outnumbers us in regular vessels, which means he owns more firepower. But we've more keels and men in total. The way for us, therefore, is to close in as fast as may be and try to carry the day with boarding parties. I can see Dzenko and his fellow nobles—but mainly him, I'd guess—are doing a fine job of busking us for that strategy."

"He's very able, isn't he?" Charlie asked.

Mishka nodded. "Yes. Mayhap a shade too wily. But no. I'll not speak ill of my lord. Although," he added, "he's only my lord under you."

"Now, I—Mishka, please—"

Before noon the force was ready, and the tide had begun to ebb. Tartan standards went to mastheads; trumpets rang above chanteys; sails unfurled, oars came forth; and the ships stood out to sea. Females, children, aged kinfolk crowded the docks, shouting, waving, sometimes weeping, till the last hull was gone from sight.

About midafternoon Olaghi's armada hove in view. There was no very strong breeze; wavelets glittered blue and green. Some kilometers off, a small island known as Stalgesh displayed a village, grainfields that had started to turn amber, timber lots where leaves blew silvery. The air was fresh and cool, tinged by a clean hint of pitch. It was hard to believe that this would be the theater of war.

But strakes and spars crowded the northern horizon. Rising from them were dozens of aircraft. And between familiar bulwarks went a roar as males fetched their gear and sought their battle stations.

On the quarterdeck, Mishka helped Charlie armor himself in mail crafted to his measure. Himself an iron tower, the chief guardsman said, "Let's just go over our doctrine again, shall we, Prince? Frankly, I wish your royalty didn't require you be in the strife." So did Charlie, though he managed to conceal his nervousness. "But at least we'll have no useless heroics, agreed? You've had no real training. You'd not last three breaths in a clash, and your fall could doom our cause."

Mishka gestured at a score of troopers who stood nearby. "We'll hold a shield wall around you. Never stick a finger outside it." To Hector, who stood leaning on his basket-hilted sword with kilt flapping from beneath byrnie: "You too, my friend. Stay beside him if you insist, but keep out of our way."

"Aye," said the Hoka cheerily. "Ever was it my proud preevilege to guard his royal back."

Meanwhile, Hasprot, the minstrel, smote his horpil and chanted:

Fearlessly faring and frightful to foes,
The Prophecy's Prince will prong them
   on bladepoint.
Happily goes he to hack them to hash.
No sweep of his sword but will slay at
   least five. . . .

With agonizing slowness, the fleets worked toward each other.

Hostilities commenced in the sky. Olaghi must have assembled his entire air force. It could virtually ignore the few blimps the barons were able to muster. Awkward but ominous, it hovered above ships to drop things on them.

Unfortunately for it, fickle breezes kept shoving the fliers around. Thus almost all their missiles fell in the water. Those which landed did small harm. Alert soldiers and sailors shielded their eyes against splinters from glass globes and suffered only minor cuts. More to be feared were the fire bombs. One set a fishing craft ablaze, but the crew launched lifeboats and arrived on other decks. (Crews downwind did complain bitterly about the smoke from a hull which year after year had been packed full of fish.) As for the rest of the incendiaries, their fuses either went out as they fell or burned too slowly and could be plucked away before they ignited the spilled oil.

In a second attempt, the bombers descended to mast height. That brought them in easy range of catapults throwing giant quarrels. Bag after bag hissed itself limp and left its aeronauts splashing in the waves till boat hooks hauled them up to captivity.

If anything, the onslaught was a pleasant diversion, which took the minds of Charlie's followers off the serious business to come and greatly boosted morale. "I have heard," said Mishka, as he watched the survivors limp away, "that Olaghi has a slogan: 'Victory through air power.' "

Time wore on. Charlie, a mere spectator, saw Dzenko in bare glimpses. The lord of Roshchak was in overall command, which kept him moving. His regular and auxiliary units had only a crude system of signal flags to send him information and receive his word; his irregulars had nothing. Both winds and enemy dispositions kept changing; Olaghi must be making full use of his radios. Yet the baronial fleet responded well to every shift and always kept good order. Its professional center kept excellent order.

In spite of his growing distrust of Dzenko, Charlie had to admire the noble. Calm and self-possessed, he went about his work as if it were routine, not a clash which would decide the fate of the kingdom and his own life or death.

From historical shows he had seen and books he had read, Charlie unconsciously expected firing to begin long before it did. But the effective range of catapults, mangonels, bows, or air cannon was only a few hundred meters.

Thus combat erupted quite suddenly. Closer the nearest hostile vessel drew, and closer, and closer, until he could count the fangs in its figurehead and hear the shouts of its officers, yes, the creak of its tackle. The first strike was with quarrels and arrows, from archers perched high in the rigging. Shafts whistled in flocks, thunked into wood, and quivered.

Troopers crouched, made wary use of shields, but never flinched. Half-naked sailors took their chances and did their tasks. Charlie thought what courage that spelled: when the best that a surgeon could do for a wound was a rough stitching or an amputation, without anesthetics, and the sole guard against infection was a red-hot iron applied to the flesh, if this was not too likely to kill the man.

Man? Yes, he thought. If a man, or a woman, was a being intelligent, sensitive, brave, basically decent, then, regardless of biology, the New Lemurians were men and women as much as any Earthling. And that gave them the same rights, the same ultimate claim upon him, as his own kind had.

Artillery opened up. Staring across the waters, he saw most shots miss, and it flashed across him how ridiculously wasteful war is. But occasional ones went home. Barb-headed catapult bolts flew low, unstoppable, across decks, hunting prey or nailing down bundles of burning tow which set whole vessels afire. Stones from mangonels smashed yards and masts or punched through a bottom and sank a craft. It came to him how gruesomely wasteful war is.

Before the wheelhouse, in helmet and mail, Dzenko kept the poop deck. His voice drifted down to Charlie in snatches, through the clamor. He addressed the captain, who gave due orders to the steersman and, via stentorian boatswains, to sailors manning capstans, lines, and sails: ". . . We don't want to close, not with these. It's Olaghi we're after. Can you wear ship to get us between them . . . ?"

They passed so narrowly through that gap that Charlie saw the faces of his adversaries. Arrows sang. Mishka's squad made him a roof of their shields. An enemy cast a grapnel, which chunked its hooks into a bulwark. At once, regardless of what sleeted around them, men with axes were there to cut the thing loose.

The flagship sailed on. For a while smoke from a burning galley blinded Charlie. When he could see again, through reddened and weeping eyes, he found that the lines of both fleets had splintered into scattered individual combats. Dzenko had counted on that. In close coordination with two other vessels, he had broken straight through.

And dead ahead, Charlie saw in a strange blend of fear and fierceness, dead ahead was Olaghi's.

The great aircraft carrier loomed over the three craft which neared it. And they must tack, while its propeller should make it independent of the wind. Yet they beat onward.

"I see what my lord has in mind," Mishka said. "We'll grapple on either side and board."

"Board?" Charlie gulped. "How?" The flanks of the carrier extended three sheer-meters above the topmost deck of its opponents.

"Not easy," Mishka admitted. "However, in this case we've the firepower over them. We'll keep their heads down."

Charlie recalled how intensively he and, especially, Hector had been quizzed about what they saw while they were prisoners. He had described the gunports which once again bristled menacingly before him. Hadn't Dzenko believed?

Dzenko had, and rejoiced. The facts he learned became the heart of his entire battle plan.

Olaghi's air cannon got busy. Dzenko's made no response. Instead, his crew stood to catapults, mangonels, crossbows, longbows . . . and sent forth a storm. The royal ship carried similar weapons, of course. But they were few in proportion to its deck area, and they were undersupplied with ammunition. Too many lockers were full of what the cannon delivered, feebly and at a much lower rate of fire.

Moreover, a large number of its crewmen who might have been in direct action were below, exhausting themselves on the treadmill which worked the propeller. Windjammers were no such energy eaters. Though the carrier had sails of its own, it was not designed to get maximum work out of them. Thus it wallowed, unable to bring to bear its useful armament.

Mishka waved sword aloft. "Ho, ho!" he roared. "And earlier were those silly fliers! Olaghi's gotten too flinkin' modern to operate!"

Charlie thought of resources tied up in sophisticated technology that might better have been spent straight to the purpose. Had Earth nations ever made the same mistake, back in the days when they fought wars? Surely not. At least, surely the most advanced countries, those most familiar with engineering, had known better. . . .

The sun was getting low. Its light lay golden across waters on which here and there bobbed wreckage or a slick of blood.

The ships came together.

But however much he had overdone progress in some respects, Olaghi was no fool.

He had an efficient fire-fighting corps, equipped with hand pumps. It doused conflagrations. And when grapnels sank into his planks, he unlimbered a secret weapon.

Abruptly his cannon wheeled back from the gunports. Instead, those ports opened to man size, and gangplanks extended out of them like tongues. Spikes at the ends bit fast. Down them, to either side where his foemen lay, his shock troops thundered.

"They're boarding *us!*" Charlie wailed.

Mishka spoke harshly through the din. "There's no such thing as a certain fight."

Battle clattered below the quarterdeck. Swiftly outnumbered, Dzenko's crew reeled back. "Why stand we idle?" Hector cried.

"Go if you must," Mishka answered. "Here we ward our Prince."

"Ye hae richt," the Hoka agreed. "Yet och, the bluid o' my clan does seethe in me like whisky."

With a crash, one of Olaghi's assault planes struck centimeters from Charlie.

It hit Mishka and another guardsman a glancing blow, and pinned down the trooper between them. All at once, the wall around the Prince was broken. Through the gap, iron aflame in the evening glow, came the king's men.

Hector bounded to meet them. "Ah," he exulted, "the bra' music o' steel upon steel!"

In a shattering clang, his "claymore" smote a shield. The Talyinan behind it flew halfway across the deck fetched up against a rail, and lay quietly twitching. Hector cocked his head. "Aye," he decided, "E flat."

A huge royalist stalked toward Charlie. In both his hands he whirled an ax which looked huger still. The Hoka saw. "I come, lad, I come!" he shouted. "Ever wull Hector MacGregor ward the back o' his Bonnie Prince!"

"Not my back, you dolt!" Charlie screamed. "My front!"

Hector skidded on a heel, whirled his body through an arc, and caught the descending shaft on his sword blade. The ax tore out of its owner's grasp. The blade snapped across. Hector gave it a regretful look before he gripped the soldier's belt, raised the struggling shape over his head, and, after taking a proper sight, dropped him on top of another Olaghist on the main deck.

Battle ramped. Hasprot prudently stayed below the ladder to the poop and declaimed, not very loud:

> *How grossly ungrateful. No glory goes ever*
> *To us who do also face anger-swung edges,*
> *That tales of the deeds may be talked of in towns,*
> *We careful recorders, we war correspondents. . . .*

Mishka, briefly stunned, recovered. He lent his great strength to that of the Hoka and to the lesser but valiant efforts of his troopers. From above hastened Dzenko and his own guards. In red minutes, the quarterdeck was cleared.

Yet elsewhere ruin drew nigh. Better armed, better drilled, and in greater numbers, Olaghi's warriors drove back the baronial company. At masts, deckhouse, bulwarks, aloft in the shrouds and along the yards, clusters of crewmen fought with desperate courage. But the iron tide moved in on them.

Dzenko's voice came bleak: "It appears we are done for, after all. Well, we strove. Our names will endure."

"Our folk have lost their leaders," Mishka groaned. "If only—"

A volcano burst in Charles Stuart. "I am their leader!" he cried.

"What?" Mishka lifted a shaky hand. "No. You'd be cut straight down."

"Won't we be if we do nothing? Look, I don't mean to fight myself. But if they see me—I'm supposed to be the Prince who can't lose—"

"Whirlwinds and seaquakes!" Mishka bellowed. "Right you are! Oh, but there's heart in you, my King!"

He swept Charlie onto his shoulders. The Earthling unbuckled his helmet and cast it off. When the coif and cap beneath had followed, the level sunbeams flamed in his hair.

"*Behold your Prince!*" Mishka bugled, till it rang from end to end of the beleaguered ship. "*Now strike for your freedom!*"

He went down the ladder. Behind him came Hector, Dzenko, and the guards.

Swords belled. Axes banged. Arrows whistled. Men shouted. And they danced together to a terrible music. Across the deck did Mishka's band advance, hewing, hewing. Banner-high above them flared the russet head of Charlie—the red mane of the Prophecy.

The word flew among screaming seafowl: "He has come, he has come, he is here, and he leads us." Spirits rose anew in the men who would be free. Mightily they smote, carved a way to each other, then walked forward shield by shield. Soldiers sworn to Olaghi resisted them stoutly. But impressed commoners tossed their weapons aside and lifted hands in surrender—or, more and more, turned those weapons against their oppressors.

The ship was regained.

The usurper's men streamed over their gangplanks and cast these loose. Relentless, the Prince's men raised ladders and swarmed in pursuit. When aboard the carrier, they engaged its crew so fully that warriors off their companion ships became able to join them.

Charlie's memories were partly clear about the end of the battle. At first, Mishka, whom he rode, had been at the forefront. But when it grew plain to see that the revolutionaries would overcome, the sergeant hung back, not from fear but because of the very precious burden he carried. No longer in a maelstrom of violence, the rider could again look through sober eyes and understand what he saw.

The carrier was all but captured. Olaghi's standard was gone from its staff and masthead, where tartan flags blew in the sunset light. Elsewhere across the waters, royalist crews noticed, and despaired, and struck their colors. On many vessels the sailors mutinied in order to yield.

Still one forlorn combat raged. Olaghi himself and a few men held the bows. Against them came a band which Dzenko led. King and baron crossed blades, and Charlie never knew which of the twain showed more skill or courage. It was the baron who won. He forced his rival out from the rest of the defenders. Men of his fell upon Olaghi, pressed him between their shields, held him trapped. Then the last of the king's following lowered their steel, and peace descended with dusk.

In later years, Hasprot would chant of how the victors cheered until the western clouds were shivered apart and fell as a rain of gold. At the time, however, those remaining were too weary, too wounded. They croaked forth some dutiful noises while they wondered when they could go bathe their hurts, swallow a goblet of shmiriz, and sleep.

Wrists bound behind him, spears at his back, Olaghi went to meet Charlie, where the Prince sat on a bollard under stars and a lantern. The prisoner's eyes were hawk-proud. Dzenko, in the best of moods, didn't mind consulting the human. "What about this wight?" the baron asked. "We can hang him in the main market square of Bolgorka. That would be a useful demonstration. On the other hand, since you're tender-livered, maybe you'd rather give him an honorable beheading at once. I leave the choice to you."

Charlie met the noble's gaze, and the fallen king's, and answered quite steadily, "Set him free."

Dzenko stiffened as if a lance had gone up along his backbone.

"We've had too much killing," Charlie went on. "Any killing is too much. I've thought about it while I waited here. . . . Amnesty. We start fresh, Talyinans together."

"*Him?*" somebody cried in the darkness.

"I think in his way, he tried to do his best for the country. And I think it's wrong to destroy people just because you don't like their politics." Charlie smiled. "What are you afraid of? What possible harm can Olaghi do? He's completely discredited. If he wants to save his life, he'll get out of this kingdom in a hurry and stay out forever."

The captive flushed angrily but did not speak.

"We'll give him a sailboat and supplies enough to reach the mainland," Charlie continued. "I'm told the dwellers there are savages. Maybe Olaghi can teach them something. That'd make the rest of his life useful."

"No!" Dzenko cried. "This is nonsense! I won't have it!"

Charlie gave him a cool stare. "Oh, but you will," he commanded. "I am the Prince. And doesn't the Prophecy say 'In terror, the tyrant who caused all the trouble, the false king, goes fleeing, unfollowed, in shame'? We have to see the Prophecy fulfilled, don't we?"

15
THE PRINCE

Reaction set in. He was no hardened warrior. What he had witnessed shocked him more deeply than it would have a native civilian used to horrors long banished from Earth. Nor had he simply watched. He had run a high risk of being killed or maimed. He had pitted his will repeatedly against that of strong and ruthless veterans.

For a week, he spent his time in a dull daze or choking awake out of nightmares. Dzenko opined that it would be unwise, as well as bad for the patient, did the Prince arrive at the capital city in this condition. Yet it was important to ride the crest of success, take possession of the throne, reorganize the royal household, get started on a restoration of order and commerce throughout the realm. The baron proposed to lead the regular navy off and see to that. Charlie would remain behind until he recovered for a triumphal entry.

No one objected. The fleet steered for Bolgorka. It included those ships, with officers and crews, which had been Olaghi's. Medieval types of aristocrats had elastic loyalties. None of them accompanied the fallen usurper into exile. On this account, too, it was vital to nail down the victory, before any warlord might grab power for himself.

Volunteers dispersed to their widely strewn homes. They bore the news: that the liberating Prince had come into his own at the Battle of Stalgesh and now remained awhile on that island in order to meditate how best he might improve life for his people.

Only Hector stayed with him. Dzenko had pointed out that he, the baron, would need every able-bodied man he could bring along, as much to prevent trouble from starting as to quell it should it arise. The injured should be carried straight back to Glats. But Charlie would need a less hectic atmosphere than that of the court. The villagers would provide as many guards and as much service as he could possibly require.

Indeed they did. Their hospitality was humble, but what they lacked in facilities they more than made up in devotion.

So during that week, Charlie got well. Sunshine, fresh air, plain food, ample rest; later swimming, boating, fishing, hiking; the company of people who loved him, at first anxiously tender, afterward cheerful, chatty, eager to swap songs and stories—these things healed him.

He did feel as though there had been some basic changes in him. No longer was he unduly shy, and he didn't think he would ever again prefer daydreams to real-world action. At the same time he had grown more thoughtful, more aware of the troubles which haunt the universe but less ready to find simple causes or instant cures for them.

It was in this mood that he wrote a long letter to his father, after he learned that the spaceship still waited on Shverkadi Island. A miniradio wouldn't reach that far. Besides, Dzenko hadn't left him any of those captured from Olaghi—an oversight, no doubt. Charlie resigned himself to sputtering along with a quill pen and fish-gland ink on sheets of flexible bark.

He told the tale of his adventures, pointing out that on the whole he had never got a chance to turn back from them. Yet now, he declared, he must act of his own free will. No longer was he in danger. The same local skipper who delivered this message would gladly have taken him and Hector in person. But he *must* go to Bolgorka. If the Prince did not make an appearance in the capital of Talyina, doubts were sure to spread; ambitious barons would conspire; a full-fledged civil war might well ensue, instead of a single decisive clash such as they had mercifully gotten by with. Dzenko was obviously right. Between them the two could work out a formula which would enable Charlie to go home without disrupting the kingdom.

He begged everybody's pardon for this. He knew it might not be legal, but he also knew it was moral. And . . . the presence of outsiders would be disastrous.

The Talyinans had always found it difficult to believe that the mighty Interbeing League really did not plan to conquer them. Their trust in its good intentions was often fragile. Did a band of spacemen accompany Charlie to Bolgorka, many natives would jump to the conclusion that the Prince was a stalking-horse for human imperialism. The new government would collapse in a storm of rebellions and secessions. Whatever leaders arose afterward would tend to shun the Plenipotentiary and reject his advice.

"Please, please, Dad," Charlie wrote, "sit tight, and get Mr. Pomfrey to do the same. I won't be gone more than another month or so. Why don't you continue your route? I can use royal funds when I'm finished here, to buy passage to a planet where we can meet. Meanwhile, I'm perfectly safe, I swear I am."

He left for Bolgorka the day before his courier raised sail for Shverkadi. He would not directly disobey his father. Therefore, he wasn't about to chance getting an order to come straight back.

After all, he knew wryly, from now on he expected to enjoy himself.

Like Glats, the royal town stood at the end of a bay which formed a superb natural harbor. It too was built on hills. The island whose name it bore was still more rugged than Lyovka. To the west and south rolled a great river valley, intensively cultivated, but mountains walled those horizons, haloed with snow and jeweled with glaciers. Northward, the highlands thrust a tongue out to sea in the form of a long and steeply ridged cape. Too rough for farming, it was forested almost to the outer bastions of the city. A good road did go across the neck of it.

Several boats escorted the one which bore Charlie to his throne. Pennons and streamers adorned their rigging. The swiftest vessel went ahead to tell the people. Thus a mighty crowd greeted the Prince. Troopers lined the streets, holding back throngs whose cheers echoed off heaven, or slammed their thousands of boots down on paving behind his horse-drawn carriage in the parade which conducted him to the palace. Their mail and helmets shone like new-minted silver; plumes and cloaks blew about them, as colorful as the banners beneath which their pikes gleamed and rippled; drums boomed, horns winded, deep voices chanted aloud the Prophecy. He wore brilliant fabrics and rich furs; he carried in his hands, naked, the sword which had been the Founder's; his head stayed bare, that the red locks might blow free. Beside him stood Hector, bowing right and left, waving, beaming, blowing kisses. The Hoka had been given a sack of coins to toss to the populace but did not think that became a thrifty Scot.

In glory they reached the stark stone pile of the kingly dwelling. Almost at once, Dzenko got the Earthling off in private for a business discussion.

It was curiously like their first encounter. They were alone in a guarded tower room, so high that they saw through the narrow windows only sky and wings. The chill of masonry was not much relieved by woven tapestries and skin rugs. The furniture was massive and grotesquely carved. Dzenko sat cool-eyed. Charlie perched on the edge of his chair and, bit by bit, felt sweat prickle forth on his skin.

"Yes, I have matters in hand," the baron said. "We must see to it that they remain thus. It will take quick and precise action to get you back where you belong, uncrowned, without provoking upheavals. I'll need your unquestioning cooperation."

"Uncrowned?" replied Charlie. "Why that?"

Dzenko twitched his whiskers. "Have you forgotten? The fifth Feat is left for you to do. It happens to be impossible. It's equally impossible, politically, to hold your coronation until you have done the deed. And, since the Grotto of Kroshch is quite near town, you would perform before many witnesses. There is no way to, ah, make prior arrangements."

"Well, what do you have in mind then?"

"That you stay here for, hm, about a twelve-day. You will move around, inspect your capital and its hinterland, meet people, attend ceremonies—a more extensive and elaborate version of what you did in Glats. Hence no one will afterward be able to deny that you were indeed present, victorious. Mostly you'll be seen in my company, and will show me every mark of favor. I'll give you a schedule for the honors you heap on me.

"Meanwhile, we'll start a new story going. I have some reliable priests, minstrels, and the like, ready to help as soon as they get their instructions. Probably you can give me a few ideas, though I've already decided in a general way. Essentially, the tale will be that while the Prophecy is true, it is not complete. Before he can settle down to reign over Talyina, the Prince must still overcome certain other difficulties—abroad—especially among the starfarers in whose image he has been incarnated. He must go suppress warlords of theirs who plot to overrun us. This will take time, but at last he'll return successful. Then will be the proper moment for him to enter the Grotto, and come out alive, and assume his throne here.

"In his absence, he will naturally require a regent. Who but his well-beloved Dzenko? And should Dzenko not outlive the years during which the Prince is away striving for the people, why, the heirs of Dzenko will succeed him. After all, since the Prince is to reign forever, it's reasonable that he may need a few centuries yet to complete his labors."

The baron smiled and bridged his fingers "There," he finished. "A most excellent scheme."'

Despite Bolgorka's being the largest and wealthiest city in Talyina, Charlie found many sections antiquated as he toured it. The Sword

Way, up which he had been paraded, was broad and straight, but most streets were crooked and stinking lanes creeping between overhanging walls. One reason for this was that earlier kings had had much reconstructed in expensive stone or brick. Consequently, it had not suffered the fires which, every generation or two, made most towns start fresh. It was frozen into a primitive pattern. Well-to-do homes, warehouses, marts were like fortresses here and there in the middle of slums whose wretchedness appalled Charlie. He thought of doing something to help the poor—then remembered that he wouldn't be around and Dzenko was not especially interested in reform.

Nobody showed Charlie bad conditions on purpose, or tried to hide them. They were incidental, taken for granted. One simply had to shout or flick a whip to get the filthy commoners out of the way while one was guiding the Prince from historic monument to quaint shop to stately mansion, then back to the palace in time for a major speech, a formal banquet, and picturesque traditional entertainment. If from time to time he stopped and tried blunderingly to talk with some work-broken navvy, crippled beggar, or gaunt woman carrying an infant, why, that was just his whim. Let him pass out a few coins if he wished and get him moving again.

Besides Hector, a hundred crack guardsmen were always with him in public. He recognized none of them and learned they were mercenaries who had formerly served Olaghi. "Where're my travel friends?" he demanded of Dzenko. "Where's Mishka?"

"I have to send my most reliable men out to handle special problems," the noble answered. "For instance, if a baron fell at Stalgesh, we must make sure the right successor takes over his province. Mustn't we?"

The sergeant of Charlie's troop was not very communicative. He would reply to direct questions, of course. Thus, while inspecting the fleet, the human saw a number of sailors tied wrist and ankle in the shrouds of ships, under a scorching sun. He asked why. The sergeant told him casually, "Oh, mutineers being punished."

"Not mutineers, Highness," said the captain of the vessel on which they stood. "Such we'd flog to death. These conspired to petition for discharge. That only rates spread-eagling for one full day."

"What?" Charlie exclaimed. "They can't even petition?"

The captain was honestly surprised. "Highness, how could we let impressed men do that? It'd imply they had some kind of *right* to go home before it suits the king's convenience."

"You're still keeping them, this long after the battle?"

Charlie contained his anger. But that night, in English, he told

Hector he meant to take the matter up with Dzenko, force the baron to release his quasi-slaves.

"Maybe ye can," the Hoka said doubtfully. "Yet is it no a waste of effort, when soon ye'll gang awa'? Dzenko wad simply haul them back after ye're gane or catch himsel' ithers."

"Why does he need that big a force, anyway?"

"A vurra eenteresting question. What say ye I poke aboot on my ain? I'm nobbut your funny wee companion; nae guardsmen wull clank alang behind me; and I've found the Talyinans wull talk wi' me richt freely, once they're used to the sight and pairhaps a drappie or twa hae wetted their craws."

"All right." Charlie sighed. "I'm not sure what good it'll do—and I'll miss you in that hustle-bustle and dull ritual I'm stuck with—and lordy, lordy, how glad I will be to get through here!"

Hector did join him on an excursion to the Grotto of Kroshch. For this was a famous local wonder, its general area a picnic site for the aristocracy and bourgeoisie of Bolgorka. Dzenko himself wanted Charlie to visit there. Such a trip would lend credibility to his eventual announcement that the Grotto could wait until the Prince had disposed of what serious threats remained to the well-being of Talyina.

The Hoka was unwontedly silent, even glum. Charlie wondered why but didn't press the issue. After six days of officialism, it was too delightful to be out in the country again.

His yachi bounded along a winding, climbing road whose dirt lay vivid red under fragrant green of woods on either side, blue of sky and flash of gold off wings overhead. He had got used to riding native style, and his muscles fitted themselves happily into its thudding rhythm. Ahead of him, a section of guards made a brave sight in their armor and cloaks.

Behind him came the rest, along with scores of curious civilians.

The trip across the cape took a pair of hours. From the crest Charlie saw a narrow fjord, mercury-bright against the darkling cliffs of its farther side. Toward this the road descended, until it reached a cleared spot above the very end of the inlet. There stood tables, benches, fireplaces, and other amenities. Cooks had gone ahead to prepare a barbecue for the Prince. By now he had made his tastes known. Their simplicity was widely admired. With only salt for a condiment, the meat which he got was delicious. His wellborn seatmates were affable, flattering, proud to dine in his company.

After lunch, the party climbed down a trail carved out of the precipices to the water. Their outing had been carefully timed. The tide was low. Waves lapped quietly on rocks which formed a strip of beach. At its end, a mouth gaped black in a sheer granite wall.

"The Grotto of Kroshch, Highness," said the foremost of the magnates present. "The end of your destiny. No, the beginning of it." Awe freighted his tones.

Charlie knew what awaited him. He approached boldly. Yet he too felt a certain inner dread. The dimness down here, hemmed between dizzying heights; the opening before him, darker still, from which chilliness billowed forth; the mark of the sea, meters above its top—

He stepped through. Beyond was a passage, twice a man's height. For a while, light seeped in from outside, and he stumbled along on water-slick loose cobbles. Thereafter the murk deepened until he had to wait for flint and steel to kindle the lanterns his attendants carried. Shadows and glimmers ran eerily over the stone which enclosed him. He breathed damp cold. Afar he heard the ocean growl, through his ears and footsoles and bones.

The passage suddenly gave on the Grotto itself.

This was a roughly hemispherical chamber, perhaps the remnant of a volcanic bubble, about twenty meters in width and up to the ceiling, seamed with crevices, ledges, and lesser holes. The lantern bearers climbed along these until their firefly-bobbing burdens gave wan illumination to the entire cavity. He stared toward the roof. Blacknesses betokened hollows in it. But none, he knew, reached as far aloft as did the high-water mark he had seen outside.

Dzenko had explained beforehand. This fjord formed what on Earth was called a roost. It forced incoming tides to abnormal rapidity and power. Twice a day a wall of sea roared through, smashed against the cliffs, and wholly drowned the Grotto.

"Had you gills, you might wait in there and come out alive, as the Prophecy says," the baron sneered. "But you haven't. Nor have you along such diving gear as I'm told your people possess. In any event, the witnesses would never accept your going in with a load of equipment. If I remember aright, you're allowed a horpil, nothing else. No, I fear this is one test where I cannot help you. Luckily, you don't want the crown of Talyina."

As he stood in the sounding gloom, fingers plucked his sleeve and a nervous voice said, "Best we go, Highness. The tide will soon turn. Hear you not an awakened hunger in the noise of the waves?"

*   *   *

Back on top, the party waited to view the tidal bore. Charlie and Hector wandered a little distance aside. They stood near a verge amid blowing grasses, and gazed across the sky and down to the now-uneasy waters. Wind whittered; seafowl shrilled.

"I've found what's become o' Mishka, laddie," the Hoka said in English. "I wadna hae heart tae tell ye, save that a rough, tough Hieland clansman doesna ken hoo tae keep a secret frae his chief."

Alarm knocked in Charlie. "What is it? Quick!"

"He's a slave in the inland quarries. They say such canna hope tae live lang."

"What? But—but—why—"

"I learned this last nicht, in a low dockside dive whaur I've won the confidence o' the innkeeper. Ye see, I've sought tae make clear that everything done in your name isna necessarily done wi' your knowledge. But I canna say this tae the nobles or the well-off or even the small burghers, for then word might well get back to Dzenko. I've therefore gane amang the vurra puir, who hae naught to lose nor aught to gain by blabbering to him. For they're no a' slum-bred, lad; mony and mony o' them waur freeholders or boat owners, till Olaghi's greed uprooted them. They nourish a hope the Prince'll mak' it richt for them again, and they ken me for your friend.

"Yon landlord's hiding Kartaz in his cellar. Ye'll reca' Kartaz, o' Mishka's men, he who fought bonnily at Stalgesh. He waur wi' those who stood behind Mishka when the sergeant went before Dzenko tae protest, no alane the continued impressment o' seamen, but the new taxes."

"New taxes?" Charlie said. "I didn't know—whatever for?"

"Och, ye'll no hae heard, syne they're levied on little folk, crofters and foresters wha' dwell far frae towns. 'Tis clear, though, I think, that if Dzenko ha' a'ready begun wi' them, ithers may look for the same or fiercer erelang. Anyhoo, he dootless expected this deputation, for he had it meet him alane and unarmed. But then his new guards burst in at the ring o' a bell and arrested Mishka and the rest at crossbow point. The preesoners waur hustled off to the quarries that selfsame nicht. Next day their comrades waur fed a cock-and-bull story like the ane ye got, laddie, aboot special assignments in the ootlands, and syne, they're scattered far and wide on errands which hae no purpose save to scatter them. This I hae established frae ither reliable soorces.

"Kartaz got a chance tae escape and tuk it. His last sight o' Mishka was of our auld fere in chains, breaking rock, wi' a lash to hurry him alang. So Kartaz tauld me, and I've aye found him truthful."

Sickened, Charlie stared down into the gorge. The rising waters snarled at him.

"I'll collar Dzenko tonight," he whispered. "I won't have this. I won't. I'll denounce him in public—"

For now he knew what the baron intended: the identical thing Olaghi had tried to build, "an up-to-date absolute monarchy." That was why the navy must be maintained at full strength. Talyina had exchanged one dictator for another. And indeed it was worse off, because Dzenko was more intelligent, more efficient. And he ruled through Charles Edward Stuart, the Prince of the Prophecy!

Hector gripped the human's elbow. "Nay, laddie," said the Hoka. "Ye'd nobbut fling your ain life awa'. Surely yon scoundrel ha' made proveesion again' such an emairgency. Belike he'd stab ye the moment ye spake, then denoonce ye for an impostor and hope to ride oot the storm what wad follow. He might well succeed, too. Dinna forget, ye still lack the final proof o' wha ye are. Besides, when ye waur supposed to rule Talyina forever, your slaying wad in itself discredit ye.

"Nay, laddie," he repeated sadly, and shook his round head. "Ye canna but deepen the woes o' the realm, an' alienate Dzenko frae the League, which otherwise might pairhaps meetigate his harshness a wee bit, and yoursel' perish, when yonder lies a univairse for your exploring. Come hame wi' me! Hoo could I e'er face your parents or mysel', did I no bring ye back?"

"But how can I ever face myself again," Charlie shouted, "if—"

The sea drowned his words. Rising and rising, the tide crashed into the fjord, violence which trembled in the rocks beneath him. It marched like destiny, against which nothing may stand.

Nothing?

Charlie came out of dazzlement to see the many eyes upon him, made fearful by the trouble they saw in him. He dared not stop to think further, for he knew that then he would grow afraid. High above the noise of the bore, he yelled, "Hear me! Tomorrow I go into the Grotto as the Prophecy tells! And I'll come forth again—alive—*to claim my crown!*"

16
THE DEEP RANGE

Once more the sea was low, but drawn by a moon which hung day-pale above the cliff of the cavern, it was starting to rise. Sunlight flickered off wavelets whose chuckles took on an ever more guttural note. Chill and salt, a breeze piped farewell.

The dignitaries who had accompanied the Prince down to the beach lost their solemnity as they sweated and panted their way in single file, across the switchbacks of the trail toward the brink where a crowd of witnesses already stood. Hector wrung Charlie's hand. "We maun be off the noo," he said thickly. "Unless—lad, wull ye no reconseeder this madness? 'Tis ane thing tae hae read summat in a pheesics textbook; 'tis anither tae set your life at hazard."

"I've got to, Hector," Charlie said. He pointed at the watchers, forestlike on the steeps. "For them. They trust me. And I can help them, if—" He clasped the Hoka to him. "I *will* come back to you. I promise."

Hector gave Dzenko an ominous glance. "If ye dinna return, there's more than me wull regret it," he muttered in Talyinan. Again in English: "Good-bye, Bonnie Prince Charlie, until we meet anew and ye enter upon your heritage."

The Hoka waded to a lifeboat in the shallows. Its ten rowers were not guardsmen; they were ordinary fishers and sailors, but each was armed, and each likewise looked grimly at Dzenko. They paused no longer, for already it would be difficult to escape from the fjord. No craft could live there while the tidal bore raged. The plan was for them to wait outside and come in after Charlie as soon as possible, in case he wasn't able to leave by himself.

Their coxswain struck up a chant. With Hector in the bows, oars bit water and the hull departed. Charlie and Dzenko stood alone. They were in sight of everybody but in earshot of none.

Except for a scarlet cloak, the baron was also dressed simply, in light tunic, trousers, and shoes. Both wore the usual knife, but his was long and heavy, a weapon rather than a tool. Charlie clutched to his breast the horpil he carried and met the stare of his rival with more resoluteness than he felt.

"Well, at last you grant me a private talk," Dzenko snapped. From the mask of his face, fury sparked.

"I wasn't going to give you a chance to pull some trick or . . . or assassination," Charlie retorted. "I made sure the whole town knew I'd do my final Feat today, and I stayed in public view till my bedtime, and Hector got those boatmen to watch over my suite, and you were the reason why!"

It was strange, he thought, how well he had slept. But as his moment drew near, every nerve was tightening.

Dzenko stroked his whiskers. "You are not overly courteous to your mentor, youth."

"I'm nicer to you than you've been to my people."

"*Your* people, eh? Your people? Well, well. A few of us might have something to say about that."

"Not after I've been in the Grotto."

"Ah, yes," Dzenko said with a sour smile. "You've gnawed your way to the secret of the Grotto, have you? I did myself, weeks ago. You might bear in mind, however, the Feat is dangerous just the same. For example, suppose the waves throw you against a wall and spatter your brains."

"Suppose they don't," the Earthling replied. "Somebody must've survived high tide in there once, to get the tradition started."

"Belike you're right. Yet I am anxious for you. Really, your suspiciousness hurts me; yes, it cuts me to the liver. I mean to wait low on the trail and myself be the first who goes in after you. This I will announce to the watchers." Dzenko bowed. "Therefore, fortune attend you, my Prince, until we meet anew."

He turned and strode off. A gust of wind swirled his cloak aside, revealing the pouch which bulged and banged at his hip opposite the knife. Charlie gulped. Chill went through him. What did Dzenko mean by that last remark?

Sarcasm, probably. He didn't expect his rival would live. But if that proved wrong—well, Dzenko would have to mend his own fences. It was understandable that he would make a point of hailing the new king before anybody else did.

Ripples lapped cold across Charlie's feet. The time was upon him.

He too was loaded down with a weighted pouch, which annoyed him by its drag and bump as he crossed slippery, toe-bruising rocks. Wasn't he supposed to be a legendary hero, above such discomforts and inconveniences? Instead, he stumbled alone through bleak, blustering hugeness.

He stopped at the mouth of the cavity. Far off, the boat which bore Hector was a white fleck under the cliffs. Closer, but still remote, patches of color along the trail marked the nobles. The commoners gathered at the top were a blur. Charlie wondered if they could even see him.

Yes, no doubt every available telescope was pointed this way. He must go through the motions. He plucked a few forlorn twangs and shook a few weak rattles out of his horpil. His lack of skill didn't matter. Nobody else heard him.

Quickly, before he lost courage, he entered the tunnel.

When well inside, he slung the horpil on his back and opened his pouch. It bore a glow lantern. This was a Talyinan invention, a glass globe inside a protective wire frame, filled with water which contained phosphorescent microorganisms. The dim blue light it gave was of some use to divers.

Nobody minded the Prince's bringing such a commonsense piece of equipment. He and Hector had kept quiet about the item which next he drew from the pouch. He didn't feel he was dishonest in taking it. But why give his enemies a chance to make snide remarks? The whole future of Talyina depended on his prestige.

The object was the bag from the Hoka's pipes. He blew it up and closed it with a twist of copper wire. He might have to stay afloat for well over an hour. This would let him do so. Otherwise, if nothing else, cold would sap his strength and he'd drown.

It boomed in the gloom. He hurried onward.

When he entered the Grotto itself, the floor was already submerged a few centimeters. He splashed about, searching. Except at very short range, the glimmer from the lantern hung about his neck was less help than his memory of how his guides yesterday had scrambled around the irregularities of the walls.

Yes . . . this ledge slanted upward to a fissure, along which it was possible to creep farther to reach a knob, and from there— He took off his shoes and climbed. The rock was slick. It wouldn't do to fall, no matter how loudly the water beneath had begun to squelp and whoosh.

After what seemed like a long time, he got as high as he could go, onto a shelf which jutted from the wall and barely gave space for him to sit. He clenched fingers on every roughness he could find, and waited.

Here came the bore.

The tide noise grew to a monstrous bellow, rang through his skull, shook him as a dog shakes a rat. Spray sheeted over him. With one arm he squeezed the bag to his ribs. It was the last thing he had left.

Onward plunged the sea. Yet that vast mass could not quickly pour through a narrow shaft. Its vanguard struck the inner side of the Grotto and recoiled on what came after. Waves dashed back and forth, whirlpools seethed.

Through that brutal racket, Charlie felt a sharper pain lance his ears. He worked throat and jaws, trying to equalize pressures inside and outside his head. Amid all the chaos, his heart broke into a dance. The pain was a benediction.

It proved his idea was right.

When the tunnel filled with water, air was bound to be trapped inside the cave. As the tide rose farther, that air would be compressed. At some point, it must counterbalance the weight of liquid. And thus, no matter that the water outside stood higher than the roof within, here would remain a bubble of breath.

Charlie had no way to determine in advance where equilibrium would occur. He could but cling to his ledge.

The tide mounted. As the hollowness grew glutted, waves damped out. The earlier crashing diminished to a sinister mumble. At last the water was almost calm.

When it reached his breast, he decided to seek the middle of the room. He hugged his life preserver to him with both arms. His feet paddled him along until he guessed he was about where he ought to be. There he halted, lay in the sea's embrace, and thought many long thoughts.

This was what it meant to be a king, a real king—not wealth and glory, not leadership into needless wars, but serving the people, and if necessary, dying for them.

Yet kingship was not enough. The people themselves might want a Landfather to lift from them the weight of decision. But if they did, the people were wrong. The highest service a king could give was to lead them toward their own freedom.

Charlie smiled at himself, alone in the dark. Wasn't he self-important! Did he imagine he could save the world?

No, of course he couldn't. But he might leave it a little bit better than he found it.

Again the water roughened. Remembering what he had seen the

day before, he drew a glad breath. The tide had turned. The Grotto was draining.

But that brought fresh dangers. The height of the tide would recede almost as rapidly as it had entered. Charlie recalled what Dzenko had said: A current might smash him fatally against the stone around him. Even after the tunnel was partly clear, he shouldn't try to go out. The swift and tricky stream could easily knock him down, snatch away his life preserver, and drown him in the hour of his victory.

No, he must wait inside for quite a while, until it was perfectly safe to walk forth. . . . Maybe not that long. Hector's crew would row in as soon as they were able. But at any rate, what he should do now was find a wall and fend himself off it as he sank.

He did. The effort was exhausting. He was overjoyed when by the wan light of the glow lantern he identified a broad shelf newly uncovered. He could sit here till the Grotto was emptied, if the boat didn't fetch him earlier. It would then be an easy scramble to the floor. In fact, already the tunnel must be only about half full. He thought the darkness had lightened a trifle.

The rest of the ebb would take considerably more time than had the showy bore and the initial outflow. Charlie tried to summon patience. Miserably chilled, too tired to warm up by vigorous exercises, he slapped arms across body.

Maybe he could divert himself with the horpil. Besides—he grinned—the Prophecy did say the Prince would make music while the waters retreated. He unslung his instrument. Soaked, its strings twanged dully and its rattle gurgled. Scratch one more piece of glamor.

Wait. What was that new noise? Charlie peered around. A vague blueness flickered and bobbed; eddies gave back the least sheen of it.

Following the beacon of Charlie's own glow lantern, it neared. A tall form climbed onto the ledge. The glove beneath its neck picked out the face in a few highlights and many shadows.

"Dzenko!" Charlie exclaimed. He leaped to his feet.

The baron's teeth flashed. "Did I not promise I would be first to come after you, my Prince?" he said, low above the lapping and swirling of the tide. "All praised my faithfulness, when I doffed cloak and shoes and plunged into the fjord. Fain would many guardsmen have come along, but I claimed for myself alone the honor of leading you back to the day."

"Well," Charlie said uncertainly, "that's very kind of you. I do want us to be friends, and I do need your advice. It's only, well, we don't think a lot alike, do we?"

"No," Dzenko agreed. "In many ways we do not. I believe your notion of slipping the ancient anchor which holds the commoners in their place is madness. Yet in some ways we are kinsmen, Charles. We share bravery and determination. My sorrow will not be entirely feigned, Charles, when I tell the people that I found you dead."

"What?" Echoes rang fadingly back, *what, what, what.* . . .

"You drowned." Dzenko reached forth crook-fingered hands.

"No—wait—please—"

The baron trod forward. "I suggest you cooperate," he said. "If you keep still, I'll cut off your breath with a throat grip. You'll be unconscious in a matter of pulsebeats. You'll never feel it when I stick your head underwater. And I'll always honor your memory."

Charlie whipped forth his knife. Dzenko sighed. "I too am armed," he pointed out. "I have a better weapon, a longer reach, and years of experience. I would hate to mutilate your body with rocks until the wounds are disguised. But the future of Talyina and of my bloodline is more important than any squeamishness."

Charlie sheathed the knife. "Excellent," Dzenko purred, and sidled close. Charlie slammed the horpil down over his head.

The string jangled and broke. The frame went on to enclose Dzenko's arms. He yelled, staggered about, struggled to free himself. Charlie left him in a clean dive.

Cursing, Dzenko got loose and came after. Charlie unshipped his glow lantern and let it sink.

From the set of the currents, he could probably find his way to the tunnel. He'd have to take his chances with riptides and undertows. Dzenko was more dangerous.

Charlie was no longer afraid. He hadn't time for that. He swam.

A splashing resounded at his rear. It loudened. Dzenko was a stronger swimmer than he, and tracking him by the noise he made. Charlie stopped. He filled his lungs, floated on his back, paddled as softly as he was able.

The baron's call came harsh: "You think to hide in the dark? Then I'll await you at the door."

Charlie saw in a white flash that his enemy was right. Either he, the prey, swam actively, and thus betrayed himself to a keen pair of ears, or he stayed passive, in which case the flow would bring him to the exit where the hunter poised.

His single chance was to find another surface halfway level and broad, and dodge about. He was more agile than Dzenko, surely. He struck out across the ebb. Behind him he heard pursuit.

Light broke upon his eyes, the yellow gleam of an oil lantern. Hector held it aloft, where he stood in the bows of the lifeboat. "Ahoy, lad-die!" he piped. "Laddie, are ye here?"

"Help," Charlie cried.

"Aha!" said Hector. His free hand reached forth to haul a kicking, cursing, but altogether overpowered Dzenko across the gunwale, help-less in the powerful grip of the Hoka. "What *is* this farce?" demanded Hector sternly.

17
EARTHMAN'S BURDEN

For three terrestrial months, the Honorable Athelstan Pomfrey, Plenipotentiary of the Interbeing League to the Kingdom of Talyina and (in theory) the planet of New Lemuria, had received no direct communication from the royal town.

At first King Charles had been eager to talk with him, as soon as a man in an aircar brought a radio transceiver powerful enough to bridge the distance between Bolgorka and Shverkadi. He related what happened, to the moment of his coronation: "—And I sent Dzenko after Olaghi, into exile. His family and a few old retainers went along. I think they'll actually be a good influence on the mainland. They'll need to make friends with the savages there, which means they'll teach them some things. I did this right away, before I was crowned—"

"You!" Pomfrey had interrupted, furious. "You the king? Of Talyina? How dare you, fellow? How dare you?"

"I hoped you wouldn't blame me, sir," a subdued voice replied from the set in the compound. "Haven't I explained how I sort of got swept along?"

"Up to a point, yes," Pomfrey conceded before he reddened afresh. "But accepting the lordship of a native country— Don't you know, Charles Stuart, I can charge you with imperialism?"

The voice strengthened. "I don't think you can, sir. I mean, well, the plan Hector and I've worked out— Oh, I guess you haven't met Hector MacGregor, exactly. Anyhow, we figure it's the direct opposite of imperialism. But maybe I should ask a lawyer first. Look, is my dad around?"

"No," said Pomfrey. "After my courier assured him that you were, indeed, safe, but wouldn't come back for some time, he wanted to visit you, but I forbade that. So he continued his voyage." His jowls went from crimson to purple. "If you have, in addition, the sheer gall to demand I obtain legal assistance for you— No!"

"Then maybe we'd better not talk anymore," said Charlie.

No total curtain fell between kingdom and League. Messengers went back and forth. Charlie was a gracious host to whomever Pomfrey sent. By degrees, the Plenipotentiary cooled off. At last he decided it might be best for himself that he check with a competent attorney. What he heard, coupled with what information he got from Bolgorka and from Talyina as a whole, made him very thoughtful.

When word came that the king would pay him a state visit, and requested off-planet transportation be available, Pomfrey got onto his subspace communication set. The *Highland Lass* was still in this galactic neighborhood.

Thus Captain Stuart was on hand when his son returned.

A sizable fleet docked at Grushka. The next morning a procession started north for the compound. At a leisurely pace, with an overnight stop, it arrived toward evening of the following day.

The humans who waited at the gates of the compound gasped. Not even their airborne scouts had prepared them for what they now saw and heard.

Autumn lay cool on the land. Leaves flared in multitudinous colors. The sea danced in whitecaps beneath a merry wind. High overhead went southbound birds. And up the road came the King of Talyina and his household troopers.

He rode in the van, on a horse rather than a yachi. His slender form was plainly clad for travel, but the sword of the Founder hung at his waist, and on his red hair sat an iron crown. The two who flanked him were similarly mounted. On his right, in kilt and bonnet, was a Hoka. On his left, in gleaming mail, was one of the biggest New Lemurians that anybody had ever seen.

Behind them tramped the guards. Banners fluttered; pikes nodded; boots smote ground in heart-shaking cadence. But something new was here. Below their armor these warriors wore kilts, in the same tartan as flew above their helmets. And at their head, setting the time of their march, went the wild music of a hundred bagpipers and as many drummers.

The giant drew rein and wheeled his mount around. "Com-pan-ee-halt!" he roared. The troop snapped to a standstill. "Salute!" A thousand swords flew free. "Sheath!" Blades entered scabbards with a hiss and crash, as the pipes droned away to silence and the last drumroll lost itself in surf noise.

Charlie leaped from his horse and sped to his father. "Dad!" he shouted.

They hugged each other. "Sorry I made you so much trouble," Charlie whispered.

"I'm not, not anymore," Captain Stuart answered, low in his throat. "By all that's holy, you've made me prouder of you than I ever dared hope for."

They straightened. Pomfrey, gorgeous in formal dress, advanced upon them. "Ah . . . welcome, your Majesty," the Plenipotentiary said. He cast a nervous glance toward the soldiers, where they stood at statuelike attention. "I hope we can, ah, provide hospitality."

"Shucks, don't worry about that, sir," Charlie replied. "We brought supplies and everything. They can camp in the field yonder, can't they? It's only overnight."

"Indeed? I assumed . . . a certain amount of ceremony—"

"No! I've had enough ceremony! We'll throw a farewell party on the campground and enjoy ourselves, and that'll be that!"

"Well." Pomfrey was not displeased. "As you wish. I can understand it if you wish to abdicate quietly."

"Huh?" Charlie stared at him. "Abdicate? What're you talking about? Didn't I make it clear to you?"

Pomfrey began to swell. "Young man—I mean, your Majesty, *I* thought that in obedience to the laws prohibiting imperialism, you would retire as soon as feasible. It was on this basis that legal counsel advised me to file no charges against you."

Captain Stuart bristled. The Hoka, who had joined their group, broke the tension. "Plenipotentiary," he said, "dinna ye ken that to renounce the power isna the same as to renounce the title?"

"That's it," Charlie said in haste. "I . . . well, I am supposed to— Well, the Prophecy says, 'Righteous, the red-haired one rules us forever!' A mortal can't do that. But a legend can. If not forever, then long enough."

Pomfrey calmed. He stroked his double chin. He was not actually stupid, in fact, rather intelligent. "I believe I see," he murmured. "The last few messages you sent were pretty garbled. No doubt you were too busy to pay attention to their exact wording. . . . Ah, yes. You propose to take, shall we say, an indefinite leave of absence?"

"Yes," Charlie answered. "I've told the people this is part of my mission. I couldn't quite explain to them why it is."

Nor would he ever tell how that had been his last, greatest ordeal—the decision he must make, wholly alone in the night.

He could stay on as king. If he avoided the treaty zone, League law could never touch him. Rather, the Plenipotentiary would have to cooperate, like it or not. He, King Charles the Great of Talyina, could rule justly, bring in the benefits of civilization, and cover himself with glory. Nor need he be lonesome for his own kind. By offering trade concessions and well-paid jobs, he could attract as many humans to his court as he desired.

And he wanted to stay. Here was his realm. Here were his tested friends. Here dwelled his people, whom he had come to love.

But he harked back to a certain darkness in the sea and remembered that the highest service of a king is to give the folk their freedom, whether they ask it or not. Their descendants will bless him.

He, Charles Edward Stuart, must return to being an ordinary student on Earth. He could never visit this planet again.

"I'd have come sooner," he told Pomfrey and his father, "but it took a while to establish a Parliament—House of Lords and House of Commons, you know, and Commons has the purse strings—get organized, lay down some ground rules, hold our first election—that kind of thing. I'm ready to leave now."

"I see." The Plenipotentiary nodded. "If you, as the king who's supposed to reign forever . . . are not on hand . . . then nobody can succeed you, and the people will have to learn how to run the country by themselves."

" 'Tis like British history," said the Hoka. As he spoke, his burr shifted toward an Oxford accent. "Bad though the early Hanoverians waur, yet they'd one advantage. The wee, wee Gairman lairdie—that is, the initial two Georges—couldn't speak English worth mentioning. So they didn't preside over meetings of Parliament. From this grew the practice of having Cabinets, Prime Ministers—in short, the whole jolly old structure of democracy, don't y'know? We trust the Talyinan national folkmoot will follow a similar course of development. QED."

"In other words," Captain Stuart said to Pomfrey, and his tone clanged, "my son has accomplished what the League has only dreamed of doing since it found this whole world."

The spaceship departed soon after dawn. Charlie and Mishka waved to each other all the time the human went up the gangway.

When the last airlock had closed, the warrior turned to his men, "Ten-*shun!*" he shouted into the frosty mists. "Salute your king!"

Swords flashed free and clashed home. A drumroll thundered.

Engines hummed. On silent drive fields, the ship lifted.

Mishka, Prime Minister to his Majesty Charles, Eternal King of Talyina, drew sword of his own. It was his baton, to direct the pipes which began to skirl. From the ranks of the fighting men, deep voices rose in the tongue of the Highlands.

> *Will ye no come back again?*
> *Will ye no come back again?*
> *Better lo'ed ye canna be.*
> *Will ye no come back again?*